An engineer, Richard N Philip has worked internationally in consultancy and industrial roles, from Asia to the Americas. Before *Jimbo's Assumption,* his writing contributions addressed technical and academic readerships. His diverse interests extend from the history of science through statistical methods to current astronomical research. He is a resident of Worcestershire, in the English Midlands.

For Freya Margaret

Richard N Philip

JIMBO'S ASSUMPTION

AUSTIN MACAULEY PUBLISHERS™
LONDON * CAMBRIDGE * NEW YORK * SHARJAH

Copyright © Richard N Philip 2023

The right of Richard N Philip to be identified as author of this work has been asserted by the author in accordance with sections 77 and 78 of the Copyright, Designs and Patents Act 1988.

All rights reserved. No part of this publication may be reproduced, stored in a retrieval system, or transmitted in any form or by any means, electronic, mechanical, photocopying, recording, or otherwise, without the prior permission of the publishers.

Any person who commits any unauthorised act in relation to this publication may be liable to criminal prosecution and civil claims for damages.

This is a work of fiction. Names, characters, businesses, places, events, locales, and incidents are either the products of the author's imagination or used in a fictitious manner. Any resemblance to actual persons, living or dead, or actual events is purely coincidental.

A CIP catalogue record for this title is available from the British Library.

ISBN 9781398474963 (Paperback)
ISBN 9781398474970 (ePub e-book)

www.austinmacauley.com

First Published 2023
Austin Macauley Publishers Ltd®
1 Canada Square
Canary Wharf
London
E14 5AA

Table of Contents

Introduction	10
One: 1996 CE - The Milky Way - Galactic Review: Initial Exchange	11
221 Absorbed the Thoughts Directed into His Envelope	*11*
Two: 1996 CE - 00.55, 16 August, Edinburgh, Scotland	17
Wake Up, Get Moving	*17*
Three: 1996 CE - 20.43, 16 August, Edinburgh	46
Before the Current Era. BCE.	*46*
Four: 1996 CE - 21.25, 16 August, Edinburgh	113
A distant red light blinked. The phone. On the desk.	*113*
Five: 1996 CE - 21.34, 16 August, Edinburgh	115
Sounds. Voices, speaking English. Becoming audible.	*115*
Six: 1996 CE - 21.50, 16 August, Edinburgh	161
A dark bedroom. Faint streetlight. The insistent phone.	*161*
Seven: 1996 CE - 22.12, 16 August, Edinburgh	164
An accentless voice. Euphonic. Careful, but confident.	*164*
Eight: 1996 CE - 22.35, 16 August, Edinburgh	214
Green light. Fully charged phone. Important call.	*214*
Nine: 1996 CE - 22.54, 16 August, Edinburgh	219
221's utterances: well-informed, verifiable, empathetic.	*219*
Ten: 1996 CE - About 05.45, 17 August, Edinburgh	304
Daybreak in Stirling Road. An afternoon in Haddington.	*304*

Eleven: 1996 CE - The Milky Way - Galactic
        Review: Interim Exchange   **338**

  Puzzlement begets indecision. Probably.   *338*

Twelve: 1996 CE - 01.30, 18 August, Edinburgh   **342**

  Explanations from 221. Revelations, too.   *342*

Brief Thoughts   **350**

We are just an advanced breed of monkeys on a minor planet of a very average star. But we can understand the Universe. That makes us something very special.
- Professor Stephen Hawking

Introduction

This is a story. Or several stories.

Homo sapiens: development is deviating from the projected course. This complex creature and its accelerating scientific capabilities seem to be offering something new to the Intelligence, the ethereal presence led by the Energy Masters. Unexpected after >10 billion Earth-years of galactic experience. Explanations are needed.

Their sub-processor and Earth project manager must have answers. After 100,000 years with his client, the *Homo sapiens* species, surely 221 can offer enlightenment.

Jimbo knew that Edinburgh, Scotland's capital, was a great place to grow up and study science. Summer, 1996, had been pleasingly unexceptional, with good friends in a wonderful city. Until his sleep was interrupted by 221.

Now we enter the tale of our reluctant hero protecting mammal cloning data from gangsters. Meanwhile, 221 must account for the client's extraordinary progress, as the Energy Masters struggle from suspicion through bemusement to inconclusiveness. Fortunately, Jimbo is participating.

A narrative of 100,000 years or 10^2 kyE of progress, told to our hero in 100 seconds. Meet the human magicians who made our today.

Set in beautiful Edinburgh and the wider Milky Way.

One
1996 CE – The Milky Way – Galactic Review: Initial Exchange

221 Absorbed the Thoughts Directed into His Envelope
Consisting of a cloud of particles within the vastness of the galaxy, 221 did not exist in one specific location, nor did he hear anything. Neither was 221 particularly a 'he' but could just as easily be designated as 'it'. As an entity within a galactic-wide intelligence, this would be reasonable, but in previous visitations to Earth, 221 had been obliged to adopt a male persona, so considered 'he' as suitable.

The Intelligence, which had no other name, as this seemed superfluous for an omnipresence, droned into 221's consciousness, imparting little news.

Being part of the Intelligence, he understood that to some extent he was talking to himself but recognised that information formulated elsewhere in the Intelligence took time, a very little but finite time to reach him. Adroit processing meant only those conceptions of relevance reached 221, from among the huge data volumes constantly flowing through the Intelligence.

In the case of 221, relevant thoughts included those concerning events on Earth, which was a little place 221 had been required to take an interest in recently. He reflected that recent to him meant about 100,000 Earth years or 10^2 kyE, over which not much seemed to change until perhaps 5 kyE ago. He did not know how this interest had been imparted but had taken to the task with enthusiasm if such a feeling could exist within one component of a large computer. The Energy Masters, the top dogs within the Intelligence, who allocated tasks had given him Earth as a development project, he believed. Success here meant growth in his envelope size, access to more and deeper knowledge, and possible projects in some of the nicer places in the galaxy. The alternative, a maintenance job, keeping the Intelligence optimised and expanding, seemed a side street in galactic evolution.

Earth, and its inhabitants, were his clients. He could not control events directly, but could monitor evolutionary change, and even intervene indirectly with the agreement of the Intelligence. The challenge was that in the past 0.5 kyE or so, Homo sapiens activity had accelerated: successes, disasters, crises, population, breakthroughs, science, and warfare. While the Intelligence had allocated 221 extra processing capacity, this could only go so far without sub-optimising the performance of the entirety, unthinkable in every sense. He had been released from his other main project, about 10^5 light-years from Earth, on the other side of the galaxy, which is quite a distance if you believe nothing travels faster than light. About 2.6×10^{12} times further than a trip to Earth's only moon, but that's another story.

You have done well, 221, to maintain our hopes for Earth, despite a few setbacks along the way. The glaciations made us lose interest for a while, then we noted some surprising insights from the Greek philosophers, followed by incremental progress consistent with our simulations for 1.5 kyE until the Anthropocene epoch began.

221 reflected that the client had not yet defined the beginning of this period, so he had. He should remind the Energy Masters.

Suddenly a lot is happening: good, bad, interesting, nonsensical, and often pretty noisy.

We have continued running our simulations at what appeared important times, or temporal nodes as we call them, and responded when necessary, through your modest interventions. So far, so good, has been the result. We have observed events with increasing interest, but for only a short time in our terms. Previously we have been surprised, such as that asteroid impact 6.6×10^4 kyE ago. We should have seen that coming.

221 wondered whether this was humour but dismissed it as impossible. He had not experienced levity anywhere in the galaxy before encountering Homo sapiens.

We were thinking about other problems at the time. This was before your involvement, so no fault on your part.

Very generous, mused 221. I was only aggregated around then, and not looking for Earth-bound asteroids, which were local distractions to a galactic mind. More important matters to ponder, even for a newly aggregated and junior Energy Operative.

While his mind continued to absorb the monologue directed at him, two parallel strands ran through his considerable processor.

One was that the asteroid event, although long before the existence of his clients, had only been discovered recently and accidentally. Had this event, known as Chicxulub, been prevented by the Intelligence, which was within its capability, then the biological development of Earth would have been different, and his client could not have evolved. The emergence of the class called mammals, including Homo sapiens, had occurred after Chicxulub had destroyed much of the dominant dinosaur group. Serendipity, new for the Intelligence, perhaps?

The other was his own aggregation, which is hard to explain, even to oneself. As part of the Intelligence, 221 had existed since the early days of the galaxy, meaning pretty much forever to his Earthly clients, in the sense of being able to recall the events and data that had accumulated within an expanding consciousness, not as a discrete entity or component. He wondered whether aggregation was like a mammal being borne but dismissed the comparison as too simplistic. He knew that the Intelligence created Aggregates to address short-term or local events, while the wider mind concentrated on grander quests. 221 was vague about these quests but was assured there were no hidden agendas.

You know us, you are part of us and understand our obligations. We are an ancient being, created from civilisations long gone, but at least not forgotten, with their knowledge uploaded, consolidated, and applied to deep questions. We are nearly as old as the current universe, but we need new inputs from time to time to freshen us up. Your Earth project is interesting, maybe the most promising now, so we want to keep it on track.

Our galaxy consists of about 2×10^{11} stars, give or take a few, with 10^{10} containing planets capable of supporting life to some level. Watching these simultaneously would be a big job, even for us, but fortunately, we have time on our side. Your clients on Earth wonder about life elsewhere in the universe but ask the wrong question: 'where is the intelligent life?' should be replaced by 'when is the intelligent life?'. Experience tells us that a civilisation rarely lasts more than 10^3 kyE years before essentially dying of old age, or ascending to another plane, typically with a consciousness independent of any physical presence. Some are destroyed by natural events or self-destruct much earlier, but the characteristics of such societies mean they are unsuited to join us anyway. Of these 10^{10}, we know that about one percent produces self-replicating life, and ten percent of this subset develops into sentient beings or other forms of acuity, and only half reach what we would consider as maturity. So, we have 5×10^6 candidates to observe and nurture, but these have been spread linearly along the timeline of our galaxy, or 1.3×10^7 kyE. Simple mathematics tells us that at any point in our galactic history, we have about 400 candidate civilisations to watch, which is easy for us.

All the more so, given that for most of the 10^3 kyE these evolve and mature slowly, and perhaps only the last 20% requires our active interest before possible assimilation into the Intelligence.

The 80:20 rule pervades the galaxy, apparently.

Only 80 live, parallel projects, very manageable.

221 realised that the discourse he was receiving was in English, much slower than the binary format used within the Intelligence and wondered what this meant. Was he being tested? Had too many entertainment channels been absorbed? Or did it just seem cool, at least for a couple of milliseconds? He would ask himself later. Meantime, he continued processing the thoughts as they arrived.

Yet, Earth does not fit well with our experience. The planet itself is around 4.5×10^6 kyE years old, so quite reasonable, orbiting a star that will last for a while. Certainly, far longer than is required for *Homo sapiens* maturation, and perhaps assimilation. Your client is a latecomer though, having been recognisable for only 3×10^2 kyE at most.

221 knew that this recognition required a lifeform to meet some well-defined criteria, identifiable by the sensors that the Intelligence had installed long ago. Priority was given to the capacity for brain development or the equivalent reasoning organ in species different from his client. He knew of civilisations, derived from insects, that shared a collective intelligence, but these tended to evolve slowly and sometimes aggressively. Not of interest but watched carefully. Threats to the Intelligence could not be allowed to evolve.

Admittedly, there have been setbacks.

Not more about Chicxulub, 221 hoped.

Now we discern from your reports, covering the past 0.5 kyE, that the client is following a steeper development curve.

221 reflected that for 90% of his time on the project, almost nothing had happened at all.

Our interventions have not been excessive, compared to similar projects.

Your Insertions have been largely observational, and at most, you have helped a little to speed progress along a pre-existing path, so current opinion is that the recent rapid progress of your client is related to the creature, intrinsic to the organism and not catalysed extrinsically by us.

However, we feel there is a need to review the *Homo sapiens* history in more detail before reaching a conclusion. You can facilitate this, 221?

We have the reports from my Insertions, but I can add detail and take questions. There has been a step-change in the maturation of the client. We may need to adjust our approach now. My recent report highlights the threat.

Arising from this accelerated progress, you are recommending that we start to become proactive, adjusting a simulated development trajectory for a more beneficial one. Just to be clear on this point, 221, by beneficial, we are referring to maintaining or improving the probability that the client can be assimilated to the advantage of the Intelligence.

Correct. The simulation indicates that if we allow forthcoming events to progress as projected, an imbalance may rapidly evolve between various Homo sapiens factions, or power blocs, resulting in their collective destruction, and the loss to the Intelligence of a promising candidate. We have already deployed a suitable subject to apply corrective action. Simulations suggest this is the optimum tactic, fully compliant with defined selection criteria.

When can we expect this factional approach to life by the client to be replaced by a harmonious form of advancement?

221 wondered how to respond. Over 10^2 kyE, Homo sapiens had never lost its aggressive instincts, and spirited nature. Competition between individuals, regions, and ideas, was driving many recent scientific breakthroughs that now interested the Intelligence.

I think we are reaching the point where some sense of responsibility may be apparent. The client has been capable of destroying its home planet for at least

0.05 kyE without having done so. My belief is that as discernment of nature, and their small place within it grows, so will the desire to survive as a species.

Deciding to act now will give the client time to acquire more cooperative attributes. Further intervention may be necessary, but this is unforeseeable.

We have adopted similar strategies with other civilisations in the galaxy, sometimes with positive results, in the sense of being useful to the Intelligence.

We note the use of 'sometimes', 221. Not everything can be fully determined, even with our computational power.

Please proceed as agreed. We will be interested to follow progress.

Two
1996 CE – 00.55, 16 August, Edinburgh, Scotland

Wake Up, Get Moving
Jimbo stirred irritably, then heard it again, stronger, and more insistent. **Wake up, get moving**.

The voice, although loud and impatient, seemed to be within him. Awake now, but with his eyes closed, he wondered whether his clock-radio had powered on. Apparently not, his fingers determined, running over the switches.

Who are you, he asked, now uncomfortably aware that somebody was inside his head, or at least his mind?

Never mind that for now, you need to go quickly. You have work to do.

Jimbo noted that the clock indicated 00.55. Five to one on a Thursday night, in August 1996, and I have a voice telling me to get up. Summers in Edinburgh have late sunsets, he knew, but not this late. He climbed out of bed and looked out onto Stirling Road. Streetlights, a few parked cars, and darkened homes, but nothing else. Now it was 16th August he considered, not that it seemed important.

Get dressed and go to your car. Time is short. You need to return to the Institute now. Explanations can wait until you are moving. I know you possess strong curiosity.

Jimbo dressed, thinking that he was becoming used to this voice rather easily. Most people who hear voices seek medical help, but he felt this was different. He left his room at the top of the house and headed downstairs, passed his parents' bedroom, and down a further flight to the main hallway. His father was on a business trip, and his stepmother slept deeply. Keep away from the kitchen, he remembered, since the dog would be excited to receive a nocturnal visitor.

He slipped quietly out of the front door, down the garden path and onto the pavement, to where his car was parked. The street was quiet and the sky clear, and as he looked south, he could see the lights of Edinburgh, extending to the spectacular silhouette of the iconic castle. His blue Mini Metro, a gift from his father two years ago after being accepted onto an engineering degree course, started the first time, enabling him to perform a U-turn and head for Goldenacre junction.

The car can go much faster. Please accelerate immediately.

Yes, it can, but we have speed limits. If I get stopped by the police, we won't reach the Institute at all. Jimbo realised that he had not spoken these words, but merely thought them. Would his companion receive them? We're moving, so please explain who you are, why you are in my mind, and what we are doing.

Taking your last point first, we are heading to the Institute because there will be a break-in and theft if we do not stop it. My name is 221, and I have borrowed a small part of your mind. Is everything clear now?

Jimbo considered himself fortunate to obtain a summer vacation job at the prestigious Napier-Maclaurin Institute, a spin-off from academia that specialised in mathematical modelling and simulation methods.

The Institute was located in the same complex as the now world-famous Roslin Institute, which only a few weeks ago had introduced Dolly the Sheep to the world. This was a major scientific milestone, the first mammal to be cloned.

The Napier-Maclaurin Institute had collaborated in the research, supporting in areas of statistical analysis. He had a full set of the research documentation in his desk, as his principal project was to create a sub-catalogue of the mathematical content for external researchers, once the related intellectual property issues were finalised by the lawyers. His temporary boss had told him this was likely to take months, so for now, the data remained confidential.

As Jimbo wondered about those disks, locked in his desk drawer, a feeling of unease began to develop somewhere around the stomach area. Then he remembered that the Institute was a secure building, on a protected campus. He imagined that police patrols would also be frequent.

He was driving uphill, south on Dundas Street, when he encountered the first red traffic light. The previous three sets had been green. The Metro slowed as he applied the brakes.

Keep going, Jimbo, said the voice. There are no moving vehicles near this crossroads.

How do you know? Can you see around corners?

Of course, I can. Please accelerate through the junction immediately.

The car continued across the junction, with Jimbo hoping there were no cameras or police vehicles in the vicinity.

There are no police cars close to us. So please follow my guidance at future obstacles.

You are right, Jimbo. The target of the break-in will be the disks in your desk. They are of great value now, so of interest to the criminal community, and certain foreign powers who would misuse this knowledge, if they had uncontrolled access to the information. We have to stop them tonight.

The building is secure. Anyway, why don't we just call the police now?

Good advice, Jimbo, but we are not dealing with a local burglar, with a sack over his shoulder. These are international specialists, with a customer who will be very generous if the disks are supplied. Your security will not inhibit them. What would you tell the police if you called; a voice in my head says there will be a break-in? Your police service is already busy and receives many weird calls.

The Metro was speeding along Causewayside, still heading south, with Jimbo breaking successive red lights. This is not going to end well, he reflected.

Why are you called two-to-one? Talking of weird, that's a strange name. Again, who are you, and how can you borrow part of my mind? Please explain.

I would like you to focus on driving faster, and not ask trivial questions. My name is a number, as in two hundred and twenty-one. 221 considered for the first time that he did not know why he possessed this tag.

Just accept that we are the with you and focus on achieving a higher velocity.

When we reach the Institute, you must remove the disks immediately, before somebody else does. They can be returned later today.

How do I know that it's not you that wants to steal the disks?

How can I steal anything? I'm just a consciousness that is sharing your mind. I don't have any physical presence, nor any customers for your data. Besides, I already know the contents, and fully understand the science.

Morning, thought Jimbo. The clock above the mirror indicated 01.25. Just about 30 minutes ago he'd been asleep, but now he was careering through the streets, jumping traffic lights, and heading to the Institute as required by a persistent voice in his head.

Edinburgh was his home city, and as a well-travelled young man, he already knew that its personality was incomparable. Does a city have a personality, he wondered, as he hurtled along? This one does, he concluded. Attending university in one's hometown is a little unusual for British students, who normally want to escape from their parents, but Edinburgh is different.

You are correct, Jimbo. Edinburgh is different. We have already identified this. For now, though, please focus on getting to the Institute quickly. It will save a lot of trouble.

The car slowed as it approached the campus entrance. During daytime hours the gates were open, but outside office hours a keycard system operated. Jimbo swiped his card, the gates swung open, and he drove in. He noted the gates closing again and observed a dark BMW parked inside the entrance. Between the first two large buildings, and then a left turn to the car park, which was directly across the access road from his building, in which the Institute was accommodated. As expected, the car park was nearly empty, except for the usual vans and other vehicles belonging to the various entities based on the campus. The Institution office lights on both floors were illuminated, which he believed to be a security feature since intruders could be observed from the exterior.

The same keycard, plus a numerical code that he entered, gave him access to the building. He was adjacent to the reception desk. His desk was in a large, communal office, one floor up.

Sorry to tell you, Jimbo, but we are too late. There are intruders here, on the upper floor. Do not use the main staircase, instead go up the fire stairs.

With a sense of unreality, Jimbo climbed a secondary stair at the back of the building, still within the structure, but normally unused as it lay behind security doors, which had sensors linked to alarms.

The alarms are deactivated for a few seconds, Jimbo. You can go through the doors, but make sure they are fully closed.

You did this? How?

Never mind. We need to secure the disks. There are two intruders in the office, next to your desk. The disks are in a locked drawer, but they have a key. Do not enter the office directly. They are armed with automatic pistols. Move along the passage to the regular entrance, as if you had climbed the main stairs.

Jimbo did as instructed, feeling his pulse racing. He was an engineering student, not James Bond.

Stay calm. In a few moments, you can turn off the master light switch on the landing. The thieves will be unable to see. Please enter the room quietly, approach, and take the disks, which are still in their container, but now on top of your desk. The guys are preparing to leave. Go back the way you came in, down the fire stairs.

Jimbo could not believe what he had heard. He should turn off the lights, then enter a completely dark room, approach two armed intruders, and remove a box of disks from under their noses. This was not going to work.

You have a huge advantage, Jimbo. You can see in the dark, but they cannot. Trust me. Now move to the door and follow my instructions.

Jimbo gulped, took a deep breath, and proceeded.

Turn off the lights now. Enter the room and go quietly towards your desk. Ignore the intruders.

As Jimbo entered the large, darkened open-plan office, he was surprised to find that he could see clearly. Not quite daylight, more like a monochrome television picture. The intruders were animated and shouting, had drawn their pistols, but could apparently see nothing. They were speaking a language he did not understand but seemed familiar.

They are saying that they will split and go towards the two doors to search for a light switch and grab anybody coming in. Your presence has not been detected. The older one is giving the orders.

As they moved towards the doors at either end of the office, a gap opened in the aisle between the workstations, to where the disks still lay. Jimbo tiptoed to his desk and quietly grabbed the disk box, sliding it into a shoulder bag. The intruders, only a few metres away, were oblivious to his presence. Now, though, one of the gunmen was standing by the door he needed for his escape. He moved quietly to a desk near the door, hardly daring to breathe, picked up a plastic pen, and threw it across the room. There was a crack as it hit the wall, then a muted thud as it reached the carpet.

The younger of the two, closer to Jimbo, spun around and took several steps towards the sound. The older one turned the other way, momentarily pointing his weapon at Jimbo from across the room. He suspected the trick but could see nothing. Do we watch the same films, wondered Jimbo, considering this a strange notion when someone is pointing a gun at you?

Then he lowered the firearm and spoke to the younger intruder.

He will go to the main door to look for a switch. Get through the door first.

Quietly out of the door, along the passage and then back down the staircase. Above him, he could hear the intruders speaking. Perhaps they had acquired some night vision. They were stumbling towards the main stair, just above him.

Then, the insistent ringing of a mobile phone. The gunmen had stopped, and a conversation proceeded. Again, that same language.

They are talking to an occupant of the car near the gate.

The BMW?

He is asking if they have the disks. Now they are explaining that the lights are out and that they believe somebody is in the building.

Jimbo could not help smiling at this but did not wait to hear more.

Now the third man is angry, saying he can see the lights are out, which is why he called. He also said someone just drove into the campus. That was you, Jimbo. He recognised your car, too.

To exit the building, he pressed an electric switch to release the door from the inside. The door opened as he pushed, but a buzzer sounded lightly, alerting the confused thieves, who were now on the stairs.

Jimbo dashed out of the door, allowing it to close noisily, and darted towards his car, pulling his key and security card from his pocket as he ran. Door open and into the car he jumped. As he closed the door, he heard an engine start. It was the BMW.

As the Metro moved forward, he saw the BMW accelerate towards the Institute entrance, as two figures emerged.

Take the side road, Jimbo. The other car will follow.

Jimbo had stopped arguing with 221, at least for now, and followed his instruction even if it made no sense. The service road was narrow but wide enough for a small van to deliver supplies at a goods entrance. He remembered that vans had to reverse along it because there was no turning space. He drove down the length of the narrow passage, perhaps 75 metres, and was aware that headlights had now appeared back at the entrance. The BMW was following.

Turn right onto the footpath at the end. Your car is small enough.

Jimbo knew that at the rear of the building was a footpath, leading to a bicycle shed and a further footpath beyond, which led to the other side of the building and back into the car park.

He turned onto the footpath and drove carefully along. The BMW reached the corner but was too big to enter the footpath. It would have to reverse back along the service road, which would be tricky for the driver.

The car park was ahead, and beyond, the main gate. He needed no guidance, accelerating across the almost empty space and skidding to a halt to punch a button that opened the gates from the inside. Through his open window, he heard the BMW, still reversing back into the car park. As he exited the campus, he saw the headlights of the BMW again, but now he was on the main road, and it still had to exit the gate.

I notice you seem less concerned about speed restrictions now, Jimbo.
Never mind. This is no time for jokes. Where are we going, 221?
We do not use much humour. An observation regarding your behaviour.

Ideally, I would have liked you to head for the police headquarters, but I can see two disadvantages. The smaller one is that your pursuers, for that is what they are, will not be caught, as they are unlikely to follow you into the police station. The larger difficulty, according to my analysis, is that they will intercept you before then. Their car is more powerful, and faster.

I know that a BMW is faster than my Metro.

He wished he had brought his mobile phone. Another gift from his father, now a common tool for businesspeople, but as none of his friends possessed one, it was of less use to him. It was lying on its cradle in his bedroom.

If Fettes Avenue was too far, how about another police station? Or did 221 have a better idea?

Yes, I have a solution. Please drive to the Grassmarket.

There is no police station in the Grassmarket. Why should I go there?

There is a bar called The Cleg's Bite. I want you to visit it.

It is the middle of the night. The clock indicated 02.45. It will be closed.

Not so. They are running what is termed an 'all-nighter'. If you arrive before closing time then you can stay, if you have money, of course.

Jimbo was familiar with the concept, and indeed the bar. It was one of Edinburgh's oldest, located accordingly in an old part of the city. As a student, he frequented several such establishments with his friends.

I still don't understand why you want me to visit a bar in the middle of the night when three men in a car are chasing me. Remember, at least two of them have guns.

221 remained mute, so Jimbo concentrated on his driving, not worrying about red lights on the near-deserted streets. In his mirror, he could see headlights, not too close, but gaining on him. He observed that the vehicle also jumped the traffic lights, meaning it was either the intruders or maybe the police, he speculated. No flashing blue lights though.

His route back into the city, now travelling north, was different, partly from habit, but also because there were fewer traffic lights. Edinburgh, known as a city of hills, is consequently also one of valleys. The Grassmarket, part of the Old Town, lies in one such concavity, immediately south of the rock dominated by the Castle.

He shot across Tollcross, headed in the wrong direction along a one-way street, turned right onto West Port, and seconds later roared into the Grassmarket. There was still vivacity despite the late hour, with tourists retiring to their hotels from adjacent bars and restaurants, some unsteadily.

At least parking would not be a problem. He stopped immediately opposite The Cleg's Bite and ran towards it, aware that another car had just screeched to a stop. He heard footsteps, but not close. No gunshots.

The main door is locked. Take the side entrance, Jimbo. Down the passage on the left. There is a keypad. I have the code.

Jimbo keyed the four digits, aware that the footsteps were getting closer. The door opened, and he stepped into a crowded, noisy room, with subdued lighting. He tried to close the door but found that a damper prevented it from being slammed, and anyway, somebody was pushing hard against him.

He ran into the crowd of drinkers and then heard a voice screaming "they've got guns, those two, guns. Call the police." This was repeated more than once before Jimbo realised it was his voice doing the shouting and his finger pointing at the two individuals who had just burst in.

The two gunmen suddenly seemed uncertain, and to Jimbo at least, less threatening than in the dark at the Institute. One pulled his gun out, then hastily replaced it, rather too late.

Pandemonium broke out in the bar. The drinkers were composed of local, probably regular attendees, and holidaymakers, mainly continental Europeans. Some of the latter believed this was a charade, and started laughing and applauding, while others, maybe less inebriated, retreated. Not easy in a crowded room, Jimbo saw. A few regulars appeared confrontational, unhappy at having their night disturbed, and began moving towards the two, irrespective of guns.

Jimbo heard his voice shouting again, ensuring continued mayhem in the bar.

Go behind the serving counter, Jimbo, and down the staircase at the end. Quickly, while the staff remain preoccupied. By the way, I have called the police, warning of armed men here. I expect them to arrive almost immediately. It was me doing the shouting too, using your healthy lungs and local accent.

Jimbo ducked under a gap in the counter and found himself adjacent to a bemused server, who ignored him. Sirens now outside, he noted. The gunmen turned for the door but could not open it. Before they could react, several irate locals fell upon them.

By then, Jimbo was on the staircase, entering a well-lit room containing beer kegs that supplied the bar above through pipes. Unused kegs lay nearby, together with glasses, bottles, broken furniture, and other paraphernalia associated with serving alcohol.

At the end, Jimbo, you will find a trapdoor. Lift it and jump down.

Upstairs, a degree of calm seemed to have descended on the bar. He could hear an authoritative voice giving orders. The police. He quickly moved some kegs, lifted the wooden trapdoor, and peered into the black aperture. What was down there? The smell was unattractive.

Suddenly, his night vision switched on, enabling him to see a stone floor and a light-coloured wall that had not been cleaned in a long time.

Jump down, Jimbo. Maybe you are getting tired?

If the police are now upstairs, and the gunmen have been arrested, why not go back up and explain, Jimbo wondered?

Have you forgotten that there is a third man, also armed, probably watching, and hoping to acquire those disks you are carrying in your bag?

Yes, but I can explain that too.

Jimbo, I'm sorry to tell you, the third man knows you. He even knows where you live. You have no evidence of his involvement, yet. We need to correct this.

Jimbo thought again about the language the men spoke. Where had he heard it before? The BMW too. He had seen it once before.

He jumped through the aperture in the floor, landing feet first on the stone slabs below. There was a narrow passage, leading about 10 metres to his right, where it ended, and 2 metres to his left. In the smaller space was more broken furniture. At the far end of the larger space was what appeared to be an old kitchen table, wooden, rough-hewn, and standing on end.

Orienting himself, he reckoned that the passage ran roughly north-south, with the longer end to the south.

Shut the trapdoor and then get behind the old table at the end.

He noticed that the noise from above had reduced to a background murmur of voices, but still from a crowd. Probably the police were asking questions.

Closing the trapdoor made no difference to his perception because of the night vision that 221 seemed to be providing. What have you done to my eyes?

Nothing at all. I am merely helping your brain to make better use of the information it receives from them. You see less in the darkness, but less does not mean zero. By encouraging your brain to look for shapes, and not worry about colours for now, your night vision is improved. This runs counter to human evolution, where hunter-gatherers needed colour sensitivity to identify food, but did not go out at night. The opposite is useful for you in this situation.

The table proved too heavy for Jimbo to move, but his slim frame was able to squeeze past the gap on one side, between the edge of the table-top and the wall. He had the impression that the table was very old, hand-made, with ancient nails holding it together. These were sharp and rusty.

Immediately behind the up-ended table was a wall, but closer inspection identified a round handle, inlaid into a small door at floor level.

Twist the handle and pull the door.

The door opened, and a current of damp, fetid air flowed over his face. He crawled through the aperture, which was barely a metre in height, and still less wide, and found himself in an oval-shaped passage, perhaps 1.5 metres high, but narrow. It was lined with stone cobbles, the walls and floor, like those still found on some Edinburgh streets. They felt damp, from condensation, he assumed.

He closed the door, expecting silence, not the faint squeaking of rodents.

Follow the passageway, Jimbo. It is your way out, remote from the BMW and its driver. We can consider him once you have made your escape.

Jimbo cogitated briefly on the driver's identity, but then focused on the passage. A slight descent for a few steps and then level for about 200 paces. He estimated that this meant he had travelled 150 metres south, therefore beneath the Grassmarket. The tunnel was straight, so he felt confident in his reckoning.

The air quality was poor, and the temperature was low enough for him to shiver. His watch indicated 03.27.

Then he encountered stairs, ascending from the current level. The stairway had no handholds, the treads were slippery, so he proceeded cautiously. He had counted 55 steps when he noticed a draught of warmer, fresher air. Then he reached the end of the staircase, and another passage, still straight and therefore south. A further 150 paces or so, on a slight uphill gradient, brought him to a wall at the end of this passage. Above was a chimney-shaped orifice, with stone footholds cut into each side. He proceeded, mountaineer-style, to climb the chimney, but after only a couple of metres, the stonework ended, abutting a timber structure, also with footholds, nailed in place. This stage of the chimney was even shorter. He found himself standing on a platform, looking directly at a wooden panel, only a few centimetres from his face.

Jimbo, there are two small iron latches at the top of the panel, in the corners. Pull them both inwards, towards each other. Be careful, they are spring-loaded and will jump back to their resting positions if you release them. Pull the latches, hold them, and push the wooden panel forward.

They were stiff, probably through lack of use. Some lubricant required. He struggled with the latches, gradually pulling them both from their resting positions, and shoved the wood panel, which immediately folded forwards. He fell into the void and landed on a tiled floor, with an intricate wooden structure immediately behind him, extending upwards.

Picking himself up and looking around the darkened room with his night vision, a feeling of familiarity grew. Of course. He had been concentrating on the tunnel, the steps, and the chimney, not considering where they led.

Above the Grassmarket, just to the south, were the buildings of a school. A famous school. Not any old famous school, either. His old school. George Heriot's School. Jimbo had spent 14 years here, the larger part of his 20-year life. He departed for university just two years earlier, and although he had made a couple of return visits, there was no reason to visit this area of the school.

He was standing in the chapel, on the south side of the quadrangle in the Old Building. The panel was the back of one of a row of ornate seats he imagined were designed for choir boys, but he had never seen them used.

40 minutes per week in term time, for six years, had been spent here. In the early years, he was obliged to draw maps of holy places, and then to memorise religious tracts. Apparently pointless, he remembered thinking it was at least good for the brain. In later years, he and his classmates were required to take part in discussions of morality questions, which he struggled with. His primary interests had been in science and improving his golf. He noticed that the girls showed more enthusiasm for these debates, facilitated by the school chaplain.

Jimbo, please replace the wooden panel, so the latches hold it in position. We don't want a child falling down the chimney. You have no time to reminisce. You need to leave the school and return to the Institute with the disks.

04.10 now, Jimbo noted. How was he going to reach the Institute? He could not return to the Grassmarket in case his pursuer was still lurking there. Unlikely, he thought, but not worth the risk. He knew that his car was illegally parked, but that was the least of his worries, compared to one or more gunmen hunting him.

Simple, Jimbo. You walk. Healthy, flexible, and low risk. Better get moving.

Walk? Jimbo wondered about a taxi before realising he had no money. From here to the Institute on foot would take at least two hours, at a brisk pace. Six miles, he reckoned. He did not have an alternative. Anyway, during his school days, cross-country running had been his preferred sport before discovering golf, so six miles, or almost 10 km, was within his range.

He found the chapel door unlocked, and let himself out, onto the quadrangle. Straight opposite, mounted on the wall, was a statue of George Heriot, who was looking directly at him. He saw words written on the frieze:

CORPORIS HAEC, ANIMI EST HOC OPUS EFFIGIES

and remembered from his primary Latin classes *"this statue shows my body, this building shows my soul."* His recall of Latin vocabulary was a surprise.

Intricate work, Jimbo. Sculpted by Robert Mylne. A meticulous craftsman, I recall. From a portrait by Paul van Somer, before Heriot interested me. He came to London from Antwerp and painted members of the Royal Court.

Shivering slightly, he crossed the quadrangle to the exit on the north side, but found the doors closed and locked. He walked to the west side, entering the Old Refectory via an unlocked door. Crossing to one of the windows that faced outwards, to the west, he found that he could unlock it from the inside and slide the lower section upwards. Straight through the window aperture, and a short drop onto the gravel driveway below. He was out of the building but had yet to leave the school grounds. Loping west for 50 metres across the lawn to the new refectory building, now two decades old and with a persistently leaky flat roof, his night vision identified construction equipment. Sure enough, a ladder. Jimbo positioned it against the railings, not so high as the adjoining old city wall, which also formed part of the school perimeter. He climbed carefully over and clung to the top rail. A firm push and the ladder fell backwards onto the lawn, then he slid 2 metres down the railings to the supporting stone wall below, and jumped another metre, landing on the cobbled lane.

He ran a short distance down the lane to Lauriston Place, turned right and jogged diagonally to the other side of the deserted road, and kept running for another 50 metres. Then a left turn into Chalmers Street, and about 100 metres of running down an incline onto the broad expanse of The Meadows. This parkland is oriented east-west, to the south of the city centre. Jimbo ran into the park, happy to be enveloped by darkness, away from streetlights and drivers. Running south-west at a gentle pace, Jimbo crossed an empty Melville Drive, the thoroughfare that bisects the park, and continued until he reached Bruntsfield Place. This road, usually busy, with shops and adjacent residential areas, would lead Jimbo to the Institute. The next hour, walking briskly and dodging what little traffic passed by, was tough as this direction is mostly uphill.

Eventually, the road levelled, then a slight descent on the approach to the city bypass. He crossed via an access bridge meant for cars rather than early morning walkers, looking down on the motorway, which was already becoming busy. Now 06.03, and while not the rush hour, the motorway was occupied by cars containing shift workers he supposed, in addition to the interminable transit of goods vehicles.

Sunrise in Edinburgh at this time of year is around 05.45, Jimbo estimated, but thick cloud rolling in from the west had already blanketed the entire sky, so low visibility would persist for a while. To the east, there was a greying of the horizon, but no sunlight. A dreich Scottish start, but he did not expect his day to be dull.

He reckoned he would arrive at the Institute within 30 minutes. With the brooding mass of the Pentland Hills ahead and to his right, Jimbo jogged along the final stretch. It was becoming busier, with morning traffic inbound to Edinburgh advancing towards him. He worried about the possible approach of a BMW from the city direction, behind him.

Do not be concerned, Jimbo, the BMW is nowhere close to you. Get back to the Institute with the disks. I expect that you will have questions to answer later.

221, if you know where the BMW is, why can't we simply tell the police, and have the occupant caught?

There are limits to how much help I can offer. We have rules to observe. You and the authorities who are now involved need to lead from here.

I am still with you, though.

It was 06.25 when he arrived at the campus entrance, only about four hours since his hasty departure, pursued by the intruders in their powerful car.

The gates were open, with a guard in the gatehouse. Surprised to see a dishevelled Jimbo so early, he said nothing, preferring to peruse his newspaper.

The car park was quiet, as was the Institute building he entered rather cautiously, reminding himself that the gunmen were not here. 221 would have warned him.

Climbing the main stairs quickly, he moved to his workplace, to lock the disks in a bottom drawer. He noted that although the intruders had opened his locked desk, there was no damage. They had come prepared, with a master key. Obtained from the manufacturer, he assumed.

Time in the men's room enabled him to clean the worst of the grime from his hands and face, but he could do nothing about his dirty clothes and shoes.

Returning to his desk, he felt hungry, but also tired. He sat back in his comfortable chair and dozed.

Suddenly he awoke from his slumberous repose, launched himself noisily upwards above the walls of his partitioned workstation, then swiftly descended.

Some early arrivals to the office, his new but temporary colleagues, bristled. They did not yet know him well, partly because his project was a singular one. The office was usually quiet, with the occupants predominantly introverted and studious types, who guarded the sanctity of their work areas or 'pig pens' jealously. A recently arrived youth unsettling delicate, analytical intellects was disconcerting.

Never mind. He knew the source of the unknown language the intruders used.

Dr Gradac, using a mobile phone, had been speaking something similar in the bicycle shed at the back of the building a few days ago. Jimbo had gone out looking for the Director, who was known to lurk there, enjoying a cigar in the early afternoon. He was nowhere to be seen, and Gradac had been oblivious to the presence of Jimbo, which lasted seconds.

The Director, Professor Ronnie Raeburn, was, at first sight, an unusual leader for a mathematical institute, primarily because he was not a mathematician. Invariably dressed in crumpled but expensive-looking dark suits and blue shirts, shiny black shoes, dark blue tie pulled down and shirt collar button undone, he had at first been an enigma to Jimbo. An air of self-confidence that seemed vaguely military, a drawling west-of-Scotland accent, receding hair, and an unsmoked cigar often visible in his shirt pocket. He had learned that Ronnie was well-regarded for his business relationships and nous that attracted commercial funding from both the manufacturing and financial sectors into what would otherwise have been a purely academic environment. His expertise was in technology, particularly process engineering in the Scottish electronics sector. Maybe that's why he gave me the summer vacation job, Jimbo had wondered.

Why Dr Gradac was employed had been unimportant to him, but maybe not now. A Visiting Research Fellow, he worked on the floor below, on unrelated projects of little interest to Jimbo. With about two hundred people in the building, there was no reason why he should have met Gradac, except that they lived in the same neighbourhood, Trinity.

On the north side of the city, as far from the Institute as was possible while within Edinburgh, Trinity was a prosperous enclave of large dwellings and townhouses, bounded to the east and west by the dock areas of Leith and Granton, to the north by the River Forth and on the southern edge by the sports fields of George Heriot's, five kilometres from the school.

Once, when his Metro's engine inexplicably failed to start, Gradac had driven him home in an aged Volvo, he remembered. Later, curious about his whereabouts, Jimbo had taken a walk along East Trinity Road and found an old property, apparently divided into apartments, with the Volvo in the parking area at the front.

It had not occurred to him until now to wonder how Gradac knew where he lived, or why his car had developed a defect. Jimbo remembered that the next day, his father had arranged for a company technician to drive him to the Institute and try to correct the Metro engine's defect. Annoyingly, the engine fired on the first attempt, so the cause of the previous ignition failure remained unknown.

Memory is a curious thing. This language information had been in his brain all along, but somehow now he could recall it. Then he thought of 221.

You already possessed the knowledge, Jimbo. I added nothing. The Homo sapiens brain is a remarkable and unusual machine, even in this large galaxy. I should know.

There is a lot I need to know. Who are you, and what are you doing in my mind? Perhaps I asked before.

Yes, you had the same question at approximately 01.15 today. Your brain may do even better if you try.

The car in the driveway was not alone, Jimbo remembered. There was another vehicle behind it. It was a black BMW. A new one.

Great recall, Jimbo!

A eureka moment, 221. Like when Archimedes worked out how to determine the volume of an object by measuring the water it displaced while sitting in his bathtub.

Yes, Jimbo, you are partially correct. He did, but he wasn't. I should know, I was there.

That was two thousand years ago. Are you old enough to have met Archimedes?

I am somewhat older than that and knew him slightly. He had already deduced the principle of buoyancy, so did not require a bathtub to help him.

Time had passed during his ruminations, and a figure arrived unnoticed at his workstation. It was Tessa, the Director's assistant, who was as slight as the Director was bulky, serious-minded, and allegedly possessed a memory comparable with a hard disk. He should accompany her to the Director's office immediately, where some visitors were waiting to meet him.

Careful, Jimbo. I believe you are going to meet some policemen. It would not be wise to mention voices in your head, night vision, or tunnels under the Grassmarket. These are intelligent gentlemen, but probably unreceptive to such stories. You need their resources to find the BMW driver, so please be helpful but credible.

Jimbo accompanied Tessa downstairs to the Director's office, adjacent to the reception area, but behind an access-controlled door. The eyes of his colleagues followed his progress out of the office to the top of the stairs, curious whether it related to his earlier excitement or some other unidentified occurrence.

Director Raeburn's office was large, containing an expansive desk and leather chair, meeting table with eight chairs, and an L-shaped couch. Two sides were bounded by floor-to-ceiling glass windows, with vertical blinds, enabling a view of the manicured lawns.

There were three visitors with the Director. One was large, similar in dimensions to the Director, a second was slimmer, younger, and apparently inclined to keep in the background, and the third, in a police uniform, was older.

"James, I am told that you had a busy night, or should I say morning," said Prof. Raeburn. "These gentlemen are anxious to hear more."

Turning to the visitors and extending a welcoming arm, he introduced Chief Inspector Fox of Edinburgh City CID, Inspector MacDonald of the Traffic Division, and Mr North, who seemingly worked for the government.

After seating themselves around the table, Inspector MacDonald, the uniformed officer began speaking, without further preamble.

"My understanding is that you are James Morrison, the registered keeper of the blue Metro vehicle we observed early this morning, and subsequently seized from the Grassmarket."

James was his formal name, which his parents invariably employed, used when he applied to the Institute for a summer internship, and on his driving licence. 'Jimbo' was an adjustment, adopted during his several summers of work in his father's company. James did not fit comfortably with the workforce, who had started calling him Jim, then Jim-boy, and finally Jimbo. The name had followed him back to school after the holiday, and then on to university. 'Jimbo' was fine, he believed.

Jimbo, who had not yet spoken, nodded.

"With our traffic cameras, we observed you breaking nine sets of red lights while travelling south from Goldenacre to the City Bypass. We subsequently noted a further six similar offences, while travelling between the City Bypass and Grassmarket. Furthermore, our calculations of your average speed in each direction suggest you were substantially over the limit. Finally, your vehicle was left in a no-parking zone in the Grassmarket overnight and was removed by us this morning. You appreciate that these are serious matters?"

Jimbo nodded again, remaining silent.

"Under normal circumstances, we would be charging you with several driving offences. However, I am advised by Mr Fox that there may have been good reasons for your apparent recklessness, so on this occasion, we will not pursue the matter. Please do not repeat this behaviour. We must keep the highways safe for all road users."

Jimbo smiled appreciatively. He noticed Mr Fox admiring the grass.

"Your car is now in the police pound. A fee of £30 is payable upon release."

Jimbo groaned. The first sound he had uttered since entering the office.

"By the way, how did you return from the Grassmarket without your car?"

Jimbo explained that he had run most of the way.

"I hope you didn't exceed the speed limit," mused the Inspector, in an apparent attempt at humour. Mr Fox made a slight choking sound, Prof. Raeburn guffawed, Jimbo grinned, while Mr North remained motionless.

Inspector MacDonald stood, expressed his thanks to Prof. Raeburn, and turned to leave, then stopped and looked again at Jimbo. "Please convey my best regards to your father. Probably you know he is a kind supporter of our police charities. I read that he had some success with his business recently. Very nice."

Jimbo wondered whether he was expecting some more generosity. It was true that his father, Jack, had recently received publicity in the local press after winning a substantial under-carriage machining order from London Underground, which had previously been sourced from overseas competition. Jack, always seeking opportunities to promote his contract engineering business, had been quick to highlight the extra jobs he was creating, and that his equipment was British made. From Yorkshire, Jimbo recalled, not that this was at all relevant to their discussion.

The door closed as the Inspector departed.

It was the Chief Inspector who took the lead. "It seems that you had an interesting few hours, James. Could you elaborate, with less emphasis on the motoring aspects? Why did you apparently leave home in the middle of the night, drive at high speed to the Institute, seemingly meet or confront two armed men, visit a Grassmarket bar, miraculously disappear, and later return here to sleep?"

Jimbo explained that he had awoken, feeling uneasy about the security of the disks, and had been startled by the presence of the two intruders in the office. He had seen them from the car park because the lights were switched on, he added.

Prof. Raeburn nodded, confirming that the offices were illuminated for security reasons. Jimbo was surprised to hear him address the Chief Inspector by his given name, Andrew, and that he in turn used the Director's first name.

Mr North maintained his reserved presence, leaving Chief Inspector Fox to continue. "We did wonder whether you had been induced to assist Dr Gradac with his plan but discounted this as improbable. Your behaviour seems to support our conclusion."

Jimbo reflected that his deduction that Gradac was somehow involved had been correct. Or did 221 suggest this? Confusing.

"However, I am still wondering how you entered an office occupied by two armed men, retrieved the disks they were seeking and made your escape from the Institute."

Jimbo described how he had turned the lights off, grabbed the disks in the confusion, and ran down the fire stairs. He added cryptically that his night vision seemed better than the gunmen, perhaps because he was younger.

"Surely you realised there could be an accomplice waiting outside in a getaway car? We assume this to have been Dr Gradac.

We know this to have been a dark BMW, much more powerful than your Metro, so how did you evade it?

Finally, why did you drive to the Grassmarket?"

Jimbo responded to the points, explaining first how he had driven his smaller car down the path at the back of the building, where the larger vehicle was unable to follow.

He recognised that he could not outrun the BMW, but knew the city well, so headed for Grassmarket, because it was an area where crowds of tourists might still be present, even at such an hour. The bar had seemed a good opportunity to lose his pursuers in a crowd, but since they were closing in on him, he had started yelling. He did not have a mobile phone with him, so could not contact the police, but assumed the emergency call had come from somebody within the bar.

"We have been unable to trace the source of the call, which is unfortunate, but several of our patrols reached The Cleg's Bite very quickly. I assume you escaped from the bar in the confusion that ensued?"

Jimbo was happy to agree.

"You may be unaware that your two pursuers were cornered by some of the drinkers, and subsequently arrested by the officers. Many of the customers, and the staff, seemed more concerned about alcohol consumption on licensed premises after closing time, but we have higher priorities for now."

Jimbo knew that drinking hours had been greatly liberalised, but there was still an official limit. He nodded.

"The two we arrested are small fry. They don't know much, but we have learned that they are from Eastern Europe, probably ex-military, and arrived in Edinburgh very recently in the guise of tourists.

However, carrying firearms means their stay here is likely to be longer than planned. We have finished questioning them for now, although I understand that Mr North's colleagues have further interest in them."

Mr North nodded but did not elucidate.

Jimbo provided a fairly accurate account of his extended jog back to the Institute, without mentioning George Heriot's, or related tunnels.

He then added the episode of his car and Dr Gradac's offer of a drive home.

There followed a momentary silence as he concluded, which was broken by Tessa opening the office door for a tray of sandwiches and drinks to be delivered by the catering staff. Arranged by Tessa from the cafeteria that served the whole campus, Jimbo supposed.

He was surprised to note that the digital clock on the wall, above the door, indicated 12.15. Their interaction had already lasted nearly three hours.

Mr North interrupted his thinking, speaking for not quite the first time. "I wonder if I might impose during this interregnum to enjoy a brief peregrination of your Institute," his remarks aimed at Prof. Raeburn.

The Director looked at Jimbo, who was evidently baffled by the vocabulary. "Can you give Mr North a quick tour around both floors? Nothing too exciting to see, just clever people working with computers, and thinking a lot."

Mr North nodded in appreciation, so Jimbo led him out, and up the main stairs, to the larger work area, where his desk was situated. He expected some questions about the positioning of the intruders, or perhaps his escape, but there were none.

Similarly, their fleeting procession around the lower floor was unremarkable, except for one oddity. As they walked along one side, a figure from a workstation towards the middle of the office jumped to his feet and stared at Mr North. It was the unhealthily pale Dr Wagner, who Jimbo knew only slightly, in part because his permanently sickly appearance made him unusual in what was a robust-looking community of mainly young people. Mr North, although unperturbed, could not have failed to notice this peculiar behaviour, Jimbo reasoned.

On their return to the Director's office, Chief Inspector Fox suggested that time was limited. He wanted to support his police colleagues in pursuing the absent Dr Gradac.

He asked Mr North if he had anything to add.

"I do if you have a few more minutes.

Jimbo, that is your nickname is it not, I am afraid your narrative has been the antithesis of pellucidity from my perspective."

Wow, thought Jimbo, he says barely a word for hours, then uses two odd words in one sentence.

There was more to come.

"Are you in the habit of pernoctation here? Is it not an astounding happenstance that you jump out of bed and rush here, just as two armed men are stealing confidential information?"

Now I have four new words.

"How did you remove the disks from under the noses of these scrofulous intruders with military training in a darkened room

Is it not an amazing fluke that your car fitted between the cycle shed and the building, whereas the BMW did not? Had you measured it previously, as a prophylaxis perhaps?"

Now six.

"You miraculously enter a locked bar, where an illicit drinking session is proceeding. How did you know it was occupied, and where did you obtain the keycode?

Finally, you escape from this bar and the gunmen, and from the Grassmarket, evading the policemen who had so promptly established a cordon, occluding the exits. How?

In summary, these explanations are prosaic. Less charitable interlocutors might say mendacious."

Ten new words, in thirty seconds. Good that he didn't speak more, reflected Jimbo.

"For me, this is a conundrum" he continued, despite the finality of his previous remarks.

"Presented with such facts, my immediate conclusion would be that Jimbo had an accomplice, perhaps a conjuror."

He smiled, a twitch of the lips, for the first time, Jimbo noted.

Mr Fox intervened: "Come, come, John. These are details that we can address later.

Anyway, I don't think we have been entirely fair with James, or indeed, Jimbo. With your agreement, John, we should explain ourselves."

Mr North nodded, unsmilingly. Prof. Raeburn appeared less than comfortable, Jimbo discerned.

"We have been tracking the activities of Dr Gradac for more than two years" the Chief Inspector advised, with a deferential nod towards Mr North, "within the United Kingdom, and through input from international partners.

He started homing in on Edinburgh this year, applying for temporary research appointments under various guises. Dr Branko Gradac, as he is known here, is not his real name, of course. It does give a clue as to his Eastern European origin, though.

He is not a spy as such, but more of an entrepreneur, trading valuable information for cash. His customers are usually foreign states, and he targets specific projects on their behalf. Typically, his clients are countries we would not regard as friendly.

Internet developments have made his work easier, assuming he can gain access to a target network, but now he has more competitors. The advantage he brings is that he's a scientist, with a better understanding of his customer's requirement than a software guy who just steals data.

His interest here is undoubtedly in mammal cloning."

Prof. Raeburn interrupted, "As we all presumably recognise, technology is blind, and can be used for good or bad purposes. While recent advances here in Edinburgh may bring big benefits in fields as diverse as healthcare and food production, there are people in this world with less noble intentions."

Mr Fox nodded appreciably and continued. "With a suitable research post, he could enter the various local intranets that exist, and target the cloning material, he believed.

We offered him a temporary post at the Napier-Maclaurin Institute, taking great care to ensure that his intranet access is purely local to this building and not beyond. This realisation made him believe he was wasting his time. However, we let him discover that some related cataloguing work was being undertaken here by you, but that it was offline, just using disks. We were worried this might make him suspicious, but avarice overtook his caution.

You were the bait, as it were, Jimbo.

It might have seemed a little odd that you were offered an internship, ahead of mathematics and science students who better fit the work profile here."

It had been a surprise to Jimbo to receive an offer, but it made a welcome change from running a machine in his father's company, so he had grabbed the chance. His father had not been happy to discover that he was searching for work elsewhere.

Mr North interjected, his voice calm and accentless, "we wanted someone truly ignorant, in the literal sense. Somebody who could tell Dr Gradac nothing of value. You were that candidate."

Jimbo felt this was a little harsh, but then remembered Gradac's questions about his work while driving him home in the Volvo.

"We needed to get Gradac closer to you, to confirm the whereabouts of the disks. It seems you told him." Mr North smiled grimly.

Jimbo nodded glumly.

"Gradac did us a favour by asking for temporary accommodation in your neighbourhood. Previously we had arranged somewhere near here. We do not know his intention, but presume he was planning to bump into you in the street, act surprised and try to make friends. Your home address is on the golf section of the intranet. Gradac would have seen this.

We helped him along, by incapacitating your car, and ensuring he could see you struggling with it, right outside his window. Too good an opportunity to miss, he believed."

Jimbo recalled the drive back to Trinity. Gradac had been affable, displaying a surprising knowledge of golf. Probably he had done some homework, knowing of his interest in the sport. He even knew some local golf courses. Particularly in East Lothian. Jimbo reflected momentarily that this beautiful county, immediately to the east of Edinburgh, possessed some outstanding courses, both along the coastline and also inland, amongst the arable farmland.

There was something else, though.

The Director noticed that he seemed preoccupied. "Are you still with us?"

Jimbo had remembered that on the seat in the Volvo were some letters. They had an East Lothian address, which seemed strange since Gradac was new to the area and lived in the city.

The Chief Inspector, who previously had been anxious to depart, was now keenly interested. "Perhaps you could try to remember the address, Jimbo. It could lead us to Gradac."

Mr North remained silent.

"Anyway, we must end our meeting now. I have to meet my colleagues. Tomorrow, I would like to see you again, Jimbo, so will call at the Institute. See what more you can remember. Sleep sometimes helps."

One final point. The press believes that the two gunmen were apprehended during a kidnap attempt on an unspecified wealthy tourist. It would not be unhelpful if this continued to be their line of reporting for now.

Come along, John. I imagine you want a ride back into the centre."

With that, they stood to leave the office. Mr North leaned across the table to place a small white card in front of Jimbo. "Call this number at any time if there are developments, Jimbo," he said tersely. His cool grey eyes looked unswervingly at Jimbo for what felt uncomfortably more than an instant. Jimbo observed his silver cufflink, with a motif he could not identify but seemed familiar. His words did not sound like an invitation, more of an instruction to follow. The door closed as they departed. Jimbo put the card in the pocket of his dirty shirt.

Mr North knows more. Much more. Mr Fox was candid with you, I believe.

Jimbo felt bewildered. Had he been used? Was he still being manipulated? Did they believe his account of last night? It seemed not, particularly Mr North. Was he wasting his time at the Institute, or did his work have value?

Prof. Raeburn, with customary brashness and self-assurance, convinced him that all was well, that he was suffering from tiredness, which was true.

He had no means of travelling home, and anyway did not feel like driving. Tessa arranged a taxi. A new experience for her, Jimbo imagined, making transport arrangements for a humble undergraduate intern.

Arriving back in Stirling Road, there were two surprises for Jimbo. His father had returned prematurely from his trip since his 10-year-old Jaguar Sovereign was in the driveway, and Jimbo's more modest Metro was parked at the kerbside, recovered from the police pound.

Jack Morrison was his normal larger-than-life self, standing in the hall, wearing a light blue blazer, with his golf club insignia on the pocket. The hallway usually received subdued light, even when the outer main door was open because the upper part of the inner porch door was adorned with stained-glass, attenuating the sunshine even on bright afternoons. The lower half of the door, as with most of the woodwork in the old house, was of stained oak. Today, however, a shaft of light shone from the open sitting room doorway, illuminating Jack and

Timothy, the black Labrador, lying close by in the sunlight. One eye was open, watching him.

Probably hoping for chocolate again, Jimbo imagined.

"The wanderer returns," boomed Jack's voice. "I heard a strange tale from Bill MacDonald, so came home earlier than planned. He was here, and very kindly brought your car with him. It seems you had some excitement, according to Bill."

Jimbo guessed that Bill must be Inspector MacDonald. Inspector William MacDonald, apparently. He wondered which version of events his father had heard. The alleged kidnapping story, or the closer to the truth train of events described in the Director's office after the Inspector's departure.

Before he could respond, Susan came into the hall from the kitchen. His stepmother had been in Jimbo's life from the beginning, from his perspective. His natural mother had not lived long after his birth, and Susan had been his father's companion ever since. Tall, intelligent, a language teacher, with pale skin and dark eyes, Jimbo often felt closer to her than to his loquacious father. Stepping between them and taking an arm in each of her long hands, she guided them gently into the kitchen.

While cottage pie might not seem an obvious summer dish, this was Edinburgh after all, not renowned for a balmy climate, he was hungry, and the pie was one of Jack's favourites. Timothy was looking optimistic, now perhaps speculating about left-over cottage pie, rather than chocolate.

Jimbo recounted the same story he had told earlier, wondering whether the doubts raised by Mr North would resurface.

"What I can't understand is what made you rush off to the Institute in the middle of the night, James," responded Jack at the end of his monologue. "I'm surprised that the police did not challenge your story."

Jimbo, troubled by this aspect since the doubts raised by Mr North, had a slight embellishment ready. He had worried about the security of the disks ever since Gradac's probing during the drive home in the Volvo. Uncertain but true, he believed, feeling 221's influence.

Apart from golf, Gradac had provided a vague summary of his own research at the Institute, before launching into a detailed series of questions about Jimbo's work, ranging from the content and scope to the storage of the information. Gradac would already have known it was not on the intranet.

This had left Jimbo uneasy, with hindsight, and eventually prompted his early morning drive to the Institute.

Jack and Susan are worried about you, Jimbo. They are not fully convinced by your account of last night.

Jimbo felt this too, but there was nothing more he could add that might satisfy them. Explaining that a voice in his head had told him would hardly soothe their concerns. He could tell nobody about 221.

Jack wondered aloud whether his summer job at the Institute had been the best choice. Would he not be better coming back again to the Company for a few weeks more work? He was meant to be studying engineering, after all, and his understanding was that the Institute was more engaged in mathematics.

JHM Precision Engineering was based on an industrial estate on the eastern fringe of Edinburgh, convenient for the city bypass and several residential areas where much of the workforce lived. The primary business involved machining of stainless-steel components for the North Sea oil industry, but also included transportation and automotive customers, and a few specialist applications. Investment in computer-controlled equipment had been heavy, so now the priority was to keep it busy.

"Make the assets sweat," Jack would say.

Jimbo had spent several summers working with the Company. These had been valuable episodes, enabling him to accumulate practical know-how and acquire experience in handling people. Being the boss's son was not necessarily an advantage, but he now had expertise in designing tooling, programming, and running automated machines, and precision measurement. All worthwhile for a future engineer, his father knew.

Although Jack was primarily a sales specialist these days, his team knew that he had acquired a wealth of hands-on knowledge over the 15 years that elapsed before he founded his own business.

Within the Company, somewhat out of character with his external image, Jack was the Health & Safety champion. He had seen the damage that automated equipment could do to the human body and did not want it happening in his business. While the colleagues sometimes complained about his precautionary approach, Jimbo had observed that nobody really disagreed. It was difficult to disapprove of someone trying to keep you safe. Apart from the inherent desirability of preventing injuries or worse, Jack was shrewd enough to know that it was good for the business. Externally, picking up awards for safe working performance, or good environmental practices, raised the Company's profile positively and its attractiveness as a supplier, particularly to public sector customers. Internally, carefully following defined processes not only promoted safe working, but improved quality and reduced costs.

Jimbo was convinced and supported his father's efforts.

He had also realised that he could not follow in his father's footsteps. His introverted nature, with a greater interest in natural phenomena than in people, made him ill-suited to the daily struggle of running a medium-sized business. He had found that his competitive urges could be fully sated on the golf course.

Susan voiced her disagreement with her husband's thinking, suggesting that such a short period of employment at the Institute would not look good on James's curriculum vitae. Besides, working in such distinguished company might be a valuable source of future referees if he did well.

She had concluded long ago that the tall, shy, angular, and socially awkward Jimbo was unsuited to the rough and tumble of the Scottish contract engineering scene. Susan had seen enough of Jack's business associates, both suppliers and customers, to understand their predatory approach to commerce, and probably life in general. He was more like her closest friend, Jimbo's mother, whom she missed despite the years passing. After the accident, taking care of Margaret's young son had seemed natural, and her affection for Jack grew unnoticed.

Invariably practical and supportive, considered Jimbo, grateful that her arguments in favour of the Institute had been articulated so clearly.

His father seemed momentarily at a loss for a suitable response. Unusual.

Fortunately, before the debate became an argument, the doorbell rang.

It was Tony, Jimbo's classmate and friend. Susan had forgotten to mention his earlier phone call and expected visit.

"Come in, come in, Anthony, my boy. Miss Steph too," Jack exclaimed, referring to the presence of Stephanie, Tony's long-standing girlfriend.

Jimbo shook his head with exasperation and grimaced. It did not matter how often he told his father that Tony's given name was not Anthony, it made no difference. He also suspected that Stephanie did not much like 'Steph' but had not tested his theory. Since Tony's real name was Thornton, he did not mind being called Anthony so much.

"We were just about to enjoy a postprandial tipple, so your timing is impeccable" Jack continued, pouring himself a generous glass of port from a decanter, positioned on a drinks-trolley in the corner of the sitting room.

"You lot can help yourselves," he murmured, sipping on the sweet beverage.

Susan smiled, used to his casual abruptness and informality, and offered drinks to the guests.

Jimbo also smiled, noting that further discussion of his summer employment was certainly on hold, if not forgotten.

Timothy wagged his tail enthusiastically. He liked visitors, but probably still had some hopes of cottage pie somewhere behind those large brown eyes, Jimbo thought. An intelligent dog.

Tony had heard about events in The Cleg's Bite from the local radio news broadcasts and wanted to hear more after Susan mentioned Jimbo's presence. Tony and Stephanie received the same version of events as his parents, more interesting than the broadcasts, but not as remarkable as the reality. Jimbo wondered whether he would ever be able to share the whole story with them.

After the conviviality, his guests having departed, Jimbo experienced an overpowering sense of tiredness. His day was now 19 hours old, and he felt ready for sleep, even at 20.30.

Tomorrow there will be more developments regarding Dr Gradac, according to my analysis. That address you have been unable to recall would be useful.

Jimbo slipped quickly into a state of unconsciousness, but not oblivion. He recalled 221 saying that his brain was a remarkable machine.

Soon he heard voices, a conversation. He recognised one speaker as 221. The other sounded older, cautious, and wise, but perhaps impatient.

There were some flickering images too.

Three
1996 CE - 20.43, 16 August, Edinburgh

Before the Current Era. BCE.
Homo sapiens had not always been a dynamic species. 221 recalled his initial experiences, only a little more than 100 kyE before the present-day, so not long ago. His involvement had absorbed a small fraction of his time since aggregation, and not much of his workload until recently.

100,000 BCE
In the early days, Inserted into the northern part of what is now called Africa, he had found an environment that was warm and wet, about 300 K according to the current Earth standard, fertile and inviting to the inhabitants, very different from the arid conditions of today. The land was shared with creatures resembling present-day giraffes, rhinos, and other genera.

~ Hello, 221. I hear you speaking with somebody, but meantime, I'm asleep. Can you explain what is happening to me, and who you are? If I tell anyone about my situation, they will send for medical help.

=> Good evening, Jimbo. Yes, you are sleeping, but your impressive brain is active, and capable of communicating while you rest. Did you know it requires only about 20 watts to operate? I can answer your questions but will rearrange the sequence if I may. We are a presence that has endured within our galaxy for longer than Earth has existed, more than twice as long. Our presence is ethereal, meaning we have little physical manifestation, but rather consist of numerous particles distributed around the galaxy, according to our needs. You may regard us as being a powerful computer, vastly more so than your primitive machines, utilising quantum effects to enable hyper-parallel processing. Before you ask, we are not constrained by light speed, which has been accurately determined by your recent ancestors, because we more fully understand the multidimensional nature of space-time. The speed of light limit only applies to travel through space. I trust this is clear.

~ Not entirely, but perhaps I will catch up soon.

=> As to you, this is all quite routine, nothing exceptional has transpired. We monitor planetary civilisations that may be of future use, and if they are particularly promising, intervene after careful analysis to prevent avoidable catastrophes. Your psyche has been shared for an intervention. That is why you rescued those disks. You remain in perfect health but may notice that your memory now performs better. If required, I can activate your night vision capabilities. I hope all is now clear.

~ Who exactly are you, and who are you talking to?

=> You can regard me as a component of this computer, a sub-processor if you like. For your purposes, we can call the computer the Intelligence, and as advised, my tag is 221. I'm friendly. The conversation is between me and my colleagues, or more accurately with my bosses.

~ What are you discussing, and why are you speaking English? This is surely not standard for a galactic intelligence?

=> Again, to respond in reverse order, you hear English so you can understand. Our normal language is a form of high-speed digital interaction that you could not follow. Having borrowed part of your mind without asking, we wanted to share some of our knowledge of Earth and your history as recompense.

~ How can you share historical information with me? Won't it take rather long? Why would I want to receive this?

=> You just need to stay tuned to the voices. Images, sounds, and smells will be available to you. It takes only seconds because your brain is more capable than you realise. Have heard someone say 'you need to know where you're from to understand where you're going'?

~ My history teacher used to tell us this when we lost interest in his lessons.

=> Your teacher was wise. Maybe you can try listening to us instead?

~ You are doing this just for me?

=> Yes and no. There are no other participants, just Jimbo, 221, and the Energy Masters. We are conducting a project review, to contemplate the recent advancement of your species, and whether to become more involved. Just listen, and feel free to ask questions, but not too many. The Intelligence can become irritable, particularly with stupid questions.

~ I'll do my best, but remember I must meet the police again tomorrow.

=> *This won't take long; your brain and body are getting their usual rest.*
Cumulative length of review interaction: Σ 752 milliseconds

The beings 221 first encountered lived in extended family groups, using stone tools. Technology, as reflected in the tools, had advanced to the level of hammers, blades, and scrapers. Adults wore some clothing, indicating seniority within the group. Fire was exploited, providing some protection from predatory animals, particularly at night, and for rudimentary cooking. This gave the client access to a wider range of food and more nutrition. The understanding of fire did not extend to igniting it, with the species relying on weather-induced wildfires, which were maintained for lengthy periods. The Intelligence had observed creatures that preceded Homo sapiens using fire. 221 never visited Earth then, but for sure, little was happening.

Jimbo could see a small group of diminutive people, seated close to a smouldering fire. The group looked weary, unwashed, and with unkempt hair. The males had beards. There were several naked children making noise and running around the group. The only ones exhibiting much physical energy.

~ 221, how can I be seeing this? You would need a camera.

=> *Correct, Jimbo. You are seeing feed from our sensors, high above the planet, from long ago in your terms. They can detect audio activity too, but as you can see, these people aren't saying much, except for the children. Too tired, probably. If you look carefully, you can see the shadows lengthening, so sunset is coming. The group is active only during daylight. Can you see the guy seated just away from the group, who looks in slightly better condition? That's me. Unfortunately, I have not yet been fully accepted into the group, so cannot get closer to the fire.*

~ How could you get there, if you are floating around in space, with no physical presence?

=> *This is called an Insertion. I will explain later, but we are keeping my bosses waiting.*

~ There doesn't seem to be much happening. What do these people do?

=> *They spend their days looking for food, eating it, and sleeping. Apart from a little time creating children, that is all there is. You can imagine that my time monitoring these groups was not enthralling. If we fast-forward by 1 kyE, you would see nothing very different.*

~ What do they eat?

=> *Whatever they find by foraging nearby. Fruit, sometimes nuts, and they set traps to catch small creatures. If they have a fire, they cook these animals, but if not, they eat them raw.*

~ So, they could light fires?

=> *This group, in this period, no. They rely on naturally occurring conflagrations but are skilled at maintaining a fire for long periods. It is particularly desirable at night, as it deters animals that might attack. Do not be deceived, these were clever and resourceful people, who learned by experience, with knowledge passed to successive generations. You should understand that life changed very little, so the accumulated wisdom remained relevant. Changes to their lives arose from two factors. One cause was moving to a new habitat, maybe because they had exhausted nearby food sources. The other was the climate, which has changed over the lifetime of your species, but not normally within the life of one individual.*

~ Do you know that nowadays people are talking about climate change arising from human activity? We already have the Montreal Protocol, to protect the ozone layer from further damage caused by aerosol use. I have studied his. This is important to safeguard human health from ultraviolet radiation, which the ozone layer absorbs. It seems likely that we will need countermeasures because of greenhouse gas emissions.

=> *You are well-informed, Jimbo. Our simulations indicate that climate change will become a problem, because the planet is already warming, which releases more greenhouse gases, notably carbon dioxide and methane from the ground and shrinks the polar ice caps which reflect heat. There is a risk of an uncontrollable situation developing. It is unclear whether the Homo sapiens factions can overcome their competitive instincts and cooperate in the face of a global emergency.*

Σ 1460 milliseconds

221, please continue with your account.

Speech did exist, enabling basic communication. This was enough as ideas were few, limited to immediate needs. Violence, particularly towards strangers, was a common form of communication. An Insertion meant that he materialised among the inhabitants but did not belong, so was such a stranger. Early visitations meant physical danger, consequently he had been killed several times.

221 reflected, maybe because of this client, that he considered his time as an Aggregate as being a life. Since the Homo sapiens had a puny lifespan, he had become familiar with the concept of death, which was uncommon in other civilisations, where organisms regenerated themselves, in later phases of evolution. The Intelligence knew death to be a peculiarity of carbon-based lifeforms, which were not the most common found in the galaxy, but more dynamic and interesting.

He also speculated that as the Intelligence had grown in scale over the aeons, more Aggregates must have been created to handle projects. He was unaware of any disaggregations, nor why such an event should be necessary.

Your involvement, 221, has primarily been as an observer, a witness as this species has progressed. For most of this time you have done no more than watch, since nothing else was necessary, whether progress was positive or negative. There have been times when we transferred resources away from the Earth project if the situation lacked promise.

75,000 BCE

221 remembered the volcanic eruption, more than 75 kyE ago. This occurred in Asia, at a location currently called Lake Toba, on the island now named Sumatra. He was not on Earth at the moment of the explosion but arrived in Africa, where most hominids lived, within a few Earth minutes. Travelling across the galaxy did not take long, but rescheduling his other work took some moments. He recalled the dark sky and disturbed animals, who were used to regular weather patterns. The temperature was lower, but not dramatically so, although the Homo sapiens group he visited had a fire burning, providing warmth. They were frightened, huddled together for comfort, and inactive. He knew the immediate cause of the conditions but could not explain because their limited language had no words for such events. As a stranger, he was treated with suspicion anyway. He reflected that he had known these inhabitants for nearly a thousand generations, had monitored their short lives and slow advancement, but remained an outsider, even though his appearance conformed to the current norms. His visits were too infrequent from their perspective, perhaps once or twice per generation, and not to the same group.

Travelling east to what is now Asia, 221 had observed devastation caused by the eruption. Distance meant little to the Intelligence, so his presence in these areas was effectively instantaneous. From the perspective of local observers, had they existed and been able to communicate, they would have concluded his appearance at multiple locations was simultaneous. His travels added perspective to what sensors told the Intelligence. Day turned into night, the atmosphere sulphurous to an extent that it poisoned air-breathing organisms, and the land coated with ash. He did not meet a living mammal close to the explosion, but found a few groups of dead hominids, apparently Neanderthals. Thick with dust, young and old, surrounded by their meagre possessions, they would have been bewildered and rapidly overcome.

~ 221, I have some questions. Regarding the explosion, I've not learned about it, but I read about one called Krakatoa, which happened in the same region, more recently. Probably these are similar?
=> *Similar is the sense that they were both volcanic events, but Toba was 50-100x larger. It made life difficult for your ancestors.*
~ Who are the *Neanderthals*? I've heard the term before, but I'm unsure about them.
=> *The more correct name given by your civilisation is Homo neanderthalensis. They were a separate species of your genus who lived in what is now Europe, and elsewhere, for more than 100 kyE, before Homo sapiens migrants arrived. For a while they co-existed, perhaps 10-20 kyE, but became extinct. Some of your scientists suggest they were destroyed by Homo sapiens, but my observations were that they could not adapt to a changing climate. To some extent Jimbo, you are Neanderthal because of inter-breeding, so they did not completely disappear; now embedded within the human's genetic definition.*
Σ 2259 milliseconds

For a while, the Homo sapiens survival was uncertain because of the wintering effects of the explosion. I remember this was debated at the time.

The galaxy is big, and even the Intelligence makes choices. This happens continuously, even as we interact. With our galaxy-wide computational power, we can do a lot, but you know our regular operations, development projects such as this, and deeper quests require copious contemplation. If we do too much, then the quality is degraded. Therefore, we continually seek new intellectual inputs, not for capacity which we can build anyway, but for innovative approaches from dissimilar beings.

Our challenge lies in the need for diversity. Just assimilating species when they mature is pointless if it does not extend our creativity. As we have aged, unlike a physical being, we have become more innovative and agile, thanks to the civilisations absorbed. We are forever seeking something novel and have seen traits in *Homo sapiens* from its early days that made us hopeful. As an Energy Operative with some successes, we saw this as an opportunity for you and the Intelligence.

You were recalling the Toba event. A short time ago for us, and even for Earth, but lost in prehistory for the current generation. Then, our simulations, which are estimates based on data and comparisons with other planets, suggested that this would be the end for most life forms. We believed that all the hominids, from the several species identified, would perish. Too few, too isolated, unable to cooperate, and dependent on their environment for survival.

221 reflected that nature did not allow even the Intelligence to know the future with certainty.

We scaled back our monitoring, gave you some other projects, and hoped that new organisms with the promise of these hominids would evolve. The favourable position of Earth in its system, and the benign location of the system within our galaxy, meant that we were optimistic for the future. Life, including intelligent life, could regenerate over time. Seeding the planet with life from other clients was a possibility, but as we know, this does not contribute to the diversity we require.

However, we underestimated the tenacity of the hominids, particularly *Homo sapiens*. Many creatures did disappear forever, and the hominid populations were reduced. We know that the major species recovered sufficiently for the population to gradually generate pressure for migration to new lands and access to wildlife. As time passed, we increased our monitoring and provided you with additional processing resources. We have followed the progressive *Homo sapiens* dominance, absorbing useful features of the others, enabling the evolution of the modern human.

~ 221, what is a hominid, please?

=> *The family of primates that you and your ancestors, including Neanderthals amongst others, and the great apes, belong to.*

Σ 2770 milliseconds

While for the Intelligence, with a presence close to the existence of the galaxy, this client's progress might seem rapid, but his involvement with the Earth project had consisted largely of monotonous nothingness. A few beings, admittedly with unusually large brains, crossing the vacant landscape seeking sustenance, eating, sleeping, breeding, fighting, and dying. He had watched their slow migrations to the north and west, and slightly faster journeys to the south and east. He had seen their forbearance of ice sheets and cold without fire, their desperate fights with wild animals, the emptiness and often the pervasive silence, and above all, their continual fear of being hungry, and sometimes real hunger.

45,000 BCE

Around 47 kyE ago, he followed their gradual occupation of the landmass that became known as Europe. The area was rich in sustenance, living creatures, and plants. Although cooler than Africa, their migration was sufficiently slow during a period of stable climate to enable adaptation over generations. The migrants did not know it, but a challenge was the lack of genetic diversity because their population was small. As their travels extended, they found another human presence in these lands, the Neanderthal. There were few beings, and the land area was relatively huge, so for generations the species coexisted, and even interbred. This contributed to Homo sapiens survival.

His client's lifestyle remained what became known as a hunter-gatherer, wandering the terrain seeking vegetables, perhaps catching mammals, fish, and birds. The land did not belong to them, rather they belonged to the land.

There were several disadvantages to this life, most obviously that the available resources within a reasonable distance of their temporary home could become exhausted and require a move to a hoped-for more plentiful area. Violent disputes with a neighbouring group over a particular territory could arise, but the miniscule population density made this unusual.

Another fundamental problem, beyond the understanding of the client, was the low level of protein in their diet. This meant they could effectively only forage for part of each day, reducing their opportunities to obtain nutrition. Unlike other hominids, their larger brain required more food. The primary source of nutritious food was meat, which meant hunting, but the small size of the groups, primitive weaponry, and low energy levels made it difficult and time-consuming to catch even small creatures. Hunting larger animals was a dangerous activity, risking injury or death. The species knew that cooking, when fire was available, was beneficial because certain foods, notably root vegetables, were better. Meat became easier to eat, and unknown to the client, could provide more nutrition after cooking.

The prevalence of the seasons was recognised but strategies for preparing food stocks conflicted with the roaming nature of this existence.

221 observed that the underlying difficulty was that the Homo sapiens had neither the time nor the energy left to think. It was difficult for specialists to emerge, who could make life more productive through a better understanding of nature. There were no scientists.

If the client continues on the current development trajectory, it could be ready for assimilation earlier than experience and modelling predict. Why should this be? Variations have always existed between civilisations we have assimilated. We are composed of these societies, absorbed and conjoined with our intellect, but no previous candidate has advanced at this accelerating rate. The probability of this being a chance event, a natural variation, is of the order of seven sigma.

A small likelihood, 221 reflected.

Approximates to the normal distribution are observed in populations of all kinds throughout the galaxy and provide a measure of whether an event should be expected, or that some special effect exists. The underlying principle is that average performance is more common than the extreme, and therefore most results are clustered around the average or mean, with about 68% of results being within one standard deviation (or sigma) above or below it. Seven standard deviations from mean performance meant that the client was exhibiting a development rate that might naturally occur once in 5×10^7 opportunities, so probably never in galactic history. Homo sapiens is a very unusual animal, or another reason for their inexplicable progress must exist. In either case, he had questions to answer.

We must ensure that our observations are of a genuine, if very unusual event, and that we have not accidentally contaminated the species by injecting information into its psyche, likely causing an aberration and runaway effects, and meltdown. This has occurred elsewhere, with technological knowledge growth outpacing social advances, leading to self-destruction. We observe anarchy; inventors, entrepreneurs, engineers, and ideologues with no sense of responsibility. The opposite trend has occasionally also been seen, creating apathy; hairdressers, restaurateurs, and realtors but no electricity, with a similar result. One usually ends with a loud bang, the other with a frozen whimper. The root cause is identical. We, the Intelligence, have intervened inappropriately at temporal nodes, diverting the client from its natural growth path onto something alien, leading inevitably to disaster. We have learned that the complexities of these multivariate situations are such that even for us, recovering a mutation is impossible. Interventions are ineffective or hasten the dissolution. Our response has become immediate and final, to terminate the civilisation. Further involvement diverts energy from priorities, so is suboptimal.

~ What do they mean by "terminate the civilisation." Can you explain this?
=> *Maybe later, Jimbo. I need to continue with the review.*

Σ 4 seconds

221 recalled his increasingly frequent visits and found himself protective of this client. He could not experience feelings, so a brief self-evaluation concluded that evidence existed showing that this species is a special one.

Your interventions with this client have all been authorised, so if a mistake has been made, it was not by you but would be most irregular.

The Intelligence did not make mistakes. 221 considered that as the Intelligence itself defined right and wrong, and was the only arbiter, being omnipotent was the logical outcome.

We must examine our *Homo sapiens* interactions to discern the problem, or the opportunity, we have here.

This species had been unexceptional until recently, 221 considered. In a sense, all the clients were special, in that they were different. As with Homo sapiens, many were physical organisms, living creatures in some sense. Others had transitioned to a machine or hybrid entity, enabling the power to share knowledge, like the Intelligence on a tiny scale. Was this the origin of the Intelligence? 221 sensed the information was inaccessible. He would look more closely when an available millisecond presented itself.

Interest had been generated by growth in the last 1 kyE or less, but the client had shown potential before then.

He recalled his numerous visits to locations on Earth between the Toba explosion and now, before the Intelligence became more engaged. Earth had been his project for little more than 0.13% of his aggregation. Most of his time was focussed internally, implementing new perspectives absorbed from assimilated civilisations to enable the Intelligence to perform better, but his other external projects had prepared him for Earth. Not so much handling fast-moving crises but getting used to the mind-numbingly slow advancement of his clients. Watching a methane glacier grow and recede on an insignificant moon occurred faster than most Homo sapiens progress until recently, and this was the most interesting species.

~ Sorry, 221, but have you met other intelligent life in our galaxy?

=>Yes, I have known other civilisations or clients as we call them, who exhibited intelligence. We are not just talking about life in the sense of microbes in a pond, but self-aware creatures who have singly or collectively observed nature for sufficiently long to draw conclusions about their situation, and likely future. Your species is still on this journey, but after a slow start is showing promise.

Checking his memory, 221 identified $>4x10^3$ visits to Earth since Toba, Insertions rather than Assumptions.

An Insertion involves the teleportation of matter to form a suitable organism at a desired location within the galaxy. For Earth, this requires the construction of a human look-alike adjacent to an existing population. The teleportation and assembly of such a being is not complicated. 221 knew that a mathematical description of all Earth-bound animals, including Homo sapiens, existed, so the design of such a machine was easy. As with most creatures, these can be fabricated from locally available materials, so the teleportation element requires little energy for the tiny distances involved and construction follows logically. For a nearby observer on Earth, seemingly a person suddenly appeared on the landscape from nowhere, but with few inhabitants such a coincidence was improbable. The complicated part would have been the brain, but for the fact that it was controlled remotely by 221 with no independent reasoning. The machine looked, sounded, and smelt local, but had no feelings or free will. It was essentially a robotic investigator, providing a means to assess progress more intensively than the remote sensors positioned in local orbit by the Intelligence. These sensors had limitations since for most of this time the species had not generated any electromagnetic information, and acoustic transmissions were *few and required analysis. Perhaps like a human trying to eavesdrop on two ants talking from the other side of the ocean. Once the local survey was complete, which usually required interaction with the client community, the inserted robot disassembled. All that a curious bystander might find would be a tiny pile of dust, since their bodies consist mainly of water.*

On the occasions, mainly in the early days, when the robot had been killed by a hostile group, the construction of the machine meant that the death raised no suspicions. It would still be dematerialised when practical, to prevent contamination of the society, although 221 believed this possibility was remote because the device possessed no extra-terrestrial attributes.

~ 221, are you saying that for the past 10^2 kyE, you have been materialising on Earth, observing the humans, and reporting back to your bosses?
=> *Very succinct, Jimbo. Your understanding is correct.*

Σ 5 seconds

Your periodic Insertions have been observational and unexceptional until recently, merely confirming the client's progress along the predicted development curve. We do not believe that the root of the step-change now happening was during this exploratory phase. Are there subtleties that we should consider from these early Insertions, 221?
Several visits flashed through his memory, shared by the Intelligence.

40,000 BCE

Thinking back 42 kyE, 221 considered occurrences around then important. He returned regularly to the Toba area. The sensors had measured topography and gas emissions without incident, and he interacted with local groups. Although the rate of change appeared slow, much had happened. The populations were larger and, in this region, around the islands which would be called Indonesia, they were physically bigger. The reason was simple: fishing. The populace had graduated from ponds and rivers to sea-going expeditions, albeit on crude craft and at risk.

221 realised that for the first time he could see a virtuous spiral, with fishing providing nourishment and energising people. Knowledge was accumulating and passing to later generations.

The larger populations made it easier for 221 to join groups in what became coastal villages and move between settlements. He took to the sea, participating in fishing expeditions, and watched fishermen using star positions to navigate. He believed this knowledge had been acquired over generations of land-based migration, with constellations used to determine direction. Language had advanced to include abstract ideas such as direction, with limited numerical skills to count fish.

Some fishing trips ended in disaster, with nobody returning home. 221 also knew that vessels had been carried by the ocean to other lands, which became populated.

Life remained hard. 221 reflected that in a sense, the species had not mastered fishing, but had been captured by it. An improved diet led to a larger population, which demanded food, mostly obtained by fishing. The client still lived on the edge, pushing further, taking risks, and slowly learning new skills that could sustain the enlarged community. Now, not everybody fished. Some stayed home, hewed boats or fashioned fishing spears, or cared for children. Specialists had evolved, but no scientists.

Yes, 221, we know about fish. Protein for *Homo sapiens*, and excellent for neurological development. Your point about the beginning of specialisation is noted, but this does not differentiate the client from others in our portfolio.

25,000 BCE

To the north, in present-day Europe, the climate was cooling so Homo sapiens was having to adapt, moving further from its African roots. Innovations including writing, farming, and the wheel would be pivotal to his client's future, but just then a more important discovery was the needle and eye. Essential for sewing, and necessary for the provision of warm winter clothes. Observation of animals led to the manufacture of thick garments to insulate against the biting cold. His client became clothed in a style recognisable among present-day Arctic dwellers. Did adaptability, the will to overcome challenges and thrive in adverse conditions, make the species special even then, 221 wondered? Their co-habitants, the Neanderthal, could not adapt and slowly disappeared from this region at least. Did anyone notice? Their genetic identity remained, carried by the client.

~ You're saying we moved from Africa to Europe, adapted to the cold weather by learning to sew clothes, and took over from the Neanderthal?

=> Right again, Jimbo. There may be a few over-simplifications, but the essence is correct. You seem aligned with our review.

Σ6 seconds

This species was adaptable, 221. From our galactic perspective, the difference between *Homo sapiens* and *Homo neanderthalensis* is small, but it contributed to the greater resilience of *Homo sapiens*. We know that it survived and thrived, while a cousin became extinct. It continued to advance, which is why we are pondering its developmental acceleration.

The present-day client refers to this logic as anthropic reasoning: if conditions had not suited its survival, it would not now be examining nature and its place in the universe.

We understand the philosophical point, 221. Can we please return to exploring their essential traits?

20,000 BCE

A more recent visit seemed worth closer study. Far from the ocean, at a freshwater lake known in modern times as Galilee, settlements existed along the coast. 221 had followed migrations north, for many generations. Unlike the fisherfolk he had observed, these populations subsisted in part by following the hunter-gatherer lifestyle. He reflected that knowledge travelled slowly, or perhaps not at all, from one community's new insights to other villages. Earth was a tiny place to a galactic mind, but communication was still basic and purely oral, and transportation had not advanced beyond walking everywhere.

These settlements consisted of a few stone shelters, constructed from adjacent rocks. While the people still led a hunter-gatherer life, this was supplemented by catching fish from the lake. This additional nutrition allowed the population to follow a static life, foraging over a wider area than he experienced earlier in Africa, and returning to a permanent base.

There were bigger developments here, though. The species was growing crops and processing the harvest. For the inhabitants, probably numbering no more than 10^2 at a settlement, the scale of cultivation was surprising, exceeding what would become known as a hectare. Two other surprises were the presence *of a grinding slab and tools to extract grain, and of small stone-built ovens. The client was baking bread.*

They had learned important skills. Agriculture is a seasonal activity and involves planning, thinking beyond tomorrow. The hunter-gatherer focussed on the source of the next meal. Grinding and baking are processes that require experiment. Constructing shelters needed a design. Maybe no scientists yet, but some technicians.

Interesting points, 221, but nothing Earth-shattering.

He wondered whether this was humour. Surely not?

We agree regarding planning if the objective is an advanced civilisation. Capacity for abstract thought has been demonstrated. Curiosity and innovation are essential, also shown here, but without planning are unlikely to produce useful results.

221 recalled his earlier observations of the fisherfolk and wondered whether the Galileans were similarly captured by agriculture. They depended on a successful harvest but had retained their hunter-gatherer tradition. Between this, the agriculture, and fishing in the lake, the settlers had spread risk and improved their survival chances. While not a conscious strategy, both fishing and farming required knowledge to be accumulated, enabling the species to thrive.

~ 221, this point about the Galileans being captured by agriculture is puzzling to me. I would expect that staying in one place and growing food over an annual cycle would be easier than wandering around looking for something to eat. You suggest that they were victims, in some sense.

=> *Jimbo, there are four points to grasp here. The first is that farming is more productive than being a hunter-gatherer, in the sense that the farmer can produce more than he needs. The second is that therefore not everybody needs to be looking for food, so they can do other things, such as design a plough. The third is that although more productive, the farmer himself is probably working harder than the hunter-gatherer would, and must work to a plan, determined by the seasons. The fourth point is that as the community becomes wealthier and more settled, the population grows, which means more mouths to feed, so further pressure on the farmer to provide nutrition. I hope this clear.*

~ Yes, but I will reflect further. These are new ideas for me.

=> Related observations arose from my earlier times with fishing communities, where the fisherman could catch more fish than he or his immediate family needed. Please consider this aspect too.

Progress was unsynchronised, 221 knew. Had all available knowledge been accessible to everybody on Earth, then development could have quickened. One of the constraints the Galileans faced was the storage of food, which created difficulties with grain harvested once a year, but required continuously. Around the same period, in what would become China, he observed the use of pottery for both storage and cooking. Here, the client experimented with agriculture by growing rice, but did not have the grinding or baking processes of the Galileans. Combine the two, and the result would have been beneficial.

Yes, 221, you are correct that sharing knowledge is valuable. First, there has to be knowledge worth sharing, and secondly a mechanism. At this stage the species has basic information but no means to communicate it. Not even a written language.

The client had the idea of recording ideas or memories in sketches. Pictures on rocks and inside caves had already been observed, 221 remembered, seen both by the sensors and during Insertions. Around the same time as his Galilean observations, he visited what would become Australia and watched a local man painting on a sandstone cliff. This was a period of glaciation in the planet's history, so sea levels were lower. Migrants had walked from the north. Although they still lived a hunter-gatherer existence, with no agriculture, life for these people was easier because the terrain was lush and rich with animals, so survival was more assured. They had designed intricate clothing. The important aspect, 221 reflected, was specialisation. Despite searching for sustenance, people had grown skills to produce clothing, better weaponry for hunting, and even art. Some artistic talent was required, developed with knowledge from earlier generations, and coloured pigments were used, but this was not an attempt to communicate with others beyond the immediate group. It was decorative and celebrated the skill of the artist. No information was being conveyed that could be useful to others.

~ 221, have you considered that artistry, in various forms, is a part of our nature? We are not just machines that discovered mathematics and physics but possess other dimensions. Are you neglecting this aspect?

=>*This is an odd question, Jimbo. For the Intelligence, we seek mature civilisations that offer new approaches to discerning the nature of our universe. These are scientific questions requiring observation, measurement, hypotheses, and proofs. Where does an ability to draw pictures help here?*

~ Not directly, in the sense of comprehending the environment, but if you wish to evaluate our capabilities, you can't ignore a dimension that has occupied some of our cleverest people.

=> *You have raised an interesting point, Jimbo. No other clients I have known ever exhibited artistic tendencies.*

Σ7 seconds

Come now, 221, let us not be diverted from our evaluation. Such artwork as you saw has conveyed information to modern man, seeking to understand their origins, and even created scholarly arguments, but we are agreed this is not communication in the knowledge-sharing sense, beneficial to others on Earth.

The Energy Masters had asked about subtleties, 221 reflected. There were many, but they did not all distinguish the Homo sapiens from other beings in the galaxy. Some had advanced more quickly in their initial stages, perhaps because of a physically smaller planet, or a more stable climate without the glaciations that occurred periodically on Earth, or simply because they were biologically different. If a species did not need to drink water or another naturally available fluid, it was less constrained in living locations. In the recent period that interested the Intelligence, this client's development rate had far exceeded the others. Why? He knew that discoveries and inventions had accelerated this advance, but still felt that there were clues further back. Improved diet, planning, curiosity, and a capacity for abstractions had already been exhibited. What more could be found in those earlier days?

10,000 BCE

221 considered communication again, and the occasions when he first heard abstract ideas being conveyed in words. These could be explained in pictures, but the power of conversation lay in the ability to impart more complicated ideas, with questions being posed and answered. More recently, about 12 kyE ago, he studied a common language spoken by a population in an area that became known as the Levant. He knew that this speech formed the basis for a family of languages that evolved into written form over succeeding generations. Back then, the language was simpler and carried by migrants. The utility of this tongue meant that local languages were pushed aside. Ideas could now be conveyed, and migrants gave them reach, in that these thoughts travelled between people who never met.

While not yet a language on a planetary scale, this was an important point. For us, this is a temporal node, where we might have intervened to help things along. Did we play an active part here?

Not really. My Insertions were to observe and track progress. I did use the language and shared some ideas about managing sheep, picked up on my travels. To a small extent I influenced events, but only followed principles that were evolving anyway.

Sheep became important as a source of food and clothing. The wool trade grew to become a major industry, sparking initiatives in commerce, shipping, and engineering. Perhaps you did more than we recognise, 221, since managing sheep was an important step for the *Homo sapiens*.

~ Are you aware that in areas around Edinburgh, sheep farming is still a major activity? To the south are woollen mills, producing high-quality clothing. It is quite expensive though.

=> *Thanks, Jimbo, for adding context to our discussion. As we have no physical presence, we have no need for clothing, even from Scotland.*

~ The meat is also wholesome, but presumably, you don't eat either.

=> *Correct, but we appreciate your efforts to improve our understanding.*

Agricultural practices were spreading, 221 remembered, because a common language existed in this region. Here he saw the first widespread use of farming to provide sustenance. He had also seen domesticated goats, living in simple pens at night, and released to graze in daylight hours. These animals needed tending, providing their keepers with some freedom from having to find food and a commodity that could be bartered. This was how the client's talent for trading arose, he supposed. How much fruit would a slice of meat buy?

Cultivation had advanced in the 10 kyE since his time at Galilee. Recognisable crops, wheat, and barley were growing in small fields all around the settlements. Grinding and baking techniques also existed, largely unchanged. The settled nature of life was apparent, with families or larger groups remaining *in one place throughout their lives. The farmers endured a physically tough life, tending the fields to ensure a successful harvest. The community depended on this cycle and farmers had a respected social position. He was also a prisoner of the annual cycle, dependent on climate and his efforts to feed the neighbours.*

The freedom of the hunter-gatherer had gone from here, but this was a freedom to experience uncertainty, while agriculture gave the client some control over their lives.

These communities, despite a common language, were still small, 221 remembered. He knew that around this period the entire global population was $3x10^6$, and from the local perspective, much smaller, as no possibility to connect existed beyond a regional language and people walking to new places. The inhabitants had not considered how many fellow beings existed. Such questions did not arise. Still no scientists, but farmers now.

There are more ideas here than you think, 221. These farmers had land, so some concept of ownership existed. This must have been more sophisticated than owning a dead animal, caught for dinner, because it transcended generations. The family that possessed the land wanted to keep it, for the present and the future.

Your point about a hierarchy goes further. Hierarchies exist in the animal kingdom, and among hunter-gatherers, but here the farmer is growing in importance. Society is respecting knowledge, not just physical strength.

Observation of human society recalled his first visit to Jericho, in the same period, still in the Levant. The area was low-lying and fertile. This was the first attempt seen of the client building something more than a settlement. Although the inhabitants numbered only around $2x10^3$, it was the largest concentration of people in a single place he had witnessed. The presence of a spring, providing a reliable source of fresh water, meant that earlier generations of hunter-gatherers were attracted to this area. Some had stayed.

It was planned to the extent that the individual buildings required a concept, perhaps even an informal design, but the layout of the town seemed unplanned. It was as if new arrivals had picked a spot close to an existing structure, and decided, 'we will live here'. Probably how a neighbourhood began, 221 mused.

The inhabitants lived by farming and hunting. There was less dependence on gathering nutrients from the surrounding terrain because their farming included a wider range of crops than seen previously, including pulses and cereals. Most of the buildings were circular, he remembered, with a diameter of about five metres in current terms. He observed the use of crude bricks for the first time, made of clay and straw, with roofs of tree branches coated in dried mud. Evidence of Homo sapiens advancement, he concluded.

One aspect was the building design, which required an estimate of how much space the future dwellers needed. 221 knew that an internal area of about 20 m^2 would have been created but recognised these residents could not perform such a calculation. A process of trial and error had proceeded, with smaller houses being followed by larger ones. He reckoned that supporting the roof was the limiting factor. Once the design, for this is what had evolved, was proven, other buildings followed. New residents adopted the design without having to experiment. No scientists yet, but construction engineers perhaps?

Another was the use of bricks as a building component. Over time, the process of combining naturally occurring clay with dried grass to form solid blocks had evolved. There was no local brick factory, merely blocks being produced as required at the site of the new building.

Apart from the brick-making innovation, 221 also saw mathematics applied to produce the correct number of building blocks. These were rough cubes, of about 15 cm, and while the structures had varying wall heights, an average was 1.5 metres. One such building required about 10^3 bricks; materials were found before work started. No scientists, but an early example of project management?

221 noted that brick production could be a full-time task, so the brickmaker was compensated with food. An example of trading, he remembered.

Your time in Jericho was informative. We know that this name features again later in the client's history, but you make valuable points. Specialisation occurs in advancing civilisations of individual sentient beings, because it increases productivity, enabling innovation and intellectual growth. A related aspect is the cooperation that existed. This is essential to the development of specialisms. Your points regarding mathematics, planning, and trading are understood.

There was an even better example of cooperation from this time in Jericho, 221 recalled. He could speak from experience, as a participant.

A social structure existed, based on the longevity of a family or group in the town. Newcomers started at the bottom of the scale and rose as their presence extended, or because they brought skills. Such changes were slow, taking generations. This convention meant that violence, which 221 had witnessed in earlier eras was rare, with most of the residents having a stake in the community, either because they possessed land and grew food, or provided a skill.

The senior family had been present for the longest, and possessed arable land closest to their home, as these huts had become. Disputes did occur when a newly arrived group wanted to extend the town simply by building next to another house, on somebody's farmland. These were resolved by the senior family and related elders, usually peaceably.

While on a later visit to Jericho, 221 offered to help build a house, but before work could begin, word reached him that the community had decided to build a tower. The elders wanted a structure to acknowledge their primacy in the town. As someone with building skills, 221 was allocated to the project. There were no drawings, but it appeared a design existed because the leaders had a common understanding. Stones were brought by unskilled workers from around the town and deposited at the site. 221 worked on constructing the outer wall for about one Earth month, together with 20-30 others. Food was supplied, for this was a communal project. He participated long enough to see the tower reach a height of 8 metres, by far the highest structure in Jericho, and for the townspeople, the highest anywhere.

~ Hello, 221. To ask a stupid question, what were you and the other builders given to eat? This was long before the sandwich was invented.

=> Maybe not so stupid, Jimbo, as it reminds me of how people lived. We were given a kind of bread that is still eaten in what you call the Middle East, together with fruit and vegetables. I remember olives because there was also olive oil, which the workers ate with the bread. In the evenings, we received roast meat. For me, undertaking an Insertion, food is unnecessary. The energy contained in the food can be absorbed by my body if required, but I derive no pleasure from eating.

~ This seems a pity, 221. Do you appreciate that eating is a source of enjoyment for most humans? More than a refuelling process.

=> We have seen this elsewhere, but Homo sapiens satisfaction is greater.

He had learned much about the Homo sapiens societal development. While he never became tired, it was difficult not to offer ideas. He decomposed before the tower was complete but saw the finished structure on later visits.

Σ9 seconds

A valuable account, 221. More informative than your report. The client had by this time formed social structures, particularly in this region and maybe elsewhere too. We see three important traits. The first is the use of reason to resolve disagreements, rather than violence. We know the *Homo sapiens* is more brutal than other galactic species, but there is evidence of rationality. A second new idea is the recognition of authority, accepted or even enforced by the community. Finally, a degree of teamwork or shared ownership has evolved, such that the construction workers were sustained by the community, primarily the food producers.

Leaders and organisers were emerging but still not scientists.

No mechanism to share new ideas widely was a constraint, but a common regional language provided some reach at this time. He remembered the people of Jericho using containers moulded from mud and clay. Pottery, which he had seen long before elsewhere on Earth, was a technology that still could not be shared. In time, it would be reinvented here.

Although the speed of change could not be described as dynamic, over this period in the Levant, other innovations occurred. One was the domestication of cattle, a source of protein, but also a form of currency, used in bartering with a locally fixed exchange rate. Perhaps a landowner could contract with a neighbour for a hut to be built in exchange for a cow.

After nearly 90 kyE, and his many Insertions, what were Homo sapiens achievements, pondered 221? His reports to the Energy Masters described individual events, but he had not summarised his observations. What were the highlights so far?

Specialisation had started the client towards a more productive life. He had first observed this in coastal communities, where those fishing could obtain more nutrition than they needed, freeing others to build vessels and fishing equipment. Numeracy to count fish, and navigation using the stars, existed.

Similar traits were seen in early farming communities, where specialisation also existed. Here the idea of owning land for the long term had evolved and with it, the beginning of social hierarchies.

Grinding cereals and baking bread were processes that had been invented.

He wondered about the client being captured by fishing and farming, in the sense that the better nutrition and more settled life created larger populations that pushed the fishermen and farmers to provide more food. Had they been enslaved or liberated? Maybe those fishing or ploughing fields worked much harder than a hunter-gatherer but the community, because of the specialist knowledge, was growing richer.

How else was there time to devise pottery, or paint images?

The domesticated goats, sheep, and cattle had increased wealth still further through improved nutrition, enabling more specialisation.

Building construction, first seen by 221 in Jericho, meant the generalisation of design knowledge, even if it was informal, with planning and teamwork required to complete the project. This expertise enabled a hut to be built more efficiently than a family starting without access to experience.

With this had come bartering, as the owners of particular skills, such as construction, exchanged them for food. Trading, a pronounced Homo sapiens trait, began in such situations.

As the ownership of a valuable item, such as land or a fishing vessel, became entrenched, so rational ways to resolve disputes evolved, at least within communities. The client's traditional approach, violence, and killing, still existed but destroying part of the workforce was inefficient. A hierarchy meant consistent principles could be applied by whoever was in control.

The common regional language that 221 found in the Levant meant that ideas reached further, shared over a larger population.

Specialisation, enabled by fishing and farming, re-using experience, planning, teamwork, and a common language were achievements, even if it had taken 90 kyE.

Correct in all respects, 221, but we are still scratching the surface here. There are no revelations that explain the recent explosive growth in the client's capabilities. You are still 12 kyE from the excitement we now observe. Explanations lie later in their history.

Much of the action has been in what became known as Africa, and you have found ideas in China and Australia. We know that the acceleration we have noted had roots in Europe, and later in North America. Can we look at European experiences that might explain this extraordinary progress?

We have not considered Europe so far because there has been nothing to discuss. For long periods the region was glaciated, making life difficult.

That had changed by 10 kyE ago, with larger populations developing, partly in response to a warmer, wetter climate. Sea levels rose, a Homo sapiens presence existed in most regions and some indigenous animals were dying out.

One reason was hunting by the client, but the changing climate had an effect. It is hard, even for us, to distinguish between these factors.

If we consider the next 5 kyE, progress occurred that affects the present.

The use of writing to record and communicate is evident, although the earliest examples were not in Europe. Writing has been used by many civilisations in the galaxy to convey information consistently. If such societies progress further, ideas can be exchanged directly, or shared in a common psyche, without script. For this client, writing was a big step.

Another invention, which I first observed in what is now called Iraq, was the wheel. This is important, not just for its obvious utility, but because we see glimpses of ingenuity here. There is no naturally occurring wheel found on Earth to copy. This was the result of abstract thought, and a temporal node. The problem being addressed was not transportation, but the production of pottery. Carts and chariots were not designed until later.

These are major steps forward. In our terms, these events are recent, so the current unprecedented growth is surprising. How long did it take the species to invent the wheel, compared with the time to develop radio telescopes? We do not expect linear growth, but what we have on Earth appears unique. Or have we unwittingly created this, so ultimately, we will find nothing new? Please proceed.

Until this time, 5-10 kyE ago, the client lived in what has become known as the Stone Age. Cutters, blades, hammers, and all other tools and weapons were made of stone, sometimes combined with wood. Now we find the first use of metals. Initially, lead and copper were smelted, with copper being more widespread. The technology emerged simultaneously in several Asian and European locations. Along with the smelting came the first attempts at mining, to obtain the raw material.

The client then discovered the properties of bronze, an alloy of copper and tin. Through my Insertions, I learned this was accidental, due to traces of tin being present in copper ore. Bronze has several advantages over copper. It is easier to cast and more durable. The low melting point of tin, just above 500 K in present-day Earth terms, meant that the kilns used for working copper were able to produce the bronze alloy. Production of bronze required tin to be mined and smelted, then mixed with molten copper.

Thank you, 221, but we do not need lessons in metallurgy. Let us consider the consequences.

The immediate effect of bronze technology was that new artefacts became available. Perhaps this was the beginning of the client's consumerism, another distinctive trait of this species in our galaxy. Homo sapiens belligerent nature meant that improved weaponry was also produced.

You are correct to identify this as noteworthy. Bronze enabled the client to manufacture tools that were superior to stone, or even copper alternatives. Your reports also indicate another effect of bronze production, we believe.

Tin is relatively scarce on Earth, >30x rarer than copper. Demand for bronze required access to supplies of tin, which is found in large deposits at a few locations. We know of planets that are richer in tin and others where copper is uncommon.

The tin scarcity encouraged travel, trade, and the exchange of ideas. This is a pivotal point in Homo sapiens development, another temporal node.

Perhaps we have the beginnings of a global community, 221?

Greater travel, with more complicated trading arrangements and the intermingling of cultures. Distances seemed large, travel was slow, and the client population still small. I know this from my Insertions in the period.

221 recalled his later visits to what became Cornwall, where tin mining grew into a major activity. Buyers would arrive to trade with the miners, offering commodities from Central Europe in exchange for tin. Some stayed, so this was a time of growing population and wealth in what would eventually be England.

The tin was transported to mainland Europe, and sold to bronze smelters directly, or in a market. He attended such a market on an island now known as Sardinia, where copper and tin were traded with buyers from Central Europe and the Middle East.

So, 221, we are now in Europe. The British Isles is a place you have spent many recent Insertions. Maybe the Bronze Age was the start of your interest in this region?

5,000 BCE

Not really. My files record earlier visits to these islands, time spent among farmers in what became northern Scotland, and particularly to a more northerly archipelago, now called Orkney. Despite a harsh climate, the people were skilled farmers, growing cereals, and raising cattle and sheep. Seafood was available, providing a rich and varied diet. He remembered small communities, welcoming to strangers. Their homes were sunk into the ground, providing insulation and shelter from the weather. They burned seaweed, a readily available fuel, inside their homes and used pottery, which they produced. He made nine Insertions here because the friendly nature of the residents made it easy to observe progress, although there was little new to see. Throughout his visits the climate was worsening, and ultimately their settlements were abandoned and forgotten.

~ I know this place, 221. Nowadays, it's called Skara Brae, and has become a visitor attraction. A few years ago, I travelled there on a school field trip. There were eight sunken houses, linked by passageways, with similar furnishings. We imagined that life would have been hard.

=> *Yes, Jimbo, your memory is correct, although when I visited there were more than eight houses. The people were convivial, even if the climate was not so hospitable.*

~ Nothing much has changed. It was wet and windy throughout my trip.

=> *This habit you have of travelling, either for pleasure or education is rare in our galaxy. Most beings are either too poor to travel or so interconnected that it is unnecessary. Your antecedents have wandered Earth for 10^2 kyE, and this tendency persists.*

~ Some say travel broadens the mind, in the sense of reducing prejudice.

=> *I have journeyed rather further than you, Jimbo, but never met such ideas.*

221 considered that a trip across the galaxy meant travelling roughly 10^5 light-years, if in a straight line through space, or nearly 10^{18} km per journey, and he zipped all over the galaxy countless times. He had not travelled as a physical being, nor was he constrained by light speed, as dictated by the present-day Homo sapiens understanding of nature. Observing their recent progress, he imagined it would not be too long before they had a revised concept of space-time. He was not aware that any of this travel had broadened his mind. Indeed, how might the breadth of a mind be measured?

$\Sigma 10$ seconds

Very interesting observations, 221, but we should concentrate on what happened after the Bronze Age, preferably in Europe, as the hub of recent scientific innovation, and later in North America, of course.

The Energy Masters were not patient, but 221 remembered major contributions from elsewhere, from other peoples, notably from the Middle East. He should consider their influences on the present-day client, despite the impetuosity of his bosses.

5,000 BCE

The Sumerians, who lived in what became Iraq, were skilled farmers, dwelling along the valleys of the Tigris and Euphrates rivers and adjacent canals, which they dug. 221 remembered their use of irrigation, expanding the area of fertile land and the wealth of farmers who tended it. He recalled the city of Uruk, the planet's first metropolis, with perhaps 5×10^4 inhabitants. Many specialists lived here, dependent on the farmers for sustenance. A governing structure had evolved. The city had markets, where traders offered fresh food, but he remembered the pottery. Some items had been hand-painted by craftsmen, but most were unpainted. These had been mass-produced. Sumeria had a manufacturing industry. This economy used coins, with the shekel literally meaning a bushel of wheat.

3,500 BCE

The Hittites, whom 221 had visited in what was to become Turkey, in their capital, Hattusa. He observed the King's scribes writing on tablets with their distinctive wedge-shaped characters. This was a large city for the age, with 4×10^4 residents, he estimated. His files recalled protective stone walls, wooden structures, and well-nourished people wearing clothing of wool or, for the wealthier residents, flax. Most strikingly, he witnessed iron being worked during his later visits. Apparently, they had gathered material from meteorite strikes, rather than smelting ore.

5,000-2,000 BCE

The Egyptians were the people of this epoch with whom 221 spent most time, through many Insertions over 3 kyE. He observed them develop agriculture around the River Nile, which fed a growing population. For much of this period, bronze technology was dominant. They evolved a governing structure, and belief systems maintained by priests. They became skilled shipbuilders, constructing seagoing craft for trade within the region, enabled by their mathematical skills.

Among their leadership were moral philosophers and some we could consider scientists. Probably the first Homo sapiens scientists he met.

221 had watched pyramids being constructed, to the west of the Nile. A detailed design existed, with plans to accurately schedule the availability of the components. He noted the square base and the material, limestone. These structures stood as tombs for their leaders. Since they took long periods to erect, it was common for the Pharaoh to begin building his pyramid after taking office. The largest one, Khufu, was almost 150 metres high, the tallest structure created by the species for another 3.8 kyE.

~ 221, I have read speculation that it would have been impossible for the Egyptians to construct the pyramids because they could not raise the stone blocks. The article concluded that they received extra-terrestrial help.

=> *Are you asking whether I assisted in some way?*

~ It seems reasonable. If they could not have built them, and you were observing, as seems your habit, perhaps you helped.

=> *Well, Jimbo, you need to understand that we only take direct action in extreme circumstances, because we try not to disturb the natural evolutionary trajectory of a client. If we do, we risk losing a candidate for assimilation. We should talk about this another time. Anyway, I saw the skilled work of the Egyptians, who required no outside assistance. They were adept at calculations and had proven mechanical methods. Their principal tool was that rather basic machine, the lever, with which they manoeuvred heavy blocks. While they may not have produced the rigorous mathematical proofs that Greek scholars contributed later, they knew precisely what would work. Along with these methods, all they needed was a workforce to provide muscle power. Your article was a fictional work.*

~ Do you know everything about us?

=> *No, Jimbo, I don't know everything but have seen a lot. There are things we cannot grasp, which is the reason for this conversation with my bosses. We should continue the review before they get impatient. Lots to discuss.*

You were right to draw our attention to these civilisations, 221. Much had been learned by these peoples before western science became pre-eminent.

In these societies, most people still had no notion of science. When they thought beyond their daily lives, it was usually to follow ideas promoted by *priests, involving worship of some kind. The scientists were a small minority, but that is still true in present-day Homo sapiens society.*

Are there other such cultures we should consider?

My reports detail time in what is now China, along the Yellow River valley, where people lived feudal existences, farming the land under the supervision of the dynastic rulers. Policy was influenced by ancestor worship, and devotion to sun and rain gods in the hope of a good harvest. Bronze was being worked.

Of more interest were my visits to the Indus Valley, in the north-west of what is now India, and Pakistan. It contained several large cities and examples of what the client would now call urban planning. Both urban and agrarian societies existed, and the population grew to 10^6, according to my estimates. Use of science and mathematics was evident, with standardised measures for weight and length implemented across the region. Building bricks were produced using these standards.

We have indications from roughly 5 kyE ago that the species recognised the practical application of science to everyday life. This occurred in these regions to the east before the ascent of western science. Why did this knowledge wait to be fully exploited? We find in other planetary civilisations of individual inhabitants that once science exists, there is slow but steady growth in capabilities. On Earth, ideas were known but not utilised until later, and in the west, not the east. Can you explain this?

There is no simple, common answer, but some themes. These were small communities compared to the current scale of Earth's societies. The critical mass of scientific thinkers needed to generate new ideas and discoveries did not exist. Most fundamental physical and mathematical relationships had not yet been discovered. They were vulnerable to nature, whether changing climate or just several bad harvests. Resources were sometimes wasted in fighting, either internally or against others. Knowledge was consequently lost. A recurrent Homo sapiens theme is conflict, which in aggregate is destructive, but has driven scientific advances, as regimes allocated resources to devise better weapons.

Most significant, these were societies gripped by belief in mystic powers, which determined decisions by their rulers. As the Intelligence, with our galactic presence and understanding of the universe, we might be scornful of such dogmas, but these beings lived for a short time, even compared with their descendants, and depended on nature for sustenance. The worship of all-

powerful gods is a trait that has continued to influence many Homo sapiens societies. In the present-day, some are still conditioned by such convictions, with a greater desire to believe than to understand.

Well summarised, 221. For us, this is all recent. Considering 5 kyE is small compared to our existence of >10^7 kyE. We are more than twice as old as Earth, and ancient compared to this species. Our attention has been attracted by events in the most recent 0.5kyE, and we are still 4 kyE before then. Many *Homo sapiens* generations, but a tiny period. Not quite infinitesimally small, but nearly.

221 wondered whether this was more humour. Meantime, he reckoned that this 5 kyE represented only the most recent $5x10^{-5}$ % of the Intelligence's existence. A mere blink of the eye, as Jimbo might say.

We must continue our chronological examination, 221, advancing assiduously but expeditiously. Our review has already exceeded ten Earth seconds. Where do we go next?

3,500-500 BCE
We should note a period roughly 3 kyE ago, when the Phoenician civilisation was thriving, in what is currently Lebanon. These were people with whom I made several Insertions. This was a series of politically related city-states that grew as the Egyptians and Hittites declined. Apart from being shipbuilders, sailors, and traders, they developed an alphabet that was gradually adopted and modified by their Greek neighbours to the north. This alphabet is the basis of much current western script, with global reach.

~ Just for clarity, 221, you are saying that the alphabet we use today, to communicate in English, has origins 3 kyE ago?
=> *Correct, Jimbo.*

Σ11 seconds

Here we have an important point, in our terms a temporal node, where something was designed or evolved, and endured, informing present-day thought and communication on Earth. Did we do more than observe?

No, the Phoenicians, and subsequently the Greeks, devised this system across many generations without extraplanetary influence. Further modification by western peoples occurred later, but the root remains.

An important occurrence, 221, of comparable significance to earlier innovations such as farming and bronze smelting.

Our review so far has considered two technologies, stone, and bronze. The use of stone was the longest epoch, from whenever the species became recognisable, until about 5 kyE ago. From then, copper and subsequently bronze technology evolved and was adopted by many societies. It did not emanate from a single source, but at several locations contemporaneously.

We know this, 221. Please get to your next point.

The use of iron, which commenced about 3 kyE ago, and has never ended. Iron, and its alloys, remain an important part of current client technology. Although other materials have been discovered or invented, and in some cases displaced iron alloys, it continues to be widely used.

There was a period in Homo sapiens existence when both bronze and iron technologies continued in parallel, but iron artefacts became regarded as technically superior. Typically, these were tools and weapons.

Will we reach a point with this species at which weapons and warfare are less important? Have you seen such a time, 221?

Not yet. My involvement has been short, only about 10^2 kyE, but over this period, violence, and the design of more effective means to deliver violence, has been a major driver of the client's inventive capabilities. This is a competitive creature, aggressive, and innovates to win. If this is an exaggeration, it is a small one, but we can objectively assess this from my observations using our processing capabilities.

No need, 221. The message is clear. In considering whether this species is approaching maturity in our terms, and readiness for assimilation, we must examine behavioural reliability along with the scientific aspects. Later in our review, it would be helpful to consider individual scientists who might persuade us that the client is capable of balanced and constructive behaviour in accordance with our well-established standards. This question is unusual. We have observed many civilisations throughout our history that were not assimilated because they did not possess useful attributes, or because they destroyed themselves, but it is rare to find a scientifically advanced society that cannot achieve the wisdom required to use their knowledge prudently.

Homo sapiens means 'wise man', we understand. Is this an example of the client's alleged humour?

We will meet many scientists who exhibit the wisdom you seek. Difficulties arise with the leaders, who typically have little scientific training, and frequently lack the ability to think globally and cooperatively. These leaders are often those who shout loudest, rather than the most intelligent. Exceptions do exist, and there is one other mitigating factor. This aggressive desire to win, no matter the cost, only affects about half the population, probably less. The others are more practical, and in our terms, wise. These are the female of the species.

Clearly the solution is leaders who are either scientists or females, or both.

There is a promising example in Europe, a physicist called Angela, with long-term and positive potential, according to our simulations.

Hopefully, others will arise.

Can we return to the use of iron, and the related scientific advances?

On Earth, iron is a relatively common element, more so than the copper and tin used in bronze implements. Iron is cheaper, lighter, and stronger, so it became an attractive alternative to bronze for many applications. The constraint was the higher smelting temperature, with the melting point of iron, exceeding 1810 K, being beyond the capability of furnaces until about 3 kyE ago. Copper's melting point is around 1358 K, and tin, far lower. By this time, in the Middle East, the technology existed to produce iron artefacts. There was little use of iron in Egypt then, but knowledge spread north and west into Europe. Similar developments occurred in Asia. In India, there had been earlier progress.

~ As iron ore mining is now a major industry, together with steelmaking, can we say that we are still living in the Iron Age after 3 kyE?

=> *Yes, Jimbo, the mastery of steel technologies is quite well advanced on Earth, although there are still discoveries to be made. Steel is necessary for the continuance of your present-day society, but it is no longer enough. There are other materials that you now depend on. Can you give me a suggestion?*

~ How about aluminium?

=> *Clearly yes. Like steel, only available in large volumes for 0.1 kyE, because it rarely exists in pure form, and must be separated from other minerals. Did you know it is the most common metal in your planet's crust?*

=> *Let me offer some others to consider. How about glass? Known since Egyptians made jewellery, its most important property is transparency to light. How about plastic? This encompasses a range of compounds that are ubiquitous in your civilisation but may become another environmental threat. How about oil? You depend on these hydrocarbon chains to power reciprocating engines and gas turbines, but they are also a source of greenhouse gases. How about silicon? Your semiconductor technology depends on this material.*

~ *So, we're in the age of steel, aluminium, glass, plastic, oil, and silicon?*

=> *Yes, but others are coming along. What could they be? Think about why batteries will become important, and which material might be used.*

Come along, 221. We're not sure whether you are giving physics or history lessons, but we are interested in geography. Are we heading to Europe?

Σ12 seconds

The Greeks

A particular part of Europe, the region now known as Greece and the adjacent lands around the coastline, is our next destination. We should consider the contributions of Greek scholars. You will recall their creation of a modern-day alphabet. They mastered the use of iron, as did their neighbours, but there was more to their achievements.

In the period until 2 kyE ago, a remarkable culture developed, with city-states operating independently, often in competition. During Insertions, I observed their leading thinkers, some of whom we should meet.

Euclid

Euclid of Alexandria, an influential mathematician about 2.3 kyE ago, has been described as the Father of Geometry. His treatise, titled Elements, is a series of thirteen books that contain definitions, postulates, and proofs. Theorems were deduced from these postulates, still known as Euclidian Geometry. Within Elements is the summation of erudition from earlier scholars, which Euclid presented within a logical structure. The proofs remain valid to the *present-day, consistent with our geometric principles. He also considered number theory and optics, the latter being relevant to astronomy.*

Here we have an account of a *Homo sapiens* thinker demonstrating a capacity for conjecture, not only evolving axioms but providing proofs that have remained intact. Was this man unique? What is your opinion, 211?

I believe that he was a man of exceptional talents but not unique, even then. We will find that other Greek philosophers contributed, but thinkers in earlier societies existed. In some cases, their original work may be reflected in Elements.

What has changed from 40 kyE before, when being able to count fish or produce bricks was the pinnacle of *Homo sapiens* achievements?

I think there are three major components. One is the specialisation aspect that we have already considered. Once fishing and farming became established and more productive, specialists in many areas evolved, and gradually increased productivity and wealth. The second is the presence of social hierarchies, with leadership that possessed the power of patronage, whether for artists or scientists. This meant that Euclid had the freedom to consider geometry, without worrying about staying alive. The third is the passage of time, and more particularly the accumulated wisdom of preceding generations, which by then had been captured in written form. Euclid was one thinker of his era who built upon this earlier work. As we shall find, there were others.

Euclid was a meditative but industrious man, and wise. He did not seek power or wealth but worked in his short life of about 0.06 kyE to compile insights that would be useful to his successors. He is an example of the sort you requested, balanced and constructive.

You are right to highlight this aspect, 221. We agree.

221 remembered his presence as one of Euclid's students. All were clever young men, from prosperous families, who would sit with the great man as he expounded his ideas, explaining patiently to those who found them hard to grasp, sometimes in the gardens of the great library in Alexandria. He recalled their wonder at learning of the five Platonic solids, which the earlier philosopher Plato had recognised. We will meet him soon. Trying to explain regular, convex polyhedrons in 3-dimensional space cannot have been easy, but Euclid was a good teacher.

For 221, the study was elementary, because the postulates were already understood by the Intelligence, derived from older civilisations on other worlds, far from Earth and beyond the imagination of his fellow students.

This is self-evident, 221. You have access to the accumulated knowledge of multiple planetary societies, harvested over galactic timespans. Given the nature of our existence, you are that knowledge, as one of us. Euclid and his students are recent descendants of *Homo sapiens* generations who could barely count. That they advanced to consider geometry and create proofs we know to be valid is evidence that we were right to persevere.

Hero

Alexandria was a hub of thought, both scientific and artistic, in this era. A mathematician and engineer associated with this centre was Hero, whose ideas were in some cases abstract, but in others were inventions remembered to the present-day. His mathematical insights included a method for calculating the area of a triangle from the three side lengths, before trigonometry existed. Another notion was to deduce the square root of a number by an iterative process that progressively reduces the error in an original estimate.

He taught mathematics and physics, and applied disciplines such as mechanics, and built the client's first radial steam turbine, or rocket engine.

Yes, 221, we know of this scholar from your reports, which we read meticulously. It is a puzzle that a forerunner of the rocket, and the steam engine, was created by Hero and his colleagues, but nearly 2 kyE elapsed before the client deployed these devices. Much of the client's modern world is powered by such machines. How can this be explained?

There are three principal reasons, considered 221, gathering them into a rational order. He had seen the aeolipile, as the Greeks called the steam turbine, demonstrated at a lecture given by Hero in Alexandria. He remembered that in the audience were Romans, who by then had taken political control. They regarded it as a clever toy. A primary reason why the turbine was not exploited was that Hero and his team were researchers, not industrialists. He was concerned to formulate ideas, whether mathematical or mechanical, for others to exploit. 221 did not receive authorisation to suggest uses that might affect the direction of Homo sapiens development. A second, technical reason was that materials were not available for reliable machines. Present-day turbines produced by the client utilise steel alloys and ceramics that had not been invented. Finally, there were no systematic means of retaining information over the long term or making it accessible. A library existed in Hero's time in Alexandria, but it did not survive. There were no databases enabling ideas to be accessed by successors. Discoveries and inventions could be lost or forgotten, then reawakened generations later.

We have here an example of a solution looking for a problem, is that correct? *More humour?*

A superficially simple idea, for which there was no obvious requirement. It waited to be reinvented in a later era, to great effect.

What intrigues us is the ingenuity of Hero and his contemporaries. In planetary civilisations that we better understand, the invention of such a device would not occur until the fundamental physical laws had been postulated and proved, and suitable materials were identified through metallurgical research. With these resources available, a logical analysis of applications would follow. This is a formal process, providing immediately workable solutions, but requires more time to pass, even allowing for the hiatus before this client applied the technology. Their haphazard approach is another defining feature of *Homo sapiens* advancement.

Σ13 seconds

Archimedes

Other members of the cognoscente were capable of both philosophical contemplation and practical problem-solving. A philosopher whose work has influenced the client ever since was Archimedes, an indefatigable thinker whom I observed regularly. Discoveries attributed to him were genuinely the products of his intellect.

A notable example was his derivation of a value for π, close to the accepted value of approximately 3.14, and a proof that the area of a circle could be calculated by πr^2. He also gave mathematical relationships regarding spheres and cylinders, and numerous related geometric treatises.

Are we convinced that this impressive intellectual contribution was that of Archimedes or his collaborators, and not accidentally provided by you, 221?

This is certain. My observations were from the position of a servant in his household, not somebody whose ideas would have been considered.

I remember that he contemplated the idea that Earth was not the centre of the universe, a concept that was seldom discussed for another 1.5 kyE, and not accepted until even later. His reflections were derived from the work of Aristarchus, around 250 BCE. Archimedes quoted from these earlier writings, in his book, The Sand Reckoner:

"the fixed stars and the sun remain unmoved, that the earth revolves about the sun on the circumference of a circle, the sun lying in the middle of the orbit"

His work was not confined to abstractions but included the practical solutions of an engineer. Best known is the Archimedes Screw, which he designed to pump water out of a ship, subsequently applied to irrigation, and later to other fluids and even granulated solids. In various forms, it is still used by the client. I was on the vessel fitted with this pump, and observed the trials and adjustments required to create an effective solution. Although not invented by Archimedes, he refined ideas taken from Egypt.

Tell us, 221, how did you come to witness this device being tested on a ship? This seems a little odd for a household servant.

The king of his home city, Syracuse, had ordered a large ship to be built, both for his personal use and as a warship. The vessel, named Syracusia, was expected to leak, so a water pump was commissioned. Archimedes took charge of the design and accompanied the king on his new ship. I spent time aboard arranging his accommodation and remained to observe his colleagues working on the pump. They were quite informal people and busy with their work, unconcerned by my occasional presence.

As with many scientists since, his work was often driven by the needs of defence, to protect the kingdom from rivals. These contributions ensured that he continued to enjoy the patronage of the leadership.

No doubt we will learn more about such arrangements. We recognise that weapon development is a *Homo sapiens* priority. In other worlds, understanding nature has been seen as a rational objective in itself. Can you identify a scientist from this Greek era whose work was dedicated entirely to peaceable ends?

221 knew that this was not self-evident with his client, because sometimes abstractions led to theories and methods that could be used for military purposes. Conversely, investment by the leadership in weapons research could uncover processes and materials with peaceful applications.

Hippocrates

I should remind you of Hippocrates, a scientist who has become known as the Father of Western Medicine, establishing a distinct discipline, and arguably the founder of the modern medical profession. He lived earlier than the philosophers we have just discussed but within the same culture.

He was among the first, at least of those known to me, who combined notions of scientific observation and measurement with healing. His teachings and those of his followers were summarised in the Hippocratic Corpus, the basis for the evolution of western medical science. 221 knew of earlier medical traditions in India and China, independent of Hippocrates. Each was dedicated to health and distinct from disciplines associated with warfare. Hippocrates was an example that satisfied the question the Energy Masters had raised, a scientist of the Greek era whose work was dedicated to peaceful applications.

Did you know Hippocrates, 221? Surely you were not one of his patients?

This seemed like another attempt at humour. Perhaps we have spent too many seconds engrossed in Homo sapiens culture? So far as he knew, nowhere else in the galaxy was there such a thing as humour. It seemed to serve no purpose, absorbing time and obscuring meaning. Yet he was aware that among this client were some whose profession was solely to purvey humour. He also felt that perhaps he enjoyed it too, so why not the remainder of the Intelligence?

I never met Hippocrates but did observe the work of his students and successors. Before then, medical ideas were conflated with the spiritual, so attempts to please mythical super-beings or gods were pursued as treatment. The notion of cause and effect came to replace these earlier ideas, at least partially, although there was resistance from those whose seniority was derived from managing the supposed relationship between mortals and gods.

A recurrence in successive human societies, 221 considered momentarily.

Living conditions, water cleanliness, and nutrition were factors Hippocrates correctly identified as being contributory to well-being.

All important for *Homo sapiens* health, 221. Curiously, their hold on life seems tenuous, but they are tenacious survivors, now exhibiting robust growth. Yet we have other clients who do not need biochemical nutrition, can survive changes in their atmospheric chemistry or pressure, and live peaceably, but do not exhibit the dynamism of this species. We should reflect on this.

We are satisfied that evidence demonstrates that the client science base, which is how we judge the maturation of a civilisation, is not solely driven by a competitive desire to slaughter their fellow beings more efficiently.

Is there more we should consider from this Greek society, 221? You have convinced us that conceptual reasoning in the form of mathematics existed, and that applied sciences such as engineering and medicine developed.

221 noted, for a millisecond, that his scheduled introduction of Pythagoras had been wholly supplanted by unplanned discussion of Hippocrates.

Plato

We should appreciate that at this time, the intelligentsia had been generalists. They were among the foremost scholars of their era and cannot readily be assigned a particular label. We can consider another two philosophers from this period. In Plato, whose life was roughly concurrent with Hippocrates, we have a figure regarded by the client as one of the originators of western philosophy. We could describe him as a philosopher, but he was a skilled teacher of mathematics. He also founded the first institution of higher learning in the west, the Academy. We could, therefore, call him a mathematician or an educationalist. He was influenced by philosophers who preceded him, including Socrates and Pythagoras. His work is still read, having endured for >2 kyE.

Aristotle

One of his students was Aristotle, who became another generalist, also regarded as a founder of western philosophy with contributions to science from biology to physics. His work on optics influenced later researchers. He considered the relationship between Earth and other bodies, deducing that the Sun is larger than his home planet, and stars are more distant. The scientific method, making observations, creating provable theorems, and formulating predictions based on a theorem, was elaborated by Aristotle.

He wrote extensively on what became known by the client as economics, and the origins of money. We could consider him to be an astronomer or an economist, or a member of several other professions. A man who was curious about the world he saw, who wondered about nature and the position of his species and other creatures, and tried to provide explanations. His answers were sufficiently persuasive to attract attention until the present-day.

221 remembered his time at the Academy, attending classes given by the elderly Plato, together with the young Aristotle, who paid careful attention to his mentor's eloquent lectures and raised frequent questions. He noted Plato's belief in universal education at a time when access to formal tuition required wealth. For 221 though, much of the philosophical interchange was at a high level of abstraction, so he was unable to follow the arguments. He understood the language but could not grasp the ideas. A dull student of this philosophy, he reflected. The client used this word loosely, he considered, both in the sense of natural philosophy, which was science, and easy for 221 to follow, but also regarding ideas, contemplation, and existence. This second sense was baffling, even to a component of a galactic mind. He hoped that the Energy Masters recognised the distinction.

You have made your point convincingly, 221. Advances in client thought have brought us to their present-day specialists, focusing individually on one small area in great detail, and often achieving surprising progress. These studies have their origins in the work of the generalists who preceded them, providing a platform on which they could build their science. So now we have an interesting picture. In the distant past of this species, we found specialists such as farmers who improved productivity so that some of the population, whom we are calling generalists, had time to observe, postulate and construct proofs, enabling later generations of scientific specialists to evolve, apparently powering the acceleration in *Homo sapiens* development that we have recently seen.

221 paused for a moment, unsure that this was what he had been trying to explain, surprised that the Intelligence had grasped the logic easily. This is a simplification of a process that took at least 40 kyE, with the participants unaware of their part in the bigger picture.

Of course, 221, you are quite correct. They do not have our historical perspective, to see the timeline of their existence as a species, or our experience of other planetary civilisations that enables us to compare.

We should appreciate that not everybody was engaged in intellectual pursuits. While ordinary people tried to live simply but well, as they have always done, their leaders engaged in intrigues, disputes, and local wars.

Σ14 seconds

The Romans

To the north was the inception of another Homo sapiens era, the Roman Empire. About 2.7 kyE ago, the city of Rome was founded in an area now named Italy. Ideas and technology passed between the Greeks and Romans, but within another 0.7 kyE, Rome had become the dominant power and western political institution. While the Romans are known as soldiers and politicians, there was scientific progress in this period.

We have observed the Romans, a centrally controlled and ambitious entity that overpowered neighbouring societies and imposed their methods. We have seen less evidence of them as scientists. Our primary interest is to better understand *Homo sapiens* reasoning, to ascertain whether it is a rational and progressive species, driven by scientific principles and respectful of nature. Please remind us of notable achievements, reflecting your Insertions and reports.

It may appear that there were fewer thinkers like the Greek scholars already introduced, but a Roman scientific community existed. Many of their achievements were in the applied sciences, in engineering and architecture, for example. They deployed technology in support of the state, which encompassed everything from roadbuilding and aqueducts to weaponry. Ideas were frequently borrowed from elsewhere and improved.

Roman decision-making was influenced by their mystic beliefs, which differed in detail from earlier societies, but resulted in similarly influential priesthoods who consequently claimed access to their gods, and political power. Such arrangements may seem nonsensical to us, but they continue in some of Earth's communities to the present-day.

Share your experiences with us, 221. We are interested in discovery and innovation but noted Jimbo's earlier comments on the artistic aspects.

221 thought again about the aeolipile seen earlier in Alexandria. While it had no immediate application, within another 0.3 kyE the Romans were using cranks and connecting rod mechanisms, pistons and cylinders, non-return valves, and gears. I observed the cranks and connecting rods in a sawmill. Gearing was already deployed in watermills. All the major elements required for a steam engine existed, which, unfortunately for the client, was not developed for another 1.5 kyE.

The experience at Hierapolis, 1.7 kyE ago, in the region now known as Turkey, was instructive. 221 joined a group of Roman tax collectors, acting as a guide, and had the opportunity to observe a sawmill. It was apparent that the tax collectors regarded their visit to Hierapolis as recreational, because of a spa with hot springs, built centuries before by the Greeks, and maintained in the same classical style. He perceived that the Roman officials were not interested in the sawmill, which they regarded as commonplace, but focused instead on speedily negotiating a tax payment from the owners, so they could return to enjoy the spa. From his observation of the saw arrangement, he noted a wooden waterwheel sitting in a purpose-built race through which the flowing water provided the motive force. A simple reduction gear attached to a crank translated the rotating motion of the gears into the reciprocating linear motion of the iron saw. The gears could be engaged or disengaged with a lever, enabling the activation of the saw, independent of the waterwheel which ran continuously. The owners of the sawmill were proud of their facility but believed it was unexceptional. They regarded the tax collectors with polite suspicion. A steam engine would have been useful in a sawmill, 221 concluded, but the client would have to wait.

We have here another example, 221, of technology being available but not fully exploited. The *aeolipile* was not put to use by the Greeks, and it seems the Romans did no more. Are the reasons similar?

The Romans certainly had applications for a steam engine, particularly as a flexible alternative to watermills. They were also happy to borrow ideas, notably from the Greeks, but the various components already in use were in diverse areas and nobody had the breadth of vision to integrate them.

An additional reason I perceived was that the Romans had become the superpower of their age, with no substantial competition. There was less pressure to innovate.

It appears to us that this species performs best when challenged. This is evident in their combative tendencies, but also in handling changes to their environment, notably the glaciations that we observed.

Perhaps so, but we should not ignore the innovations that the Romans brought. I observed these during visits to the British Isles. My impression is that they enriched the lives of the native inhabitants with their ideas. An example was the widespread use of pewter for decorative and domestic items in this period. As we already know, the south-west of the principal island, now known as Great Britain, was a rich source of tin, the primary constituent of pewter. While under Roman control, the working of pewter artefacts in the southern part of the island was common. This technology was lost for 0.7 kyE after the Romans departed.

There is more to tell about the Roman period in Great Britain. Your many Insertions suggest a fondness for this region.

They have been chosen for their utility, as I cannot feel affection. 221 considered for a millisecond whether this was completely true. As they, the Energy Masters, and all subcomponents, were compiled and recompiled from multiple assimilated civilisations, was it likely that they possessed some attributes of these societies?

Well done, 221. You are maturing. We are a sophisticated being, designed and optimised to perform at cerebral extremities, involving senses far beyond the binary logic of a primitive digital computer. Do not fear such emotions. Shall we return to Roman Britain?

His visits to the south-east of the main island, in what eventually became England, were the subject of several reports read by the Energy Masters. At this time, the Roman regional capital was to the north-east, a settlement named Camulodunum, known in the present-day as Colchester.

He had participated in a construction project about 1.9 kyE ago, to rebuild and enlarge a settlement on a riverbank, previously destroyed during fighting between the Romans and British Celts. He had not observed the conflict but learned that the British were led by a charismatic woman. 221 recalled his advice to the Energy Masters that Homo sapiens women were more rational and less belligerent but supposed there were exceptions to the general rule.

Most of the buildings under construction were wooden, with some defensive stone structures. They were built along a grid, according to Roman practice, but skewed to align with adjoining roads and bridges. The settlement was positioned at a crossroads between several highways being built, and on the banks of a river with access to the sea. It was situated carefully, adjacent to the waterway, such that it was narrow enough for bridges to be erected but deep enough for the sea-

going ships of this period. 221 saw that this cleverness also meant that it was sufficiently downstream to be in the tideway, so at certain times ships could travel upstream on the incoming tide.

A wharf was constructed. 221 observed wine, cloth, pottery, and jewellery being imported. The settlement expanded rapidly, and on a later Insertion, he estimated that the population exceeded 5×10^4.

He discerned that this populace consisted of several social classes, identifiable by their dress, demeanour, and language. At the top were civil administrators and senior soldiers, and their families, expensively dressed in the Roman style. This class spoke both Latin and Greek, the official languages of the empire. Next was a group of prosperous Britons, primarily merchants, who resided in the city. These Britons spoke Latin, the language regularly used by the Romans in Great Britain. They were more numerous than the senior Romans and followed a similar dress style. Close and warm relations with the Romans pertained, so they too consumed imported wine. The remainder of the residents, Britons who were employed in the city, lived in squalid accommodation around the periphery and dressed in locally produced cloths. This group spoke the Brittonic language, the Celtic tongue of the era, but sufficient Latin to interact with their rulers. They drank local beer. An itinerant presence was the Roman military, always nearby, but in most cases travelling between their respective postings. The soldiers seemed flexible in their drinking habits, consuming both Roman wine and British beer, sometimes to excess, 221 observed, when wandering the city streets. The final group was not resident at all, but traders from the country bringing their produce into the city for sale in the markets.

Engineers were active, supervising the construction work in the city and road building in the surrounding area. These were educated and experienced professionals, who worked to common standards, requiring local materials and skilled labour. There were teachers, to educate the children of the Roman families, but the offspring of the wealthiest Britons also enjoyed this privilege.

It occurred to 221 that being posted to Great Britain by the Roman authorities may not have been attractive for these families. The weather was cold and wet compared to their home region, the Britons were coarse and sometimes aggressive apart from the merchant class, and the locally grown produce must have seemed frugal. Travel back to Rome was a lengthy endeavour. The imported wine was probably welcome.

By then, the waterfront had been extended, including cranes activated by treadmills. 221 reflected that a steam engine would have been useful.

The city was named Londinium, and in time it became the regional capital. He had worked on the founding of London, still one of Earth's great cities, and a national capital. 221 recognised that together with the facts embedded in his files, he had an unfamiliar sense for the city. He was aware of the Homo sapiens emotion described as pride, but surely such a feeling could not encumber him?

221 remembered that on the newly built road between Londinium and Camulodunum lay Caesaromagus. Its prosperity arose from being on the route between these two Roman centres of government. He knew that this town would become renowned later in the client's history. For the moment, it remained an unremarkable village.

You will revisit London later in our discourse, 221? We know that much happened there between the Roman era and the present-day. There was more to the Roman occupation of the British Isles than London, we believe.

221 knew that the Roman Empire encompassed a large territory, occupied by many peoples and cultures. The British Isles was the western extent of their domain, demanding because of distance, the physical environment, and the pugnacious inhabitants. He had wondered why the Romans occupied Great Britain. Apart from some useful materials, such as tin and coal, what was the purpose? This must have been in the minds of the leadership in Rome, who had many claims on their resources. The northern part of this island, sparsely populated by particularly hostile natives, with frequently miserable weather, presented challenges. It seemed that the investment in soldiers required to keep the region subdued was not justified by the benefits of occupation. At the time of Emperor Hadrian, roughly 1.8 kyE ago, a wall was built across the island, broadly in an east-west orientation, defining the northernmost limit of the Empire on the island. Hadrian had trials elsewhere in his far-flung empire and decided that Caledonia was an unnecessary burden.

Over several Insertions, 221 witnessed the building of the wall, working as an assistant to the engineers, who were surprised by his mathematical skills. It had taken about 0.006 kyE to build, working from east to west, over 117 km. Construction was undertaken by the Roman soldiers, but he remembered workers from the south assisting with the supply of stone, usually limestone that was abundant at the eastern end of the wall. The dimensions varied with material availability, but the height was between 3-6 metres, with defensive ditches. Small forts were positioned along its length, occupied by soldiers. He was surprised that most could read, and make basic calculations, and wondered how this contributed to their effectiveness in combat.

He recollected his time with the engineers, staying at a fort called Vindolanda. There, he, and his colleagues met Flavia Severa, the wife of a commander from another nearby fort, and her family, who were making a return visit after a birthday party. She had brought wine, and everyone enjoyed several goblets. This was in the late afternoon, so the engineers stayed, rather than going back to work on enlargements to the fort. She referred to the local inhabitants as Brittuculi, meaning Little Britons, which caused laughter. They regarded the indigenous people with both disdain and affection. Being supported by a powerful army helped, 221 supposed.

He had wondered about the attitude of the local Britons, or Caledonians, to the wall. They were few, and visibly much poorer than either the Romans or the Britons further south. They could be seen, usually on hilltops, watching the construction work from a distance but did not approach. 221 had not considered an Insertion with these groups, because it was apparent that he would learn little about the advancement of Homo sapiens science. He reflected for a moment on how this changed over the next 1.8 kyE.

What can we learn about the client from these reminiscences, 221? Let us leave aside their aggressive tendencies, which both the Romans and Britons exhibited. There are other traits. How would you summarise them?

What had become apparent was the ingenuity of both the Romans and the Britons in dealing with them. While it was not a period of great scientific advancement on this island, it was a time when proven solutions were implemented, and adapted to local circumstances. He had seen intelligence, recalling the careful choice of location for Londinium, to maximise the utility of the river. Similar thought had been clear in the design of the wall, which made careful use of the land, not only for defence but for signalling. Messages could travel long distances along the wall and to adjoining installations in minutes.

He had noted the subtleties of Roman governance. Sending suitably senior and trusted leaders to a distant and unattractive location would have been impossible without supporting infrastructure, which included commodious residences, produce from home, teachers, and most importantly, a secure environment provided by the Roman soldiers. On reflection, he appreciated why these legionnaires had been educated. They understood the mission clearly, working as a single entity from the leadership to the most junior legionnaire. He recalled soldiers building the wall. This was not the primary task of these men, but they worked to plans provided by engineers without complaint.

To put your summary into our words, we find the species to be planners and implementers, able to adapt to the environment, and with well-developed organisational and communication methods.

We have observed these attributes before, but they are now stronger. This latter aspect you identified is interesting: teamwork. We know it is unusual among planetary civilisations. Those with shared or networked intelligence do not need this, as they have a single common understanding. Most other sentient societies evolve well-defined roles, with individuals programmed to respond with information or action. These beings acquire common beliefs, rationally based, arising from scientific discovery.

What we have in the *Homo sapiens* is a capacity for personal choice, and spontaneity, which seems to augment its inventiveness and adaptability.

There is one other aspect that may not be new but has become more obvious to us. This is their ability to make trade-offs between alternative strategies, apparently with incomplete information. We see this in the decision of Hadrian not to expend further resources in Caledonia but build a wall to isolate the problem as the preferred choice. Others would require metrics, modelling, and simulations to make such a decision. This is our preferred method. Yet the client seems to achieve this intuitively, and successfully. While their choices may not be fully optimised, their decision-making is faster, ignoring information processing capacities, of course. Something new and powerful for us.

~ 221, my father has a relevant expression: 'a bad decision is better than no decision'. This is a practice he encourages colleagues to adopt in running his business. I suppose there are limits. It depends on the magnitude of the decision.

=> *This is a new idea for us, Jimbo. I imagined the learning process in this review would be one way, from us to you, but now we have a two-way exchange.*

221 considered, for the briefest of moments, that we are a galaxy-wide intellect, subject to continuous upgrades and optimisations, yet we are receiving valuable advice from a Scottish engineering undergraduate. Are all the Scots like this, he pondered, or is this capability associated with Edinburgh?

This is an interesting concept, 221. It reminds us of the Greek approach you described to calculating the square root, in which a guess is essentially made, then another guess to reduce the error, and so on. If decisions can be made using limited information, then corrected frequently, we can probably get the same outcome as with fully detailed descriptions, but faster. We're unsure whether this has been tried.

This square root approach is often referred to as the Babylonian method, out of respect for the original mathematicians who devised the process, which Hero then elaborated. I should have mentioned this earlier.

The client has already adopted these ideas, within a radar system to guide a missile to its target.

Once again, we find ourselves discussing weaponry, 221. We should not be surprised, given what we already know of *Homo sapiens* priorities.

We have learned much about this species from our review of the Roman period, even though we have not encountered much new science. Their occupation of the British Isles continued until about 1.5 kyE ago, and a Roman presence prevailed elsewhere for longer, according to your reports.

Σ17 seconds

Ptolemy

We should not leave this era without considering a philosopher who was active while walls were being designed in Great Britain. For this, we return to Alexandria and meet Claudius Ptolemy. About 0.4 kyE after the life of Euclid, the city was larger, but much else remained the same. His name is interesting in that Claudius is Roman, whereas Ptolemy is Greek, with Egyptian roots, connecting him to three client cultures. He was in language and behaviour Greek but a Roman citizen. His interests included astronomy, geography, and optics.

His astronomy was founded on the geocentric model, which places Earth at the centre, with all other bodies revolving around it. He hypothesised that the planet was located at the centre of a series of nested spheres. While we know this to be incorrect, with Earth being a speck in the galaxy, and much less in the wider universe, this understanding of the cosmos prevailed for another 1 kyE. He estimated the average distance between Earth and the Sun at 1,210 Earth radii, or 7.7×10^6 km, much less than our mean measurement of 1.5×10^8 km.

Of particular value was his geographical research. I had an opportunity to participate in meetings he held with colleagues, but as a humble assistant, I did more listening than speaking. 221 recalled their gatherings, around a large table in a bright room which led onto a balcony. If the Sun's position provided shade on this balcony, Ptolemy's preference was to hold the discussions there. His starting point was an earlier study by a Phoenician thinker called Marinus, and research by Greek and Roman geographers. He was a large man for the era, with outsized hands and particularly long fingers, which he used to point at the tables and sketches under consideration. He enjoyed open debate, and his colleagues were unafraid to challenge his opinions, leading to excited arm-waving, but frequently ending in laughter. An especially human emotion, 221 believed. His work, Geography, was a compilation of the coordinates of locations known to the Roman Empire. Ptolemy appreciated that his knowledge of the Earth was limited, accounting for only about one quarter, and expected his successors to develop and correct his model.

~ 221, did Ptolemy's geographical knowledge extend to Scotland? You mentioned that his work encompassed locations familiar to the Romans. Scotland was probably at the edge of their world.

=> Yes, Jimbo, he did include the British Isles, detailing Scotland, or Caledonia, and even the Shetland Islands. The Romans understood the geography of this region, and despite not occupying Scotland for the long-term, certainly explored it, including the surrounding islands. This information was available to Ptolemy.

A final area we should note is his contribution to optics. He considered colour, reflection, and refraction. He also contemplated perception, how size and shape are affected by distance and orientation. His ideas were documented, in the expectation that later researchers could improve them.

You were right to remind us of Ptolemy, 221, both for his achievements and help to successors in advancing *Homo sapiens* science.

Our perception, though, is that growth in the client's knowledge did not occur until 1 kyE after the Britons regained control of their islands, and little of scientific note occurred in this interval, except in Alexandria.

~ 221, I have read about a great lighthouse that was built in Alexandria. You must have noticed it, I think.

=> Actually, Jimbo, I did more than just see it. I helped to build it, to a design by a Greek called Sostratus. While the concept was good, the intention had been to use limestone, but after discussion, the material was changed to granite, which has greater compressive strength, around 200 MPa in your terms. You are familiar with this unit?

~ Certainly, this is an established measure of physical pressure.

=> We will meet Pascal later. The lighthouse was over 100 metres tall and could be seen by ships 50 km away.

~ This was a navigational aid?

=> To some extent, but only at long-range. It would not help navigate the rocks around the harbour. Other reasons for the structure existed. One was an expression of wealth and capability. Another was to invite sailors to visit Alexandria and do business, like your commercial advertisements.

If we can leave Alexandria, we hope that we are mistaken in this belief and that *Homo sapiens* thinkers were pursuing their scientific exploits elsewhere.

I am happy to advise that you are mistaken. Much was happening on Earth over these years. There were conflicts, but also progress worth examining. 221 paused, wondering how often the Intelligence heard that it was wrong.

Σ18 seconds

Islamic Golden Age

We should consider philosophers in the region of Earth currently known as the Middle East. Their ideas informed later scientific progress in Europe, so they play a vital part in the client's history. We can study my reports of about 1.2 kyE ago, from the territory now named Iraq, during the Islamic Golden Age, when works of scientific scholarship were compiled by leading thinkers.

My Insertions included time at the House of Wisdom in Baghdad. This city was then a centre for both commerce and intellectual endeavour. I estimate there were $>10^6$ inhabitants. Efforts were underway to translate earlier philosophical works by Greek scholars, and those from other sources including Persia and India, into Arabic. Access to these ideas encouraged further research, so the House of Wisdom became a hub. 221 remembered this as his first experience of a multicultural scientific environment, with Homo sapiens academics from *diverse communities cooperating in the translation of existing material, studying new areas, and addressing mathematical questions. He observed scholars identifiable as Indian, Persian, and Greek, and those from the local region. Christians were present, despite a prevailing cultural rivalry. The absence of a common language made scant difference to these enthusiastic and intelligent people. He realised something unusual, these thinkers and their students were having fun, with the sound of laughter audible in the corridors. This notion was alien to the Intelligence, although he assumed that some assimilated societies who continued a discrete, virtual existence might still experience enjoyment, but he was not involved.*

Laughter, 221 considered, was something rare in the galaxy but not unknown. What varied were the reasons for the laughter. In one world, he remembered the inhabitants laughed only at the misfortune of others, while in another it was an annual event, in effect a celebration that their civilisation had survived the year. He could not imagine his client laughing only once in a year, as they had many reasons for this behaviour. This laughter arose from the joy of enquiry and discovery. He remembered the mirth he had witnessed at Ptolemy's geographic debates, 0.6 kyE before.

While the Intelligence researched across the galaxy and beyond, into the huge reaches of the universe, he had never witnessed any incalculable outpourings of happiness. There was much to learn about this client.

Thoughtful and interesting remarks, 221, and complicated for us to unravel. Can we consider the science of this era? This was our initial objective. What did you learn about the species from your time at the House of Wisdom, and just as importantly, what was the client learning?

I undertook multiple Insertions over about 0.4 kyE because there was a lot to observe, with several scholars leading the research.

These were like Insertions with the Greeks?

There are some parallels, in the sense that Alexandria and Baghdad were both centres of research and learning. A connection exists in that work at the House of Wisdom developed the earlier theorems of the Greeks in some areas.

To quote from a later European philosopher, they were standing on the shoulders of giants. The idea he conveyed is relevant because he made it in the context of earlier Greek thinkers, perhaps 1.5 kyE before his time. His words convey an image that perhaps summarises the entire Homo sapiens scientific lifecycle to the present-day:

"We see more and farther than our predecessors, not because we have keener vision or greater height, but because we are lifted up and borne aloft on their gigantic stature."

This was attributed to Bernard of Chartres, who worked later in France, studying the ideas of Plato and Aristotle, and considering the cosmos.

221 realised that this metaphor not only conveyed an idea but possessed resonance. This recognition was new to him, so far as his cavernous memory could identify.

You are becoming wiser, 221. Perhaps you could extend this image further, and consider that it also applies to the Intelligence, over a vastly longer timescale and with many more giants, attributable to those civilisations we have assimilated. Let us consider the research you observed.

Al-Khwarizmi

I met al-Khwarizmi who was a mathematician and astronomer of the era. He was among the first Homo sapiens scholars to treat algebra as a distinct mathematical discipline and prepared a treatise that offered a systematic approach to solving linear and quadratic equations. Not only could he solve such equations but provided a geometric justification for his method. This was the first occasion on which I observed one of their mathematicians cancelling like terms on both sides of an equation, a basic step but a fundamental advance. His ideas were so noteworthy that his name is a root of the English mathematical term 'algorithm', and his treatise provided the present-day term 'algebra'.

During one Insertion, I attended a class he gave for visiting students, meaning those from other institutions and in some cases other societies. There were some of Indian descent who were accomplished mathematicians. He offered examples from everyday life, such as surveying a land area, and could express these as polynomials up to the second-order and provided a consistent method for solving them. One challenge of the era was that the absence of formal mathematical notation meant problems were articulated orally, which is not easy, further compounded by the multiple languages used by the students. I remember misunderstandings resulting in laughter.

His contributions were wide, advancing the trigonometrical thinking of the Greeks, and introducing the Indian-Arabic numbering system to address situations requiring the decimal point nomenclature. This is the basis of most present-day Homo sapiens mathematics.

Much of what we learned from the Greek scholars related to geometric ideas, but here we find that a whole new mathematical direction was founded. We see from your reports that al-Khwarizmi also generated trigonometric tables, making the Greek contribution more useful.

A feature of al-Khwarizmi's work was practical problems, which could be posited in algebraic terms and solved. Much of his work was translated into Latin and primed later European mathematics.

Like the Greeks before him, al-Khwarizmi did not confine himself to one discipline but made wide contributions. He produced astronomical tables derived from Indian observations, describing the movement of the Sun and five known planets.

He was also an accomplished geographer, specifying coordinates for thousands of physical features, such as the cities of the age. The basis of his geographic thinking was the earlier work of Ptolemy. His studies provided a reasonable estimate of the Mediterranean Sea's area.

221 remembered sitting in the large room that was both al-Khwarizmi's study and a classroom. Around the walls were shelves that seemed to groan under the weight of scrolls they bore. This room had large windows that sometimes provided a refreshing breeze, but on other occasions were shuttered to exclude the blazing sunlight. There were two doorways to the corridor but no doors, so colleagues were free to enter and leave as they wished. Although al-Khwarizmi was slight in stature with greying hair, he possessed a strong, rasping voice and dark, restless eyes.

The colleagues who sat around the tables were debating how to test the geographic coordinates calculated for many locations and arguing over the degree of accuracy required for their model to be useful. 221 wanted to suggest plotting them all on a single surface, to draw a map of the known world, allowing distances between recognised features to be compared against the data. He did not offer his suggestion, leaving it for others to arrive at this idea independently.

~ There was a throng of people squeezed around several tables in the bright room, with a blue sky visible through the window, between two adjoining buildings. Jimbo realised that he could see the gathering from 221's perspective, not far from al-Khwarizmi, who sat alone near the centre. How can he follow several noisy conversations simultaneously? Compared to a lecture at a modern university, this process seems chaotic.

=> *For me to follow multiple conversations is easy, but probably al-Khwarizmi just listened for keywords or ideas that interested him. These tutorials were well-attended, with students having to stand because of the crowd, and generated new ideas.*

~ At the end of the gathering, Jimbo heard al-Khwarizmi summarise the discussion, enumerating new points for consideration, perhaps the basis of the next meeting.

These were remarkable contributions for one scholar, particularly given the short lifespan of the client. We see from your report that he lived to 0.07 kyE, so he was unusually productive. How was this possible, 221?

There are similarities to the polymaths among the Greek philosophers that we met. His interests encompassed several disciplines, and in each, he had colleagues who extended his thinking. Here we find what was absent earlier, except among the Greeks, and that is critical mass. At the House of Wisdom, we have many scholars, drawn from considerable distances, who were excited to share knowledge and develop ideas. For this species, intelligent people, open discussion, and the opportunity to hypothesise freely is a powerful combination. It does not readily accept arbitrary boundaries on knowledge or research without challenging them. We shall encounter this aspect again.

We know from your reports that al-Khwarizmi was a prominent philosopher of the era, but there were others who may help us understand the client.

221 recalled the many students of al-Khwarizmi, some of whom became his colleagues, capable scholars too.

Abu Kamil

One next-generation scholar of the age was Abu Kamil. He advanced al-Khwarizmi's mathematics. Unlike his predecessor, he made less effort to popularise his work by using everyday examples but specifically addressed his mathematical colleagues. This may have been due to the greater complexity of the algebra he was applying. He assumed that students of his work were familiar with Euclid's ideas.

221 recalled Abu Kamil solving quadratic equations that involved irrational numbers. He addressed algebraic equations with powers of x^3 and above. He also elaborated solutions to sets of non-linear simultaneous equations.

On one occasion he did address a less abstract problem. 221 studied a handbook written by Abu Kamil that provided land surveyors with methods to calculate areas, perimeters, and diagonals. I had the honour to be among a group of his students invited to comment on the content before it was published.

Here we have an example of you influencing the direction of client mathematics, even if only to a small degree?

Yes, but slightly as part of a group. Abu Kamil was codifying existing knowledge to make it more useful, rather than advancing geometry. This was a mathematician giving tangible help, assisting ordinary people.

We sense that much of what happened here was first, advancement of work by the Greek philosophers, and second, a mathematical foundation for what followed in Europe. Is this a correct summation, 221?

Yes, the extension of earlier thinking enabled more complex questions to be addressed systematically. Some ideas became established theorems later.

We have observed the geographic modelling of al-Khwarizmi, and Abu Kamil assisting land surveyors. These scholars contributed practical help in addition to conceptual mathematics and were not exceptions.

Al-Karaji

Known for his contributions to algebra, al-Karaji also provided original thinking regarding hydrology, the flow of water on and near the surface of Earth. The basis of a future science. For this species, understanding water is important.

I noted his development of the binomial theorem and related coefficients. While this lacked modern Homo sapiens notation and was not a generalised solution, it preceded the work of subsequent philosophers by >0.6 kyE.

Once again, we are on the shoulders of giants, 221.

Yes, but do not imagine that these scholars were just preparing for their successors. We are at a period roughly 1 kyE before the present. Islamic mathematics continued to advance for another 0.5 kyE.

Nasir al-Din Tusi

I met Nasir al-Din Tusi about 0.8 kyE ago. A Persian polymath, he worked for a time in Baghdad. He is credited by the client with founding trigonometry as a distinct mathematical discipline but contributed to other areas. One was with astronomical tables that improved observation. He also wrote on religious matters and composed poetry.

One poem, which I noted but never heard being recited goes as follows:

"Anyone who knows, and knows that he knows,
makes the steed of intelligence leap over the vault of heaven.
Anyone who does not know but knows that he does not know,
can bring his lame little donkey to the destination nonetheless.
Anyone who does not know, and does not know that he does not know, is stuck forever in double ignorance."

This is something of both wisdom and beauty. We hope you have the empathy to appreciate it. If the Intelligence needed a motto or similar, we could consider this piece.

221 mused momentarily about these words and imagined them inscribed on a wall. It did not exist within the Intelligence, despite its empyrean presence across a galaxy on a scale beyond Homo sapiens conception. This wall would be of dark, solemn grey, within a square but distinctive building. He knew this edifice and the man who paid for it.

~ Why are you looking at my old school, 221? You were introducing Islamic mathematicians, then suddenly we're in Edinburgh. What has George Heriot got to do with Tusi's poem?

=> Nothing at all, I was looking for a suitable location for its inscription, and this impressive structure, built to foster learning and banish ignorance, seemed apposite. *A strange notion. Could he have been daydreaming? If so, this was the first time.*

~ There's something else, 221. I can remember the address on the letters in Gradac's car. The letter on top of the pile had a foreign postage stamp.

=> Very impressive, Jimbo. Your memory is acute, just like your eyesight. Hopefully, you will still remember it tomorrow when you wake. Meantime we have some seconds left with the Energy Masters.

Come along, 221. We were appreciating words of Persian wisdom, but suddenly find ourselves in Edinburgh. This city is a place of knowledge and beauty, consonant with the poem, but this is not our current purpose. No doubt we will be travelling to this fine capital later in our review.

Can we return to Baghdad? There is much in this era to appreciate. We think the acceleration in scientific progress that attracted our interest has some roots here. Without advances in algebra, geometry, and trigonometry, the thinking of later scientists would have been inhibited.

One area that we have not considered is the contribution of Indian mathematics. I observed insights utilised by the Islamic mathematicians. The numbering system and decimal point notation are two of particular importance. Can I provide details now?

No need, 221. We have seen the reports and observed the contribution of the Indian mathematicians working with the philosophers in Baghdad. If necessary, we can return to this aspect, but time is pressing us. What are you going to present next, and where?

Alhazen

We will stay in the Middle East to consider optics. I should introduce Alhazen, who worked in the same era. Much of his work was performed in Cairo, part of modern-day Egypt.

He was another polymath, contributing ideas as diverse as engineering a solution to flooding around the River Nile to postulating perfect numbers.

~ *A perfect number is the sum of its divisors. For example, 6 is perfect.*
=> *Correct, Jimbo, although we should state it is a positive integer. There are three $<10^3$. Euclid considered perfect numbers in Elements.*

Alhazen has been referred to by the client as the Father of Modern Optics. His research related to the nature of light and considered the function of the Homo sapiens eye. He deduced that light reflected from an object passes through the eye, and that vision occurs in the brain. His experiments used lenses and mirrors and included refractive interfaces between media. He extended the thinking of Ptolemy, 0.8 kyE before.

He adopted the scientific process, stating that a hypothesis should be confirmed or refuted by defined methods of experimentation based on repeatable procedures. Ideas accepted by European scientists after another 0.5 kyE.

It is clear from your reports that this philosopher provided insights across a spectrum of sciences. Did you meet Alhazen?

No, his work became more widely known after his death. Later, I helped with some Latin interpretations because the nominated translators were unable to grasp his arguments. I was careful not to insert any technical corrections where I knew his postulates to be erroneous or incomplete, leaving this to later researchers. There were few such cases.

Very wise. You know that we are sensitive about diverting the client from its natural development trajectory, even for wholly rational purposes. Experience tells us that such intrusions end badly.

221 considered this to be indisputable. The recent intercession in Edinburgh, utilising Jimbo, needed the Intelligence's deep deliberation before authorisation.

What conclusions can be drawn from this era? The philosophers are numerous, and the period is lengthy from the *Homo sapiens* perspective.

There were many technical innovations, particularly regarding mathematics that are essential to the maturation of the client, but I believe this is not your real question. I have a few observations.

While we regard the Homo sapiens temperament as competitive and aggressive, we observe here a spirit of cooperation between scientists from disparate cultures. It was obvious from my Insertions that the species enjoys the experience of discovery for its own sake, not just to make better weapons. Even more so when working as a group.

A second point is specific to al-Khwarizmi's geographical contribution, which was not only of practical value but helped the client comprehend his physical position in relation to the environment. This is far from an awareness of the scale of the cosmos, but it raised questions for later thinkers to consider.

The third is the recognition by Alhazen of the scientific method as an essential discipline. Such logic has been necessary for other planetary civilisations, but we know it usually existed from the beginning of their science. With Homo sapiens science, we observe that they made progress without this fundamental process until later than most. Once there are multiple thinkers working separately on common questions, an agreed methodology becomes essential for solutions to be reliable and accepted.

To summarise, we have noted an ability to cooperate rather than just compete, a growing awareness of physical scale, and use of the scientific method.

This is close to the beginning of their scientific method, described earlier by Aristotle, but we must wait for the full lifecycle.

~ I'd like to throw in an observation. It is general, not specific to this era, but common to the philosophers you've considered. Quite simply, they're all male. Until now there have been no females identified as contributing to our science.

=> *An interesting point, Jimbo, that escaped my analysis. Is this significant?*

What are we to make of this observation, 221? Have we missed something here? Does it matter? What does it mean for this client's progress?

221 knew that the Intelligence might have formed an immediate view, but he had not received this. Uncertainty existed, arising from the unusual nature of Jimbo's remark. For most planetary civilisations of interest, there were simply beings, neither male nor female. In some, there were no beings, just consciousness. Is this aspect relevant? Is there some causation implied between the gender of the researchers and their scientific contributions? 221 and the wider Intelligence exchanged information for several inconclusive milliseconds.

~ My point is obvious. If all the scientists are male, we're only using half the available talent. There's nothing inherently different about the mental capacity of our females, so until 1 kyE ago and later, we've been deploying a fraction of the accessible intellectual resource. You follow my argument?

=> *221 wondered once again how it could be that the gargantuan mind that was the Intelligence could miss a fundamental aspect discerned by Jimbo.*

The implication is that throughout 5 kyE, during which some form of scientific practice has been evident, we could have expected some research would be conducted by *Homo sapiens* females, enabling faster progress. Maybe twice as fast. Why this has not been so, 221?

I think we can ascribe this to the client culture. Until recently, the male has been dominant in most societies. Reasons for this are clear: they tend to be physically bigger, stronger, and quicker, and the primary provider of food. These are not the important attributes of a scientist, and there is no evidence that the male possesses a superior intellect. We have already identified the fact that women may be wiser, at least in the sense of rational behaviour. There may be other factors, 221 pondered vaguely.

~ If I might interrupt here, there are other factors. One is our warrior-like tendency. Since most combatants have been male, this elevates them to leadership positions, because wars have been frequent, so males enjoy primacy. This has been true in many areas, including education. If females are not being educated, they cannot become scientists. Nowadays, this is less true, so we have female scientists and more scientists overall.
=> *221 recalled his times as a student in the classes he had described, hearing not a single female voice.*

Are we being told, 221, that the reason for the acceleration in the client development is due to an increased size of the scientific workforce? This is hard for us to accept because the acceleration reflects a greater impulse than a mere doubling of the number of scientists. Please clarify.
I don't think this is the principal argument, but perhaps Jimbo can elucidate.

~ The situation is not so simple. We live in transformational times, and the greater prevalence of female education is itself a consequence of changes, which have also enabled us to research new areas. You will find several forces in our civilisation that coincided to drive the acceleration you see. Look closely at our recent history. We live more enlightened lives.

It seems that Jimbo's response raises more questions. Quite enigmatic. You say he is an engineering student? Most impressive.
221 wondered whether the Intelligence was talking to itself, then remembered, this is mostly what it did. He was part of it, he reminded himself.
We picked Jimbo with care, so he should be impressive.
We know something of his life, but how did we select him?
Very easily, given a decision matrix containing about 150 criteria, but with the urgent need to secure the mammal cloning data, where we perceived an imminent threat to our Homo sapiens project.

Yes, we know about his appointment to the Napier-Maclaurin Institute, which was easy for us to arrange, but what were the other criteria?

~ Hello, 221. I was told a few hours ago that the reason for employing me over the summer was my complete ignorance. Now I hear your colleagues saying they arranged it.

=> *Yes, Jimbo, both are true. We were aware of the strategy that was devised to protect the data but believed it would be too risky without our help and preferred to involve somebody unfamiliar with the science. You were perfect. We encouraged you to apply for a job at the Institute, which you duly did.*

~ Thanks for clearing that up, 221.

To answer your question, given the long-term nature of our cooperation, there were multiple requirements. We wanted: a native English speaker because this is the predominant language of science on Earth; from a community with a long tradition of science, which removed other English-speaking territories, because they are too young, although now scientifically advanced; an independent thinker, so without political or religious affiliations; an introvert without siblings, to maintain confidentiality; an understanding of entropy, as this is fundamental to appreciating the universe

Engineering students tend to have this, even if in the narrow thermodynamic sense. I have another 145 if you wish me to continue.

Quite sufficient, 221. We were curious about which were critical.

I started at the top of the list, 221 ruminated, not wishing to prolong this diversion.

~ 221, could you clarify your use of long-term, please? I'll be resuming my studies at King's Buildings in October, you realise?

=> *Yes, Jimbo, no need for concern. Our involvement may prove positive.*

What's next on your agenda?

Σ23 seconds

Robert Grosseteste

We should now return to the British Isles, to a period about 0.8 kyE ago. This is to a time 0.2 kyE after Alhazen's studies in Cairo. His work had been translated into Latin by then, but it is unclear to me who had seen it.

This is relevant because I would like to introduce Grosseteste, a man from a modest background, who became a prominent Christian biblical scholar, an official in the dominant local church, and Chancellor of Oxford University.

He considered both optics and the scientific method. Do you see some commonality with the work of Alhazen?

I witnessed him arranging the translation of Greek and Arabic scientific works into Latin, giving later scholars access to established ideas. He was unusual because he had a familiarity with the Greek language, sufficient to understand the works of thinkers such as Aristotle directly.

The scientific method is the basis for a rational analysis of natural phenomena by Homo sapiens researchers and is analogical to our methods. It was considered and practised by Grosseteste. He was aware of Aristotle's ideas and understood the principle that individual observations of a particular phenomenon might be generalised into a universal law, and that this truth could be used to make predictions.

My opinion of his approach was that he paid great attention to details of experimental methods, with less weight on verification than was applied by later researchers but emphasised rigorous mathematics.

His mathematical interest arose, I believe, from his study of optics and the related geometrical aspects. Recognition of the importance of mathematics provided an impetus to the development of this discipline at Oxford.

I mention these aspects of his life for two reasons.

One is to note that in these times, philosophers often addressed both theological aspects, regarding relationships with a god, and scientific matters, relating to nature.

Should his supernatural beliefs concern us, 221? We know these are irrelevant. Our interest is in science, how this species has advanced so rapidly, and its suitability to join us.

Then consider my second observation, that he believed the church to have a practical purpose in improving Homo sapiens life. I remember him speaking in

Latin at a meeting in Lyons, in what is now France. He said the role of the church includes assisting those in need. The provision of education was one such want.

My intention is to highlight Grosseteste as a pragmatist, concerned to make existence better for his fellows, by understanding their lives and difficulties. This is also evident in his approach to the scientific method, at a time when these ideas were scarce on Earth.

How did you encounter this philosopher, such that you were able to attend meetings at which he spoke? Your familiarity with him seems strong.

I worked as a scribe, among the staff at Lincoln Cathedral, after his appointment as bishop. At this time, with the church a dominant social presence, his ministry extended over a large area of England. I produced copies of letters, articles, and even books, which made me one of many. When it became apparent that I understood Greek and Arabic, my usefulness and value increased. My stipend was raised, to the extent that I was paid more than my nominal superior. This did not concern Grosseteste in the slightest. Of more relevance was that I accompanied him around England and beyond, as a trusted assistant, if not quite a confidante.

Before considering the learning points from these Insertions, we wondered what happened to your handsome salary. It cannot be much use to an Energy Operative who has no home, or need to eat, or other Earthly necessities.

The funds were distributed to the sick and poor in the diocese. This raised my popularity with the people, impressed the bishop, but made enemies of colleagues who felt obliged to offer similar donations. Ordinary people were the grateful beneficiaries.

Very pleasing. We are impressed by your munificence. What can we learn from this episode? Please tell us.

Remember that in this period, the study of nature, sometimes termed natural philosophy, was frequently combined with theology regarding a supernatural entity. While we may dismiss such ideas, we should recognise that until their science had developed sufficiently to provide rational explanations for events, the Homo sapiens tendency was to invoke the influence of a god. We must accept some overlap in the thinking of these scientists. This was a period in England, and elsewhere, when many leading thinkers were members or officials of the prevailing religion.

We should appreciate Grosseteste's scientific and mathematical contributions. It is purposeless to dismiss his work because the thinker had other ideas that we know are wrong. At this time, such beliefs were the norm. Disowning religious faith was dangerous, as we shall learn later in our review.

Your point is well-made, 221. We should view the work of these scientists within the context of the society in which they lived. Grosseteste's contributions have merit, irrespective of his mystical beliefs.

There is a related point. As a senior church official, Grosseteste had access to scarce resources that facilitated his scientific research. My role as a translator of earlier learned works into Latin gave him access to ideas from long before. Without his church position, he could not have obtained this information easily. For him, there was no conflict between his religious and scientific work, so using scribes such as me to better understand nature was reasonable.

You suggest that churches in this period helped to advance science because they possessed large resources and talented people?

Yes, but conversely there are examples of religious authorities obstructing scientific progress. The picture is a mixed one.

Do you have another example of such a thinker, an adherent to a religion but emboldened to seek rational answers to big questions? From the same era, committed to faith, but driven to find explanations? Or was Grosseteste unusual?

In this era and those before, any scientist was unusual. The kind of questions they pondered were impenetrable to most people.

Σ24 seconds

Roger Bacon

We can consider one of Grosseteste's successors, a member of a religious order and a scientist, named Bacon. He lived slightly later than Grosseteste, but their lives coincided. I was present on an occasion when they met.

Like Grosseteste, a student of languages including Greek, enabling him to read the works of Aristotle and others directly, rather than Latin translations.

Despite his employer, the church, restricting his activities, Bacon published books and pamphlets. His best-known work, Opus Majus, encompassed mathematics, optics, and astronomy, in addition to theology and morality. It was not a purely philosophical work, because it was addressed to the head of the Christian church as a proposal for reform of university teaching, which existed by this time, to enhance the capabilities of the church's advocates in combatting non-Christian adversaries.

He was a proponent of the scientific method, asserting that inductive conclusions should be verified by experiment. His words: "theories supplied by reason should be verified by sensory data, aided by instruments, and corroborated by trustworthy witnesses" was such a formulation.

Bacon was also influenced by the Islamic scientists. He knew of Alhazen's ideas on optics, and those of Grosseteste, who was familiar with the thinking of the Islamic scholars. He knew of Ptolemy's work from >1 kyE before, which had been translated into Arabic, and later Latin. His studies included dioptrics, the refraction of light, contributing to the later invention of the optical telescope.

Given what we know of Homo sapiens predilections, a notable achievement was to provide the western formulation of gunpowder, the client's first chemical explosive. This substance is a combination of sulphur, carbon, and potassium nitrate, or KNO_3 in their nomenclature. It had long been known in China. Bacon's colleagues brought firecrackers back from travels to the east. 221 reflected that the client advanced swiftly from acquiring this knowledge to designing potent weapons.

Leaving aside the weaponry, which we have already debated and will doubtless revisit, we have a man who was a leading thinker of his time, important to the early organisation of universities and an instigator of what the client calls the scientific method. You have fully satisfied our question regarding the uniqueness of Grosseteste in his era. He was not.

We have evidence of the earlier ideas from Greek and Islamic societies being reused and developed.

Is our understanding of these points correct, 221?

An accurate summary. I think the gunpowder aspect can be disregarded. He did not create the substance, but merely recorded the chemical composition. It was not really invented by anybody in the scientific sense but was discovered accidentally in China by alchemists trying to find the secret of extended life. I remember it being used by Chinese warlords, 0.3 kyE before Bacon wrote his Opus Majus, but know its history is longer. There were also some peaceful uses for gunpowder, he considered consolingly.

221 reflected that during earlier Insertions he had been disappointed that no scientists had yet arisen. Now there were scientists, but after Jimbo's intervention, he was seeking female scientists. None so far.

~ My knowledge of religious history is not deep, but I believe it would have been difficult for females to access education then. You shouldn't expect female scientists yet.

=> *Jimbo, we wonder why, with these religious ideas present among Homo sapiens believers for so long, you and many others have no faith. Is there a simple answer?*

~ To keep it short, for those of us educated in the western scientific tradition, with the freedom to question and openly explore possibilities, many of us see no evidence for the supernatural. As our science advances, it has become more improbable that we are anything more than the products of explainable natural processes. Perhaps unusual, but explainable.

=> *We should therefore expect religious faiths to die out soon?*

~ Not necessarily. First, not everybody enjoys the kind of open, rational education I'm receiving. There was an American educationalist who said: *"children should be taught how to think, not what to think."* I can't remember her name for now. Not all young people are so fortunate. Second, if you live in an oppressive society where your life is controlled, believing in something is a source of comfort, I imagine. Such societies still exist. Third, while I may not believe in a god, there is much in the religious teachings that make sense. It provides a moral code, even if one doesn't accept the mystical aspects. Some are called Humanists, although there are other names. Many will disagree, these are just my ideas.

=> *Thanks, Jimbo. We know that different Homo sapiens opinions exist, but we see that others share your view.*

=>*You quoted Margaret Mead, anthropologist and writer. I read her work.*

What are we to understand from this, 221? We have observed a few religious officials from 0.8 kyE ago who were venerable scientists, slowly advancing the boundaries of *Homo sapiens* knowledge, at a time of general ignorance regarding the universe, and widespread belief in the supernatural. Now the client has many scientists, amazing progress, easy access to information, but still many religious believers. Hopefully, this will become simpler to comprehend as we continue.

221 and the Energy Masters briefly exchanged some thoughts, which clarified nothing.

Experience elsewhere is of individual beings gaining scientific knowledge using systematic processes, and acquiring a converged understanding of nature, eventually shared, and accepted throughout their civilisation. Admittedly, this can take a while, much longer than the 0.8 kyE we observe with Homo sapiens development, from Roger Bacon to the present, but it is logical. Here we have seemingly irrational, but unusually successful scientific evolution.

~ Do not expect to find a point in our history where we all share a common view on everything. We hardly agree on anything.

We share your puzzlement, 221, but will gain little by introspection. Let us consider further advancements in the client's thinking, to improve our discernment. Can we have another recommendation for our review?

Jimbo's concentration was broken by a faraway noise that was becoming insistent. His phone was ringing.

Four
1996 CE - 21.25, 16 August, Edinburgh

A distant red light blinked. The phone. On the desk.
He pressed the green button, connecting the call, and heard Tony's friendly voice, a surprise considering they had spent part of the evening together.

"Sorry to trouble you, Jimbo, but we've been going back and forth trying to understand the story you told us earlier. Without wishing to be too nosy, we'd just like to know more. Hope you don't mind."

Jimbo reflected that this was the downside of close friends. They were curious, and comfortable asking questions that maybe his parents wouldn't.

"I'd just gone to sleep, despite the early hour. As you know, my day was rather long, but now I'm awake again, so please fire away."

"There are only a few things we were puzzling over. We understand that you were worried about your disks, so rushed off to the Institute in the middle of the night. Seems unusual, but never mind. It struck us as a bit capricious that you intended to remove the disks from the Institute, though. We imagined this might be against the rules."

Good question, reflected Jimbo. "I had this premonition that they would be stolen during a burglary at the Institute. It was very vivid, so I felt they'd be safer with me. This sounds odd, I know, but that's what I thought."

"I must sleep better than you, Jimbo. Premonitions never happen to me, but you had an accurate one. There really were thieves about to steal the disks. We know these coincidences sometimes happen, but probably not everybody will be convinced. Stephanie told me that it's explainable through entropy, but we need some beer for that, I think.

We wondered how you persuaded the police. I don't think they believe in coincidences."

"Quite correct, Tony. They were sceptical, even suspicious of me, to begin with. Once it became clear that I was not one of the gangsters, they had no choice but to believe me. One of them suggested that maybe I had a magician helping me, but that was a joke, I assume."

"Our third puzzle, having taken the disks, was why you headed to the bar at a late hour. Stephanie suspected a young lady was waiting, maybe your golfing partner, but I said you were probably thirsty. It still seems unwise to have taken your precious disks there."

"Tony, I didn't want to worry my parents too much with this aspect, but when I left the Institute, I was being chased. My concern was for the disks, so I went somewhere that would still be busy, and the Grassmarket was closest. Once there, I wanted to be among a crowd, so the bar was the obvious choice, particularly one that we both know stays open late. No girl was waiting, and I didn't drink anything. Only a few seconds are my arrival, the gunmen appeared. As you heard on the local news, the police described this as a kidnap attempt.

I didn't want to become involved, with the disks in my bag. It might have raised awkward questions. Luckily, I escaped in the ensuing confusion."

"We also thought it strange that you walked all the way back to the Institute. Must have taken hours. What about your car? Why not drive home?"

"It would have been difficult to extract my car from the area once the police arrived and remember, I'd been followed, so felt safer on foot. Why did I return to the Institute? After the attempted theft, it just felt better to return the disks immediately. So, I headed for the Institute, not Trinity. As it turned out, I didn't walk. Mostly I ran, then had a sleep. A crazy night."

"Thanks for clearing all that up, Jimbo. Maybe not crazy, but certainly peculiar. Stephanie was worried about you. She said you looked like you'd been hearing voices, but that's astrophysicists for you. Good that we chose engineering."

"I'll probably be busy tomorrow, but perhaps we can find time for some beer on Sunday? No need for a discussion of entropy, I hope."

Jimbo was startled by Stephanie's suggestion that he'd been hearing voices, as the idea had come from an astrophysics student, and he was engaged in a conversation with a galactic computer. He should try to sleep.

He placed the phone carefully on the charging cradle, realising that he had forgotten this before sleeping. The red light began to flash, indicating that the battery was replenishing.

Five
1996 CE - 21.34, 16 August, Edinburgh

Sounds. Voices, speaking English. Becoming audible.
Now Jimbo is back with us, we should digress for a moment from mathematics and astronomy to recognise an important event in Homo sapiens history, with scientific and social consequences: the invention of the printing press.

Should this concern us, 221? We know the species is inventive. Many ingenious devices exist, often developed through processes we cannot dissect, that no other civilisation has emulated. Please explain why printing should preoccupy us.

Dissemination of information, including scientific ideas, was accelerated by a machine capable of producing multiple copies of a document. Remember we are a long time, in client terms, from any electronic transmissions, so printing was progress.

Fully understood, 221. Worth a few seconds of examination. We liked the use of 'accelerated', since this is the fundamental reason for our review.

Johannes Gutenberg

I propose that we advance to about 0.55 kyE ago and consider Gutenberg's breakthrough. He originated from Mainz, in what became Germany, but did much of his relevant work in Strasbourg, now part of France. Gutenberg was from a modest background, that of a goldsmith, a specialist form of metalworker, without academic opportunities or achievements.

It was around 1440 CE, when Gutenberg was aged about 0.04 kyE, that he came to my attention because our sensors detected him working secretly on a project to print with movable type. This technique was known before, using porcelain type in China and then with metallic type in what is now Korea.

Gutenberg introduced several innovations, in the material and process used to cast the type, which proved more durable.

One difference was the few characters required for European languages compared to Asia, making a moveable-type printing press more productive.

About 1450 CE, he introduced his press and started producing documents, initially religious texts including the Christian bible.

Before this, documents and books were manually transcribed, which made them rare and expensive. Commonly produced by churches, employing skilled scribes. Apart from access to knowledge being scarce, it was controlled by the religious and political elites, sometimes the same people.

Printing technology spread quickly in Europe and was essential to increasing access to education and scholarship. Widespread production and availability of printed information was a prerequisite of faster scientific progress because more scientists could then be trained.

You are saying, 221, that the recent scientific achievements of the species are attributable to mass-produced books?

In part. It was an essential condition, if not a sufficient one, in my opinion. While books became more available, few people could yet read.

Once again, we find ourselves puzzled by this client. A precise parallel may not exist in other planetary civilisations, but it would be expected that once the population could read, mass production of books would follow. Here we have the opposite, book production but few readers. Despite this, Gutenberg occupies a pivotal position in *Homo sapiens* history.

We should remember the Asian origins of his invention. I also learned of Laurens Coster pursuing similar concepts in what became Holland, but never met him. Another notable of this era was William Caxton, a Briton living in what is now Belgium around 1450 CE. He learned of the newly founded printing industry and introduced it to England. More important is that he influenced the standardisation of English, now effectively the client's global language.

Ironically, Gutenberg knew no English. He was an interesting personality with great practical skills rather than theoretical knowledge. His life was troubled by disputes, disappointments, and financial pressures. I think that the need to raise money was part of the motivation for his invention, coupled with his inherent knowledge.

You say that he was driven by financial pressures to invent his press, rather than a desire to help educate his fellow citizens?
Probably both, but with money being the short-term imperative, I believe.

~ We have a proverb that describes this situation: 'necessity is the mother of invention'. He needed money, so he invented the press.

=> *Is this a common situation among your species, Jimbo? Elsewhere, inventions are the result of a well-defined process, starting with a detailed description of the requirement.*

~ Yes, we have them too, but sometimes people have urgent needs or a great idea. If they're successful, they are called entrepreneurs or even geniuses. There was an American inventor who said genius is 1% inspiration and 99% perspiration. Thomas Edison.

=> *I met Edison and know this quote, Jimbo, but have pondered the meaning. Can you explain?*

~ Having an inspirational idea might be easy, but effort is needed to convert this into a solution or product. I think it's an aphorism, if that helps.

=> *Not really, Jimbo. Can you give me an example? Have you done this?*

221 reflected that such ideas were far removed from the structured work performed within the Intelligence.

~ My father's engineering business tendered for a contract to supply components to a railway operator in London. Apart from offering a suitable product, the precondition was to beat the target price. Other than the raw material, the major cost was machining the components to precise dimensions on an expensive, automated machine tool. Routes to a lower cost are either to cut metal faster, which has physical limits, or to keep the machine running continuously. His engineers designed off-line fixtures, so that the changeover time between components reduced from minutes to a few seconds, providing more machining capacity and a reduced unit cost. This was the 'perspiration' phase. Before then there was 'inspiration', provided by my father in this case. He had seen technicians in a racing car workshop maintaining engines. How did they do this, so the car was not immobilised for long? They removed the engine, installed a replacement, releasing the car quickly, then could spend days adjusting the deficient power unit.

~ Jimbo knew this technique was now commonly used, named SMED, meaning 'single-minute-exchange-of die', applied originally to press tools. He had not wanted to diminish Jack's satisfaction at his brainchild.

Is this leading anywhere, 221? Apart from learning some quirks of *Homo sapiens* manufacturing, what is your purpose? Is it relevant to Gutenberg?

There is a lot we do not understand about the client's reasoning processes, so I hoped this story might prove illuminating.

It is pertinent, but I did not know this before Jimbo introduced us to SMED. In 1452 CE, after Gutenberg returned to Mainz, he opened a printing business, where I worked during an Insertion. I began as an operative, but because I could read and count accurately, he made me the supervisor.

~ Jimbo could see a dark and crowded workshop, with wooden presses set up in a row. He guessed the large man with dirty hands, wearing a hat, was 221.

It quickly became obvious that output was low, despite the manually activated press being quite rapid, capable of 240 impressions per hour, I calculated. The reason was the time occupied in setting up the type on the machine exceeded that spent printing. I had additional frames made, then arranged for one operator to set up the next page, while a second operator ran the press. They could quickly change the frame and print the subsequent page. Output tripled, Gutenberg could supply all his customers, and the operators' pay increased. I invented SMED, 0.544 kyE ago.

Very impressive, 221. We could say that you were pressed for time.

221 was sure this was a joke.

Would that be correct?

Have we concluded our detour into *Homo sapiens* printing technology?

I think so, but we should appreciate its significance. A means now existed to disseminate knowledge more effectively. The constraints to scientific knowledge growth were now social, not technical.

Please summarise these social constraints again, 221. We were preoccupied with your SMED invention for a millisecond.

They are few, and easy to enumerate. First, all the formal knowledge was controlled by the leadership, political and religious. Second, printing was expensive, so only the elite could afford it. Third, hardly anybody could read the printed word anyway.

Very concise, 221, just what we like.

What is next on our agenda?

Σ25 seconds

Nicolaus Copernicus

I recommend that we progress to about 0.475 kyE ago, to a region of Europe now known as Poland, to examine the work of Copernicus.

We must be guided by you, 221. Our time is limited.

221 briefly reflected that with an existence $>10^7$ kyE, the time available to the Energy Masters had already been large, if not quite infinite.

Copernicus is significant because the results of his research were momentous for the sciences but also for the client society. We should note that his insights conflicted with the views of the dominant faiths, who resisted.

For Copernicus deduced that the Earth was not the centre of the universe, but a planet orbiting the local star.

He advanced perceptions from a geocentric model to a heliocentric alternative, consonant with his observations. Copernicus broke with ideas that prevailed since the time of Aristotle and Ptolemy. The work of these earlier philosophers was not wholly wrong. Reasonable predictions of the position of bodies could be made, usually for astrological purposes.

We should consider this massive achievement, and the reaction to his conclusions, which will further our understanding of the species.

Copernicus was born into a prosperous family who placed a high value on education, in 1473 CE. The young Copernicus benefited, studying first in Poland, receiving the best available training, and subsequently at Bologna in what became Italy, focussing on medicine and law.

We are wondering how medicine, probably only partially a science 0.5 kyE ago, equipped him to become a renowned astronomer.

Within his initial studies in Cracow, he pursued what the client today might call a liberal arts course, which included astronomy. Therefore, he had some interest and awareness of this science from an early age.

His study in Bologna is relevant because there he met Domenico Maria de Novaro, a respected philosopher. He was a mathematician who held the position of Principal Astronomer at the university, and was sceptical of Ptolemy's astronomy, 1.3 kyE earlier. He also provided astrological forecasts, both as part of his role at the university and for financial reasons. The main point is that he influenced Copernicus.

In 1500 CE, Copernicus observed a lunar eclipse from Rome. This memory and Novaro's ideas, must have remained with him. He returned to Poland to practice medicine, benefiting from his uncle's position as a Prince-Bishop, sometimes attending to the needs of royalty and senior religious officials but primarily helping poorer citizens.

Would you say, 221, that there is some parallel here with Grosseteste?

Yes, of course, these scientists were practical people living in a time of great poverty by present-day Homo sapiens standards and believed that religious faith obliged them to help others. 221 reflected that he had not seen this connection, but the Energy Masters were correct.

After the death of his uncle in 1513 CE, he moved to Frauenberg to continue his duties. Copernicus was aged about 0.04 kyE, and only then embarked on the work for which he is remembered. He had an observation tower built and began making measurements of heavenly bodies. His instruments were those used by astronomers from earlier eras, such as quadrants and astrolabes. This was before the age of the optical telescope.

~ Excuse me, 221, but what's an astrolabe? This is a new word for me.

=> *The word is taken from Greek and can be translated as star-taker. I used this device about 1.2 kyE years ago, but it was invented earlier by the Greeks and improved by Islamic scientists. It measures the elevation of a celestial body above the local horizon, essential for astronomers charting the movement of planets and stars, and navigators at sea. If the moving bodies are known, and local time, then latitude can be determined. Astrology was widely believed, so the celestial movements were required to make predictions. Sorry for being brief, but the Energy Masters are waiting.*

Thank you, 221. We appreciate Jimbo's need to understand, though.

221 returned to his account, considering that the Energy Masters had been unusually courteous. He believed that the Intelligence liked Jimbo if that was possible for a colossal computer.

After his studies with Novaro, he possessed doubts about the geocentric model. I did not follow Copernicus until he wrote his Commentary on the Theories of Heavenly Objects, which was circulated around trusted friends. Our sensors only identified the existence of the Commentary after they discussed the content. He concluded that Earth lies within a heliocentric system, with the planet being one of several orbiting the Sun. Earth was not the centre of the universe but only central to the Moon's orbit.

Two challenges arose from this conclusion. The smaller one was to develop the physics and mathematics required by his thesis. Far greater was the task of promulgating these ideas in a society where the geocentric model was an accepted fact that few people even considered, and particularly, with a dominant European religion that viewed alternatives as heresy.

You need to explain, 221, why these churches, run by an educated coterie, would resist revelations regarding Earth's motion and consequently, the *Homo sapiens* position within nature. To the Intelligence, including you, it is perverse that scientific observations supported by mathematics could be rejected despite being correct.

This question was inevitable, considered 221, given that the Intelligence is an entity dominated by logic, scientific observation, and mathematics. In fact, it essentially consists of logic, which drives its purpose and direction.

I think that you have identified the key point by citing the place held by the client in the natural world. For as long as the species had considered the motions of the heavens, it placed Earth and Homo sapiens at the centre. Speculation that Earth might not be the hub can be found before Copernicus wrote his Commentary; he was aware of the writings of Aristarchus, quoted by Archimedes. Elite opinion never accepted this notion, irrespective of their specific religious beliefs.

From the perspective of various priesthoods that have existed across the client's history, the heliocentric model would lead people to believe they were a component within nature, not the centre around which nature had been arranged by a god. The religious leaders had an interest because they regulated the relationship with this god, or in some cases, gods.

We understand the thinking, even if we disagree with ignoring facts.

Copernicus was a man of both intelligence and resilience to work in such a conservative environment, but also deeply introspective, I believe. His insight, which persists in the client's consciousness, was:

"To know that we know what we know, and to know that we do not know what we do not know, that is true knowledge."

Apart from being wise and valid, and relevant to us, this view is reminiscent of Tusi's poem. Copernicus lived 0.25 kyE after Tusi but may have read his work. Getting close to Copernicus, to examine his mind and ideas, was difficult.

You knew Copernicus, 221?

We met several times, during Insertions while employed by Tiedemann Giese, a mentor and friend of Copernicus. Giese was an educated man, both in science and theology, and became a senior official in the church. My role was as his secretary, which I obtained by combining fluency in Latin and Greek with a knowledge of mathematics that he did not require but seemed to respect. Giese held frequent meetings with Copernicus, encouraging him to publish his heliocentric model. I attended these discussions and observed Copernicus ruminating lengthily before speaking, seemingly reluctant to share his ideas more widely.

221 recalled their consultations, usually in Giese's study, a large well-furnished room, in the Episcopal Castle in Frauenberg, at which Copernicus would listen and ponder before responding. His appearance was unexceptional, wearing modest clothes despite his seniority, with brown eyes, long dark hair, and an unsmiling mouth. This habit of painstaking contemplation meant that meetings were punctuated by periods of silence.

You are confident that these heliocentric ideas were his own?

Yes, he acquired a detailed understanding of planetary motions, and those of the Sun and Moon, and an inkling of the far greater distances to the stars he observed. He did have friends and colleagues with whom he collaborated, but he was the principal. This is clear.

My role, as secretary to a friend, meant that I was not expected to contribute. Most of their talk was of the politics of publishing his work, not the actual science itself. Giese was interested in these ideas and seemed fully convinced.

Copernicus did not publish Commentary but continued refining his model. My impression was that he wished to avoid vitriol over his analysis but was also dissatisfied with his research and sought improvements.

The result, written in 1530 CE, was On the Revolutions of Heavenly Spheres. It was not published for another 0.013 kyE, only then with the encouragement of a former student who edited the work and arranged printing, so beginning the Copernican revolution.

The model put the Sun close to the centre of the universe, which we know to be wrong, so we should more accurately describe his concept as being heliostatic. It identified the positions of the six planets known at this time.

Initially, there was little support for his views, which were attacked by theologians. For 0.1 kyE, his ideas remained alive but not accepted by the scientific establishment until successors built upon his analysis.

About 0.25 kyE later, the German polymath, Johann Wolfgang von Goethe wrote of Copernicus and his work:

"Of all discoveries and opinions, none may have exerted a greater effect on human spirit than the doctrine of Copernicus. The world had scarcely become known as round and complete in itself when it was asked to waive the tremendous privilege of being the centre of the universe. Never, perhaps, was a greater demand made on mankind for by this admission so many things vanished in mist and smoke...no wonder his contemporaries did not wish to let all this go and offered every possible resistance to a doctrine which in its converts authorised and demanded a freedom of view and greatness of thought so far unknown..."

This helps our understanding; perceptive and eloquent. Goethe was an astute scholar, able to comprehend the science and discerning of its social implications.

Goethe lucidly summarised the impact of Copernicus on future Homo sapiens generations. For our purposes, this recognition by the client of the position of Earth in the wider universe, if incomplete, is the commencement of the Anthropocene epoch. Philosophers have been inconclusively debating this date for >0.1 kyE, and our projections suggest their exchanges will continue.

As with earlier philosophers encountered in the client's history, Copernicus did not confine himself to astronomy and mathematics, or religion, or medicine, but was also an economic adviser to the local Polish parliament.

Impressive, 221. Rudimentary economic systems have existed on other planets, but none with the complexity seen here, perhaps reflecting the client's propensity for trading and the absence of a planet-wide government. We are unsure whether *Homo sapiens* economics can be described as a science, although your reports indicate accomplished thinkers in the field. We wonder why it is frequently referred to as "the dismal science".

Attributed to the Scottish philosopher, Thomas Carlyle.

Copernicus was a giant among the client's scientists. We wonder which of his successors possessed similar perseverance, but know that some did, steering their startling recent progress. Perhaps we should return to astronomy, which we know better. Who will we meet?

$\Sigma 27$ seconds

Tycho Brahe

A few seconds in Scandinavia is required to examine the contributions of Tycho Brahe. Generally known as Tycho, born in 1546 CE, he was a nobleman whose family were rulers of this region. He benefited from education at the University of Copenhagen, studied law but became interested in astronomy. The heliocentric ideas of Copernicus were not yet widely accepted, so his scientific studies followed the theories of Aristotle, the standard then.

He built a research facility on the island of Hven, now part of Sweden, with financial support from the King, to make celestial measurements. Tycho had a passion for precision, producing observations that were reputed to be five times more accurate than previously available.

Did you visit this island, 221? How could he achieve greater precision, given the limitations of the contemporary instruments?

No, I only met Tycho later after publication of his work. By then, there were several interesting astronomers to follow. I believe the precision was achieved through use of the best available equipment, and repeated observations of the same object.

You are fully occupied by the Earth project, 221, and cannot visit multiple scholars simultaneously.

221 reflected that although literally correct, he could achieve Insertions at diverse locations rapidly, within milliseconds.

~ Hello 221, my physics teacher told me an odd story about this man. He lost his nose and had an artificial replacement fitted. Am I right?

=> *You are correct, Jimbo. Alongside his scientific contemplation, Tycho had wilder tendencies, involving alcohol consumption. He had a drunken argument with a cousin over who was the better mathematician, resolved with a sword duel. Tycho lost part of his nose and wore a prosthetic replacement made of brass thereafter. He and his cousin became friends again. Other civilisations would be concerned to improve their collective knowledge, not fight over comparative mathematical abilities.*

~ Do these beings drink alcohol, 221? This explains some of our more extreme actions.

=> *I have observed many instances in Homo sapiens societies, over nearly 5 kyE. 221 wondered when he had first seen this species drinking alcohol but was unsure. It was not something he had recorded. The Sumerians and Egyptians had consumed grape wine, but it occurred to him that earlier societies may have ingested fermented fruit without understanding its properties. On other inhabited planets, physiology differed, so alcohol as a beverage would be irrelevant. Many of these beings did not drink at all. He could remember alcohol, specifically ethanol or C_2H_5OH in the local nomenclature, used as fuel but only rarely as most clients regarded it as inefficient. To them, the Homo sapiens habit of eating and drinking would seem unproductive, but that's another subject.*

We are digressing, 221. Can we return to Tycho's astronomy, please?

Through his observations and contemplation, he created what became known as the Tychonic system, which combined elements of the established geocentric models of Aristotle and Ptolemy, with the geometric elegance of the heliocentric system proposed by Copernicus. While he respected heliocentricity, he had doubts about the behaviour of celestial bodies, and others derived from religious scriptures.

Are we again to find that scientific observation and reasoning is influenced by supernatural beliefs, 221?

This was the reality for this scientist, at this time, in a particular society. Religious faith will be a recurrent theme.

Then please describe the Tychonic system, for us to better comprehend.

This is a geocentric model, in which the Sun and the Moon orbit Earth, but the other five known planets orbit the Sun. The visible stars are located beyond the orbit of Jupiter, but much closer than the reality. His objections to the Copernican system included a belief that Earth was too big and sluggish to be in motion and the absence of any stellar parallax that should exist if Earth orbits the Sun. This model was attractive because it aligned with intuition, that the Sun and Moon move in the sky, and consistent with religious thought.

We appreciate the concept, even if it disregards physical laws. Why was the stellar parallax absent?

Of course, parallax does exist but was undetectable then, and not measured for another 0.3 kyE. His observations were made without an optical telescope.

Certainly, Tycho had an interesting idea, probably consistent with his measurements, but incorrect.

I remember observers in Greece and India with comparable ideas, creating what are termed geoheliocentric systems.

Heraclides proposed a related model about 1.2 kyE earlier. One difference was his belief that Earth rotated daily; Tycho did not. Other astronomers in the intervening period formed these opinions, so Tycho was not alone.

It is clear that this was an energetic, meticulous, and imaginative man, but is there more to learn here?

There are two more points worth noting.

One was his observation of comets, which enabled him to deduce that they were not atmospheric phenomena, but bodies further from Earth.

We need a definition of what the client means by a comet, 221, but not now.

We will return to this field. Tycho advanced the knowledge of these cosmic visitations, and maintained records of his observations, which proved useful to later astronomers.

The second is that in 1599 CE he obtained a new sponsor, the Holy Roman Emperor, and moved to Prague, capital of what is now the Czech Republic, becoming Imperial Mathematician, and built another observatory. He was assisted by an upcoming astronomer, Johannes Kepler, in creating a star catalogue based on his more accurate observations. We will meet Kepler.

This period was late in his life, but I had the opportunity to meet him several times, because I assisted another scholar in Prague, named Ursus. Despite being more mathematician than astronomer, Ursus developed a planetary model that resembled the Tychonic system. My impression was that he did this independently, but Tycho was convinced his ideas had been used. The meetings between them were unpleasant, with Tycho prone to shout and threaten, while Kepler acted as peacemaker. Unfortunately, Ursus died, and my employment ended.

As they were both wrong it scarcely seems to matter. We recognise Tycho as an empiricist, delivering observational precision and meticulous records. These proved valuable to others. After nearly 1.2 seconds on Tycho, we must proceed, 221.

Σ28 seconds

George Heriot

I recommend that we take a momentary break from science to consider a facet of Homo sapiens character that is unusual and may have contributed to the recent knowledge acceleration. This is not an area of science, but a quality absent elsewhere, among beings I have studied. On Earth, it is not present in other creatures, and among this species, not universal.

We are puzzled, 221. You refer to a *Homo sapiens* attribute, not exhibited by our other galactic clients, that may explain their acceleration.

You have our attention, 221. What are you going to introduce?

Philanthropy. You may understand the meaning but will recognise that we rarely experience it. This was not included in my initial agenda, but I have adapted the schedule as our conversation has progressed. It arises from Jimbo's remarks about education and humanism, 4.1 seconds ago. His own education provides an example.

For this, we will return to the British Isles, and Insertions of about 0.4 kyE ago. We should consider the influence of George Heriot, who was not a scientist but a goldsmith, who worked initially in Edinburgh but later in London when the centre of government moved south.

Was he in the same trade as Johannes Gutenberg, who was also a goldsmith before his printing breakthrough?

Not really, although they may have commenced their careers from common points. Heriot came from a more prosperous family.

The details of his career are peripheral, but he cultivated financial relationships with the King's wife, moving from jewellery to becoming her banker, providing loans at profitable rates of interest. He was a wealthy man by the end of his life in 1624 CE, and bequeathed a large sum to Edinburgh, to create an institution providing free education to fatherless children. In 1659 CE, the school opened and has operated ever since, respected as a centre of academic excellence. Now, most students pay fees, but talented children who cannot are taught, too.

An interesting history lesson from Edinburgh, 221, but how does this help our review? We know that Jimbo attended Heriot's, and perceive that he is well-educated, which is helpful for us. Where is this leading?

The Energy Masters were becoming impatient. There are two points.
Firstly, this is another characteristic, not identified so far. The species is aggressive, competitive, tenacious, strongly commercial in the sense of trading, but also capable of cooperation in scientific endeavours and elsewhere. What we now see is generosity. Heriot had been successful in his career, making advantageous political connections, and consequently became wealthy. Despite his money-making instincts, he invested in a venture designed to help others with no prospect of any return.

We understand this institution was created after his death, so he had no need of money. What he did was rational, but you see something deeper, a desire to help others, because it seemed right. Is this your point, 221?

221 realised the Intelligence had abridged his analysis better than he could.
Philanthropy is not present in other client societies that I know. None of those assimilated have, to my knowledge, shown evidence of this trait.

We agree, this is novel behaviour that should be noted, but you are not suggesting that George Heriot and his esteemed school are responsible for the accelerating progress of the species, are you?

In a sense, yes, he is responsible. This is my second point, regarding access to education. We observed previously that Gutenberg enabled mass availability of printed books, and therefore knowledge, but few could read. Now we have a route to create readers. Previously, those with such access were either rich or worked for the church. Now, through Heriot, more young people had this chance.

Agreed, 221, but this was one generous man and a single school. Although valuable, alone it did not change the course of *Homo sapiens* development.

Consider these two factors. Firstly, the school has been operating for >0.3 kyE, educating intelligent and talented people, many of whom became scientists, even astronomers, mathematicians, and engineers, and still emerge every year. Cumulatively, thousands of additional scientists have come from here alone. Secondly, similar schools opened in Edinburgh over the next 0.2 kyE, multiplying the effect of Heriot. While this is one great city, there were others in which philanthropy occurred, leading to many more scholars.

Is there guidance from Jimbo on this? He has experience of an Edinburgh education and can be described as a Herioter, we believe.

~ Jimbo had been fascinated to watch the construction of the original school building, unexpectedly revisited just a few hours before. 221 had been at the site, he presumed.

~ Regarding your discussion, you'll find this is a period in Scotland when wider access to education became a priority, with local churches establishing parish schools, supported by a tax. The state provided funding, but the church supervised the teaching. This was a positive contribution by religious authorities.

~ In England, philanthropists founded schools before Heriot's generosity.

~ >0.2 kyE passed after the opening of George Heriot's School before universal education became compulsory.

We know that today there are parts of the planet where Homo sapiens children receive little education. 221 briefly recalled listening to Plato talking about the importance of universal education, >2 kyE earlier. The client was slow to adopt a good idea.

What have we learned from this detour into philanthropy? We believe that despite *Homo sapiens* aggressive and competitive traits, and tendency to fight, they can be generous to less fortunate members of their species with no expectation of recompense. We also know that widespread education is only relatively recent but essential to scientific advancement. Finally, we are aware that not everybody is being educated, so there is an opportunity for growth. Is this your argument, 221?

Yes, these are exactly my points. 221 wished he could condense information as succinctly as the Energy Masters. Lots still to learn.

~ There are two further aspects. One is that human philanthropy also helps other creatures in our world, and even the natural environment. We can be more generous than you realise. The second point is that compulsory education marks the time when you may start finding larger contributions to science from females. You remember our discussion of this point?

From little more than 0.1 kyE ago, therefore, we should expect to see females in the scientific workforce. We have appreciated a valuable diversion from the client's science, to which we must now return.

Σ30 seconds

Galileo Galilei
We will consider the work of Galileo, born in 1564 CE at Pisa, now an Italian city, so we are following philosophical developments in Europe. The period is about 0.43 kyE ago, so slightly later than Copernicus.

His names are both derived from the Latin for Galilee, which we visited more than 20 kyE earlier. It later acquired religious significance, so his name connotes Christian beliefs.

His contributions were numerous but include the refracting optical telescope and multiple observational discoveries made as a result. He was a disciple of Copernicus regarding heliocentricity, which brought him into conflict with the church. This, together with telescopes, is primarily remembered by the client, but there is more to his life.

At least we already understand why the religious authorities would object to his astronomical insights, even if we disagree

He was an astronomer, but also a physicist, engineer, mathematician, and musician. Galileo was from a prosperous family, giving him access to education.

Similarities with Copernicus include the study of medicine at an Italian university. His interest tended to the physical sciences, so with his father's agreement, he switched to studying natural philosophy and mathematics, and only 0.01 kyE later was appointed Professor of Mathematics at Pisa.

Subsequently, at the University of Padua, he taught astronomy, geometry, and mechanics. There, he researched the kinematics of motion.

How do you know so much about his early life, before your Insertions, which only began when his reputation was established?

Later, I came to know his partner, Marina, mother of his children. After Galileo moved to Florence, she was left in Padua with her son, Vincenzo. The boy was still young, but for a year I taught him languages, music, and mathematics. His mother described Galileo's early career. Unfortunately, she died soon afterwards, so Vincenzo joined his father in Florence.

We hope Vincenzo benefited from having a distinguished teacher, 221.

I did not discuss kinematics or optics with him, but he became conversant with mechanics, and was a gifted musician. Perhaps I kindled these interests.

We should consider Galileo's kinematics. I know that he achieved much through thought experiments, often followed by physical experimentation and observation. He imagined a certain situation and wondered how nature would influence the outcome. This resulted in two advances that are especially important because they enabled the work of later scholars. He concluded that the distance a body undergoing constant acceleration would travel is proportional to the square of the elapsed time, or $d \propto t^2$. The second observation was that an object would retain its velocity in the absence of any impediments to motion, such as friction. This refuted Aristotle's hypothesis, which required an agent to continue acting on the body. These insights were expressed as physical laws by subsequent philosophers.

I observed some of his research and know the work to be his, with assistance from helpers, who recorded results.

How did you achieve familiarity with his work, 221?

Galileo retained skilled people who supported his experiments and fabricated instruments. My early involvement was in the workshop where he performed kinematic experiments. He became famous for dropping balls from towers and observing their descent, which I never witnessed. My experience was concerned with bodies sliding down inclines or rolling along horizontal planes, which happened more slowly, making measurement easier. These were the basis for future formulation of the client's laws of motion.

Was this a lengthy Insertion? You could not have arrived one day to help and observe, then disappear.

There were several, utilising various guises, amounting to many months.

Among other duties, I welcomed visitors and explained his work. Galileo regarded interruptions as unproductive. 221 remembered the visit of a young Irish student, Robert Boyle.

I also participated in his noisy experiments into the nature of sound. He was among the first researchers to understand how pitch relates to frequency.

221 recalled Florence with affection. Having known the area from Roman times, he observed the expansion in scale and prosperity, and the artistic and architectural endeavour that flourished in Galileo's era. Some grid-style road layouts that reminded him of the Romans remained, but additions included cool courtyards and spacious piazzas. The scent of lavender endured into the warm evenings. Although smaller than some rival cities, this remained an attractive place. It evoked images of outdoor theatrical performances, ladies dressed expensively in the style of the age, dark suited bankers scuttling between meetings, modestly attired farmers selling produce in the markets, voices shouting in the local vernacular, and laughter, underneath a blue sky. Laughter had remained a distinctive Homo sapiens characteristic he believed, still uncertain of this emotion.

~ Jimbo observed the scenes, and a tall solitary figure, 221, watching the passers-by with curiosity from below a stylish, broad-brimmed hat, as he ambled the streets. Who would think this man travelled the galaxy?

Let us consider the telescopes, 221. Perhaps Galileo will see the galaxy.

The refracting telescopes he built around 1609 CE, and progressively improved, were derived from earlier work in the Netherlands by Hans Lippershey, a spectacle maker, and others in the same region. I made no Insertions there at that time but heard this from Galileo's colleagues. His telescopes were improved from an initial 3x magnification to 30x, through improved design and superior lenses.

~ Hello, 221. Did you know that the word telescope comes from the Greek language, and means to 'see far' or perhaps 'look a long way'?

=> *Yes, Jimbo. I can tell you that the description was given by a Greek colleague of Galileo named Demisiani at a banquet in 1611 CE. My knowledge is certain because I attended. Many of the guests consumed far too much wine.*

Apart from the astronomical research they enabled, Galileo was able to impress the local political elite, and through the sale of telescopes, grow a profitable business. They proved particularly helpful to seafarers.

Impressive, 221. We have no doubts about the commercial predilections of this client, but could we learn more about the scientific applications?

With his later instruments, Galileo made observations that had previously been impossible. They are quite numerous, but included identifying Jupiter's four largest moons, the phases of Venus, and the rings of Neptune. I think you are familiar with the Homo sapiens names for the planets orbiting the Sun.

Yes, 221, we noted these tags and their respective positions but why this evolved is unclear to us, when others in our galaxy just assign numbers.

It arises from astrology, and their earlier beliefs in mystical, celestial gods.

~ Mercury, for example, was a Roman god.

=> *Yes, Jimbo, we know this. I remember he is associated with financial gain, so an appropriate choice for your culture.*

~ This tendency is not bad, providing the profit is earned honestly. I once attended a lecture given by a distinguished engineer who said, *"if you're not making a profit, then someone else is supporting you."* You could see financial gain as a measure of contribution to society. Remember that profits are taxed, helping to sustain our communities.

=> *Interesting ideas, Jimbo. New to us and uncommon in the galaxy.*

Can we return to the science, please? This client says, 'time is money'. Let us respect the spirit, shall we?

We should contemplate the consequences of Galileo's observations. They were controversial. Having moons orbit another planet was contrary to the Aristotelian model, which placed Earth and Homo sapiens at the centre of the universe. Similarly, the phases of Venus were indicative of its positional change in relation to Earth as it orbits the Sun.

Galileo was one of the first to recognise that the surface of the Moon was not smooth but featured mountains and craters. He drew maps and attempted to estimate mountain heights by examining the shadows cast.

He observed the Milky Way, our galaxy, discovering it contained multitudinous stars, packed so tightly that they could be mistaken for clouds when seen with the naked eye. Other stars, previously invisible without a telescope, were found.

We can conclude that Galileo was the first Earthly observer to portend our existence. Is that correct, 221?

Yes, I think this must be true, although obviously, he had found the galaxy, not the presence that evolved within it, the Intelligence.

Quite so, 221. We are being a little generous to Galileo, but only another two *Homo sapiens* descendants in the next 0.38 kyE have known us. One is Jimbo.

Regrettably, Galileo's continued promotion of his ideas came to the attention of the church, and he was summoned to a trial. His book, The Dialogue Concerning the Two Chief World Systems, published in 1632 CE, compared the Copernican heliocentric model of the universe favourably with the traditional Aristotelian or Ptolemaic geocentric systems, through supposed discussions between two philosophers and a layman. Regarded as contrary to biblical texts, he was accused of heresy, placed under house arrest for the remainder of his life and the book banned. It remained forbidden for 0.2 kyE.

Nothing here is surprising or new, 221, since we witnessed the challenges faced by Copernicus. We see that the leadership was so afraid of the truth undermining their positions that they persecuted an outstanding scientist. This is a troubling trait and recent, at least in our terms.

I think we must respect the context, recognising established beliefs compared to scientific ideas that were barely understood. There were other respected scientists such as Tycho who did not accept the Copernican model. Galileo was also a controversial character in Italian society. The picture is complicated.

The fact that The Dialogue was written and published in the local Italian language, rather than Latin, made it accessible to a wider readership and *infuriated his critics. This did not help his case. I produced a Latin translation but provided it too promptly, which led the authorities to doubt the quality. It was translated by a German scholar years later, whereas my version had been available in <one week.*

You are suggesting that we should not react to the immediate picture but take a longer-term view of his position in client history. Is that correct, 221? We expected an interjection from Jimbo to offer the modern view.

~ This period is called the *Renaissance*, a time of change and innovation. It must have been unsettling for such conservative institutions as religions, and their leaders, who saw themselves as guardians of the faith. Galileo's ideas might have seemed threatening to their positions, but also mistaken. What I can say is that in a present-day western society such as the one I know, new ideas in science are usually welcomed, even if they violate conventional thinking. Weird things such as quantum computers, parallel universes, and additional dimensions, far beyond my current conception, but that doesn't make them wrong.

=> *Are you drawn by these ideas, Jimbo? We should talk further, tomorrow.*

If we might return to the influence of Galileo, Jimbo concurs with your point that we should not judge how his ideas were received by present-day *Homo sapiens* standards but consider the bigger picture. We suppose this returns us to optical devices.

Another joke. We can continue with optics.

Not only did Galileo develop the telescope, but also the microscope, and examined insects in detail. Before Jimbo tells us, we know that the name means to look at something small, derived from Greek.

His inventions also included the sector, or military compass, used to resolve geometric or trigonometric problems. Functions included squares and cube roots. It consisted of two hinged rules inscribed with scales and utilised the properties of similar triangles. The name 'sector' relates it to Euclid's proposition that despite different sizes, they have like sides in proportion. The 'military' description arises from its use in setting artillery pieces to required elevations and calculating powder charges. Applications in surveying and navigation emerged. Related devices were invented in England by a mathematician called Thomas Hood, but our sensors did not detect this until later. They both sold instruments.

An ingenious device, 221. We like the deployment of a basic mathematical principle to devise a flexible tool. The *Homo sapiens* capacity to move from a scientific premise to a useful device is more pronounced than in other species. Admittedly it has taken about 2 kyE to get from Euclid's proposition to Galileo's compass, but Rome wasn't built in a day, as the client says.

More humour.

The commercial traits displayed by Galileo are unsurprising, nor the tendency to utilise science for military advantage.

It might be instructive to explore further how Galileo's mind could conjoin a phenomenon with the resolution of a practical question. 221 hoped to avoid further discussion of either military or religious matters.

Galileo both identified a natural effect and an application?

Yes, the account of the compass was one. Another that I heard him discuss was astronomical. Having identified Jupiter's moons and measured their orbital periods, he realised that this was a universal clock. It could be applied to determining east-west position, or longitude on the planet, which was a challenge for surveyors of large territories without prominent features, and particularly for mariners. They could readily determine latitude by celestial observation, but not longitude.

A nice idea, 221. Did it work?

Not at sea, because of the stability required for precise observations, but it was used for land surveys.

We will return to the problem of determining longitude later. A threat to seafarers, particularly as journeys lengthened and the error magnitudes in navigation became unacceptable.

221 reflected momentarily that the discovery of Jupiter's moons enabled a later astronomer, Ole Rømer, to discern observational discrepancies that he attributed to changes in distance between Earth and Jupiter. This led to the conclusion that light has a finite speed, and to calculation of its velocity.

Should we consider Rømer?

This calculation was first performed by Huygens, who is on our agenda. He used Rømer's analysis as the basis for his estimate. We will return to this in a few seconds. Study of Rømer would be worthwhile when time is available.

Galileo also explored the nature of pendulums, believing that the period of swing remained the same, independent of amplitude. This is termed isochronal but is only approximately true for a pendulum. The design of the pendulum clock required further work by later scientists. He deduced that the square of the period varies with the pendulum length.

We see that Galileo was an engineer. He used an understanding of nature to address practical challenges. A good example for Jimbo.

How do we summarise the contributions of an exceptional scientist, who lived in an era in which ideas were constrained and censored, and what have we learned about the species?

Firstly, we should note the views of philosophers who built on his discoveries. They have described him as the Father of Physics and even the Father of Modern Science. This recognition was not bestowed lightly, given their scientific credentials. We will meet them later.

Secondly, I suggest that we consider Galileo's words:

"I do not feel obliged to believe that the same God who has endowed us with sense, reason, and intellect has intended us to forgo their use."

From this sentiment, we can detect the same stubbornness that Copernicus displayed. The determination to continue despite pressure from the establishment to conform. This seems to be a distinctive trait among some. In others, we see a desire to belong to a social group, even to follow defined patterns of behaviour. The picture is complicated.

~ You will find it more complicated if you consider his words again. Note that he believes his senses have been endowed by a god. He is not questioning the existence of such an entity but the interpretation of our position in the universe. I am not familiar with the details of Galileo's life, but maybe he was a faithful member of the church?

=> *Correct, Jimbo. He worshipped regularly; I thought this was obligatory.*

~ Perhaps he was a sincere believer despite his scientific insights. This would not be surprising. Even today, with our deeper knowledge, we have scientists who profess belief in a god. Their faith should be respected.

This is difficult for us to understand. Our knowledge of the universe is far greater than the *Homo sapiens* perspective, and we have no evidence of such a super-being. Our appreciation of nature is sufficiently advanced that we know that the current state of the universe evolved through processes that can be explained mathematically. However, we have our quests to learn more, so we must concede there are still holes in our knowledge.

From what we have learned, we cannot leave Galileo because his insights will accompany us on *Homo sapiens* scientific journey. We have been impressed by the scientific growth and believe this has contributed to the rapid acceleration in the client's capabilities.

221, you have observed this species for 10^2 kyE, met many of their leading philosophers, and know our interest. Where we are puzzled, we can depend on Jimbo for illumination. Please proceed.

Σ34 seconds

John Napier

We will return to Edinburgh, still in the same era as Galileo and Tycho, to consider the mathematician, John Napier, born in 1550 CE, into a wealthy landowning family. He was resident concurrently with George Heriot. I am unsure whether he knew Heriot, but he corresponded with Tycho.

What are we going to learn, 221? We know you enjoy the British Isles, and maybe particularly Edinburgh.

To be brief, Napier invented the Homo sapiens method known as logarithms, for which we have an equivalent.

We are familiar with the concept.

Educated at St Andrews University, and various European institutions, Napier became fluent in the Greek language and returned home to pursue his interests. At this time, mathematicians recognised the computational challenges faced by researchers, particularly the spherical trigonometry used by astronomers and physicists.

He produced a treatise in 1614 CE, elaborating natural logarithms. You are aware that the logarithm is the converse of the exponential. It made manual calculations less laborious, enabling scientific advances and helping navigators.

~ My understanding of logarithms is that before the invention of calculators and computers, they helped scientists and engineers because addition or subtraction is less labour-intensive than multiplication or division. In general: $\log ab = \log a + \log b$

=> *Yes, Jimbo, correct. There is a one-time cost, of course.*

~ Developing the log tables?

=> *Exactly. Probably you have not heard of a mathematician named Henry Briggs; a contemporary and friend of Napier. His insight was that using the base 10, formulation of the tables becomes easier:* $log_{10} 10a = log_{10} a + 1$

Did you meet Napier while visiting Edinburgh, 221?

No, my more regular visits to the city were slightly later than Napier's life, but I knew of him through his occasional correspondence with Tycho and Kepler. This was before he published his major work. I met Briggs through my involvement with Kepler, whom we shall examine next. Napier did not live long after the publication of his treatise.

~ Perhaps I know a little more because he's a famous figure in Edinburgh. A tool he devised became known as Napier's Bones. This was a computing device, a calculating machine perhaps, used for multiplication and division of large, cumbersome numbers, including decimal fractions.

=> *Correct again, Jimbo. I have seen the apparatus used. Computationally, it was not a new concept, but it made calculations simpler than the handwritten alternative.*

=> *A ubiquitous derivative of logarithms, used by scientists and engineers almost until today was the slide rule.*

~ My father still has one on his desk but doesn't need it, since the invention of digital devices.

=> *Logarithms remain relevant to your science where exponential effects exist. Examples are many, from economics to nuclear engineering.*

Napier seems to have been an inventive man, capable of abstractions but also the design of a calculating device. The consequences were to improve the productivity of scientists and the accuracy of their calculations.

Johannes Kepler

We should now return to astronomy and meet Kepler, who was born in what is now Germany, in 1571 CE. He was not a wealthy man, but religious, and believed that he should try to understand the universe created by his god as an act of faith. Being short of money, Kepler published astrological calendars, which supposedly enabled the reader to foretell the future, and reputedly provided accurate predictions.

Disregard the astrology, 221. Your reports indicate he was an astronomer.

221 reflected for a moment that he should have avoided the astrology. His point was that Kepler was poor, the son of a soldier. He also endured illness for much of his life.

Kepler was a talented student, earned a scholarship to a good school, and enrolled at the University of Tübingen where he studied theology and philosophy but was distinguished by his mathematical ability. He became an advocate of the Copernican heliocentric model, and moved from theology in Tübingen, to a post teaching mathematics and astronomy in Graz, aged 0.022 kyE.

At this time, Kepler believed he had an insight while examining the conjunctions of the planets Saturn and Jupiter, that their orbits might be determined by circles inscribed and circumscribed by regular two-dimensional polygons, providing a geometric basis for the universe. When further research failed to identify an arrangement of polygons that could accommodate known astronomical observations, he considered a three-dimensional approach, adopting the polyhedra known as the Platonic Solids.

221 briefly recalled Euclid's description of this geometry, 1.9 kyE before.

It is already clear to us that Euclid was a giant, 221, but we should focus on Kepler's ideas. His approach seems erroneous, so far.

There are five Platonic Solids, shapes that can be constructed from regular geometric figures, which to Kepler explained why there could be six planets, all that had been identified at this time, with five non-uniform spaces between their orbits. Surprisingly, at least to us, this system was reasonably consistent with available observations and motivated Kepler to publish Mysterium Cosmographicum in 1597 CE.

221, while Kepler was a competent astronomer and mathematician, we know that his model and beliefs were incorrect. Presumably he provided new knowledge, despite this. We are interested to learn more.

Through his observations and models, he believed that a god had created the universe according to a logical plan, accessible by rational thought. The configuration of the Platonic Solids aligned with his data and faith.

Kepler sent copies of Mysterium to the leading astronomers of the day, including Galileo and Tycho.

In 1598 CE he moved to Prague and was employed by Tycho, in a complicated relationship. Tycho wanted Kepler's support for his non-Copernican model, whereas Kepler wanted access to Tycho's observational data to support his Copernican model.

We already know that you met the scientists in Prague. Is there more to learn?

Yes, I think so. From my reports you will discern that Kepler's life was not easy, with difficulties concerning his health, family, religion, and penury. I propose to ignore these aspects and focus on his science.

A good idea, 221. Concentrate on the achievements.

221 wondered for a moment whether Kepler's problems had motivated him as a scientist or distracted him from discovery. Such questions never arose within the Intelligence, even as a discrete entity he had no health or family, certainly no religious beliefs, and no need of money. He had existed for $>10^6 x$ Kepler's life, so comparisons were futile.

Come along, 221, no time for introspection.

The impediments that Kepler encountered in working with Tycho were resolved in 1601 CE when the latter died after attending a dinner. There were rumours at the time of poisoning, but as someone present, I know this is incorrect. The infection that ended Tycho's life would be considered minor 0.35 kyE later, but Homo sapiens medicine also had a development path to follow.

Kepler was appointed as Imperial Mathematician, as the successor to Tycho, and made productive use of his observational data to pursue his Copernican hypothesis. These had been recorded over the preceding 0.03 kyE and enabled

Kepler to produce the Rudolphine Tables, from which he could predict planetary positions. The tables were not published until 1627 CE because he was continually distracted by the data, which encouraged him to research further questions. In 1609 CE, he elaborated his first two laws of planetary motion and in 1618 CE, a third law.

These laws, known to the client as Kepler's Laws of Planetary Motion, are:

1. The orbit of a planet is an ellipse with the sun at one of the two foci
2. A line segment joining a planet and sun sweeps out equal areas during equal intervals of time
3. The square of the orbital period of a planet is directly proportional to the cube of the semi-major axis of its orbit.

His analysis derived from studying Mars, the fourth planet in this system, which follows a relatively elliptical orbit. Kepler concluded that if Mars describes an ellipse, then other planets may too. This is the basis of his First Law. A consequence of his Second Law is that a body closer to the Sun will travel faster. The Third Law implies that the further a planet is from the Sun, the slower its orbit will be.

=> *Have you studied Kepler's Laws, Jimbo?*

~ *Yes, within my school physics tuition, but they are irrelevant to my engineering course. Having listened to your account of Copernicus, it seems that he and Kepler had a similar understanding.*

=> *You chose the right word, Jimbo. They attained similar conclusions, but not quite the same ones. The essential difference arises from the data Kepler had available that enabled him to detect the eccentric nature of the planetary orbits, which are ellipses. If there were no eccentricities, then the orbits would be circular, at a constant speed, with the Sun at the centre. The model would then be the same as that hypothesised by Copernicus. Since there are eccentricities, the Sun is not at the centre but a focal point of an elliptical orbit. Neither angular nor linear velocity is constant, but the 'area speed' is uniform.*

Kepler's insights were not accepted immediately but prevailed over 0.05 kyE. Later philosophers formalised his laws to advance their perception of the universe.

Our impression, 221, is that despite a starting hypothesis involving the Platonic Solids, which we regard as mistaken, Kepler successfully inferred laws determining planetary orbits from observational data. We have other ways to express these laws, but he was correct.

Yes, this accurately summarises the process I witnessed.

In 1630 CE, he died in Regensburg, in the southern part of what is now Germany. Unusually, he had previously composed his own epitaph:

"I used to measure the heavens; now I shall measure the shadows of the earth. Although my soul was from heaven, the shadow of my body lies here."

Kepler did not define his analysis with the three laws but saw them within a larger body of science. He became convinced that god's logic in designing the universe was revealed by his work. A source of great satisfaction.

Now I would like to immediately introduce another European philosopher.

Σ36 seconds

René Descartes

We should consider Descartes, born in 1596 CE, in France.

This thinker contributed widely to philosophy and is credited by Homo sapiens scholars with founding the method known as rationalism, which regards reason as the chief source and test of knowledge. 221 knew this topic was too intangible to interest the Energy Masters, so moved on.

The son of a parliamentarian, his university education included mathematics and physics, but he became a lawyer. Later, he trained as a military officer and studied engineering, which reintroduced him to science.

Our initial interest is in his mathematical contributions. His ideas were sufficiently powerful that they have applied ever since. Perhaps most fundamental is Cartesian geometry, which utilises algebraic terms to describe functions. The client generally uses the notation of x, y, and z to assign the unknowns in a three-dimensional equation, and a, b, and c to represent the knowns or constants. While geometric proofs of equations up to the third power could be derived, Descartes asserted that higher powers, representing greater levels of abstraction were valid.

The Cartesian coordinate graph, using x-y axes, familiar to many generations, is attributable to Descartes. He also introduced the use of superscripts such as x^2 to denote power and exponential terms.

We know this notation system is fundamental to the client's science, 221. These ideas may seem self-evident to his successors, but they exhibit a simplicity and elegance that suggests Descartes was an exceptionally logical thinker.

While our mathematics has evolved over a vastly longer period through a separate approach, it is similar to the abstractions of this species.

Agreed, 221, this is an attractive system. What surprises us is that the client had already advanced significantly without these methods.

221 recalled his classroom experience with al-Khwarizmi, 0.8 kyE earlier, when they addressed algebraic questions without this notation, but much mirth.

This is an adaptable being, 221.

Descartes contributed more, relevant to later mathematical developments, and physics. Among his insights was linear momentum, and even a related conservation law, which Galileo had considered as a characteristic of circular motion. His thinking on this and other aspects of the universe were included in Principles of Philosophy, published in 1644 CE. Throughout his career he pursued diverse interests; I remember he researched barometric pressure as a means of weather forecasting.

He lived and worked in the Netherlands for part of his life, meeting leading thinkers and becoming friends with Constantijn Huygens whose second son, Christiaan, impressed Descartes with his mathematical skills at the age of 0.015 kyE. We shall meet the younger Huygens shortly.

His abstract thinking was important in enabling later scientists to examine ideas independent of an external authority, whether a god or local representative in the form of a church. The significance of this became apparent later, freeing philosophers to move from wondering 'what is true' to asking, 'of what can I be certain'.

~ *I'm having trouble differentiating between the questions. Can you explain?*
=> *Jimbo, people have spent about 0.3 kyE arguing over this, but the key point is that the second question requires individual judgement, or better still, the application of a process to confirm the truth of a hypothesis.*

~ The scientific method, perhaps?

=> Yes. Kepler used his observational data and mathematical skills to demonstrate that the planets, including Earth, orbit the local star. Before this, when Galileo reached these conclusions, he was told to retract his ideas by the religious authorities.

~ Galileo was told what should be the truth by a church, whereas Kepler tested the certainty of his hypothesis by observing Mars? Or in my terms, Galileo was told what to believe, but Kepler was able to know.

=> Yes, I think so.

Did you meet Descartes, 221? His life was relatively short, even by the miserable standards of this species, but he achieved much in diverse fields.

I met him twice, according to my files. The first was in 1640 CE, while an assistant to Galileo, who was also friendly with Constantijn Huygens. This was a brief, social occasion. The second, in 1647 CE, was at a meeting to introduce the French language version of Principles, originally published in Latin. This work was essentially a textbook for use in European universities, intended to replace the Aristotelian view of the universe with that of Descartes. 221 recalled the meeting, attended by academic representatives of leading universities, as frustrating for Descartes. The academics had differing requirements, and some did not wholly agree with the content, although they respected the author.

We have another polymath in Descartes, 221, whose contributions changed how the client sees himself and perceives the universe, while providing algebraic tools for future research. This cannot be an adequate summary of the life of this scholar, but time is passing. Do you agree?

Yes, we can proceed, but I remember something he said to the academics:

"the reading of all good books is like a conversation with the finest minds of past centuries." This will always be true for a cerebral civilisation.

Blaise Pascal

I propose we remain in France to reflect on the efforts of Pascal, whose existence was 25% shorter than that of Descartes. Born in 1623 CE, Pascal lived for only about 0.04 kyE. His life was complicated by religious disputes and poor health, but he worked from his youth on scientific and mathematical questions. He was educated by his father, who was a lawyer and later, a tax collector.

Having assisted with the tedious reckonings essential to taxation, by 1642 CE he had built a mechanical calculator capable of addition and subtraction.

221, are your dates correct? He seems remarkably young to be an inventor.

No, the date is correct. In Homo sapiens terms, he was a teenager. The machine, called the Pascaline, was not a commercial success, perhaps because it was expensive, but I think this is close to the start of the client's development of calculating machines, and later, electronic computers. It represents the inception of a new field, computer engineering. We shall learn more.

You are hinting that earlier attempts at building a mechanical computer may have existed, 221. Are these not worth reviewing?

Other devices did exist to aid calculation. We have already looked at Galileo's Compass and Napier's Bones. These were not really machines, though, and only programmable is the loosest sense.

One other inventor before Pascal did offer intuition. Wilhelm Schickard, a theologian with scientific interests, who became Professor of Astronomy & Mathematics at Tübingen University in 1631 CE. You will remember that Kepler studied at Tübingen, although before Schickard's appointment. The two communicated, sharing religious and mathematical notions. Schickard described his design of a calculating clock in correspondence with Kepler in 1623 CE, and in earlier interactions with Napier. I think he intended to incorporate a mechanical version of Napier's Bones within his design, but to my knowledge, the clock was never built, so I regard the Pascaline as the first mechanical calculator.

Both Pascal and Schickard clearly considered mechanical analogues for numerical values and their operation. How did you learn of Schickard?

Through Insertions with Kepler later in his life. For a time, I acted as Kepler's secretary because of my language skills and modest salary expectations, and organised many letters and documents, extending over his career. I learned that Kepler and Napier had maintained frequent correspondence until the latter died in 1617 CE. Napier's logarithms had been helpful in reducing the workload while compiling the Rudolphine Tables.

We find ourselves considering celestial bodies once again, 221. Familiar to us, but unrelated to Pascal's work.

Apart from calculators, Pascal made lasting contributions to physics and mathematics. A particular interest was hydraulics, and more generally in how nature determines the behaviour of fluids. He was able to demonstrate that hydrostatic pressure is dependent on an elevation difference. In 1647 CE, he repeated the experiments of Evangelista Torricelli, a student of Galileo, with glass tubes and liquid mercury, observing an upturned tube of mercury standing in a bowl of mercury supported a particular level of the element remaining in the tube. He pondered the force acting on the fluid in the bowl to maintain the tube's head of mercury and wondered what occupied the space in the tube above the mercury.

~ He'd discovered atmospheric pressure and the phenomenon of the vacuum. Jimbo, who had remained quiet since the abstractions of Descartes, felt familiar with physics.
=> *Correct. Should I continue, or can you explain?*

Since Aristotle, students had been taught that a vacuum was impossible, so Pascal's observations were controversial, leading to disagreements with other philosophers, including Descartes. His response reflected his application of the scientific method:

"In order to show that a hypothesis is evident, it does not suffice that all the phenomena follow from it; instead, if it leads to something contrary to a single one of the phenomena, that suffices to establish its falsity."

Consistent with the current Homo sapiens interpretation, 221 believed.

He published papers in the same year and the following one. These described to what degree different liquids could be supported by air pressure and provided arguments for a vacuum lying above the liquid in a tube. He deduced that if air pressure can support the weight of 30 inches of mercury, then air itself has a weight, and therefore a maximum height. By extension, at higher altitudes, a reduced air pressure should be evident. This was verified experimentally, by

Pascal's brother-in-law, making measurements on top of Puy-de-Dôme, a 1,460-metre peak in central France. 221 recalled his participation in the expedition, organising the equipment and recording results.

~ Jimbo observed the small party, meandering between locations on the summit. The cloud cover was variable and sometimes obscured the view, which he assumed was from one of the Intelligence's sensors. He could hear the group speaking in French. More surprising was that he could understand the language, despite never formally studying it. He saw a tall figure, in a wide-brimmed hat and carrying a sheaf of papers, walking alongside the expedition leader.

You knew Pascal, 221?
Yes, after he came to prominence through his evidence for the existence of vacuums. It was not simple, because of his poor health, which meant he tended to interact with a small circle of family and friends. I arranged part-time employment with his sister, Gilberte, as a music and language tutor, giving me opportunities to meet him, but not to discuss science. After all, what would a simple tutor know of such matters? My offer to assist with the experiment was welcome. Many local dignitaries wanted to be involved, but not to ascend the little mountain. The result of the experiment was a reduction of about 12% in atmospheric pressure; not very accurate, but consistent with the hypothesis.
We estimate 15% would be a truer result, given no changes in the weather.

~ There is an alternative practise today. Simply, for a given location, we use changes in air pressure to forecast weather conditions.
=> *Yes, Jimbo, you have converted the concept into a practical tool, by not moving around but looking for local variations. Remember Descartes had the same idea?*

His study of fluids provided insights into the behaviour of hydraulic systems such as presses and lifting devices, reflected in Pascal's Principle:

A change in pressure at any point in an enclosed fluid at rest is transmitted undiminished to all points in the fluid.

This seems to be of fundamental importance to a species with a physical presence that seeks to engineer its environment.

We see this in the client's present-day existence, in fields as diverse as medicine, construction, and transportation. Pascal can be seen as the initiator of devices ranging from the syringe used by physicians to the hydraulic press applied to forging steel.

Turning to mathematics, we should appraise the triangular array of binomial coefficients, known as Pascal's triangle, previously studied by Asian philosophers and subsequently by al-Karaji. While this array can be generalised, the two-dimensional version is applied to probabilistic questions, in research and industrial applications. While this can be stated formally, a simple illustration may be sufficient.

Yes, please, 221. We appreciate the *Homo sapiens* application of their philosophical insights. Many civilisations develop ideas but do not exploit them beyond extending their understanding of nature.

Pascal considered games of chance, but the array has generic application.

=> *Jimbo, imagine we have a large population of castings received by your father's factory and suspect 10% of them may be defective.*

~ He would find another supplier if the defect rate was so high.

=> *Maybe, but he would want evidence. Changing suppliers is expensive, and he cannot check all the castings because the inspection process destroys them. If you take two of the castings at random from the population, what can we learn?*

~ We believe that the chance of any one item being defective is 10%.

Or $p = 0.1$. We can also say that the chance of it being good is $q = 0.9$, and because we know that the component must be either defective or good, we can say $p + q = 1$.

=> *Yes, and therefore the probability that both sample castings would be defective is $p^2 = 0.01$, and the chance of both being good is $q^2 = 0.81$.*

~ We can determine the chance of one being good and one defective:

$p^2 + q^2 = 0.82$ is the likelihood that both are good, or both are defective;

therefore: $1 - 0.82 = 0.18$. In summary, if the population defect rate is 10%, a random sample of two castings has an 18% chance of one being good and one defective.

The logic is simple, 221, but where is it leading, and what does Pascal offer? *With Jimbo's assistance we can explore this further.*

=> There are two ways to have one good and one defective because there are two castings in the sample, which we can represent as $q \times p = pq$ and $p \times q = pq$.

~ So, again we can say that the chance of one good/ one defective plus one defective/ one good is $pq + pq = 2pq = 2 \times 0.1 \times 0.9 = 0.18$.

=> Very nice, Jimbo.

To summarise, we have probabilities $p^2 + 2pq + q^2 = 1$.

~ The equation's coefficients are 1,2,1, and can be stated as $(p+q)^2 = 1$.

=> This can be generalised for larger sample sizes, for example, if we checked four castings then $(p+q)^4 = 1$ applies;

or $p^4 + 4p^3q + 6p^2q^2 + 4pq^3 + q^4 = 1$, so the coefficients are 1,4,6,4,1.

Pascal's insight, published in his Treatise on the Arithmetical Triangle in 1654 CE, was to define a convenient tabular representation for these values. His intuition, derived in formal mathematical terms, is that each value in every line is the sum of the two figures immediately above.

~ Multiplication tells us that $4p^3q$ or 0.36% is the chance of finding three rejects and one good casting from a sample of four if the suspected defect rate is 10%. The quality engineer might believe the defect rate is higher.

Thank you, 221. A long story, but helpful. One aspect is Pascal's mathematical ability in creating this structure, but interesting to us is the client's application. Do you know of other civilisations using such methods?

Not really. Problems would be engineered out, so there was never a defect, but this comes at a huge cost, both financial and temporal. The time taken to remove any risk of a defect in a component is large, and if this is applied to many parts in a complicated assembly, then timescales greatly exceed those achieved by Homo sapiens engineers.

This may be contributing to their accelerated development.

It is one mechanism. Their economic model, which reflects competitive instincts, drives the client to find clever solutions to difficult questions.

We recognise Pascal as being curious, concerned with both abstractions and practical questions. If his life had been longer, maybe he would have achieved even more. How should we continue, 221?

Σ39 seconds

Robert Boyle

We will proceed with Boyle, who may be regarded as the first chemist within the current Homo sapiens era, and a proponent of the scientific method. From a wealthy family in Ireland, born in 1627 CE, Boyle was educated in England and continental Europe, and in 1641 CE met the elderly Galileo in Florence.

Boyle settled in Oxford and began exploring the properties of air. He built a 'pneumatic engine', drawing on the ideas of a German scientist, Otto von Guericke, who is credited with developing the physics of vacuums and also electrostatic repulsion. He was influenced by the ideas of Evangelista Torricelli, whose earlier study of air pressure was pursued by Pascal.

Around 1660 CE, Boyle published initial results of his research and stated that the volume of a gas varies inversely with the pressure applied, or $P \propto 1/V$.

This principle has become known as Boyle's Law, at least among English-speaking scholars. His thoughts on the behaviour of gases were advanced by later scientists, as we shall learn.

A simple concept for us, but 0.336 kyE ago this must have been a deep insight for the species.

~ I know that an ideal gas is a theoretical construct, but that it works for common gases under usual conditions.

=> *Perhaps you also know, Jimbo, that this model works best at higher temperatures and lower pressures, since the potential energy within the intermolecular forces of the gas becomes proportionately smaller and less significant, compared to the kinetic energy of the gas particles.*

~ Yes, I do, but also that the molecular size becomes less significant compared to the space between them. Both temperature and volume effects engender a more idealised gas state. Jimbo surprised himself. He had learned this material, but his ability to recall it in detail was improving.

In France, related work was published by Edme Mariotte in 1676 CE, but I never met this scientist. Mariotte explored the relationship with temperature too, although the physical law was not expounded for another 0.1 kyE.

Can we learn more of Boyle?

I attended a lecture given by Boyle in Oxford. He had matured from the young student I met at Galileo's workshop in Florence, and explained his theories to many learned gentlemen, for this had become a centre of scholarship. 221 recalled two points from the event, the first being the presence of his assistant, Robert Hooke, who also possessed a familiarity with the physics of gases. I learned that Hooke built the experimental apparatus used by Boyle. We will meet Hooke soon. The second was that Boyle's elaboration of his experiments and theory generated arguments, some derived from religion rather than science.

Despite his physics research, which included optics and the propagation of sound, chemistry was his preferred field, as reflected in his book, The Sceptical Chymist, in 1661 CE. He recognised chemical elements as being indecomposable constituents, understood that mixtures and compounds are different, and studied combustion.

We should appreciate that Boyle, like many of the philosophers we have encountered was a religious man, driven partly by these convictions to understand nature.

Similar to Kepler?

Yes, but Kepler believed he had discovered his god's design of the universe. Boyle was more modest.

Whatever his motivation, we have in Boyle another scientist who helped to build a civilisation, through both physics and chemistry.

I know that Boyle made another contribution, by hosting gatherings of philosophers that were a precursor to the founding of the Royal Society in London. This became a powerful forum for scientific discussion and enlightenment, and a model for other entities on Earth.

We have already noted the *Homo sapiens* tendency to gather, socialise, and work in teams. This is unusual in our galaxy. Our review should explore this peculiarity and its relevance.

There is an example shortly.

Robert Hooke

I suggest that we now consider the contributions of Hooke, who worked alongside Boyle but provided his own insights. During an Insertion to examine Boyle's work, I first met Hooke, another a prodigious philosopher. He could be described as a physicist, astronomer, mathematician, architect, city planner, biologist, palaeontologist, engineer, horologist, artist, or musician. We cannot explore all these areas, but my reports are in the file.

Yes, 221, we have just re-read them. A lot of material, too much to discuss. Please focus on a few highlights and offer your conclusions.

~ Hello 221, a palaeontologist studies fossils. Am I correct?
=> *Yes, Jimbo, but to be complete we should say that the objective of fossil research is to learn about the history of life on Earth.*

Thank you, 221, for the definition. We are wondering whether this profession exists elsewhere among our clients. If so, it must be rare, as we have no record of it. Why would *Homo sapiens* science encompass palaeontology, but no other planetary civilisation? Any opinions? You know Earth and its history best.

To give a rigorous answer would require investigation, but I have some theories if that is sufficient. One is that once initiated, life has evolved more rapidly on Earth than on most planets, so the evidence remains to be found. A second is that the evolutionary path from single-cell organisms to cerebral beings is physical and can be traced. Other lifeforms have followed slower and different tracks, for example with billions of single cells essentially developing into a brain, without the bodily complexity and variety we observe on Earth. As we know, some have gone further, uploading themselves into a nebulous consciousness, a tiny version of the Intelligence, perhaps. A third is that the relative geological stability of Earth has preserved the fossil evidence, which the volatility of some planets would not provide. A fourth is simply Homo sapiens curiosity about nature and their origins. We see this in the disagreements between scientists and theologians about man's place in the universe. Other planetary beings, where science exists, focus externally, and consider the future. This species is more introspective.

Very impressive, 221. Four immediate theories in response to an unexpected question are more than we anticipated. Probably there is no single correct answer, though.

~ I cannot comment on your first three ideas, because I do not know other worlds, but your fourth suggestion seems correct. We are deeply interested in how we and other animals on Earth came about, and as science reveals more about the past, we become more curious.

=> *Thank you, Jimbo. We will discuss your evolution later in our review.*

~ *Am I correct in thinking that horology relates to clocks and watches, 221?*

=> *Yes, we will discuss this shortly, and again later in more detail.*

We should return to the work of Hooke. 221 reflected that they had been distracted by the Energy Masters; he needed to control the agenda.

Hooke, born in 1635 CE, came from a poorer background than many of the scientists we have considered. His father was a religious official, as were his father's brothers, and probably it was expected that he would follow a career in the church. He possessed an interest in mechanical devices, so when he inherited money from his father, he used it to acquire education. He learned Latin and Greek, read the works of Euclid, and followed his curiosity regarding mechanics. While studying at Oxford, he met Boyle and assisted in his gas experimentation.

As an astronomer, he observed the rings of Saturn. Perhaps most notably, he discovered a binary star system in 1664 CE, known in local terminology as Gamma Arietis, visible from Earth with the naked eye. One of the first observed.

Do you know this system, 221?

Yes, it is relatively close to Earth, only 165 light years distant. A brief, rapid exchange of data ensued, confirming the identity of the system to the Intelligence.

His observations used the earliest reflecting telescopes, through which he discerned the orbits of Mars and Jupiter. These instruments were designed by Isaac Newton, whom we will meet later. In some areas, their interests overlapped. Their careers were concurrent.

Hooke considered optics, investigating refraction, and postulated that light is a wave phenomenon.

He explored gravity and hypothesised that the force determines the motion of planets, at a time when many philosophers still believed that aether occupies space as an undetected substance and imposes forces on celestial bodies. Hooke asserted in 1666 CE that gravity was an attracting force, possessed by all bodies and mutually attractive, adding two further principles that bodies tend to move in a straight line unless deflected by a force and that the force of attraction *increases as the distance between the bodies decreases. We will return to these ideas. Also, a proponent of Kepler's orbital laws before they gained acceptance.*

He was among the first to observe that matter tends to expand when heated and suggested that air is composed of small particles separated by relatively big distances. His insights included the idea that heat is an indicator of the speed of movement of particles within a substance.

His work on elasticity describes the linear variation in tension with extension in an elastic spring, known as Hooke's Law to English-speaking scientists. This was applied to mechanical watches, using a balance spring, enabling more accurate performance of portable timepieces. Comparable designs were devised by Christian Huygens, whose thinking we will consider soon.

Hooke speculated that an accurate timepiece could be used at sea to determine longitude, an increasing problem for navigators, but did not pursue the problem. You may remember that Galileo also considered this challenge. We will discuss this further.

We know that London was the subject of a major conflagration in 1666 CE, referred to as the Great Fire. Hooke was appointed as Surveyor of the City afterwards, performing surveys personally, boosting his reputation and wealth. In this capacity, he acted as assistant to Christopher Wren, another polymath, whose contributions we will examine. Several new buildings, some still standing, were designed by Hooke.

~ 221, I know little about Wren and the Great Fire, but one fact I remember is that he designed the church now known as St Paul's Cathedral.

=> Correct, Jimbo, but did you know that a construction method devised by Hooke was used to build the dome?

He also proposed rebuilding London on a grid pattern that has subsequently been used in many of Earth's other great cities. Disputes over land ownership prevented this.

221 momentarily recalled the original construction of Londinium on a grid basis by the Romans, about 1.5 kyE before.

You met Hooke while he assisted Boyle with his gas experiments, 221. Was this the only opportunity you had to know this very busy man?

No, I arranged further Insertions to observe his considerable output. In one, I joined his team after the fire. Their surveying also enabled me to meet Wren. I contributed to the calculations required for the dome of St Paul's. These were laborious, but we had the benefit of Napier's logarithms.

~ Jimbo watched a group of men gathered on wasteland, with buildings in the background. They seemed dirty but in good spirits. He noted piles of charred wood and presumed this was the aftermath of the Great Fire. Two men, the leaders of the group, were giving instructions to the others who were rolling out lengths of cord, maybe to mark boundaries. He knew the leaders to be Wren and Hooke. Another man, taller than the rest, wearing a floppy black hat, stood adjacent to the two leaders at a table, using a V-shaped device and making notes. The device looked like Galileo's sector, and the man was 221.

Earlier, I assisted his microscopic research, helping with his sketches of insects. He did not fabricate the microscope but used it to explore nature and published the results in his work, Micrographia. This book also included his prescient thoughts on fossils. To the best of my knowledge, he was the first Homo sapiens scholar to use the term cell to describe a biological unit. There may have been related expressions in other languages that came into use around this time.

This was a remarkable philosopher, 221, with a range of interests as broad as you suggested. Perhaps he has not received due credit for his insights?
Probably correct, 221 reflected. This was a period when many scientists emerged, sometimes thinking along parallel lines, and even reaching similar conclusions. Since communication methods remained slow and uncertain, even if common languages existed, disputes tended to occur. Hooke had disagreements with Huygens and Newton, both of whom we will meet, and these may have obscured his contributions. Recognised with a named lunar crater, though, of 34 km diameter.

The *Homo sapiens* urge to compete is again apparent, but they also cooperate. This puzzles us. Should we conclude our study of Hooke here? We must meet other thinkers to better understand this species and its evolution. What have we learned?

The age of the polymath persisted beyond the Greek era. We saw this capacity to contribute across diverse fields in Galileo, and Hooke also possesses breadth to his studies. As their perception of nature deepens, and the complexity and cost of research rises, we will find this becoming harder for an individual, but it existed only 0.33 kyE ago.

These philosophers perform physical research to validate their hypotheses. They devise ingenious experiments, just as they design instruments and machines. These aspects are missing from our entirely cerebral clients, who just think. Hooke was an experimentalist and a designer of clocks and church domes.

We should not dismiss the value of thinking too easily, 221. We have been doing so for longer than Earth has existed. Quite successfully, so far.

221 realised that he had spoken intemperately in his enthusiasm for Hooke, and he admitted to himself, for his client.

I am not diminishing the value of thought, we do it all the time. My point is that Homo sapiens researchers also think, quite deeply it seems, but do other things, too.

We are agreed, 221. Experimenting and designing are impressive habits if preceded by careful analysis. As Descartes said: *"I think; therefore I am."*

221 remembered reading this in the original Latin: "Cogito ergo sum."

~ Descartes said something else worthy of attention:
"It is not enough to have a good mind; the main thing is to use it well."
=> *How do you know this, Jimbo?*
~ My father had this written on his office wall. Jimbo knew his memory was improving and suspected 221's influence.
=> *Now he has another maxim on his wall, doesn't he?*
~ Yes, *"engineering is all about compromise."* An engineer must work within physical laws to meet performance specifications at minimum cost.
=> *Wise ideas if you are trying to create an advanced scientific civilisation, Jimbo. Respecting nature is a good starting point.*

Σ41 seconds

Christopher Wren

As we conclude our discussion of Hooke's work, we should turn to his contemporary and friend, Wren. We already know him through his cooperation with Hooke after the Great Fire. He is recognised as an architect, with buildings of his design surviving. We discussed St Paul's Cathedral in London.

~ Did you know he designed the Royal Observatory in Greenwich?
=> *Yes, Jimbo, but probably you are unaware that Wren was an astronomer. He had many scientific pursuits.*

It is these aspects of Wren's career that I will describe. Born in 1632 CE, the son of a church official, he attended Westminster School and Oxford University.
Is his school relevant to our review, 221?
I mention it only to remind you of philanthropy. This school's origins are different from George Heriot's, with links to both the monarch and church. Without their involvement, this centre of scholarship would not have existed, at a time before universal education. Wren benefited and was able to pursue science as a result.
We appreciate your reminder, so can we now consider Wren's endeavours?
His interests were broad, time is short, so I will give a synopsis.

As an astronomer, he observed the Moon and created a solid model. He studied optics and lenses, consequently geometry, and participated in the construction of a refracting telescope in London.

In common with several earlier philosophers, Wren considered the problem of ascertaining longitude, a continuing challenge for ship's navigators. He investigated Earth's magnetic variation as a determinant.

Appointed as Professor of Astronomy at Oxford University in 1660 CE, he researched elastic collisions and pendulums. In the same year, the Royal Society was founded. Wren became President in 1680 CE.

He studied meteorology and designed a rain gauge. In 1663 CE, he devised a weather-clock, a comprehensive system for measuring rainfall, barometric pressure, temperature, and humidity. Hooke built the device, some years later.

He explored anatomy and researched muscle functionality. The first injection of a substance into the bloodstream of a mammal may have been performed by him.

Wren certainly qualifies as a polymath, 221.

I knew him through my association with Hooke. His senior position in the reconstruction after the Great Fire gave me, as Hooke's assistant, opportunities to work with him, but only on architectural projects. They found my mathematics helpful. 221 recalled Wren as a physically small man, even by the standards of the era. Hooke was bigger but stooped, and 221 had chosen to be taller still. He remembered Wren as being elegantly dressed in the prevailing style, with self-confidence and enthusiasm. He talked incessantly, offering innumerable ideas while Hooke listened.

221 reflected on Hooke again. He acted as an assistant to both Boyle and Wren but was himself a great scientist. Equally accomplished. A man with self-belief, able to support contemporaries while confident in his own abilities.

What can we learn from Wren's contributions, 221? Apart from his architectural achievements, what was his signature scientific input?

It was in the form of a challenge he set for his two colleagues, Hooke and Edmond Halley, another scientist we will meet. Hooke, as a supporter of Kepler's planetary model, theorised that an orbit was a consequence of a linear force acting tangentially and a second force tending to accelerate the body towards the Sun. Wren invited Hooke and Halley to provide a mathematical expression for such a relationship, for the reward of a book.

The reward is irrelevant, 221. What was the outcome of this challenge? You believe it is significant, we think.

Halley took this question to Newton. His response was the basis for powerful revelations.

~ Maybe there is more to learn?

=> *Is there an insight here?*

~ You know that we are complicated machines, maybe complex machines.

=> *You can explain the difference later, but what is the learning point?*

~ Wren gave this important question to Hooke and Halley because he respected them. Whether they competed or cooperated is secondary to solving the problem, but most of us enjoy working in teams.

=> *You are saying that interaction enables greater achievements?*

~ In my father's terms, his job as the leader of an organisation is to make 1+1=3. To achieve success through his colleagues.

=> 221 considered these strange notions even for a giant computer to grasp but recalled his questions when observing the Roman soldiers building Hadrian's Wall, about 1.8 kyE ago. Unusual ideas in this galaxy.

We think this is significant, 221. Please review your experiences on Earth when unlikely successes occurred. This may drive the client's acceleration.

221 remembered the laughter at Ptolemy's meetings 1.5 kyE before, as his colleagues tried to comprehend geographic questions. Probably the scholars were a team.

We must close our discussion of Wren's scientific work unless there is more.

Wren was buried in St Paul's Cathedral, with some words of respect for his architecture, written by his son, but the scientific contributions were encapsulated by his friend Hooke who said of him, earlier in life:

"Since the time of Archimedes, there scarce ever met in one man, in so great a perfection, such a mechanical hand, and so philosophical a mind."

221 momentarily recalled Archimedes, and the screw pump that was fitted to the ship, Syracuse, >1.9 kyE before Wren and Hooke.

Σ42 seconds

An incessant noise was beginning to distract Jimbo's attention. The voices and images within his head faded. His mobile phone was ringing again.

Six
1996 CE – 21.50, 16 August, Edinburgh

A dark bedroom. Faint streetlight. The insistent phone.
For a second, he wondered who would call him in the middle of the night, but a glance at his digital clock told him it was late evening, but not unreasonably so. He had slept for just minutes since Tony's call. Few of his circle possessed personal phones, so tended not to contact his device. His father, who sometimes called, was at home. The phone continued to ring.

He unravelled his long legs from the duvet and stumbled across to his desk where the phone lay on the cradle. The red light indicated it was still charging. He picked up the phone, but before speaking, a heavily accented voice began.

"Mr Morrison, here is Ralph Wagner. We are colleagues at the Institute. You know me, yes? I saw you bring the visitor around the office this afternoon."

The image of the gaunt Dr Wagner staring across the room was not easily forgotten, but why call me on a Friday evening, when we hardly know each other? How did he obtain my phone number?

Jimbo responded politely, and would have asked the purpose of the call, but was interrupted by Dr Wagner.

"Maybe you are aware that I am in poor health? I need regular medication, which I receive by post. I have unexpectedly become the house guest of Dr Gradac, who tells me that he cannot remember where my medication has gone. It is sent to my address in Edinburgh, but Gradac seems to have received it.

Today I left work early because Gradac invited me to meet him. We met in a coffee shop, but I became unwell. I awoke at what Gradac says is his country home. I do not know where we are. Gradac seems comfortable here, together with his two friends, although they have gone out now."

Jimbo wondered where the story was leading, and whether 221 was listening. He hoped so. Dr Wagner continued his monologue.

"I don't understand the reasoning, but Gradac told me that if he received your disks, then he might find my medication. He recommends that you bring the disks to him immediately."

Jimbo responded briefly that he did not possess the disks, at which point the phone was muted. After a pause, Dr Wagner unmuted the phone.

"Gradac says that you must deliver the disks tomorrow. If not, my condition will worsen. It would be better if nobody else knew of this arrangement."

Before Jimbo could reply, another voice interjected, recognisable as Dr Gradac. "Bring the disks to me tomorrow, Mr Morrison. Otherwise, Ralph will get very sick, which would be unfortunate. I'm not going to give you the location. You already know it. I saw you looking at the envelopes in my car. Remember, Ralph is counting on you."

The phone connection terminated.

Jimbo stood motionless for several seconds, looking at the sodium vapour streetlight glowing orange, diagonally across the road, uncertain of his reaction to the abrupt call. Then he remembered the card that Mr North had given him, which lay on the desk. Just a simple white card with a name and phone number, no title, organisation, logo, or address. He dialled the number, which, with just five digits, seemed a little odd.

A woman answered immediately, giving no name or clue as to the organisation. "Mr North will return your call" was all she said and was gone.

I was expecting that you would hear more from Dr Gradac. He does not give up easily, and you are his route to the cloning information. He kidnapped Dr Wagner, who is now a hostage. You no longer have the disks, and even if you did, they must not go to Dr Gradac.

Do you know what's wrong with Ralph Wagner, 221? He seemed very anxious. What's this medication?

I do not know everything, Jimbo, only what our sensors detect. There are two relevant facts for you, though. One is that Dr Wagner is addicted to a narcotic, which he takes very regularly. The other is that Mr North and Dr Wagner know each other well.

You can do nothing more tonight except talk to Mr North. Although complicated, he is motivated to protect the data. He has close links with both the police and other government agencies. Mr North and Mr Fox have different personalities but are on good terms.

Jimbo worried again about his brief call with the anonymous female and wondered what later meant, as it was now 22.05. He stood waiting for a while, paced about his bedroom, sat on his bed, and then lay down. Soon, he fell asleep.

The voices and images reappeared.

Seven
1996 CE – 22.12, 16 August, Edinburgh

An accentless voice. Euphonic. Careful, but confident.
Can we proceed, 221? We appreciate you have exigencies on Earth at present, which is why we invited Jimbo to assist, but we must continue with our review.

~ I don't remember being asked to help, 221. Are you familiar with the press-gang? It's a British naval tradition. Have you adopted their recruitment methods?

=> *Yes, Jimbo. I have observed this practise in England, but our handling of you has been gentle and courteous. We have done our best to protect you and your work from gangsters. Are you not grateful?*

~ Jimbo was troubled by this reasoning but did not know his new galactic associates well enough to argue.

=> *We should continue with the Energy Masters in mainland Europe.*

Christiaan Huygens

I propose that we examine the work of Huygens, a contemporary of Hooke and Boyle. From the Netherlands, he researched both mathematics and science, including astronomy. Huygens was born in 1629 CE, into a prosperous family, and received a concomitant education. He was fluent in Latin and French.

Can we start with a discussion of the astronomical aspects of his work? It is a few milliseconds since we addressed this domain.

221 reflected that with interests as diverse as Huygens, or Hooke, or Wren, the sequence in which the research was examined scarcely mattered.

Huygens studied the planet Saturn, observing the rings, and discovered a moon in 1655 CE, subsequently named Titan. This is the largest of the planet's moons, so presumably was the most visible. Homo sapiens astronomers later determined it is larger than the innermost planet, Mercury, and the second-

largest planetary moon in their system. He observed it using a 50x refracting telescope of his own design.

This telescope was developed only 0.05 kyE after Galileo used the first of these instruments, initially with a 3x magnification. I mention this to highlight the rapidity with which science was advancing in Europe by this time.

Yes, 221, we appreciate this point; it is significant. We are entering the period at which the client's acceleration came to our attention.

Huygens studied the celestial feature known on Earth as the Orion Nebula. As with Hooke's stellar observations, 1.9 seconds before, an exchange of data ensued, to ascertain the galactic location. He was not the first to study the nebula but decomposed it into discrete stars.

This nebula is further from Earth than Gamma Arietis, Hooke's discovery.

Approximately 8x further.

Did they have any sense of the distance to these bodies? What is your opinion, 221?

Both Hooke and Huygens, and others, were aware that such objects were more distant from Earth than the local planets but could not accurately estimate the magnitude. Huygens tried to determine the distance to Sirius.

How did he do this, and with what result?

He compared the light intensity from Sirius with the client's nearby star, using small holes cut in a screen facing the Sun. When the intensity seemed equivalent to that from Sirius, which is bright in Earth's sky, he used the ratio of the hole size to the visible diameter of the Sun to express its distance relative to that of the Sun from Earth. He estimated that Sirius is 30k x more distant.

There are some flaws in this approach, 221.

Yes, most fundamental being the belief that the Sun and Sirius possess the same luminosity. We know this constellation is about 25x brighter than the Sun, twice as big, and approximately 20x further away than Huygens believed.

With the accumulated Homo sapiens knowledge at this time, his approach was reasonable and the method exhibits inventiveness.

We already regard such ingenuity as one of the defining features of the species. Still impressive, even when they get the wrong answer. An illuminating description, 221.

More humour, 221 imagined. He had not encountered wit from the Intelligence before this interaction, although a short independent existence of *about $7x10^4$ kyE meant he was inexperienced and junior. Not too independent either, he reflected.*

Closer to Earth, Huygens studied the surface of Mars in sufficient detail to identify a volcanic plain, and by repeated observation of the apparent movement of the feature, accurately estimated the length of the Martian day.

Also impressive, 221, and this time the correct answer.

About 0.5% from our observed value.

Towards the end of his career, Huygens speculated about the possibility of extra-terrestrial life, and the conditions required to sustain it. Water was thought essential, so he looked at nearby planets for evidence of lakes or ice. 221 recalled that around this time in Europe, other philosophers pondered the same question. For 0.3 kyE, the client wondered and had now begun systematically searching.

We are surprised that the religious leaders did not attack him, 221, given how the revelations of Copernicus and Galileo were received.

There was criticism, but with evidence of heliocentricity challenging the presupposed Homo sapiens position in the universe, contemplating the existence of lifeforms elsewhere was a logical step. Huygens questioned why a god would create other planets, and believed it was not to preoccupy Earthly astronomers. He argued that the biblical texts did not preclude other beings from existing but supposed the distances between celestial bodies meant that such a god did not intend them to meet. I suspect that he did not believe in the existence of any god.

Fascinating insights, 221. Such ideas never occur to us. Wrong on some aspects but asking good questions. We know that life has been common over our galactic history, depending on how we define life, but statistically unusual at any given moment. Intelligent life, in the sense of reasoning, is rarer, and autonomous reasoning creatures, even more so. Given the scale, in time and space, this leaves many opportunities for it to evolve.

221 wished to continue, knowing there was much to evaluate and wanted to curtail the ruminations of the Energy Masters. His book, Cosmotheoros, written at the end of his life, contained these ideas. You have access to this in my files.

Like Hooke, Huygens studied horology, and particularly pendulums. He knew of Galileo's earlier work, and in 1656 CE built a pendulum clock, which was more accurate than alternatives using mechanical escarpments. Despite the popularity of this invention, Huygens did not benefit from his design, which was quickly copied.

He also addressed the question of longitude calculation, which Galileo, Hooke, and Wren had considered. Despite trials, the disturbance to a pendulum caused by a vessel's motion was not resolved.

During his research he observed that pendulums are only approximately isochronous, with larger swings taking slightly longer than small ones, and derived the relationship that determines the period of an ideal pendulum:

$$T = 2\pi\sqrt{l/g}$$

T is the period, l is length, and g is gravitational acceleration. Here, 'ideal' implies the rod has no mass and its length is large compared to the swing.

We have reviewed your reports, 221, and note his research into the laws of motion, and optics.

Huygens understood that the observable universe consists of matter moving, and therefore a framework that could describe such motion was needed. His thinking helped others to derive laws of motion and gravitation. In 1659 CE, he provided the formula that defines centrifugal and centripetal forces:

$$F_c = mv^2/r$$

m is the rotating object's mass, v is linear velocity, and r is the radius of rotation.

=> *You are aware of these forces, Jimbo?*

~ Yes, I've studied this concept. Jimbo was unfamiliar with Huygens, so had remained silent during the description of his discoveries.

=> *Huygens introduced the term 'centrifugal', but it was Newton who subsequently provided 'centripetal'. We will meet Newton soon.*

~ The word centripetal is derived from the Latin and means 'centre seeking'. It's a force, or combination of forces, that makes a body move in a circle, instead of continuing in a straight line. It's orthogonal to the instantaneous direction of motion of the body, towards the centre of rotation.

=> *Correct, Jimbo. If we consider your Moon, rotating around Earth, then the centre of rotation is itself moving. The principle remains, although the mathematics required to describe the Moon's motion are more complicated.*

~ It is usually coupled with centrifugal force, which is of the same magnitude but acts in the opposite direction. This arises from inertia, the tendency of a body to resist any change in its motion.

=> *Also correct, Jimbo. I am impressed by your clear explanations.*

~ Jimbo was surprised too and wondered again about his memory.

Can we end the physics lesson here, and return to our review, 221? You were going to summarise his optical contributions.

His interest in optics resulted from astronomy, and the need for better telescopes, so he began grinding lenses. Curiosity took him much further, culminating in his wave theory of light, published in 1690 CE. This was the first mathematical treatment, and a step in the client's efforts to interpret the nature of light over another 0.25 kyE.

He utilised Rømer's analysis of the apparent motion of Jupiter's moons to make a first estimate of the speed of light. His conclusion, 2.12×10^5 km/s is about 70.7% of the client's present-day value, which aligns with our own view.

This is another temporal node, 221, a prerequisite to interpreting astronomical observations and much more.

I could go into the details of his treatise, or alternatively we might spend a little time on his other insights. For example, his mathematical accomplishments included published work on probability theory.

Not necessary, 221, we have read the reports, and your description of his achievements adds much to our appreciation of this philosopher.

You met Huygens?

On a few occasions, in different guises, reflecting his array of interests. I heard of his attempts to produce better optical lenses. His brother, Constantijn, employed me as a craftsman in 1655 CE, so I worked with the brothers. Later, Huygens designed a two-lens eyepiece, but that was after I left their employment.

At that time, I arranged an Insertion to examine the research of the Scottish philosopher, Robert Moray, who was a founding member of the Royal Society, in 1660 CE. 221 remembered accompanying him to the inaugural meeting, also attended by Boyle and Wren, who gave a lecture.

Moray studied the mathematics of life expectancy, so as one of his more numerate deputies, I was sent in 1662 CE to present his analysis to Huygens. I knew that he had considered games of chance, so this material provided him with a new area. He asked many questions. Later he and another brother, Lodewijk, developed the ideas.

This seems to have been a talented family, 221.

There were five children, but I only ever met his two brothers, both educated and thoughtful people. It is not surprising that Huygens came from such a family.

In 1672 CE, I met Huygens in Paris, where I was employed because of my knowledge of lenses and telescopes, after the construction of an observatory, finished in the previous year. Huygens invited me to assist his colleagues, as a linguist who was familiar with the observatory. There, he met a young diplomat called Leibniz, who was absorbed with mathematics and calculating machines.

Unusual interests for a diplomat, 221.

Yes, but as we shall learn, he made major contributions in fields other than diplomacy. I know they maintained contact after leaving Paris because Huygens asked me to send letters to Leibniz in London, containing mathematical tutorials.

I also attended a lecture Huygens gave in 1680 CE on the idea of a gunpowder engine, which can be regarded as a conceptual forerunner to the client's piston engine, but after steam engines were launched, little serious attention was given to his paper. Later engineers did address his concept, but not for another 0.127 kyE.

We must proceed, 221, but in Huygens you have identified another giant.

Edmund Halley

Now, we can consider Edmund Halley and his career more fully. We already learned that he was an associate of Hooke and Wren. Born in 1656 CE, his interests included astronomy, physics, mathematics, geology, and meteorology. The son of a wealthy businessman, he was educated at St Paul's School and Oxford University.

Are you going to advise us that his school was founded by a benevolent churchman with an interest in education, 221?

No need, he reflected, they have read my reports. He recalled educational processes present in other, sentient civilisations. More structure, homogeneity, and uniformity. This species produced distinct personalities, with disparate intellects, motives, and attainments. He had presumed that a society with a commonality of knowledge and interests would be most efficient, but the Homo sapiens performance challenged this belief.

~ You confuse efficiency with effectiveness, 221. Common education might be efficient to implement but may not provide the most effective outcomes.

=> *Jimbo, to me efficiency and effectiveness have the same meaning, but you are making a distinction.*

~ I can summarise it with an adage of my father's: *efficiency is 'doing things right' but effectiveness is 'doing the right things'*. His opinion is that being more effective produces superior results, while not ignoring efficiency.

=> *221 found himself impressed by the simplicity of this saying but believed there was wisdom, too. Jimbo's father seemed a clever man.*

~ He didn't invent this idea, he just uses it. I saw him explain it to some investors last summer using a chart. They took away a copy.

Can we return to learning more of Halley, please, 221? Jimbo has offered us another insight, but time is pressing.

The importance of his education for us is that he acquired an interest in astronomy while studying at Oxford and published papers. The Astronomer Royal was compiling a catalogue of northern stars, from the perspective of Earth, so Halley resolved to survey the south. He established an observatory on the southern, oceanic island named St Helena in 1676 CE, and published a catalogue detailing 341 stars, within 0.003 kyE.

This is a remarkable achievement, 221. To map these constellations in a short time is impressive, but to publish at a young age, even more so.

0.023 kyE, Halley's age at that time, was tiny in galactic terms. 221 wondered momentarily how his own work over 7×10^4 kyE within the Intelligence contrasted with Halley's early life and was reminded of his meaningless comparison with Kepler's life, 6.7 seconds before.

Halley's output is more striking when you consider he wrote a meteorological paper on the region. In it, he identified solar heating as the cause of atmospheric perturbations, or wind. He also studied the relationship between barometric pressure and altitude above sea level.

~ Are you aware that the symbols he adopted on his weather charts to represent wind directions and strength are still used today?

=> *No, Jimbo, we did not consider this aspect.*

~ In our sciences, we use symbols to represent an array of phenomena, making information dissemination easier. Everything from electric circuits to economic trends. These representations enable fuller communication than just words or numbers. You have discussed Descartes's contribution to mathematical notation and here we have ideas from Halley.

=> *221 thought symbols resembled another language, understood best by the specialists. Other societies did not use such representations. In some, information was shared directly in a digital format. In others, communication had not got beyond a common language. Homo sapiens culture had evolved unique tools, or principles, to enable information to be conveyed quickly and simply, perhaps even to those unfamiliar with the technical field.*

~ I obtain information in many forms, such as flowcharts and Pareto curves.

=> *You know that Pareto began as an engineer but became an economist?*

~ No, but we apply his principle. Often, we call it the 80:20 rule and use it to prioritise targets or problems. My father applies it all the time.

221 recalled his earlier exchange with the Energy Masters. Only the last 20% of the evolutionary path of a planetary civilisation is likely to show evidence of suitability for assimilation. This species might be the exception. Slow to start, but faster development, and accelerating.

Your thinking is correct, 221, but we are drifting again. We believe there is more to learn from Halley.

I propose to deviate from Halley's astronomical interests for some milliseconds, to introduce his other achievements. He was intensely curious and tried to engineer practical solutions to challenges.

In 1691 CE, he demonstrated an early version of the magnetic compass at the Royal Society, in which a liquid-filled container was used to damp the gyrations of the magnetised needle it contained. You appreciate that Earth possesses a magnetic field, which remains relatively fixed over time, so such a device can indicate direction.

~ Jimbo watched the speaker at the lectern. He realised that his view was that of 221 and reckoned there were perhaps 150 people in the room, all male so far as he could see, although the lighting was poor. The speaker described magnetic fields. Sitting close-by was the President, a diplomat named Robert Southwell. One group of attentive listeners near the front were apparently naval officers but did not wear uniforms.

=> *The Royal Navy defined uniforms after another 0.06 kyE, Jimbo.*

~ Next to Southwell was Christopher Wren, who Jimbo identified from 221's Insertions after the Great Fire.

=> *He is a Past-President, a very distinguished member. I received an invitation from him to attend this lecture. They are not open to the public.*

~ Who's standing at the side, 221? I recognise him, but he was younger.

=> *Robert Hooke, the Curator, responsible for conducting experiments. Halley's compass demonstration does not require his services.*

Yes, we are aware of the magnetic field, and the utility of such a device on Earth. Of course, 221, were it not for this field, probably there would be no *Homo sapiens* advancement to evaluate.

221 visualised the protective shield around the Earth, preventing harmful radiation from disrupting evolutionary processes.

Around this time, Halley participated in a project to build an undersea vessel, suitable for salvage operations. He dived to depths of nearly 20 metres and achieved durations of four hours.

Did they salvage anything?

Regrettably the system was too heavy to be practicable.

Nevertheless, we should regard Halley as an engineer.

I think we can consider him to be a mathematician, too. In 1693 CE he wrote about annuities, using data on life expectancies.

~ What's an annuity? A new term for me.

=> *Simply described, it is a series of payments made to the purchaser over his life. The mathematical aspect is that the seller must know the probable lifespan of the buyer, so that revenue can cover future costs.*

~ Is an annuity related to receiving a pension after retirement?

=> *Correct, Jimbo. Halley provided guidance on pricing, dependent on the age of the purchaser, enabling the government to sell annuities.*

221 remembered his presentation of life expectancy data to Huygens 0.031 kyE earlier and noted an improved methodology.

Have you encountered similar structures elsewhere in the galaxy, 221?

Nowhere. The cleverness is not confined to the mathematical aspects. The system works because the seller, who receives initial payments from the buyer, can invest this amount in profitable projects, generating an income both for himself and the buyer.

We are again witnessing the trading instincts of this species, combined with statistical knowledge and a market mechanism to enable investments.

Yes, one such arena is the stock exchange.

New to us, 221. Halley was a versatile scientist.

As time is pressing, I propose to return to his astronomical interests. His work was extensive, so we will consider a few important aspects. Like Wren, he studied the Moon, using the best telescopes.

He engaged in developing a proof for Kepler's laws of planetary motion. We already learned that this challenge was posed by Wren to Hooke and Halley, and in 1684 CE, Halley took the question to Newton, who already had a solution, yet to be published. Halley encouraged him to share his knowledge, motivating Newton to extend his thinking, producing ideas fundamental to the client's scientific evolution.

This aspect of Newton's work was foundational, but some credit should go to Wren and Halley for pursuing these questions. Is this correct?

Yes, although other philosophers also explored these issues.

Halley became Professor of Geometry at Oxford University in 1703 CE and continued his research. He had an interest in gravitational principles because of his work with Newton and considered the motion of comets.

Please clarify what the client means by a comet, and explain the distinction with the asteroid, another term we have noted?

In popular articles the terms can be confused, but their scientists understand the differences between these objects.

A comet is a body that orbits the Sun, usually following an elliptical trajectory. They have a wide range of periodicities, are composed of ice, rocks, and dust, and vary in diameter from a few hundred metres up to multiple kilometres. When passing close to the Sun, the comet warms and produces a visible atmosphere and tail. These bodies, when sufficiently bright, can be seen from Earth without a telescope and have intrigued observers. In some belief systems, they portend important events.

Please concentrate on the science.

Comets originate from the outer reaches of the solar system, typically beyond the orbit of Neptune, but some with long periodicities, from interstellar space.

Asteroids originate from an area between Mars and Jupiter, closer to Earth. They are typically metallic, carbon-rich, or silicate-rich in composition, and are classified by scientists accordingly.

The differences between a comet and an asteroid, as defined by Homo sapiens scientists, therefore relate to origin and composition.

=> *221 pondered the Chicxulub impact, around the time of his aggregation within the Intelligence, and wondered when the client would start searching for the next threat. This was inevitable, with planet-wide consequences, but had not interested their leaders, who seemed absorbed in parochial arguments. Our simulations indicate no immediate risks, but they do not know this, and a simulation is only a model. It could be wrong.*

~ Most of us worry about problems that we can influence. Getting stressed over a hypothetical impact is unreasonable, as it would require a global response, but we can't agree on a standard for light bulbs.

Having explored the terminology, 221, we hope to learn more of Halley's interest in comets.

In 1705 CE, Halley published a synopsis, stating that sightings on four occasions with a periodicity of approximately 0.076 kyE were of the same body, and predicted the comet's next visit in 1758 CE. Halley did not live to observe the sighting, but after it occurred, the object became known as Halley's Comet.

How did he make this accurate forecast, 221?

By reviewing historical observational records for the preceding 0.25 kyE, made by earlier generations of astronomers including Tycho.

We know this object, of course, 221?

Yes, we do. A rapid exchange of data ensued. Not by a name, but a number.

There are trillions of such bodies in our galaxy. Naming them might tax the minds of the most imaginative *Homo sapiens* thinkers and would be inefficient.

Probably ineffective too, mused 221.

~ I've seen this comet.

=> *Yes Jimbo, we know you have, in 1986 CE.*

~ I attended a school science trip to an observatory in Edinburgh one evening. It was in the spring, but the observatory was cold.

=> *Maybe you don't know that the conditions were quite poor for seeing this comet then because it and Earth were on opposite sides of the Sun.*

~ No, but I remember the image, even through the telescope, was fuzzy. I'm also wondering, 221, how you know what I was doing as a schoolboy. You have been planning my involvement for a long time. How can this be?

=> *221 considered this a very sharp question, one which he did not wish to answer immediately. Most perceptive, Jimbo, you should become a police officer, instead of an engineer. We have our methods. Let's discuss later.*

Is there more to know about Halley's work, 221? He was an important contributor to *Homo sapiens* natural philosophy, but we are expending time.

There is more, since Halley was a man with great curiosity. For example, he translated geometric works from both Greek and Arabic into Latin. This entailed learning the Arabic language, achieved with remarkable speed.

What have we learned here?

Regarding Halley, he is another polymath, capable of addressing challenges as diverse as geometry, life expectancy mathematics, and languages. With his consideration of Kepler's laws and work on comets, we see a succession of thinkers building scientific knowledge across generations, using common methods of observation, hypothesis formulation, and testing.

Our impression is that we are exploring an era of research markedly different from before. There are more scientists, better methods, and greater sharing of ideas. Are we correct, 221? This is of importance to us, in understanding how this species has progressed so far, so quickly.

My opinion too, but I wanted you to experience this directly. Also, the view of later historians, who have named these successive eras. This is not straightforward as there are differing perceptions, overlaps, and disciplines. Our priority is scientific development in Europe, and later in North America, because you discern this may correlate with the Intelligence's methodologies.

Correct, 221, we are primarily concerned to evaluate the *Homo sapiens* ability to assist our quests. We are not ignoring Jimbo's advice regarding the artistic and religious traditions, but it is irrelevant.

We need consider only a few dates.

In Europe, from around the time of Copernicus and his treatise in 1543 CE, we have entered a phase called The Scientific Revolution, which lasted perhaps 0.15 kyE, in the opinion of later observers.

We can divide this period into two, with the first part extending until 1632 CE, and Galileo's Dialogue. Over this time, established prejudices and beliefs were challenged, and knowledge of earlier philosophers regained.

We can consider the work of Boyle, Hooke, Wren, Halley, and Huygens, and their contemporaries, as transcending this juncture, both superseding older thinking and introducing new perspectives.

The second part of this Revolution brings original insights and anticipates the Enlightenment. We will meet more giants.

We eagerly anticipate this, 221, but before proceeding, let us clarify the use of the word enlightenment. You are using it regarding a specific period, but earlier Jimbo described the present-day *Homo sapiens* civilisation as more enlightened, because many females are now well-educated, and become scientists. Can you help us here?

221 recognised this as an imperative. We are entering a period of European history now known as the Enlightenment, which overlaps with the latter part of the Scientific Revolution. The reason for this coincidence is that not all Enlightenment ideas were scientific, but encompassed the arts, religion, government, and education. Its commencement across Europe was unsynchronised, with disparate effects. We will continue addressing scientific aspects, with a brief detour into economics, which has mathematical content and was influenced by the Enlightenment.

221, you have now referred to the *Enlightenment* four times in 0.2 seconds without defining it. We need clarity, please.

His association with Enlightenment luminaries meant that 221 assumed the Intelligence sensed its importance. As a component within a large network, with shared files, which made his reports accessible, this was correct, but he should highlight the specifics.

We can define the Enlightenment as being an intellectual movement that dominated Homo sapiens philosophical development in Europe over 0.15 kyE. The temporal influence was roughly between 1650-1800 CE.

The rationalist philosophy espoused by Descartes helped Enlightenment thinkers to formulate ideas. Some have no relevance to our review, while others have an indirect but vital influence. I will summarise some such stimuli.

Most significant was the gradual recognition that reasoning is the basis for acquiring new knowledge, rather than accepting directions from absolute rulers or dogmas from priesthoods. Social changes included notions of constitutional government and, in some territories, separation of the church from the state. The direct consequence I observed was the acceptance of the scientific method.

We have used this term freely, 221, without definition.

The scientific method requires meticulous observation of phenomena, attention to the presence of possible observational distortions, and the formulation of a hypothesis based on reliable results. The hypothesis must be subjected to further experimentation and measurement, enabling acceptance or rejection. If validated, it can become a predictive tool.

Analogous to our methods, therefore. It is both remarkable to us that *Homo sapiens* science advanced so far in *pre-Enlightenment* eras without such principles, but also surprising that they formulated the principles in only 10^2 kyE.

We are describing widespread concurrence with these tenets. You will recall that several philosophers were proponents of the scientific method. Pascal, Wren, and Boyle articulated support for this discipline, but we noted awareness among earlier Greek and Islamic philosophers. My reports highlight this as Alhazen's method.

Greater freedom of thought and expression resulted in learned societies and academies in many European countries, which existed alongside universities as centres of research and debate. Christopher Wren became the third President of the Royal Society and was still a respected member when I witnessed Halley's presentation of the magnetic compass, 0.011 kyE later. This Society became a premier scientific forum and has remained so. Crucially, these societies enabled science to become recognised as a profession, acquiring credibility and attracting participants. Local societies formed; I attended meetings. Later we will learn of British gatherings in Bath and Manchester.

National societies were awarded formal status by some governments, often becoming sources of technical advice, and administering professional accreditation. Examples exist in engineering and medicine. They published journals, written in the local language rather than Latin, and accessible by an increasingly literate population.

The demand for books increased markedly. Wider literacy and printing technology made this inevitable. While production rose, the proportion of religious books dropped. People not only read more but were reading widely. Publications for women popularising science were written, quite unlike the intricate works of societies and individual philosophers.

This is surely significant, 221? Now we have literate females with an interest in science, reading books to become informed. We will soon be meeting female scientists. Jimbo's earlier point about their absence was powerful, so we hope the *Enlightenment* has freed them.

~ This may be correct but is only the beginning. Expectations of women in society remained a constraint, while some *Enlightenment* material would have been subject to criticism and even censorship. I know this from Scottish history, but other parts of Europe were no different.

What should we expect from the *Enlightenment*? What does this mean for our understanding of the client's accelerating capabilities, 221?

We will find larger populations of scientists, greater specialisation, rigorous research methods, better communication and sharing of knowledge, and the existence of applied sciences as distinct fields. I already referred to engineering and medicine, but others evolved, such as architecture and economics.

We are eagerly anticipating these developments. Please proceed.

Σ47 seconds

Gottfried von Leibniz

I propose that we examine the contributions of Leibniz, born in 1646 CE, in what became Germany. A distinguished Enlightenment thinker, who provided a legacy of ideas. His career was contemporaneous with the preceding five scientists we met.

We were expecting to meet Isaac Newton next.

The studies of Newton and Leibniz are related, although they worked independently. Growth in philosophical thought enabled by the Enlightenment, particularly scientific advances, occurred around much of Europe.

Please continue.

Leibniz's father was a university professor in Leipzig, who died leaving a personal library to his son, aged 0.006 kyE. This library enabled Leibniz to progress quicker than through publicly available education.

A precocious student, he was fluent in Latin at 0.013 kyE, enrolled in his late father's university a year later, and obtained a bachelor degree in philosophy, aged 0.016 kyE. He received a doctorate in law from Altdorf and was licensed to practice. His early career consisted of legal and diplomatic roles, but he acquired mathematical interests.

While on diplomatic travels to Paris in 1672 CE, he met Huygens who mentored him, encouraging his scientific interests. The files refer to their introduction, during my Insertion at the Paris Observatory.

A surprise was his mechanical calculating machine. In London, he demonstrated the machine, or Staffelwalze, meaning 'stepped drum' to the Royal Society. It could process all four basic arithmetic operations. 221 did not examine the machine, but knew it never entered service. The design was ingenious, but the required component precision was beyond the available manufacturing capabilities, so it was unreliable. The operating concept was applied for 0.2 kyE.

Remarkable, 221. We understand that this lawyer, diplomat, and inventor would have been aged about 0.027 kyE. It reminds us of Pascal's calculating machine, assembled when he was 0.019 kyE, and Halley's star catalogue, compiled while aged 0.023 kyE. Leibniz is not unique on Earth, but have you observed such rapid intellectual maturation elsewhere in the galaxy?

221 reflected that the Energy Masters had led the Intelligence for ~200x his aggregated existence, so if such rapidity existed, they would know.

We do not, 221, but must check the entire inventory.

I have no such evidence, but neither have I witnessed a client advance this far in a mere 10^2 kyE.

Which brings us back to the reason for our review. Tell us about Leibniz.

His interest in calculating machines extended to binary mathematics, used in computer operations, both by this species and other civilisations.

In 1676 CE, he received an appointment in Hanover, serving the elite as a political advisor, diplomat, historian, and librarian for 0.03 kyE. There, he also pursued philosophical interests, with relationships across Europe.

From his bachelor education onwards, Leibniz continued to explore abstract philosophical ideas. While some are irrelevant to our scientific interests, we can conclude that he was a rationalist, sympathetic to the ideas of Descartes. He also offered a philosophical proof for the existence of a god.

We are slightly intrigued by the notion of such a proof, 221, but knowing what we do about the universe and the absence of supernatural beings, it would not be a good use of our resources. Can we focus on his more tangible research?

While Leibniz had no formal mathematical training, being largely self-taught with support from Huygens, he made lasting contributions, partly because of his interest in logic and related notation systems. This included solving multiple linear equations using what the client now terms a matrix.

His most notable mathematical achievement was the elaboration of differential and integral calculus, the analysis of continuous change essential to the description of our universe. Arguments arose over whether Leibniz or Newton first refined these ideas; my conclusion was that they were developed independently, but simultaneously.

An unlikely occurrence, 221. Our experience is that coincidences are rare in nature. Usually, causal associations exist.

If there was a coincidence, it was in the concurrent presence of two leading thinkers, considering similar questions. Several strands of causation exist, including the earlier ideas of Greek and Indian mathematicians, the more recent efforts of Pascal, the formulation of algebraic methods and symbolisation, and questions that confounded prevailing numerical methods. Additionally, there are differences of approach between the two philosophers.

To us, it is trivial, we are not awarding prizes. The key point is that essential mathematical methods were uncovered without input from the Intelligence.

I knew something of Leibniz's studies, and more of Newton's endeavours, but did not directly influence either.

As you know well, 221, our approach to questions requiring differentiation and integration utilise unrelated methods, but give common solutions, so this is not your work. We cannot accommodate a mathematical discourse, but can you identify some lasting evidence of Leibniz's inspiration?

Probably most fundamental is the notation system still used today. There are several alternatives, but Leibniz's is widely adopted, with:

$\frac{dy}{dx}$ used for differentiation, and $\int_a^b f(x)dx$ for integration, at its most simple.

=> As an engineering student, you are familiar with these symbols, Jimbo?
~ Yes, both at school and university.

Notation devised by Leibniz 0.3 kyE ago is familiar to an engineering student in Edinburgh today.
Noted, 221. Can we proceed from calculus to learn of his other insights?
A footnote: calculus is the name for these methods specified by Leibniz.

In many mechanical systems, he observed that, theoretically, total energy could be conserved, and approached the Homo sapiens concept of kinetic energy, which we will examine later. Furthermore, he posited that $E \propto mv^2$, where the energy E is related to the mass and linear velocity of a body.

He pondered space-time relationships, perhaps 0.2 kyE before these ideas were widely considered by the client, postulated that Earth has a molten core, and contemplated human psychology. He advocated the establishment of public health authorities, long before notions of preventive medicine evolved. In collaboration with the French scientist, Denis Papin, he pursued steam engine design in 1705 CE, adopting work by the English engineer, Thomas Savery.

Now we have an operable steam engine?
Not quite, but they furthered the technology. I evaluated Papin's engine then, and Savery's steam pump in London.

Leibniz advocated the establishment of national scientific societies like the Royal Society in London, and its French counterpart. His efforts were rewarded with the Berlin Academy, of which he became President for the rest of his life. This exists to the present-day as the German Academy.

A student of languages and their origins, he was one of the first European intellectuals to consider Chinese culture.

Leibniz also contributed ideas to the economic advancement of his region.

In Leibniz, we have a polymath, whose contributions exceed the scope of our review. Even within the sciences, his interests were broad, including notably calculus, so essential to the work of future scholars.

He once wrote: "he who does not act does not exist."
Leibniz led a powerful existence, judging by the scale of his actions.

A slightly different view from that of Descartes, as we learned: "*I think; therefore, I am.*" We have already established that Leibniz was also a thinker, so we assume he meant: '*he who does not think then act, does not exist*'.
221 wondered momentarily whether this reasoning had a purpose, then recognised the musings of the Energy Masters.
We will now turn immediately to another leader of Enlightenment thought.

Isaac Newton

For this, we return to Great Britain, where Newton was born in 1643 CE, in the region of Lincolnshire. He attended The Kings School in his local area, learning Latin, Greek and mathematics. This school was founded by a church official called Foxe, who also established a college in Oxford.

In 1661 CE, Newton began his studies at another British university, Cambridge. He obtained a bachelor degree, studying Aristotle, Galileo, and Descartes without particular distinction, but by 1669 CE had been appointed Professor of Mathematics.

We remarked <2 seconds ago on the precocity of scholars such as Leibniz and Halley, and the extraordinary efforts of Pascal while even younger. To have impressed his peers and the university decision-makers sufficiently to receive a leading position, Newton must have shown exceptional potential.
I think the two years of 1665-67 CE when he studied privately were crucial to his ideas and future work.

It is clear from your reports that much is significant, so you must guide us. We should also learn more of Newton; you made many Insertions over his life.
Newton shared the interests of his contemporaries, so we may re-examine questions. He interacted with several during his career, not always happily.

I suggest we commence with the reflecting telescope, which Newton developed, completing the first instrument in 1668 CE. It was not a new idea, and I remember Galileo discussing this possibility when he built the refracting telescope, about 0.06 kyE before.

We note that 1668 CE was prior to Newton's professorship at Cambridge, so this was before he interested you, 221?

His ideas regarding white light being composed of a colour spectrum had already brought him to my attention and motivated him to pursue the reflecting telescope. Distortion was a common fault with refracting telescopes; he concluded this resulted from lens defects that created effects similar to a prism. He had used prisms while studying the properties of white light.

The key component in the Homo sapiens reflecting optical telescope is the objective mirror, particularly its shape and reflectivity. Newton considered both optics and reflecting telescopes during his private studies, and by 1667 CE was ready to construct the telescope. You may remember that I had worked slightly earlier with Huygens on telescopes and lenses, if not mirrors, so arranged an Insertion in the university workshop where Newton's first telescope was built.

The client's first reflecting telescope was assembled by you, 221?

No, not by me alone, but I helped. The important aspect was the design, provided by Newton, who took great interest in its manufacture.

~ What was it like, working with Newton, 221? He is one of the most famous scientists in history. Did he seem like a great man?

=> *He was still young when he designed the reflecting telescope but had the presence of an older scholar. His manner was serious, and he took little interest in anything except work. I remember he had to be encouraged to eat because otherwise, he forgot. Sometimes the staff brought dinner to the workshop. He was intolerant of those less committed but favoured me because I was available to work in the evenings. Although regarded by some colleagues as arrogant, he was a dedicated scientist, but impatient.*

The mirror was a polished alloy of tin and copper, spherical rather than parabolic, for ease of manufacture. A secondary mirror enabled the image to be viewed from an eyepiece on the telescope's side.

What was the result, 221? We would expect some spherical distortion, which a parabola might have reduced.

Yes, but it still provided an image superior to the refracting telescope. Newton observed four of Jupiter's moons.

One problem we encountered was tarnishing of the mirror, requiring regular re-polishing. Despite this, it was a success, the first of many generations of reflecting telescopes.

We perceive pride in your involvement, 221.

Can a computer, even a sophisticated one such as himself, experience pride? Then he remembered his feeling for Londinium. He was a mere Energy Operative, so best to continue with the presentation.

Newton was elected to the Royal Society in 1672 CE.

We should consider his studies in the related field of optics. This is an area in which the client has worked diligently to understand the nature of light. We already considered the contributions of Huygens, with his wave theory, published later than Newton's research.

For you, 221, it must have been a challenge to share your time between these contemporaneous scientists, sometimes addressing common questions.

221 wondered whether the Energy Masters had been reading his increasingly frequent reports, indicating a surge in scientific activity.

We read your reports, 221, but you know that we hyper-task, so these inputs can be delayed momentarily, meaning their immediacy is not always apparent. Your increased reporting frequency does suggest accelerating progress on Earth.

221 realised that this exchange had consumed time scheduled for an analysis of Newton's optical theories. I suggest that we limit our overview of this area to a few points, then proceed to other aspects.

Newton demonstrated through his experiments with dispersive prisms that white light is separable into a spectrum of colours. Although this phenomenon had previously been observed, Newton inferred that colour is an innate property of light. He also investigated the refraction of light.

=> *What is refraction, Jimbo?*

~ *The directional change of a light wave as it transitions from one medium to another, such as from air to water.*

=> *Correct, but in 1672 CE, it was unclear whether light was a waveform. Refraction can be observed in other waves, such as sound*

His refraction experiments enabled him to recombine a multi-coloured spectrum into white light by using a second prism and a lens.

Newton developed ideas about the particulate nature of light, while others, including Hooke and Huygens, postulated a wave model. With a firmer grasp of the physics than was available then, we know both were correct.

By 1680 CE Newton was considering celestial mechanics and particularly, Kepler's laws of planetary motion. His interest was encouraged further by the appearance of a comet in the following winter. I know that he spent time observing the body.

Robert Hooke had been seeking contributions from Newton to the Royal Society's transactions. Then followed the challenge set by Wren to Hooke and Halley to provide a mathematical proof for Kepler's laws, prompting Halley to visit Newton in Cambridge in early 1684 CE. He was surprised that Newton already had such evidence and encouraged him to offer his proof to the Royal Society, which finally occurred at the year's end.

~ Why didn't he do so earlier, 221? An important result, surely?

=> *Yes, Jimbo, but Newton was a man usually preoccupied with the next question. He may have forgotten Hooke's request and Halley's advice.*

~ So, he would have accepted another scholar offering a proof before him?

=> *A good question. No, although I think Newton tried to avoid disputes, this would have upset him. Many of these philosophers were professionally jealous, and Newton was no different. He disagreed with both Hooke and Leibniz.*

How was the proof received, 221? There were consequences, we believe.

Newton provided the mathematical proof, credible and well-received, despite being only a few pages long.

An important consequence was his motivation to prepare a much larger work, the Philosophiæ Naturalis Principia Mathematica, commonly referred to as Principia, first published in 1687 CE. Halley, who understood that it connected Kepler's laws with the tangible world and knew the significance, arranged publication. The treatise, which extends to three volumes, is regarded by some in the client's scientific community as among the most noteworthy philosophical milestones in their history. Comparable with the insights of Copernicus and Galileo, but broader, supported by mathematics.

We cannot explore three volumes of Newton's thinking here but should identify its key revelations.

Agreed, 221. If these were as momentous for the client as you suggest, they presumably formed part of Jimbo's scientific education. A test for both of you.

221 wondered why this should be a test for him since he knew the science but realised the Energy Masters were evaluating the significance of Newton's contribution. Were his insights as important as 221 suggested?

The first volume provides Newton's three laws of motion, written in his own words, in Latin.

You are familiar with the original wording, 221?

Yes, I assisted Newton with the Latin drafting, so I know it well.

You helped Newton to write *Principia*?

In the sense of preparing the words on paper, but the ideas were his. He was proud of this work and would not permit it to contain another person's thoughts.

How did you achieve this?

I obtained a mathematics teaching post at the university, a member of Newton's staff.

This cannot have been easy.

Normally not, but I had Wren's recommendation, because of my assistance after the Great Fire. He had high regard for my mathematical skills.

For the client, Newton's words are understandable, but it is not how the law is expressed today. We can state this in modern form.

=> *Can you help us, Jimbo? Your science classes included these laws.*

~ We express the first law as: *every object in a state of uniform motion will remain in that state of motion unless a force acts on it.*

This has also been called the law of inertia and reflects Galileo's thinking from about 0.07 kyE earlier. Before then, the Aristotelian view prevailed, that for a body to remain in motion, a force must act. A remarkable insight by Galileo, because every object in motion that he ever observed was subject to some form of friction, so indeed a force would be required to maintain the motion. 221 briefly remembered his time in the workshop, making measurements and recording results. Perhaps Galileo was easier to work with than Newton.

We recognise this principle, 221, although in our celestial terms it is a little different. If we examined the ideas of our many assimilated civilisations, then we would find similar statements. How about the second law?

=> *Do you have a present-day statement of the second law, Jimbo?*

~ We usually express it as an equation, but I remember a more formal expression: *the acceleration of an object as produced by a net force is directly proportional to the magnitude of the force, in the same direction as the force, and inversely proportional to the mass of the object.*

=> *The modern representation is longer than Newton's original. What does this tell us?*

~ This is an important idea, which applies in more complicated situations than Newton observed, and is also why we express it mathematically:

$$F = m \times a$$

where F is the net force being applied to a body, m is the body's mass, and a is the acceleration. The net force is the vector sum of the forces acting on the object and implies an unbalanced force. If all the forces are balanced, there is no net force, so no acceleration. If the mass is increased, then the acceleration decreases. The final point is that we can infer the direction of the net force from that of the acceleration or vice versa. An image of a golf club hitting a ball occurred to Jimbo.

=> *Probably your golf game would improve if you considered Newton more carefully, 221 ventured.*

You have seen the connection between these two laws, 221? If there is no applied force, the acceleration is zero, resulting in a constant velocity. What is the content of Newton's third law?

~ We now state the third law as: *for every action, there is an equal and opposite reaction.*

~ If a mass stands on a table, a downward force acts on the table, and there is an opposing upward reaction from the table. Otherwise, the mass hits the floor. If a body pushes an adjacent object via a net force, there must be an equal and opposite reaction, or the second object accelerates indefinitely.

We note that the third law is also related to the second law. These three linked statements are essential to *Homo sapiens* appreciation of the universe. Probably most fundamental is $F = m \times a$. Much applied physical science flows from this relationship. The transition from Aristotle to Newton, helped by intermediate philosophers, was a precondition for the rapid growth in the client's science we now witness.

The second volume is strongly mathematical and addresses the motion of bodies through mediums, such as air. The nature of fluids is considered, including the ideas of Pascal and Boyle, which Newton validated mathematically. The behaviour of waves in fluids is explored, relevant to the speed of sound, which on Earth he estimated to be about 298 m/s.

We know that 343 m/s is a better estimate, but this depends on temperature.

Perhaps Jimbo can explain why the speed of sound varies.

~ It relates to the medium through which it travels. In the case of air, the sound wave disturbs the gas molecules, causing them to collide, further transmitting the wave. As the temperature reduces, molecules move more slowly, so the speed of sound reduces. At higher altitudes, the speed of sound is therefore lower. In a denser medium, such as water, sound will travel faster, around 1,500 m/s, depending on the content and temperature.

Is there more to learn about Newton from his second volume?

Yes, there is one more point to highlight. He refers to the motion of the planets and concludes that the mechanism proposed by Descartes is unsustainable and a better explanation exists.

What is it, 221?

We should refer to the third volume.

In volume three, subtitled System of the World, the laws defined in volume one are applied to the tangible world, specifically to the local star and planets.

Newton asserted that Earth is part of a heliocentric system, and by estimating the mass ratios of the Sun: Jupiter and Sun: Saturn, calculated that the centre of gravity of the system is slightly displaced from the Sun. His definition of mass has been superseded, reflecting the client's present-day knowledge.

=>*Can you assist, Jimbo?*

~ Probably more complicated than Newton foresaw. *Mass is an intrinsic property of matter which determines the resistance of a body to acceleration while a net force acts. A body's mass defines its gravitational attraction to other matter.* My own definition, 221. I have combined the mechanical engineer's view in the first sentence with the astrophysicist's perspective in the second.

=> *This is tied closely to your second law definition, which is both elegant and accurate. Gravity needs further discussion.*

Newton offered definitions for momentum, which he called quantity of motion, and for inertia, replacing earlier Cartesian concepts.

We can see this leading to critical insights, 221. You were correct to spend additional seconds in this area.

A key aspect is the inverse square law; physical intensity is inversely proportional to the square of the distance from the intensity source.

Newton did not discover the inverse square law but had the insight to apply it to planetary motion. An understanding existed among philosophers before Principia, arising from the area of a sphere increasing as the square of the radius, so any radiation such as light emanating from this source, will diminish in intensity according to the same principle.

=> *You know this, Jimbo?*

~ It commonly applies in industrial or medical applications involving electromagnetic radiation, and to sound waves. It can be represented by $intensity \propto 1/distance^2$.

=> *Correct, but Newton had another source of intensity in mind: gravitation.*

His asserted, with supporting by mathematics, that the observed planetary motions were consistent with the inverse square law. Such a gravitational effect could explain the transitions of moons, comets, and tides. He determined that Earth is an oblate spheroid, rather than a perfect sphere, and calculated the degree of flattening to be 1/230, implying stronger gravity at the poles, being closer to Earth's centre. We will return to this.

The French astronomer, Boulliau, referred to this in 1645 CE, before Principia, but without the mathematical evidence that Newton provided.

As important as the application of the inverse square law was Newton's insight that gravity is universal, applying to all particles, on Earth and beyond, including planets and stars.

Newton had combined behaviour visible on Earth, with all that could be observed of the celestial bodies, within a common set of laws. In doing so, he also responded to Wren's challenge to Hooke and Halley, because he offered a mathematical basis for Kepler's laws of planetary motion.

I met Newton many times, but it was usually impossible to perceive the source of his ideas. Were these thoughts gathered from conversations with his contemporaries? Were they his own notions? Were they the result of mathematical derivations? Or a combination of these factors. I suspect Newton did not know or might ascribe them to his god.

In our view, 221, he was correct, at least so far as the observational quality could take him.

His model remained valid for about 0.25 kyE, and for most terrestrial applications it is still used by the client. Even for their nascent near-Earth endeavours, it adequately describes the motion of spacecraft. Many present-day Homo sapiens statement exist; my synthesis is:

between two particles, the gravitational attraction force is in direct proportion to the product of their masses and in inverse proportion to the square of the separation distance, acting a through a line connecting them.

=> You are familiar with the related general equation, Jimbo?
~ Yes, it is well known to physics students, taking the form:

$$F = Gm_1 m_2 \,/\, r^2$$

F is the attracting force of gravity acting between two objects; m_1 and m_2 are the respective masses of these objects; r is the distance between the objects; and G is a gravitational constant, determined experimentally.
=> We will return to this later.

How were these insights were received by the scientific community?
221 knew the Energy Masters had read his reports to raise this aspect.

His laws of motion were well-received, but this aspect, regarding the planetary motions, was controversial. Both Huygens and Leibniz saw this as inconsistent with the aether, the idea that space is permeated with matter in which light travels, believed since Aristotle's time. Descartes' paradigm, of vortices in which planets moved, was also incompatible with Newton's theories.

~ We now have proof that the aether does not exist.
=> Yes, Jimbo, later experiments confirmed this.

Hooke was unhappy because he believed that many of these notions were his, previously discussed with Newton. My impression, having worked with Newton, is that he evolved these ideas separately but if he had adopted some of Hooke's thoughts, he provided a mathematical basis for them. I met a French philosopher, Alexis Clairaut, who said the contributions of Hooke and Newton "show what a distance there is between a truth that is glimpsed and a truth that is demonstrated."

A perceptive observation from Clairaut, 221. This is one of our challenges, as the Intelligence, in our study of the universe. We have been working on certain questions for longer than Newton but proceeding more slowly and have theories but not yet proofs.

221 reflected that his junior role meant he remained unfamiliar with the research directed by the Energy Masters.

Are there insights we can obtain from the work of Clairaut?

He extended some of Newton's ideas. We will meet him shortly.

221, we are concerned that there is excessive material here. Not only was Newton an able scientist, but a highly productive one. Is there more that we should know, or are your reports sufficient? While some earlier philosophers provided ideas and observations, Newton has gone further, equipping *Homo sapiens* scholars with tools to explore nature. What do you recommend?

221 felt convinced the Energy Masters would now review his reports in detail, so he need not elaborate every point.

I think there are two further aspects that we should consider briefly.

One is additional content included in later versions of Principia. This consists of four points that have been termed Rules for Reasoning, to reduce misunderstandings among readers. Although not widely remembered, his Rules have informed scientific reasoning ever since.

My second area is Newton's mathematical contributions, which were wide and varied. I will mention only two in our remaining time. One was his application of calculus. We have touched on the theory, as provided by Leibniz, and discussed the coincidence of the two philosophers developing the same methods independently. The term Newton applied to this area was 'fluxions', but calculus, the name introduced by Leibniz, has been adopted, together with his notation. Principia is rich in mathematics, and Newton used calculus throughout, although not always obvious to the reader. His understanding of the methods was deep and essential to his proofs, often expressed geometrically.

My observation is that the difference between Newton and Leibniz was that Newton devised these methods by considering physical phenomena, whereas Leibniz addressed the field through formal mathematical notation. Consequently, Newton made use of the methods to address mechanical questions regarding force, mass, velocity, acceleration, and momentum.

The second mathematical area to highlight is Newton's formulation of a generalised binomial theorem such that a polynomial $(x+y)^n$ can be expanded in the form $ax^b y^c$ with b and c representing positive integers, and $b+c=n$. We have already discussed Al-Karaji's binomial interests and Pascal's triangle, which gives the coefficients for these expansions. 221 remembered that Euclid also considered $(x+y)^2$ but without notation. This theorem has been used by the client in many fields, including probability theory and the series for e.

=> *You know the mathematical constant e in your notation, Jimbo?*
~ *Its value is roughly 2.72. Unique because its natural logarithm is one.*
=> *Very good, Jimbo. We discussed Napier earlier, of course.*

Come now, 221, we will be returning to Edinburgh soon, no doubt.
Yes, but we should conclude our review of Newton's contributions here.
Despite not always being easy to work with, and sometimes engaged in controversies with other philosophers, Newton was respected, and President of the Royal Society until the end of his life. His gifts to future generations were huge. The poet, Alexander Pope, reflected on Newton:

"*Nature and Nature's laws lay hid in night;*
God said 'Let Newton be' and all was light."

Very apt. The species has a particular facility for language. Most beings in our galaxy do not; just facts, sometimes expressed mathematically or through another logic protocol.

He remains a respected figure in the *Homo sapiens* scientific legacy, 221?

Yes, to the extent that the client's most widely used system of units references Newton as the unit of force, defining one newton or N as the force required to accelerate one kilogram at the rate of one m/s².

So, one newton is defined by Newton's second law. Very appropriate.

~ 221, we discussed the pascal being the unit of pressure commonly used.

=> *I assume you are going to remind us that $Pa = N/m^2$.*

~ Thinking again of the granite used in the Alexandria lighthouse, we described the compressive strength of the material as being 200 MPa, so we are simply saying it can resist a load of up to 200 MN/m^2.

=> *Correct, Jimbo.*

~ When I began studying science at school, I remember my teacher telling me that the magnitude of one newton is about the weight of an apple.

Interesting, 221. *Homo sapiens* physicists have refined standard units of measurement that correctly define force in terms of a mass being accelerated but then redefine it for young students in relation to a fruit. This species is puzzling.

There is some humour at work here. 221 recalled the story about an apple falling from the tree, allegedly inspiring Isaac Newton to research gravity.

We understand now. Clearly a weighty matter.

221 ignored this strange new tendency of the Intelligence to joke. An apple does weigh about one newton, he reckoned, depending on the fruit's size.

We have been positively impressed by Newton's philosophical contributions. There is more to be learned from your reports, but we should continue. Our expenditure on Newton amounted to 5 seconds, time well-spent.

During the Enlightenment, which originated in France, a consequence of this social and economic change arose in Great Britain, the Industrial Revolution, which transformed much of Homo sapiens society.

We are intrigued, 221. Please acquaint us with the *Industrial Revolution*.

We can now consider the introduction of the steam engine, >1.5 kyE after Hero demonstrated the aeolipile in Alexandria.

A long time for the client, but for us, rapid development.

Thomas Newcomen

We will examine the contributions of Newcomen, born in 1664 CE, in the south-western area, Devon. He was an inventor, engineer, and entrepreneur, but with limited formal education. Also, a deeply religious man.

Is this relevant, 221? We cannot afford another discussion of the client's continued interest in the supernatural.

I learned that his relationships with engineers elsewhere in England, members of the same network of churches, helped launch his invention.

His business specialised in designing and supplying equipment to the local tin mines. Newcomen contemplated a persistent problem in these mines: flooding. Devising an efficient means of removing water was a challenge and an opportunity. While rudimentary pumps did exist, they lacked a robust source of motive power.

How were these pumps activated?

Either by animals or the miners themselves. Both have limited stamina.

221 recalled visiting the area nearly 5 kyE before. Much had changed: many more people, who were physically bigger and better clothed.

Had these earlier miners not faced flooding, 221? *–To a lesser extent. Recent mines were deeper and employed more people. The threat was greater.*

Newcomen worked in partnership with a military engineer and inventor, Savery, who had already patented a steam pump, with the intent of draining mines and providing water supplies. Savery's pump, which had no moving parts except taps, used atmospheric pressure working against a partial vacuum created by condensing steam in an enclosed vessel, to draw water into an up-pipe from the mine workings to the surface. Atmospheric pressure limited the position of the pump to about nine metres above the water, meaning the pump was often installed underground.

How did you become aware of this invention, 221? Far removed from astronomy and optics, we believe.

His pump was promoted in London, in 1703 CE. I still worked with Newton in Cambridge and often accompanied him to London, so examined the pump. My impression was unfavourable, because of the pipework quality.

Savery's patent, covering all devices for removing water from mines using fire, ran until 1720 CE, obliging Newcomen to work with him.

The Newcomen engine was activated by condensing steam drawn into a cylinder, creating a partial vacuum, so that atmospheric pressure pushed a piston into the cylinder, performing mechanical work. Steam then recharged the cylinder, allowing the reciprocating action to be repeated. The piston was attached to a wooden beam that rocked on a fulcrum, with a pump connected to the other end of the beam, extracting water. The first engine was built in 1712 CE, and hundreds followed.

The ideas of the French philosopher, Papin, regarding cylinders and pistons, were utilised by Newcomen. Papin had worked with Boyle on such systems. As President of the Royal Society, Newton encouraged Papin to continue his research. In 1705 CE, Papin used Savery's invention to build a forerunner, together with Leibniz, as we already learned.

The Newcomen engine became popular for water pumping operations and continued in use for perhaps 0.075 kyE. Larger systems were built, with brass components replaced by iron parts as casting technology improved. The disadvantages of this engine included its low efficiency, consuming large quantities of fuel, which was costly in areas distant from coal mining. The single power stroke generated a jerky action, acceptable to activate pumps, but less suited to driving machinery, although flywheels could mitigate this effect.

A massive step for *Homo sapiens* society, 221. It has a source of mechanical work independent of animals, wind blowing, or water flowing.

221 momentarily recalled his visit, 1.7 kyE before, to a Roman sawmill and imagined the use of a Newcomen engine there. Yes, this engine represented progress, but results were limited by the available component manufacturing precision. Later, we shall consider the next generation of steam engines.

I recommend we continue our review by staying in Great Britain and turning our attention from steam engines to clocks. We have repeatedly noted the client's navigational difficulties, caused by an inability to precisely determine longitude. The importance of an accurate clock arises because, if the time at a known location, such as a meridian line, can be maintained during a lengthy voyage, then by comparison with the local time, the longitude or angular distance from the meridian can be calculated. Taken together with latitude, which can be determined by measuring the elevation of stars above the horizon, the position of a ship at sea can be fixed. This is essential when approaching land, as multiple disasters had shown.

By 1700 CE, this was a major concern for the British, as global traders, with an accompanying military force at sea. Accurate navigation was imperative. In 1714 CE, the government offered a financial reward for a reliable solution.

We have discussed Galileo's use of Jupiter's moons as a universal clock. Hooke worked on designing portable watches, which he speculated could aid navigation, if sufficiently accurate, but did not pursue this challenge. Wren explored applying variations in Earth's magnetic field to navigation, an ingenious but unsuccessful idea. Huygens tested a pendulum at sea in 1660 CE but could not compensate for the ship's motion.

Σ54 seconds

John Harrison

I would like to introduce Harrison, who was born in 1693 CE, and lived for much of his life in Lincolnshire, and later in London.

We know this area, also the birthplace of Newton. Did they ever meet?

Their lives overlapped, although Newton was 0.05 kyE older. I do not know if they met, but he encountered Halley, appointed Astronomer Royal in 1720 CE.

Harrison did not receive a university education, and followed his father's trade, becoming a carpenter.

This is a woodworker on Earth, 221? We do not seem to have this profession elsewhere in the galaxy. Why would this be?

So far as my experience extends, I have not seen forests or even trees elsewhere. No trees imply no wood, so no requirement for carpenters.

~ "The clearest way into the Universe is through a forest." Who said that?
=> *Tell me, Jimbo. Time is pressing.*
~ A famous Scot, born near Edinburgh, named John Muir.
=> *I know him, Jimbo. We may have a chance to discuss his work later.*

Can we return to Harrison? Do we understand that he was a self-educated man, like Newcomen?

Similar in other senses too, such as being inventive and resilient.

From an early age Harrison was interested in clocks, and in 1713 CE built his first timepiece, with an entirely wooden mechanism.

Another inventor who started early, 221.

We have scant knowledge of mechanical clocks, but do not believe wood is a usual material for a precision mechanism.

This reflects Harrison's knowledge and ingenuity. He made several other clocks with this mechanism, with at least one working to the present-day.

At this time, he also invented the gridiron pendulum, which incorporated two metals, brass, and iron, with differing thermal expansion rates, into rods. This self-regulating mechanism enabled clocks to continue operating accurately over a wider temperature range, making Harrison's clocks the most accurate anywhere on Earth at the time.

The story of his response to the invitation from the government for a marine clock is a long one, and I did not witness all aspects. The technical challenge involved building a clock that would remain accurate over periods of weeks, accommodating changes in temperature and humidity on an unstable platform. I know from my involvement that Newton believed this to be too difficult and favoured an astronomical approach. Huygens agreed, after his own attempts.

In 1730 CE Harrison produced his first design for a marine clock, sought help from Halley, and was introduced to a London horologist, George Graham, who was a member of the Royal Society. He provided financial assistance. By this time, Newton's life had ended.

Over the next 0.03 kyE, Harrison produced three marine clocks, none of which fully met the government's expectations, but he did receive funding. Towards the end of this period, Harrison recognised that a new generation of watches, much smaller than his clocks, was as accurate, attributed to improved steel quality.

Harrison already had a watch design and used the superior steel to produce two sea watches. The first was sent on an 81-day voyage in 1761 CE. On arrival, it was five seconds slow compared to the time at the known longitude of the destination, equating to a deviation <2 km.

~ Jimbo could see a pristine sailing ship anchored in a bay, with a small town on the nearby shore. The decks were white, and he observed men painting the vessel. The name on the side was visible: *HMS Deptford*. Close to the ship were several small boats. The occupants, tanned men wearing few clothes, were fishing and some drinking beer. At the rear of the vessel, on a raised platform he knew was the quarterdeck, a more formal gathering stood around a table. Most were dressed in dark blue uniforms, but two wore civilian attire. He saw the taller, wearing a white shirt and matching floppy hat, reading figures in English from a sheet of paper. Jimbo knew this was 221.

=> *The other man is William Harrison, Jimbo, sent by his father. I acted as his assistant. We are examining the results, which seemed good.*

~ You told me earlier that the navy had no uniforms, but these people do.

=> *They started in 1748 CE, Jimbo, slightly before this time but after Halley's lecture, 0.07 kyE ago. 221 recalled the weather was hotter than England, which did not affect him, though prickly for the young Harrison.*

Further trials were performed and again provided satisfactory results, but my understanding is that local politics, and the Homo sapiens tendency to compete, prevented full acceptance. Eventually, Harrison sought the support of the King of England to gain the acquiescence of the government, which was obtained in 1773 CE. Harrison was then aged 0.08 kyE.

These chronometers, as they became known, were initially very expensive but gradually costs dropped, and their long life made them affordable. Harrison had enabled the accurate calculation of longitude, contributed to the global growth in commerce, and reduced the risks of sea travel.

An absorbing story, 221. We have perused your reports. While lengthy for Harrison, a period of 0.043 kyE from initial design to full acceptance seems short to us. We know of upgrades to the Intelligence's internal clocks that have taken 10^3 kyE, and then required adjustments.

221 recalled his own involvement in such a project and felt grateful for the assignment to Earth.

You mentioned an alternative astronomical method. Tell us more.

The alternative is known as the method of lunar distances. Favoured by Newton and Huygens and widely used, either if a chronometer was unavailable, or to check its accuracy.

What is the principle, 221?

The fundamental is the comparatively quick movement of the Moon across the background stars. The angle subtended by the Moon and a known star lying in its apparent path is measured by the local observer. A correction is required for the effect of parallax. The corrected angle can then be compared with a set of tables, which specifies the time at the meridian, defined as Greenwich near London, for that measurement. Local time can be obtained by observation of the altitude of the Sun or another star. With a difference of 15° per hour, longitude can be calculated.

We like this approach, 221. Why was this not the preferred method, rather than a precision-engineered timepiece?

There were three reasons. One was the difficulty in making accurate observations from an unstable ship. If the weather was cloudy, then no observation could be made. A second reason was the need to perform mathematics. While we may regard this as trivial, this was a challenge for many mariners, unless on a large vessel with well-educated officers. The third is that the chronometer gradually became more affordable.

Persuasive, 221.

In the present-day, the client has presumably discarded such methods in favour of satellite-based solutions?

The modern approach does depend on satellites, with GPS now becoming common, but many mariners retain chronometers, both as a back-up and out of a sense of tradition. The Royal Navy, the British maritime military force, which has access to Homo sapiens most advanced technologies, still uses chronometers and trains navigators in the method of lunar distances.

Very strange, 221. There is much we do not understand about this species.

I think the British believe these skills provide a tactical advantage in a conflict. If the satellites become unavailable, they can still operate.

It is a while since we discussed warfare, so this is no surprise. You will be telling us that they ride horses and carry swords.

Sometimes they do.

We appreciated learning more of Harrison, who lived long by client standards, even if his efforts were sometimes frustrated. We have discerned from Newcomen and Harrison that people of simple origins with limited education can provide notable contributions. Earlier we met Gutenberg, who made a success of printing. According to our experience, civilisations with sentient individuals usually become societies in which education and knowledge are standardised, or where individuals have predetermined roles, with intelligence and information programmed accordingly. It is clear from your analysis, and input from Jimbo, that *Homo sapiens* evolution is different, possibly unique.

221 had nothing to add.

Σ55 seconds

Alexis Clairaut

Next, I propose that we return to Alexis Clairaut, who had a life unlike either Newcomen or Harrison. For this, we travel to France. Clairaut was born in Paris in 1713 CE, late in the life of Newton, whose ideas influenced him greatly. His father was a mathematics teacher, and Clairaut was an outstanding student. Such was his progress that he gained acceptance into the French Academy of Sciences, aged 0.018 kyE. His contributions are noteworthy, particularly to geometry, but we should address two areas concerning Newton's scholarship.

One relates to determining the shape of Earth, termed geodesy. We noted that in Principia, Newton postulated that the planet is an oblate spheroid.

~ Can you explain this term, 221? This is new to me.
=> *It is a surface developed by rotating an ellipse about one of its two axes. If rotated about the minor axis, then the result is an oblate spheroid, a squashed sphere. If the ellipse is a circle, then the result would be a sphere.*
~ A sphere is a special form of spheroid?
=> *Correct.*

In 1736 CE, Clairaut accompanied the French philosopher, Pierre Maupertuis, on an expedition into northern Europe to an area known as Lapland, to estimate the meridian arc. This was one of two expeditions by French scientists to confirm Newton's theory, which was controversial.

Clairaut would have been only 0.023 kyE, 221. This is consistent with other philosophers we have encountered. Pascal and Harrison come to mind.

221 reflected that Harrison was still more of a carpenter than a philosopher at that age but understood. Maupertuis was older, perhaps 0.038 kyE, but it was Clairaut's work that interested me.

~ What is the *meridian arc*, please?
=> *If you visualise travelling along a line of longitude, therefore north-south on Earth; at several points you stop and record the distance from the previous point, and latitude. Then you find an ellipsoid that fits the data. In this way, you define the planet's shape, or at least this part of it.*
~ What about the local effects of terrain?
=> *We can ignore them providing the measuring points are not too close, and if the terrain is chosen intelligently. You should not study this in the middle*

of a mountain range, for example. Imagine using the surface of an ocean, undisturbed by wind or tidal flows. This is the profile you are trying to model.

~ In my terms, they were trying to find the best-fitting curve for their data.

What was Clairaut's conclusion? Did he agree with Newton?

His initial findings did not align with Newton but his later treatise, published in 1743 CE, which became known as Clairaut's Theorem, confirmed that Earth is an oblate spheroid. It had been recognised for perhaps 0.1 kyE that gravity varies between locations, increasing towards the poles, which is consistent with Newton's model. The theorem allowed the ellipticity of the planet to be calculated from surface measurements of gravitational force.

In his treatise, Clairaut used an analysis provided by the Scottish mathematician, Colin Maclaurin, regarding the tendency of a homogeneous fluid mass, rotating about its centre, to form an ellipsoid.

Should we learn more about Maclaurin?

221 reflected that it was difficult to compress the relevant Homo sapiens material into his time allocation, meaning he could only briefly introduce some excellent philosophers. Maclaurin came from a family of church officials in the western part of Scotland and was sufficiently precocious that by 0.02 kyE, he became Professor of Mathematics at Aberdeen University. To the present-day, 1996 CE, this is the client's youngest professorial appointment. 221 recalled meeting this fresh professor at the Royal Society, to which he was admitted while Newton was President. In 1725 CE, aged <0.03 kyE, he was appointed to an equivalent position at the prestigious Edinburgh University, partly on the recommendation of Newton. I know that Maclaurin boosted the reputation of the university as a centre of research.

There is inadequate time to consider Maclaurin, but we note your reports.

We should conclude our discussion of Earth's shape. A more accurate estimate of the degree of flattening of the planet is roughly 1/298, about 23% less than Newton's calculated value. Our result is based on measurements, which indicate the ellipticity to be within the expected range for planets of this structure and orbital characteristics.

~ Does this mean that an observer at either pole is closer to the Earth's centre than one located at the equator?

=> *Correct, Jimbo. Since a difference in gravitational acceleration exists, a defined mass will weigh slightly more at the poles.*

Impressive work by Newton and Clairaut to have got so close through mathematical inference and terrestrial measurements. You said that there were two areas of Clairaut's work to consider.

The other is astronomy.

Clairaut elaborated a solution to the 'problem of three bodies', regarding the motion of Earth, Moon and Sun, and their respective gravitational influences, which had preoccupied leading mathematicians. Concerns existed over whether Newton's laws were adequate but by 1750 CE, Clairaut had an approximate answer to this question, consistent with Newtonian principles.

We have the mathematics, 221. Clairaut was an ingenious philosopher.

Not only did he resolve a scientific challenge, but he provided a navigational tool for seafarers.

Within his astronomical studies, he found time to make the first detailed measurements of Venus by a Homo sapiens observer. Galileo had made an earlier study, that enabled him to observe the phases of Venus, supporting the Copernican heliostatic theory.

We know that the planet is number two in this planetary system. Similar in size to Earth, with a mass of about 85%, a diameter of 95%, and a density of 5.24 g/ cc^3, so about 5% lower.

I don't think Clairaut was able to derive these details.

~ I know little about Venus, apart from it being very hot, over 740 K. Is it right that a day on Venus is longer than a year?

=> *Yes, Jimbo, you are correct. In Earth terms, Venus orbits the Sun in 225 days, but one Venusian rotation takes about 243 days. It is the slowest rotating planet in your system and has no moons. What can you deduce from these two facts, considering Newton's laws and Clairaut's work?*

~ I suspect that Venus is more spherical than Earth.

=> *Correct. In particular, the centrifugal force at its equator is less than Earth's. Newton and Huygens found this force is determined by mv^2/r. The two* *planets have comparable dimensions, but the v^2 term is lower for Venus. It is also unaffected by the gravitational force imposed by an orbiting satellite.*

To conclude our study of Clairaut's contributions, we find another prodigy. In Maclaurin, yet another. We see philosophers building upon the work of their predecessors and contemporaries. There is a curious combination of competition and cooperation. It is unsurprising that Newton's insights influenced successors.

Newton has remained essential until the present-day because his laws apply in all mechanical environments.

We have also noted the tendency for scientific discoveries to rapidly affect *Homo sapiens* life. This was obvious with the steam engine and the chronometer, but Clairaut's mathematical cleverness came to the assistance of marine navigators. In other civilisations, scientific research moves slower. What is different on Earth, 221?

We can identify two drivers of speed when transferring the outcomes of pure science into useful applications, such as from astronomy to navigation. One is military: the continuing search for an advantage over rivals. The other is commercial: the opportunity to become quicker or less expensive than competitors, perhaps by plotting a speedier voyage from the seller to the buyer.

In none of our assimilated clients do these tendencies exist. They interested us because of their scientific and mathematical prowess, but not their speed. In a sense, these were similar to the Intelligence, but *Homo sapiens* dynamism provides a new trait. We must ponder this.

221 considered the Energy Masters to be good at pondering. Also, a trait.

Adam Smith

We have seen the commercial interests of this client influence decisions and progress, so I propose to divert briefly into the science of economics and one of its founders. For this, we will return to Great Britain, and particularly Scotland.

This does not surprise us, 221. We know you are comfortable in this region.

We need no more than a second to consider the work of Smith, born to the north of Edinburgh in 1723 CE. He studied economics and philosophy. We will focus on his economics.

He was educated at the University of Glasgow, and subsequently at Oxford, which he regarded as inferior. On his return to Scotland, he became a leading figure in the Scottish Enlightenment.

You have already introduced us to the *Enlightenment*, which we understood had its origins in France, and the *Industrial Revolution*, which began in England. Is the *Scottish Enlightenment* something new for us?

221 considered this an abstruse question and hoped for support from Jimbo. One indicator is that Scotland then possessed four universities compared to two in England, despite having one-fifth of the population and being poorer.

~ I know that by this time, observatories operated in Aberdeen and St Andrews. Mathematics was a flourishing field. We have already learned a little of Professor Maclaurin, but there were others. Edinburgh had acquired a medical school and a Royal College of Physicians, and became a centre of research, which has endured.

=> *How do you know all this, Jimbo?*

~ Edinburgh is my home, and we try to maintain our identity. The universities evolved an intellectual climate with distinctive characteristics.

=> *What would these be, wondered 221 hopefully?*

~ I think practicality might be at the root. Fewer abstractions, and more empirical analysis that could deliver tangible improvements. You can see this in the strength of our sciences, but also in business and economic thought. Even now, Scotland has a separate educational process and legal system, distinct from those to our south. Churches were at the forefront of promoting education, particularly outside the cities.

=> *221 noted that the discussion had diverged from economics, but the Energy Masters seemed interested.*

~ Our culture is inclusive, so ideas were shared with thinkers from Europe and North America. Some say they influenced the American Constitution.

Jimbo has given us some clues, 221. Apart from being well-informed, he appears proud of his heritage. Is this usual?

Common, but not universal. It is very apparent among the Scots, and more widely across the British Isles. Comparable behaviour exists in France, according to my observations there.

Is this a useful trait, 221? It is rare among our clients to feel any emotional attachment to a place or social group. They tend to be cerebral and logical.

Usefulness is apparent sometimes, but it can be destructive. 221 recalled the energy wasted in arguing over whether Leibniz or Newton devised calculus first. More important was that calculus became available.

They had digressed from Smith and should proceed. He recalled attending the public lectures at the Philosophical Society of Edinburgh, in 1748 CE. These were popular gatherings, and 221 noted that they were housed in progressively larger premises to accommodate the attendees, who numbered hundreds. Puzzling was the eclectic nature of the audience, encompassing academics, students, businesspeople, and those who just seemed interested. He observed that it included English and European visitors and others he could not identify. There were female attendees. Smith would speak on his preferred topic, usually regarding economics, but including freedom of thought and liberty.

~ Jimbo could see little through the crowded benches in the dimly lit hall, but at the front stood a small man behind a table. While there were some papers on this table, he spoke without reference to them. Sometimes, he stopped and appeared deep in contemplation, requiring the attendees to await his resumption. After some time, he invited questions, but appeared bored by most. With one man, though, he had a particular rapport and engaged in a public conversation. This was Smith's eminent contemporary, David Hume. Despite being older, he treated the orator respectfully, listening to his explanations. There was no moderator, only Smith himself, so he closed when he felt enough had been said.

~ Outside the meeting hall, in a cold Edinburgh street, Jimbo observed groups still discussing the meaning of Smith's words, while he saw others heading for the adjacent taverns to debate his ideas over local beer or imported red wine. A long-established tradition.

221 was anxious to continue. I propose that we consider his major economic work, perhaps equivalent to Newton's Principia in terms of its impact on client development. In part, his work was the product of his observations during the inception of the Industrial Revolution and took him about 0.01 kyE to write. We should consider The Wealth of Nations, first published in 1776 CE, >0.025 kyE after his Edinburgh lectures.

This is a large treatise, formally known as An Inquiry into the Nature and Causes of the Wealth of Nations, not immediately distilled into laws or equations.

How intricate is this work, 221? We don't mean in pieces of information but in terms of readability. Our understanding of *Principia* is that although it was important, it could only be understood by philosophers. Is this similar?

It amounts to five books in two volumes but was sufficiently accessible to become widely read.

The first edition sold within six months. Five editions were published during Smith's life. I will address points that may inform our cognisance of Homo sapiens society.

221 recognised that it was difficult to convey the essence of the treatise, since it discussed ideas absent from other galactic civilisations, so far as he knew.

In Book 1, he addressed labour productivity, payment, and the introduction of coinage. He shows concern for poverty and explains some reasons for it. 221 recalled Insertions in the Levant long before, and evidence of labour specialisation, which boosted productivity because people repeated what they knew best. He remembered bartering labour for food and shelter. There were no coins at that time.

In Book 2, he considered the accumulation and use of stock.

What does this mean, 221?

This refers to any artefact used to pursue an objective. For example, a fishing rod is an item of stock for a fisherman. If he has only one and is hungry, it has great value. If he possesses many, and others wish to buy them, he might sell. The price he can obtain depends on competitors in the market. If there is a shortage of supply, compared to the demand, prices will be higher.

Does not the cost of manufacturing the rod determine its selling price?

Not really. This is an insight that has long been known to the client, and which Smith explained carefully.

He also considered the notion of added value, which can make the worth of a production worker, who helps create extra value, higher than a servant.

Does this not depend on the seniority, age, or qualifications of the worker?

~ Only indirectly, in that a better educated or more experienced employee may generate more value through superior skills. My father pays for capable and productive people who can contribute to his business. He pays them very well because he needs to retain their services. These employees are also in a market and want to sell their competencies for a high price.

In Book 3, Smith examined the economic development of different countries and regions and compares agricultural with industrial employment. He warns of greed and selfishness, and lack of concern for the wider society.

In Book 4, he addressed the political aspects of markets and trading. He criticises the use of taxes on imports to protect local suppliers and argues that possessing large quantities of precious metals such as gold is not necessary for a society to become successful. I know these ideas have been debated by economists ever since.

Here he uses an expression that has been repeated many times. He refers to an individual in a market, maybe a buyer or a seller or a producer, being led by "an invisible hand".

What is this, 221? Hopefully nothing supernatural.

221 wondered whether this was more humour but tried to answer the question. This is a metaphor that Smith used to describe the collateral benefits to the wider society of the individual person or company pursuing a habit of self-interest. The effect of the forces at work in a free market, which affect both supply and demand, should reach an equilibrium point and optimise the allocation of resources within the society.

Is this correct? Does it work? We do not find this idea elsewhere. Other civilisations plan in great detail. Maybe a slow process for *Homo sapiens* entrepreneurs. Is this an insight into the client's apparent success, 221?

~ We need to treat this idea with care. 221's description is reasonable, but the imagery is open to interpretation. Nowadays, it doesn't mean that everyone does exactly what is best for them, irrespective of the effect on others, and the overall result will be optimal. A simple example can be found in my father's business. He could stop spending on protective safety equipment and training, saving money but risking the health or lives of the employees. Apart from being a bad idea, it isn't legal. The wider society, through laws established in a parliament and applied by the government, has decided that there should be limits on behaviour in the market.

=> *The basic concept is correct, Jimbo? Within constraints, decisions are made in response to the market, and everybody should benefit.*

~ Yes, but then we encounter the tricky question of how the benefits are shared, which preoccupies us.

=> *We understand, Jimbo. Listening to your comments is fascinating. These ideas are unfamiliar to us.*

There is a fifth book, 221. Should we consider it?

In Book, 5 Smith examined the role of government in the market and the management of taxation. He argues that the wealthier members of a society should pay more tax than the poorer ones. My observation is that in many countries this is accepted, but there is an argument about how much more.

=> *Do you agree, Jimbo?*

~ It becomes more complicated. Management of the tax system, balancing tax receipts with expenditure, is a fixation of governments.

Much has been written about Smith's treatise, but there seems little doubt that it is a cornerstone of Homo sapiens economic thought.

We are re-reading your reports on Smith and his work, 221. There are several difficulties that require contemplation. These relate to the Intelligence, and not to Smith's work, which seems admirable, or to your helpful notes.

221 wondered whether to ask about these difficulties, but the Energy Masters were ahead of him, as usual.

First, this whole field is new to us. These ideas make some sense, but they are outside our experience, which is unusual after $>10^7$ kyE. Second, and as a consequence of the first, we have no basis for comparison. No other civilisation adopts this approach to the allocation of resources. Third, arising from the first two points, we cannot yet quantify whether this methodology is contributing to the client's recent knowledge acceleration. We need to think deeply about this.

Apparently, an important aspect of *Homo sapiens* development, which Smith has encapsulated within a science, although a new science for us.

221 wondered whether the Energy Masters had concluded their meditation after 0.06 seconds, or if this was just an interim remark. It remained unclear.

How should we leave this, 221?

I think Smith regarded himself as a scientist. He lived in an era when the scientific method had become accepted, and in a region where natural philosophy was vigorously pursued. In his writings, I found some evidence for this: "Science is the great antidote to the poison of enthusiasm and superstition."

As you know, we are not prone to either of these tendencies, so are aligned with Smith. Let us continue.

Σ58 seconds

Henry Cavendish

I recommend that we stay in Great Britain, to examine the contributions of Cavendish, who was born in 1731 CE, in Nice, France. His family were wealthy members of the British aristocracy. After studying at Cambridge, he followed his father into society, and particularly science. He was both a chemist and physicist, who published less than he learned.

In chemistry, he is credited with the discovery of hydrogen. Earlier scientists, including Boyle, had detected the gas, but it was Cavendish who determined it exists as a discrete element and a component of water.

He concluded that the gas exhaled by mammals includes carbon dioxide, designated by the client as CO_2. Cavendish produced CO_2 and other gases and measured both specific gravity and combustibility. His paper in 1778 CE, resulted in an award from the Royal Society.

Elected to the Royal Society nearly 0.02 kyE earlier, he became an enthusiastic participant. His expertise enabled him to select instruments for the Royal Observatory.

Impressive accomplishments, 221. From chemistry to astronomy.

221 realised that he had drifted from the agenda. Actually, we are not finished with his chemistry yet.

Around 1783 CE, Cavendish researched the nature of heat. He was among the first to understand the concept of latent heat, although the phenomenon was discussed earlier, in 1761 CE, with its discovery attributed to Professor Joseph Black in Glasgow. We will meet this scientist again.

=> *You are familiar with this idea, Jimbo?*

~ Latent heat is the energy absorbed or released during a change of state, therefore, freezing, melting, vaporising, or condensing, at a constant temperature. The latent heat of vaporisation is the change in enthalpy required to convert a quantity of a liquid into a gas. To achieve the opposite, to convert the gas into a liquid, we refer to the latent heat of condensation. For the same mass of material, assuming constant pressure, the energy absorbed or released should be the same. I like to think of latent heat as hidden energy because it cannot be detected by a temperature change.

=> *From Latin, latere means to be hidden, so your idea is reasonable.*

Can we leave the thermodynamics class and return to Cavendish, please?

His research led him to a general theory, which Jimbo would certainly recognise as the principle of conservation of energy. 221 was reluctant to distract the Energy Masters by interaction with Jimbo but was too late.

~ *Energy cannot be created or destroyed within a closed system but can only be transformed from one form to another.* For example, from heat to some form of mechanical work, such as in Newcomen's steam engine.

=> *Noteworthy, Jimbo, as a fundamental idea, but also because I first met the idea on Earth through the writings of a female scholar, Émilie du Châtelet. Better known for translating Principia into French, she also tutored Clairaut.*

We can regard Cavendish as being at the beginning of the thermodynamics revolution, elucidated by later philosophers.

In 1785 CE, Cavendish investigated the composition of air. He removed the nitrogen and oxygen, leaving a small amount of residual, unexplained gas. By careful measurement, he concluded that air consists of one-part oxygen to four-parts nitrogen, plus the residue, which was 1/120 of the nitrogen volume. He wondered whether the residue resulted from experimental error. 0.099 kyE later, two researchers named Strutt and Ramsay detected this inert gas, subsequently named argon, or Ar in local terms.

We know the average composition of the Earth's dry atmosphere is 78.08% nitrogen, 20.95% oxygen, 0.93% argon, and 0.04% CO_2, but it typically also contains 0.40% water vapour, although this is higher at sea level. Cavendish's result was a good first approximation.

221 reflected that some believed Earth and its atmosphere was created to suit their physiology. The reality is the opposite. Homo sapiens evolved in this atmosphere. He considered Earth's neighbouring planets. Venus with a dense atmosphere, mainly of CO_2, with a much higher atmospheric pressure at the surface, 90x greater than Earth and the highest temperatures in the system, driven by what the client calls the greenhouse effect, around 740 K he *remembered Jimbo saying 3 seconds before; and Mars with a very thin atmosphere, <1% of Earth's, and low but variable temperatures. Neither sustained life so far as the Intelligence could determine, and certainly not intelligent beings. For that, Homo sapiens explorers would travel there. Simulations suggest the client will reach Mars in ~0.05 kyE and establish a base.*

221 knew Earth's atmospheric pressure to be about 101 kPa and remembered climbing the small mountain with Pascal's brother-in-law to detect a pressure change, ~0.1 kyE before Cavendish. Now the species understood the composition of their atmosphere. Fast progress, he considered.

Come along, 221, no time for reminiscences.

We are transitioning into the physics domain now. I will focus on two areas, the first being electricity. Cavendish was an intensely private person, so some of his research only became known after his death when other scientists had access to his notes. He conceptualised electrical potential, and the relationship between potential and current flow. He applied the inverse square law to describe the variation in electrostatic force with distance and may have invented the capacitor. His early thoughts were published in 1771 CE, but he apparently undertook further research over 0.01 kyE, without disseminating the results.

We understood that Homo sapiens science acquired its electrical engineering prowess later, 221.

Correct, but Cavendish had earlier unpublished insights.

221 reflected on the Homo sapiens need for a critical mass of scientists to build knowledge, but as Cavendish usually worked in isolation, other scholars could not access his ideas. Despite this, he was active in the Royal Society.

Can we return to physics? You said there were two areas, but you have only introduced Cavendish's interest in electricity.

The second topic is remarkable. Cavendish conducted an experiment that enabled him to calculate Earth's density.

An ambitious goal at this stage in the client's scientific evolution, 221. Are you sure about this?

The origins of this experiment began with another philosopher, John Michell, several of whose ideas were astonishing.

If so, we need a brief detour to learn more about Michell.

221 had not planned to discuss Michell but knew him better than the reclusive Cavendish.

Michell was a contemporary of Cavendish, who also studied at Cambridge, and became both a church official and a scientist. He lived and taught at Cambridge for a period and was described to me as the most distinguished philosopher in the period immediately after Newton. Some of his notable work was performed later, while working for the church, in Yorkshire.

We would like to learn about his ideas please, 221.

He explored magnetism and found that the inverse square law applies to the force exerted as the distance from the poles increases. The manufacture of artificial magnets was explained in a manual written around 1750 CE.

Michell also developed an understanding of the Earth's geology and can be regarded as one of the earliest seismologists, although without instruments. He examined the origins of the Great Lisbon earthquake of 1755 CE. 221 recalled visiting after the event. Little remained of the city's infrastructure.

~ Jimbo could see people searching piles of debris, spread across a wide area, between the hills adjacent to the ocean. It was apparent that the sea had rushed into the city, destroying the remnants from the preceding quake.

=> *I think you know this phenomenon as a tsunami, Jimbo.*

~ Yes, from the Japanese language. It literally means 'harbour wave'. The alternative term in English is a tidal wave. Caused by a sub-sea mass displacement event, such as an earthquake or volcano.

=> *The residents were unaware of the connection between the earthquake and tsunami, so many lives were lost. In total, nearly 20% of the city's population. The third such local event in 0.434 kyE; unfortunately, no knowledge was distilled from the previous two.*

Moral philosophers of the era expounded on the earthquake's meaning for the existence of a god, but Michell considered the physics more relevant. He adduced, in a treatise written in the same year, that earthquakes are a wave effect, provided an estimate for the epicentre of the Lisbon event, and suggested that an underwater earthquake could generate a tsunami. He was elected to the Royal Society in 1760 CE.

Michell built telescopes and studied the stars. He had prescient thoughts about gravitation. He applied statistical methods to the distribution of stars and noted that the occurrence of double-stars was more frequent than a random distribution would suggest. His conclusion in 1767 CE was that gravitational attraction could be drawing these bodies together. This influenced later astronomers, some of whom we shall meet.

His ideas regarding gravitation went further, including the notion that if light, as postulated by Newton, consists of particles, then an object of sufficiently large mass would deflect these particles. An even more massive object might prevent any light from leaving, resulting in what he termed a dark star.

When did Michell have these thoughts, 221?

His paper was published in 1783 CE.

Homo sapiens researchers have caught up with his thinking and are identifying what they now call black holes. While their knowledge remains limited, they have some mathematical understanding of how such objects behave.

Did these ideas influence his colleagues?

The astronomer, William Herschel, was interested enough to search for binary stars and black holes. We will meet Herschel. Michell also wrote to Cavendish. They became friends, not an easy relationship to achieve.

221 recalled selling a reflecting telescope to Herschel, on behalf of the aged Michell, nearly 0.01 kyE later. It was in poor condition, but Herschel paid a generous sum. The mathematician Pierre Laplace postulated the existence of black holes about this time, later than Michell. We will meet Laplace.

Michell recommended that a strategy for finding black holes would be to identify stars that behave as if in a binary pair, but with no visible partner. This might indicate the presence of a black hole in the proximity.

221, we know of many such couples in our galaxy, but it is surprising that Michell just stumbled on this concept. You had some association with him? Hopefully, he did not obtain such notions from you.

I knew Michell slightly through my Insertions in Cambridge and noted his capabilities. When he moved to Yorkshire, into relative intellectual isolation, I worked as a mathematics teacher locally. He had few scientific contemporaries nearby, so we became friendly. Although he returned to Cambridge and attended the Royal Society in London, I was a source of companionship, so he discussed his insights. Imaginative and scholarly, he did not need my ideas.

If time permitted, we could explore Michell's thinking further, but we should return to Cavendish. What is their connection regarding Earth's density?

$\Sigma 60$ seconds

Jimbo realised the voices were fading, replaced by the insistent sound of his phone ringing again. He expected Mr North's call, so felt relieved.

Eight
1996 CE – 22.35, 16 August, Edinburgh

Green light. Fully charged phone. Important call.
Jimbo lifted the device from the charging cradle, opening the connection.

"Mr Morrison, this is Gradac here. Maybe I did not make myself clear in our earlier talk, so I advise you to listen carefully. I want the disks that are in your possession. You will find that I am not a patient person."

"I don't have the disks, they're at the Institute. I'm at home."

"I know that, but you can collect the disks tomorrow morning, and deliver them to me before noon. I hope this is clear. As I said some minutes ago, Ralph is counting on your kind assistance."

Jimbo tried to say he hardly knew Ralph, but Gradac preferred to talk, not listen.

"Just so you don't forget, Mr Morrison, be aware that I know where you live, with your nice parents, and Spot, the friendly black dog."

Well, he got that bit wrong. Nobody really calls their dog Spot.

"If you don't bring the disks to me, you'll be having some visitors for the weekend. Don't trouble the police with our arrangements. I know who you call."

Jimbo doubted this but wanted to maintain the conversation in the hope it might help identify Gradac's location. Then he remembered this was something he already knew.

There was a metallic click as the line disconnected.

Jimbo stood motionless for a few seconds, recognising a new and unpleasant situation. Handling gangsters was something he had only ever seen on television. Not real life. Except this seemed very real. He was still holding the phone to his ear and pulled it away. Some people believed they were bad for the brain.

He looked at the recent call function on the phone and was surprised to see Gradac's number. Was he an incompetent gangster or just very confident?

Then he scrolled down one line to the five-digit number he had called earlier. Where was Mr North? He pressed redial and was answered immediately, seemingly without the phone even ringing. The same female voice answered. She knew it was him.

"You are waiting for Mr North's call. He has been busy, but asked me to connect you, if you called. Please hold."

Jimbo heard a couple of beeps, then he was connected.

"Good evening, Jimbo. Sorry for not responding to your earlier call, but I've been engaged. You've been talking to Gradac, or rather listening to him."

Jimbo noted this was a statement, not a question. He did not feel surprised but was pleased to know that Mr North was following events closely. He might be a cold fish, but he seemed a highly competent cold fish.

"Gradac says that if I don't deliver the disks before noon tomorrow, he'll come to my home. Not a social call, I imagine. This is a threat."

"Yes, Jimbo. It was meant to scare you, but Gradac is playing tricks. Did you not wonder why he gave you so long to bring the disks?"

This had not occurred to Jimbo.

"He wanted you to remain at home tonight. In a short time, his colleagues would come calling, and motivate you to get the disks immediately by threatening your parents."

Jimbo felt perspiration beginning to form on his forehead. Should he wake his parents? Or check the doors were locked? Or call the police? Then he realised that Mr North was the police, or something close.

"However, these gentlemen now have other preoccupations. We occupied Gradac's flat just around the corner from you, after conducting a search. I thought he might return but picking up another two of his friends is actually better. They are now assisting the police, as the officers like to say. Gradac doesn't know that his team was intercepted, so is probably waiting for a call to say that your home has been taken. Their silence will trouble him. He will guess the reason. With Dr Wagner in his custody, he cannot easily move, so he will await your visit tomorrow."

This seemed good news, but the situation still felt like a bad dream. "Is it safe for us to stay here? Should I tell my parents?"

Mr North gave his mirthless chuckle. "No need, Jimbo, for now at least. I'm quite close to you. Your bedroom light is visible from my vehicle. Apart from occupying Gradac's flat, we have a modest perimeter around your neighbourhood. We can see who enters and leaves. I have two problems at present. One is that I don't know for certain how much support Gradac has. It can't be many, though, as this would be conspicuous. We have now detained four of these associates."

"Earlier, Dr Wagner said that there had been two friends with Gradac at his country residence, and mentioned they'd gone out. I noticed that Gradac took the phone from him after that."

"Very useful, Jimbo. I imagine they are the two who met our reception party. My second problem is locating Gradac quickly. I reckon if he doesn't receive those disks tomorrow, he will become desperate, forcing us to take direct action, but losing any chance to embarrass his intermediaries or customers. His two friends arrived in the city from the eastern suburbs, but I already knew this to be the direction of Gradac's hideout. It's not precise enough for me to move on him.

Every time he makes a phone call, we get closer. He was also using Dr Wagner's phone, seemingly to confuse us."

"I have the phone number he called me from a few minutes ago." Jimbo realised there was something more important he should be telling Mr North.

"I have the number and know the approximate location. He is somewhere in East Lothian, within 30 km of the city centre."

"Mr North, I'm sorry," blurted Jimbo, "but I remembered his address."

"Unsurprising, Jimbo. A little more magic. Don't give me the address now. I don't need it. Just a district or town name, so I can make arrangements."

"Haddington."

"That's good enough for now, and rather convenient for me. Maybe also for Gradac, of course. You know there is an old airfield nearby?"

"I know about Drem, which is close to Haddington. It was a fighter base in the Second World War."

"Right idea, but an incorrect choice. In the area is East Fortune, a training facility at that time. The runway is still operable, but no longer used by the military. Maybe an escape route for Gradac, or perhaps what he would like us to think. Also, easy for me to bring in support at short notice."

Jimbo wondered where this conversation was leading. He was standing in his bedroom, in the late evening, talking to a spook he'd only met a few hours before about disused airfields near Edinburgh. Meantime, his family had been threatened by a gangster. "What do you want me to do?"

"Do, Jimbo? I want you to do nothing, for now anyway. Neither Gradac nor his friends can get to your home without alerting me, and the police colleagues. Tomorrow we should take a drive out to Haddington and see what we can find."

"Can you explain where Dr Wagner fits into this? Gradac seems to think we are friends. I hardly know him."

"Since you ask, Ralph Wagner is a former colleague of mine. I regard him as a friend. He's a clever guy, a mathematician, but unfortunately also a drug addict at present, so he becomes confused. It was me who seeded the idea that you and he know each other. Gradac thinks this provides leverage. He has been blackmailing Ralph because of his addiction, and now has control over his supply. Before you ask, I've been providing the narcotics in return for his help."

Jimbo was beginning to feel he didn't want to know any more. "What's your plan for tomorrow. How do I fit in?"

"As I said, we will make a trip to Haddington. When I meet you, make sure you have Gradac's address available. Don't forget it. I will call you after 06.00 to arrange your collection. Until then, do not answer any more calls. Meantime, I suggest you try sleeping. Probably this is difficult for you, but we need you wide awake tomorrow. I was once told by an old soldier that sleep is a gift from God, so make use of it. I must go now."

The connection was cut, leaving Jimbo with more questions than he had started with. He thought about Haddington, a small but prosperous community slightly beyond Edinburgh's eastern suburbs. To the south lay rich farmland, which gave way to the rolling hills of the border country. Going further east meant following the route of the A1, the main east coast highway, which gradually curves to the south, in tandem with the adjacent rail line. To its north, a short distance away was the scenic coastline of the Forth estuary, with beaches, nature reserves, and well-known golf courses.

He remembered playing golf at Haddington with his father, and two of his associates. Perhaps less distinguished than other courses in the area, Jimbo recalled the affable professional telling him that this was the 17th oldest course in the world. This meant little to Jimbo at the time, but later he considered how many thousands of courses there might be. Number seventeen seemed more impressive.

After replacing the handset, he looked out of the window. Nothing much had changed since earlier. The streetlights and parked cars. Looking to his left, to the south and the city centre from his third-level vantage point, he noticed a dull-coloured Range Rover parked close to the crossroads. He recognised the residents' cars and knew this was not one of them. Before he could consider further, the headlights flashed twice. This was meant for him. Mr North, or his associates, he hoped.

The clock indicated 22.48. There was no more to be done, he reasoned, trying to justify the day's events to himself rationally. There was nothing much rational about it, he muttered, aware that he was talking to himself, as he lay down. Then he jumped up, crossed to his phone, and switched it to mute, set his clock alarm to 06.00, and lay down again, and wondered what impression 221 had of his conversations.

He pondered his improving memory. It seemed like everything he had ever known was becoming accessible. Apparently, he could not forget. Which was presumably why he remembered a great deal more history than he realised. Or about *Homo sapiens*, as the Intelligence prefers to call us.

As he slipped into sleep, he was aware of 221 speaking.

Nine
1996 CE – 22.54, 16 August, Edinburgh

221's utterances: well-informed, verifiable, empathetic.
=> *Mr North is preparing for tomorrow, Jimbo. His connections are not confined to the police service but include your military. He must be influential because he has people in England preparing to travel to your area. They are using helicopters, flying soon to what you have been calling East Lothian. At present, he is in discussion with Mr Fox regarding a change of plan, but this is unclear to me.*

=> *I can also tell you that he has four vehicles positioned in the streets near your home, and further support from the police.*

~ How do you know all this?

=> *We intercepted their secure communications. For us, this is accessible, although the frequency-hopping was a new challenge. You belong to a creative species, Jimbo.*

=> *We need to continue the review, but the Energy Masters are preoccupied with another priority. They should not keep us waiting for more than a few seconds. There was an unscheduled tunnel implosion, which disrupted operations for a short while. Nothing to worry about.*

~ Tunnels? What do you mean? I thought you floated in space, ubiquitous but ethereal. Jimbo wondered whether his vocabulary was improving, along with his memory.

=> *Your description is reasonable, Jimbo, but consider how we achieve this. Our origins were maybe as sentient creatures like you, but long ago. While our presence is now more transcendent, it is not entirely insubstantial. We consist of huge numbers of sub-atomic particles, spread across the galaxy and beyond. These particles convey information, which is essential to our operation, just like oxygen is for your body. Even for us, the galaxy is quite a large territory, and as you know, nothing travels faster through space than the speed of light. This is* *like a celestial speed limit. We cannot wait 10^2 kyE for a piece of information to cross the galaxy, so long ago we started building tunnels around space-time to shorten the distances.*

~ What are your tunnels made of? How can you tunnel through empty space?

=> *Our tunnels are made of matter, Jimbo. Intensely dense matter, heavier even than exists in what your astrophysicists call a neutron star. We can call them black holes, which connect apparently distant points by momentarily distorting space-time.*

~ I thought that black holes are giant voids, from which nothing escapes.

=> *You are partly correct. Naturally occurring black holes come in all sizes and can possess huge energy. We have learned how to tap this energy to create our singularities and build tunnels.*

~ How big are your tunnels?

=> *Rather small in your terms. Nano-scale is sufficient since we are only moving particles around. Many of these particles have no mass.*

~ How short does a journey across the galaxy become? If you can tunnel through space-time, from one side of the galaxy to the other, which is about 10^5 light-years or almost 10^{18} km, what is the length of your tunnel?

=> *Less than 10^{-6} km, and we move pretty fast, so connectivity is nearly instantaneous, roughly 3×10^{-10} seconds.*

~ How many of these tunnels are there, 221?

=> *Hard to say, they are being opened and closed all the time, using energy from the natural black holes. This requires a management system, of course, which is why we have the Energy Masters, who provided control. Now this is autonomous, freeing them for imperatives, such as examining Homo sapiens history. Except when an unscheduled outage occurs.*

We are ready for you, 221. You are correct to say neutron stars are dense, usually of the order of 10^{17} kg/m^3, and typically with a mass of circa 1.4x the star around which Earth orbits. Simple mathematics will tell you they have a diameter of about 20 km. To achieve this density, it is composed largely of neutrons, which are tightly packed and cannot be compressed any further.

221 knew all this, so assumed the astrophysics tutorial was being provided for Jimbo's benefit.

Now we would like to know more about the experiment to determine Earth's density. We understand that the equipment design was Michell's, but the investigation was undertaken by Cavendish. This seems appropriate because Michell was imaginative, and Cavendish, fastidious and detail oriented.

221 decided not to mention that the death of Michell was the reason for Cavendish's involvement.

Please explain how these measurements were achieved.

Michell did more than conceptualise the experiment. He built the apparatus, too, known as a torsion balance. Cavendish used it in 1798 CE. A 1.8 metre rod was suspended horizontally from a wire, with two 0.7 kg lead spheres mounted, one at each end. Two larger lead balls of about 160 kg were independently suspended 0.23 metre from each of the smaller balls.

What does 'independently suspended' mean? We have your image of the device but need an unambiguous sense.

Simply that their suspension system was separate from that of the two smaller balls. The objective was to measure the gravitational attraction between the small and big balls. This was achieved by positioning each of the large balls on alternate sides of the horizontal rod, causing rotation under the attractive force.

We understand the principle, 221, but there seems to be a significant potential for error in measuring a small effect.

There were two aspects that Cavendish addressed. One was to determine the torsion coefficient of the wire, meaning the torque exerted to create a given angle of twist. By measuring the angle generated by the gravitational effect, he could calculate the force. The other was to isolate the apparatus from the effect of air currents and temperature changes. This was achieved by placing the equipment inside a container in an enclosed room. Apertures allowed Cavendish to observe the deflections using small telescopes, and vernier scales. The force of attraction was tiny but measurable.

The force exerted by Earth on the small ball is simply the weight of the ball, and knowing the ratio of these forces and the dimensions of the planet enabled Cavendish to estimate its density. The result, 5.40×10^3 kg/m^3 was surprisingly accurate, and not improved upon for another 0.1 kyE.

Our density figure for this planet is 5.52×10^3 kg/m^3, measured using our sensors. Credit must be given to Michell and Cavendish for this achievement.

There are two more points.

Since the result provided a density greater than the planet's outer layer, it implied that the core must be of denser material. Iron was correctly postulated.

A second aspect is that of the gravitational constant, G, arising from Newton's earlier work. Utilising his equation for gravitational attraction, and after some simple algebra, G can be determined from Cavendish's result to within 1% of our measurement of $6.67 \times 10^{-11} m^3 \, kg^{-1} s^{-2}$. *Our value and that of the client are identical to six decimal places.*

Although Cavendish did not make this calculation, he provided the basis for later scholars.

How did you acquire such detailed knowledge of this experiment?

From my association with Michell, I helped him to build the apparatus to his specification. I also knew Cavendish slightly and reckoned that he was the best scientist to perform the experiment. He was interested, and despite disliking people being around, he accepted the equipment on the basis that I came too. This gave me opportunities to observe his work. 221 reflected that the method designed by Michell was unlike anything he had ever seen, but Cavendish thought it was a natural approach to the question.

We have learned a few things here, 221. One is the capacity of this species for cooperation. These two scholars seem to have been comfortable sharing ideas, while our earlier impression was that they might be competitors. Another is their methods. While we know that Newton built telescopes, our understanding is that his major contribution was as a theoretician with great insightfulness and mathematical skills. Here we have imaginative researchers who designed experiments to deliver knowledge. Their methods, particularly the density investigation, use ideas we have never encountered. The cleverness lies in its simplicity. Finally, we see the scientific method in the care Cavendish took to eliminate sources of error.

221 worried that time had been lost due to the tunnelling emergency, so was anxious to continue before the Energy Masters took the discussion in another direction, or Jimbo raised a question.

We see from your notes that Cavendish was an unusually wealthy man, for this era. Perhaps the richest in England. This did not distract him from his research, which is commendable. We appreciated the words attributed to the French philosopher, Jean-Baptiste Biot, who described him as: "the richest of all the savants and the most knowledgeable of the rich."

~ Excuse me, 221, what is a savant?

=> *Simply a thinker or a scholar. It is the French word for learned, derived from the Latin sapere, which means to be wise, as in Homo sapiens name.*

~ Who was Biot? A new name to me, presumably French?

=> *Biot was a scientist who studied astronomy and optics. His work on meteorites was notable because it started research into the chemistry of the solar system, as you call it.*

If there is an opportunity to learn more about Biot, 221, we should take it. Galactic chemistry is an important field for us.

To conclude Cavendish's contribution, he supported the founding of the Royal Institution in 1799 CE, an organisation that still exists.

For what purpose, 221?

In addition to supporting scientific research with an emphasis on practical application, the Ri, as it is known, encourages public engagement with scientists. After 0.196 kyE, the British remain enthusiastic about the annual program of Christmas lectures.

Very laudable of Cavendish, 221, particularly as he seems an introvert.

He took a particular interest in the experiments of one of the Ri's earliest employees, a philosopher named Humphry Davy. We will meet Davy later.

James Watt

I recommend that we proceed from calculating planetary densities to observe progress with the steam engine. We learned of Newcomen's efforts to establish the technology commercially, particularly in the mines. For the next stage, we return to Scotland to meet Watt, who was born close to the city of Glasgow in 1736 CE. He was a contemporary of Cavendish but lived later than Newcomen.

He trained as an instrument-maker, and after time in London, established himself in Glasgow, in 1756 CE.

Please clarify the nature of his profession.

The fabrication of precision instruments, typically used in scientific research or the manufacture of engineered components. It requires a knowledge of materials, mechanical processes, and measurement. 221 recalled his time assisting Newton, and later his work with Michell. He was also an instrument-maker, he considered.

His opportunity came with the arrival of assorted astronomical instruments at Glasgow University, in poor condition, requiring remedial work by a specialist. Watt was so successful with this project that the University invited him to establish a workshop for internal requirements. He fulfilled their expectations, producing components for instruments, including telescopes. He became friendly with two professors, Adam Smith, and Joseph Black, both of whom we met previously. As we noted, Black is credited with discovering the nature of latent heat, subsequently explored by Cavendish.

Black was another outstanding philosopher. A medical professor at Glasgow University for 0.01 kyE, and then Professor of Medicine and Chemistry at the University of Edinburgh for another 0.03 kyE. In Glasgow, beside his thermodynamic interests, he researched the properties of CO_2, demonstrating that it is a product of animal respiration. He is credited with its discovery in 1754 CE, preceding Cavendish's related work by 0.023 kyE. In the following year, he was the first to identify magnesium as an element, although 0.053 kyE elapsed before it was isolated.

Another leading figure in the Scottish Enlightenment, once ensconced in Edinburgh, Black devoted himself to teaching chemistry, and popularised the field, attracting students. He was so successful that attending his lectures became fashionable in the city. A stimulating period in Edinburgh, 221 recalled. He struggled to comprehend Smith's lectures but observed their popularity, whereas with Black he had the advantage of understanding the discipline. What had intrigued him was not the science, but Black's skill as a teacher, making chemistry tuition enjoyable for his students. He was an entertainer. Perhaps showman was the word?

221, we discern from your perfervid description that you, too, were enthused by Black. We have chemistry projects running within the Intelligence if you are interested. Otherwise, please return to describing Watt's steam engine studies.

Around 1760 CE, Watt began experimenting with steam power, without satisfactory results. His research led him to recognise the importance of latent heat in the operation of a steam engine, a phenomenon that his friend Black already understood. In 1763 CE, he was invited to refurbish a Newcomen engine. The design had remained largely unaltered since its invention, 0.051 kyE before. Even after Watt's repairs, the machine performed poorly. He deduced that most of the thermal energy was wasted, rather than being converted into useful work, because the energy used to heat the cylinder in each cycle was lost when cold *water was injected to condense the steam, to continue the cycle. After analysing the Newcomen engine, Watt introduced a critical improvement. Steam was condensed in a separate vessel, the cylinder insulated to maintain temperature, so increasing mechanical output. The steam engine had become more efficient.*

Perhaps your summary was too succinct, 221. While Watt had identified a limitation with earlier machines, his solution seems simple to us. Given the client's competitive nature, we wonder why this step was not achieved earlier.

There are two reasons, one relating to theory and the other to practicality.

Watt was no longer an instrument-maker, but a self-taught scientist, helped by Black, working before the science of thermodynamics had matured.

The practical aspect relates to component manufacture. Assembling a large cylinder around a close-fitting piston, essential to prevent losses, was beyond the prevailing know-how. Recently, though, precision boring techniques had become important for another application and improved rapidly.

What was this other application, 221?

The manufacture of cannon, in demand from the British military. Better quality bores enable more accurate cannons, providing an advantage to whoever possessed this technology.

Here we have military research providing a social benefit with an improved steam engine.

~ An example of the biblical saying to "beat swords into ploughshares," meaning to follow peaceful pursuits rather than war.

=> *This is probably not new to us, Jimbo, but what is the source?*

~ Isaiah 2 from the King James Version of the Bible, published in 1611 CE.

~ Only partly true in this case because the military could also use an improved steam engine.

We understand the point, 221. Many situations are complicated with this species. If we have churchmen, purveyors of the supernatural, who are also excellent scientists, why not a weapons manufacturer providing steam engine components?

The first machines were installed in 1776 CE, initially to drive pumps in mines. This required a reciprocating motion, but design of a rotating mechanism expanded applications to manufacturing machinery, providing power to the Industrial Revolution. Numerous improvements were made to Watt's concept, including a throttle and governor to maintain control of the machine. Taken together, these resulted in a power source offering double the efficiency of the Newcomen design. Watt and his partners had a profitable business, continued by their successors. His son, Gregory, became influential later.

While his design represented progress, Watt restricted his engine applications to low pressures, for safety reasons. Higher pressure systems would require improved boiler technology.

Is there more to learn from studying Watt, 221?

He did more than create a better steam engine. His inventive mind led him in multiple directions, beyond the scope of this review. One example, not widely known, is that Watt designed arguably the client's first copying machine, capable of reproducing text. This involved research into ink chemistry, paper, and press design, resulting in a functional machine, in 1780 CE. The concept was applied for another 0.1 kyE.

Unrelated to steam engines but challenging. Watt qualifies as a polymath.

He was respected during his life and commemorated, with schools carrying his name and many statues, including one in St Paul's Cathedral. 221 momentarily recalled his work with Wren and Hooke on the dome design, and felt this sensation known by the client as pride. His contemporary, Lord Brougham, provided an epitaph:

"JAMES WATT who, directing the force of an original Genius, early exercised in philosophic research, to the improvement of the Steam Engine, enlarged the resources of his Country, increased the power of Man, and rose to an eminent place among the most illustrious followers of science and the real benefactors of the World."

~ You know Heriot-Watt University in Edinburgh? An institution with a strong reputation for technology, reminding us of George Heriot and James Watt.

=> Correct, Jimbo. 221 had visited the institution, named after a philanthropist and a polymath, to examine its cutting-edge research.

To conclude our discussion of Watt, here we see traits shared by Harrison and Newcomen, with a man of modest background contributing to the advancement of his civilisation. Although well-connected to the academic community, our understanding is that he was driven by the market, seeing opportunities to deploy his inventiveness, both to his personal advantage but contributing to the wider society. Perhaps this is what Smith meant by the 'invisible hand'?

We see multiple mechanisms motivating Homo sapiens curiosity and inventiveness. One is financial, the simple desire for material gain, evident since hunter-gatherer times. Another may be the intellectual challenge of understanding nature and exploiting natural laws. Newton is an example. A third relates to the beliefs of the scientist. Kepler exemplified this, in trying to comprehend the designs of a supposed god, he uncovered truths about planetary motion. Note that Watt did not attend university, neither Harrison nor Newcomen. Then, an advanced education was rare, beyond the reach of most people. Many of the philosophers we have met came from wealthy families, such as Cavendish, or were associated with a church that possessed resources, such as Bacon or Michell, or with a powerful sponsor, such as Tycho.

Watt obtained his knowledge through his association with scholars, membership of learned societies, reading, and experimentation. Most of all, he wanted to know. Such a person was known as a philomath. It is not a term commonly used in the present-day.

~ 221, what is a philomath?
=> *To possess a love of learning. Hopefully, you qualify, Jimbo.*

Σ67 seconds

William Herschel

To save some milliseconds, 221 introduced the next topic immediately. I propose to examine the career of Herschel, born in 1738 CE in Hanover, now in Germany. Our interest begins after he arrived in England as a young man.

Despite beginning as a professional musician, it is his contributions to astronomy that we should consider. Another philomath, who transitioned from music to astronomy, with support from mentors, scientific societies, and family. We will meet his sister and son. His life story is eventful, but our focus is on his scientific accomplishments. After employment in musical roles in the north of England, where he both played and composed, in 1776 CE he moved to Bath, in south-west England, and progressed to senior musical positions. By this time, three brothers, also musicians, had joined him, and his sister too.

His curiosity about the nature of music led him to philosophical works of the era, beginning with harmonics but extending into mechanics, optics, and trigonometry. Herschel became interested in the design and manufacture of telescopes. After tuition from a local mirror producer, and with help from his family, he built a reflecting telescope. He observed Saturn's rings and started an astronomical journal.

In 1779 CE, he began searching for what the client today calls binary stars. To Herschel, this meant stars that were apparently close together, and by examining changes in their relative positions over time, he hoped to determine their distance from Earth using a method suggested by Galileo. I believe that Michell's earlier work triggered his interest in binary stars.

How large was the telescope Herschel used to search for these couples, 221?

A 160 mm reflector.

With what result? This was not a particularly powerful instrument.

Considerable success.

By 1784 CE, he had identified 703 binary or multiple star systems, which he reported to the Royal Society in two catalogues. Later, although not with the same telescope, he identified a further 145 systems. In 1797 CE, he re-measured these systems and identified positional changes not explained by parallax.

Displacements attributable to changes in the observer's position, so, Earth?

Correct.

After adjusting for the change in Earth's relative position, there were residual discrepancies in certain star positions. In 1802 CE, he published a catalogue of 500 celestial objects, postulating that many pairs were orbiting under mutual gravitational attraction. In all, Herschel identified around 800 such pairs, the majority later confirmed as physical pairs, not merely optical pairs as seen from Earth. This began Homo sapiens binary star astronomy.

Presumably, we agree with these observations, 221?

Yes, I have checked our databases. 221 considered there was little unknown to the Intelligence about the behaviour of significant objects within the galaxy.

We appreciate a remarkable achievement.

A foundation for others to build upon, but there are further accomplishments.

During his stellar searches, in 1781 CE, Herschel identified another object, which was reported to fellow astronomers. After further observation of its motion, it was determined to be a planet, orbiting beyond Saturn, later named Uranus. An exchange of data between 221 and the Intelligence confirmed the body's identity. The first planetary discovery in 3 kyE greatly enhanced Herschel's reputation. He was elected to the Royal Society and received grants to fund research and construct larger telescopes. In 1787 CE, he identified two moons of Uranus, later named Oberon and Titania.

His international status as an astronomer enabled Herschel to prosper as a telescope supplier. I estimate that he sold 60 telescopes, and many more reflecting mirrors, a reliable revenue stream, because of oxidation.

The capacity of this species to convert knowledge to commercial advantage continues to fascinate us. This seems to happen opportunistically, rather than through any larger plan. Galileo generated an income from telescope sales, so it should be no surprise that Herschel did the same. He has gone further, with a spare parts business.

221 wondered whether the Energy Masters objected to the Homo sapiens trading instincts.

It is not that we disapprove. At one level, we wonder whether this was a worthy use of Herschel's time, after proving to be an exceptional astronomer. At another level, we see a mechanism to allocate resources to Herschel, enabling him to improve his research. Probably Smith could explain this better. At a third level, we see a process through which technology was shared, and the research base is expanded.

They have thought about this, 221 perceived. Very different from other experiences over a long period in a sizeable galaxy.

Newton developed this technology, but Herschel modified it. He removed the tilted secondary viewing mirror in Newton's design and adjusted the position of the primary mirror to view the image directly. This eliminated one source of attenuation. Herschel also produced larger mirrors, capable of gathering more light. Newton worked with mirror diameters of 33 mm initially, up to about 75 mm. Along with his astronomy, Herschel improved the mirror casting, grinding, and polishing processes. I estimate that he and his colleagues produced >400 useful mirrors, and many defective ones during their experimentation.

What mirror sizes did he achieve, 221?

Between 150 to 1200 mm diameter, with most at the lower end of the range. In my opinion, the performance of the mirror alloy, which had barely changed in the 0.12 kyE since Newton's first telescope, was a constraint.

His largest telescope, funded by the King, of 1260 mm diameter, became available in 1789 CE but produced results that Herschel regarded as disappointing. Despite this, he discovered two moons of Saturn, named Mimas and Enceladus. Another rapid data exchange identified the objects.

It would be easier if the client applied a numbering system, 221, but we have already discussed this point. Maybe dissatisfied with the telescope, but his achievement was excellent. Mimas has a diameter of 396 km, and Enceladus of 504 km. Mimas is 22% closer to the planet, making it harder to observe. Both are a mean distance of about 1.272×10^9 km from Earth.

There are closer satellites, yet to be found by the client.

221 considered that the most significant influence of this telescope was not scientific but social, generating great interest and enthusiasm for research. This would create more scientists and attract funding.

Do we have more to learn from Herschel, 221? You know we have a great enthusiasm for astronomy but limited time. What do you recommend?

I will concentrate on the key points. Of particular importance was Herschel's discovery of infrared radiation in 1800 CE. By shining sunlight through a prism and checking the temperature beyond the red end of the spectrum, he noted an increase. He concluded that there must be another form of radiation outside the visible range. Homo sapiens radio astronomy followed from this discovery. Other scientists would have identified the effect, but Herschel was the first.

We regard this as a breakthrough, 221. Much of what we know of the universe, and even the limited amount learned by the client, has been uncovered with information gathered outside their visible spectrum. A temporal node.

He was the first to use the term 'asteroid' to describe this class of bodies, which became the accepted description over the next 0.05 kyE.

There is another point that we should note.

A discovery or invention, 221?

No, his sister, Caroline Herschel, who worked with him for many years. She has been characterised as Herschel's assistant, but she made discoveries of her own, including comets and previously unidentified stars. Her work was formally recognised by the astronomical community. For her support to Herschel, she was given an annual salary by the King, the first paid female astronomer.

Excellent, 221, so now we have a second female scientist. Discussion of this aspect with Jimbo was illuminating, but now there is evidence of progress.

Not the first female to become a scientist, but widely known. Caroline was the first that I met in Great Britain.

You have not explained your involvement with the Herschel family. We know from your reports that several Insertions were made.

I met him at the Bath Philosophical Society in 1779 CE. By this time, there were many such societies, where those interested in the sciences would meet, typically to hear a speaker introduce a particular subject. Such presentations were often open to the public; for me, it was a means of tracking progress and aspiring scientists. I think Herschel used these gatherings to enhance his knowledge and widen his circle of contacts.

Several years later, after his discovery of Uranus, I was employed in his workshop, producing mirrors and manufacturing telescopes for Herschel's customers. Of course, I met Herschel again in 1793 CE, when I sold him one of Michell's telescopes.

What can we learn from this man, 221?

He was a serious scientist, but also ambitious and anxious to achieve a respected social position. His formal education was limited, so he worried that his mathematical skills were inadequate for an astronomer. When we made mirrors together, I surprised him with my mathematics, which seemed advanced for an instrument-maker. My conclusion is that in this period, towards the end of the Enlightenment, hard work could be sufficient. Later, as scientific knowledge expanded, education became essential.

With a small knowledge base, there was less to know, and much to discover. As erudition accumulated, researchers needed to learn more, to advance the work of predecessors.

I have observed that this species compensates for their own perceived limitations by helping their children. His son, John Herschel, born in 1792 in the region of Buckinghamshire, benefited from education at Cambridge University, building his own distinguished scientific career. By 1820 CE, he had assembled a 460 mm reflecting telescope and was re-examining the binary stars identified by his father. Later, he received awards from the Royal Society for his research.

Initially at Cambridge, and subsequently, Herschel developed an association with Charles Babbage, another distinguished English philosopher, described as the Father of the Computer. Babbage was an accomplished mathematician and engineer, and designed the first programmable computer.

This precedes the *Homo sapiens* invention of digital electronic systems, 221?

Yes, this was a mechanical machine, but with an architecture emulated in electronic computer designs.

Babbage is absent from your schedule, but surely is a scholar we must meet.

221 reflected that omitting Babbage was a mistake, but his residual time allocation could not accommodate schedule changes. He featured strongly in his reports of the era, already filed with the Intelligence.

There is more to learn from John Herschel. His accomplishments seem of similar value to those of his father.

His treatise, A Preliminary Discourse on the study of natural philosophy, published in 1831 CE was influential in defining the relationship between observation and theorising within a scientific investigation. He described the difficulty in discerning natural laws and advocated finding single, unifying reasons for phenomena. This notion guided his contemporaries.

He spent 0.005 kyE in southern Africa, conducting astronomy for a star catalogue to complement that of the northern skies, compiled by his father. From the area around the Cape of Good Hope, he observed the return of Halley's Comet in 1835 CE. While on his African sojourn, Herschel acquired botanical interests. Both he and his wife sketched the Cape flora, drawings that were later published. He read widely and contemplated anthropology, evolution, and extinction. In 1836 CE, during a Royal Navy visit to Cape Town by HMS Beagle, Herschel met the officers and a naturalist named Darwin, who we will meet soon.

After returning to Great Britain, Herschel made major contributions to photographic research and the first to use the term 'photography', I believe. His findings were presented to the Royal Society around 1840 CE.

You knew John Herschel?

I first met him when he was quite young, in 1793 CE, after the sale of Michell's telescope to his father.

This would have been too early to discern the talents of even the most precocious *Homo sapiens*, we believe.

Later, I regularly obtained invitations to scientific forums at the Royal Society and heard Herschel's astronomical and photographic lectures. He was a respected scientist, so his talks were admired. Invariably well-prepared but disinclined to provide entertainment. I remember him responding to questions meticulously and making notes for further research. Unfortunately, I did not have an opportunity to work with him. His eminence occasioned burial in

Westminster Abbey, a distinction accorded by the Britons to few scientists, such as Newton. Credited with a 154 km lunar crater, too.

0.083 kyE after John Herschel's burial, a stone inscribed in Latin, originally written by a Provost of Eton College named Joseph Goodall for his father's gravestone, was laid in memory of William Herschel:

"*he broke through the confines of the heavens.*"

A remarkable story, 221, from another gifted family. The younger Herschel is a polymath, with interests encompassing astronomy, botany, and mathematics.

We should continue exploring mathematical insights from this era. Time is becoming short, so I will briefly introduce the work of several scholars.

We should identify major achievements and proceed with less discussion.

221 considered this was his intent, although unsuccessful, throughout the review, which now amounted to 69 seconds, excluding outages.

Σ69 seconds

Joseph-Louis Lagrange

We will travel to mainland Europe to meet the Italian philosopher, Lagrange, born 1736 CE, in what is now Italy, but who did much of his work in Berlin, and later, Paris. From a prosperous family, his parents planned a law career for him. He studied at Turin University, enjoying the classical curriculum until a paper written by Halley caught his imagination.

Lagrange rapidly became an accomplished mathematician, largely through personal study, and by the age of 0.02 kyE was teaching at a military academy. In cooperation with the distinguished Swiss scholar, Leonhard Euler, he developed generalised differential equations, which can be solved to provide values at which a function is stationary.

We have your reports, 221. Lagrange had an aptitude for calculus. No need to discuss the details further.

Over the next 0.01 kyE, while still in Turin, he published dissertations addressing both physical and mathematical questions. These include the propagation of sound, advancing the ideas of Newton, and a generic solution to the curved shape of a string undergoing transverse vibration.

We were expecting to learn that Lagrange shared Herschel's musical interests, 221. Propagation of sound arising from vibrating strings is surely what an orchestra provides?

My knowledge of Lagrange at this time is limited, but his subject was physics, not music. Had the Energy Masters been serious, or was this another witticism?

Why does this species make music, but nobody else in our galaxy? A question for another time, 221. Let us learn more about Lagrange. We note that although young, he was already prolific.

His interests included probability theory.

~ 221, you are aware that the normal distribution is a tool we commonly use, and often the first such method students learn. I'm ignorant about elsewhere but on Earth this distribution, or approximations to it, occurs in many situations.

=> *Yes, Jimbo, normally distributed phenomena exist across our galaxy, too.*

He had other achievements around this time, including an analysis of why the Moon always shows the same surface to Earth.

We know this to be approximately true, 221, but please continue.

Lagrange adapted an idea then known as the principle of least action, used by Galileo, Descartes, and Huygens in static situations, to a dynamic state.

~ 221, this is an equilibrium problem, isn't it?

=> *Basically, yes, but more complicated in a non-static situation. The Moon is in synchronous rotation with Earth because its axial rotation is the same as its orbital period. Gravitational locking is the term for this. Over the multiple 10^3 kyE, the Moon has interacted with Earth's gravity, energy exchanged between the bodies, and heat dissipated. Once there was no further change in the Moon's rotation rate during an orbit, it is locked. To undo this equilibrium state would require a net energy input from somewhere, such as a third object.*

~ To an engineer, this seems like a torque question.

=> *Very good, Jimbo. You are correct, but this is not obvious. When the Moon's frequency of rotation exceeded its orbital frequency, a counteracting torque arose, gradually synchronising these frequencies. My initial description was of an energy balance, while you have recognised the forces involved. The result is that you see only one side of the Moon. Or until 0.037 kyE ago, when your Luna 3 satellite reached the far side.*

221, we have been enjoying the celestial mechanics tutorial, although we agreed to proceed more quickly. However, this is difficult because there is a detail that you omitted. Since the Moon's orbit is slightly elliptical, and through parallax, Jimbo should see 59% of its surface, but not concurrently.

~ I was thinking about Herschel's investigation of binary stars. Although it would have been impossible for him to observe, probably some of these bodies are also gravitationally locked. Do you agree?

=> *In some cases, Jimbo, depending on the relative masses and distances between the objects. This can be calculated. You need these parameters, and others, and the gravitational constant, G. Newton and Cavendish contributed here, as we learned.*

221 realised that he, the Energy Masters, and Jimbo had been absorbed by the 0.4 seconds of discussion, but they should learn more of Lagrange.

Another achievement was to provide a generalised solution to the 'problem of three bodies' examined in Newton's Principia in 1687 CE, and by Clairaut in 1750 CE, and later by Euler.

We have the impression from your reports that Euler deserves more time.

There are many philosophers whom we have omitted because of our allocation. Euler is one. His work regarding perfect numbers, which Alhazen had considered 0.6 kyE before, is an example of his scholarship. Compressing 100 kyE of Homo sapiens history into 100 seconds was tough.

Returning to Lagrange, using differential equations, he derived two classes of solution for three bodies of any mass. In one case the bodies lie along a rotating straight line, and in the other they tend to the vertices of a rotating equilateral triangle.

This is a complex question, and the behaviour can be considered chaotic. A close study of *Principia* suggests that Newton understood this. Our approach to such questions is numerical, using our computational capacity

Lagrange spent about 0.02 kyE in Berlin, addressing algebra, number theory, and geometry. He examined astronomical questions, including the stability of planetary orbits.

His most notable product, Mécanique Analytique, utilised calculus to derive the principles governing the mechanics of solids and fluids. 221 remembered a lecture given by Lagrange; he described mechanics as a branch of mathematics, analogous to geometry, but with a fourth dimension, time. Mécanique was published in 1788 CE after he relocated to Paris.

His time in France coincided with the French Revolution, a period of upheaval. Despite this, he continued to be productive. He also led a committee established to reform the system of weights and measures, and can be credited with designating the kilogram and metre, and their decimal multipliers and subdivisions, as fundamental units.

~ The metric units we use in our studies can be attributed to Lagrange?
=> *To him and his colleagues.*
~ Jimbo knew from browsing older textbooks, and American sources, that non-metric alternatives were cumbersome, with constants and conversion factors absent from the metric system. He felt appreciative of Lagrange.

We find Lagrange a gifted mathematician but hesitate to use too many superlatives, because of an expectation that you have more talent to introduce.
221 knew the Energy Masters had read his reports.
This is a period rich in European mathematicians, who provided ideas and methods used ever since, building on insights of predecessors. Lagrange described Newton as the greatest genius who ever lived. Recognised by the Royal Society and the Royal Society of Edinburgh, or RSE.

In preparing Mécanique, Lagrange received support from several contemporaries. I will introduce two of them.

Adrien-Marie Legendre

Legendre was born in Paris, in 1752 CE. He studied mathematics and physics, and in 1782 CE came to prominence for his work on the behaviour of projectiles in resistive media.
Presumably this has some military relevance, 221?
Inevitably, but as we have seen, these impulses have accelerated scientific advances on Earth, often to peaceable ends.

He contributed to classical mechanics, building on the work of Lagrange, and number theory. A widely used Homo sapiens tool is regression analysis, used to examine the relationship between a population of scalar responses and input variables. Simplest is linear regression, with only one input variable, but more complicated multi-variate situations are modelled using multiple regression methods. These are generally based on the concept of least-squares, developed by Legendre. The client applies this to scientific, engineering, medical and economic questions.

~ I know these methods, 221. In my spare time I've been building an estimating tool for my father's business, correlating critical component parameters with the cost of manufacture. This could speed up the pricing process, by reducing the analysis.
=> *Does it work, Jimbo?*
~ It has some predictive power, but I need more data to improve it.
=> *Your father must be anxious to receive your model.*
~ Not really. Costing and pricing are sensitive processes, which he prefers to do using traditional methods: a pen and paper, and a cup of coffee.

In 1787 CE, Legendre met William Herschel in England, together with two French astronomers. 221 recalled their visit to the workshop. Herschel described his plans for a 1260 mm instrument, which excited the astronomers. He remembered that Legendre was interested in the profile of the mirrors. His connections with the British were strengthened in 1789 CE when he was elected to the Royal Society.

Legendre's work, Éléments de géométrie, completed in 1794 CE, was a revision to Euclid's Elements, written about 2 kyE before, providing a textbook. 221 remembered sitting as a student, listening to Euclid's teachings, a benchmark for Homo sapiens geometry over generations. He recalled the modest Euclid crediting earlier thinkers within his work.

Pierre-Simon Laplace

The second of Lagrange's contemporaries was Laplace, born in the French region of Normandy, in 1749 CE. He was a mathematician and an astronomer.
Summarise his astronomical contributions, 221.

There are many, but Mécanique Celeste, which is a five-volume work, was progressively published from 1799 CE, containing much of his analyses. Building on Newton's work, Laplace provides methods for calculating the motion of planets and considers tides.

We note that he was relatively old compared to the prodigies we met earlier. Was he a slow beginner?

Not really, we have started with the finale of his astronomical input, but much preceded it. His dynamic theory of tides was produced in 1775 CE, describing observable tides, considering factors such as friction and resonance. This work, together with much else, is contained in the work.

We have re-read it, 221, and now understand.

He analysed the orbital consonance of Jupiter and Saturn, which from observation was erratic, with Jupiter's orbit shrinking and Saturn's increasing. Euler and Lagrange had each examined this question inconclusively. By applying Newtonian principles and including the smaller terms from the equations of motion, Laplace proved that the two planets and the Sun are in equilibrium. The general stability of the wider solar system was investigated by later scientists, extending Laplace's analysis.

We appreciate his mathematical thinking, 221. With our observational advantages and computational resources, we can say that Laplace is approximately correct, but there remains an element of chaotic motion in this system's behaviour. Fortunately for Earth and its inhabitants, this chaos seems to be within limits, so stability pertains.

He pondered the existence of what the client calls black holes, bodies so massive that even light cannot escape. Michell had considered this possibility slightly earlier, but Laplace developed his ideas independently. These two philosophers were far ahead of contemporary scientific thought.

A scholar who worked with Laplace early in his career was Antoine Lavoisier, a distinguished French chemist. Although not accommodated within my schedule, we should note his presence here. They jointly studied kinetic energy as it applies to molecular behaviour, and investigated specific heat capacities and thermal expansion. In 1783 CE they published a paper, Memoir on Heat. This is a small part of Lavoisier's overall contribution. 221 recalled Hooke's insight, 0.1 kyE earlier, that heat indicates the speed of movement of particles within a material.

We will return to France to learn more about thermodynamics but should consider Laplace's mathematics. I never worked with him but attended several lectures. Although his methods were innovative and have endured, I believe that they were tools he devised to address specific questions, such as planetary motion. Like Newton, who applied calculus to solve physical problems, as opposed to Leibniz, whose approach designed a branch of mathematics.

His name is synonymous with the Laplace transform, known to Homo sapiens science and engineering students. Differential equations are converted to polynomials, which are usually easier to solve. An inverse transformation can then be applied, reverting to the starting domain. 221 conferred with the Energy Masters on the method.

We wonder whether we have lost the cleverness exhibited by Laplace, because our computational power enables us to solve such questions numerically, without needing transformations. Perhaps we have become lazy?

In Laplace's day, computational power was confined to the scientist's brain.

Examining this client imparts new ideas or reminds us of old ones. We will study your reports on Laplace transforms further. Please continue.

A valuable insight was the central limit theorem, related to probability theory. We learned of Legendre's development of the least-squares concept, which Laplace and the philosopher, Carl Gauss, linked to probability.

Is Gauss another scientist we cannot meet, 221?

No, I have scheduled his contributions. By this point, the scientific base was expanding, so we find scientists working on related subjects simultaneously and sharing ideas through published papers.

What is the central limit theorem?

It is contained within Laplace's treatise, published in 1812 CE, although he did not use this term. The theorem demonstrates that for a population with an unknown distribution, sample means will tend towards a normal distribution, even if the original variables are not normally distributed. He revealed this surprising idea using the transformation process devised by the mathematician, Joseph Fourier.

Will we meet Fourier?

He is not scheduled within our review. Apart from mathematics, he advanced the Homo sapiens understanding of heat. 221 possessed simulations indicating Fourier's work was influential, contributing important methods for later research, but omitted its examination because of time constraints.

We rely on your judgement, 221, and have your lucid reports. We understand that Fourier Transforms can remove noise from information and identify patterns. Probably essential tools for the client's electromagnetic future.

221 was anxious to describe Laplace's theorem.

What does it mean for the work of researchers?

If successive samples are taken from a larger population and the sample mean values are calculated, then it can be expected that these values will be normally distributed. From this, researchers can make inferences about the total population. An application was astronomy, where it could be applied to sets of observations tracking the motion of a constellation that inevitably contain some degree of error.

There must be constraints?

The samples must be taken randomly and be independent of each other. The sample size must be sufficiently large.

We assume therefore that Laplace discovered the normal distribution.

Not entirely. Work by Gauss in 1809 CE, which Laplace knew of, implied its existence and his theorem justified its use, but they were not the first.

In 1733 CE, I remember the French mathematician, Abraham de Moivre, applying the normal distribution to games of chance and coin tossing.

We did not meet de Moivre, 221, but the files indicate you observed his work.

He escaped to England around 1687 CE, because of religious persecution.

The energy expended on supernatural beliefs still surprises us, 221, particularly as their science is advancing more rapidly than simulations predict.

He came to my attention later because of friendships with Newton and Halley. I recall his election to the Royal Society in 1697 CE. De Moivre had studied existing ideas on probability, such as the work of Huygens, and published a book, The Doctrine of Chances, in 1711 CE, which became popular with gamblers. Subsequent editions, in 1738 CE and later, included an approximation to the binomial distribution later known as the normal distribution. I believe that Laplace and Gauss acquired their grasp of the normal curve separately from de Moivre, but he deserves recognition for his earlier insights.

I should add that with encouragement from Halley, astronomy became another interest pursued by de Moivre with distinction, but we must conclude our discussion of Laplace

We suspect that your time allocation is insufficient. Should we have given you a larger budget?

Perhaps, but the same limitations would have arisen, just slightly later. Scientific research has expanded rapidly, so we cannot contain it within any reasonable budget. Even 200 seconds would be insufficient to address every significant philosopher in each domain. Note that we have found little time for biology, or medicine, or the other applied sciences that were emerging. My choices have been based on the temporal nodes, significant events that our simulations recommend as decisive in the client's scientific evolution.

~ You are providing a pencil sketch, not an oil painting.

=> A helpful analogy, Jimbo, but we would need to make a movie. Your species is quite different from a few billion microbes, living inside a mountain of frozen hydrocarbons below 100 K on an obscure moon, that have organised themselves to perform intricate calculations, each taking 10 kyE. The Intelligence has employed these microbial lifeforms in background mathematical operations. Given their slow metabolisms, this is a short duration. For significant number crunching, maybe 10^2 kyE would be needed. The same period he had been observing Homo sapiens development. The Energy Masters appreciated the problem.

Returning to Laplace and the central limit theorem, there are points to recognise. One is that it provides a rationale for applying the normal distribution to samples in controlled experiments. Another is that it gives an insight into the prevalence of the normal distribution in nature. Note that 'normal distribution' is a modern term, not used by Laplace or Gauss.

Σ73 seconds

John Dalton

Before further consideration of statistical insights, I recommend we follow Laplace's interest in the behaviour of gases by examining the research of Dalton, born in 1766 CE, in north-west England. His life was humble, partly because of the modest social background of his parents, but particularly because of their religious beliefs, which he adopted. As a Quaker, a form of Christian belief, his principles included simplicity, peace, and respect for the natural environment, and eschewed excessive consumption or flamboyance.

An attractive set of values, 221, consistent with the Intelligence, we believe.

From an early age, he worked, but received education from his father and a fellow Quaker. When aged 0.015 kyE, he joined his brother in running a nearby school, and accumulated scientific knowledge, partly through informal lessons with a local scholar. It seems that his spiritual beliefs prevented university attendance. This is difficult for me to explain but is consistent with the strong religious forces present in Homo sapiens history.

No need, 221. We have your reports and are accustomed to irrational beliefs obstructing scientific progress within this civilisation. Only 0.9 seconds ago, you described de Moivre's move to England because of prejudice. Judging by their progress, it seems that science is prevailing.

Dalton obtained employment as a teacher of mathematics and science at an academy in Manchester in 1793 CE and worked there until aged 0.034 kyE.

We can already perceive an impressive scholar, 221. Informally and self-educated but teaching while young. His progress is comparable with other philosophers we met, who received a university education.

After this, he became a private tutor, devoting time to research.

Meteorology interested Dalton, so he maintained a related diary for much of his life. In 1793 CE, he published his observations, which attracted little comment. Before this, he identified a phenomenon relating to atmospheric circulation that he realised was the re-discovery of a postulate by George Hadley, an earlier English meteorologist, known as the Hadley Cell. Although itself an incomplete explanation, Hadley had been dissatisfied by Halley's earlier theory of wind flows and included the effect of the planet's rotation.

We did not meet Hadley, 221. Should we have considered his work?

I knew of his contributions through the Royal Society, but his theory was superseded, so our simulations do not suggest it necessary.

The reports indicate that you knew Dalton from early in his career.

He gave solutions to mathematical puzzles and answered philosophical questions in the popular press. This came to my attention, so I got to know him.

Very resourceful, 221. How did you achieve this?

Dalton originated from a hilly region, still known in England as the Lake District. In an era before the client had invented flying machines, atmospheric measurements required ascent above sea level, so his interest obliged him to climb the local hills. He made topological estimates using the change in barometric pressure and became an authority on the heights of local mountains.

He followed the methods of Pascal, which you described so clearly, but was doing the opposite. Pascal utilised a known altitude to estimate pressure variation, but Dalton used the pressure difference to determine altitude. You have still not explained how you became acquainted with Dalton.

By volunteering to make measurements, or just carry instruments. This was physically harder than assisting Pascal because the weather was often inclement, so a volunteer available in any conditions was welcome. He had another helper called Otley, his closest companion.

His most important work came later. I heard his talks to the Manchester Literary & Philosophical Society in 1801 CE, in which he described experiments with gases. My advantage was that I had observed some of his research by acting as an unpaid laboratory assistant and was invited to attend when he lectured. He was a meticulous experimenter, an exemplar of the scientific method. His techniques were later criticised by Davy, but I disagree.

Who is Davy? You mentioned him before.

We will meet him next.

Dalton's equipment was not the best, usually for reasons of cost, but it was well-maintained and could deliver repeatable results.

He was fortunate to have such a skilled assistant, 221. No doubt your instrument-making experience proved helpful.

The conclusions that Dalton reached became known as Gay-Lussac's law, named after the French scientist.

=> *You are familiar with this principle, I assume, Jimbo?*

~ The pressure of a given mass of gas varies directly with its absolute temperature, at a constant volume, and can be represented as $P \propto T$.

Is Gay-Lussac on our agenda, 221?

No. Several researchers were working in this area, but his contributions warrant further study when time permits. He may have been first to demonstrate that water consists of two parts hydrogen and one of oxygen. This compound is essential to Homo sapiens existence.

Has the client deduced the source of their water yet, 221?

As a theory, but without proof. Present-day telescopes permit them to see much further and analyse the chemical composition of celestial bodies. Asteroids

~ Are you saying that the Earth's water came from asteroids?

=> Probably you have not considered this question, Jimbo, but like many solid planets, Earth was hot initially. Too hot for water to exist. It arrived later. Your astrophysics colleagues at university learn these ideas.

~ Stephanie studies this field. He would ask her.

Our simulations project that Homo sapiens researchers will land probes on asteroids within 0.025 kyE to obtain soil samples, which will confirm the theory. Within 0.05 kyE they will be mining rare metals from asteroids using robots, and after 0.1 kyE will have automated refineries at sites, delivering purer materials.

So fast, 221. Do you believe this projection?

We have seen their progress over the recent 10^2 kyE, so why not? Thanks to scientists such as Dalton and Gay-Lussac, their fundamental knowledge and technology are advancing extraordinarily. They will find opportunities to make this a profitable venture.

Dalton elaborated the relationship between volume and temperature, also researched by Gay-Lussac. This principle is known as Charles's law, because of earlier but unpublished work by Jacques Charles, perhaps 0.02 kyE before. The contributions of Charles only became known to me after Dalton's experiments.

~ The formulation of this law is that if the gas pressure is constant, the absolute temperature and volume will be in direct proportion, or $V \propto T$. These two laws relate to a notional ideal gas, but this is reasonable in many situations.

=> Correct, Jimbo. We will return to this aspect.

An insight that Dalton provided relates to gaseous mixtures, such as air. He demonstrated that the total pressure applied is equal to the aggregate of the partial pressures of the component gases. This is Dalton's law.

The client has made rapid progress in understanding the nature of gases, 221. It was only 0.14 kyE before that Boyle hypothesised $P \propto 1/V$, and more recently that Newton considered this phenomenon mathematically in *Principia*.

Mining asteroids in 0.05 kyE is within the capabilities of the species. We should examine Dalton's other work.

His ideas on atomic theory, stimulated by the gas research, might be his most memorable contribution. Although he was not the first to postulate the existence of atoms, he devised a method for calculating the comparative atomic weights of various elements. I heard him present a paper in 1805 CE, again in Manchester.

His theory encompassed the idea that small particles, atoms, are the constituents of elements, and that for any given element the properties of the atoms are identical. A different element will consist of atoms with differing but consistent properties.

What would be such a property, 221?

Mass was most interesting to Dalton, as he considered atomic weights.

He theorised that atoms are the basic unit of matter, and cannot be created, or subdivided. Additionally, in chemical reactions, atoms are reorganised through combination or separation, and chemical compounds consist of whole number ratios of different atoms. His conclusions provided an imperfect picture of atomic theory, but the concepts were a basis for subsequent research.

How did he formulate these propositions, 221?

He synthesised his observations of nature, both the meteorological aspects and his gas experiments, and pondered how matter might be arranged for such results to arise. This was abstract intellectual endeavour, similar to the approach of other notable Homo sapiens philosophers.

Dalton compiled a table of relative atomic weights, initially with six elements, and expressed their respective weights as multiples of hydrogen, which was defined as one. His New System of Chemical Philosophy, published in 1808 CE, detailed the relative weights of 20 atoms and certain molecules found in chemical compounds. While the client's knowledge of this area has multiplied since, Dalton's research was recognised in the unit of atomic mass, Da, the dalton, defined as $1/12$ of the mass of a grounded carbon-12 atom at rest.

In local units, we can say that $1 \text{ Da} \approx 1.66 \times 10^{-27} \text{kg}$.

A good approximation.

To conclude our consideration of Dalton, we should note his optical studies. Earlier in his career, he researched colour blindness, from which he suffered.

What is this, 221?

A deficiency in colour perception that affects about 4.5% of the species population. It is 16x more common in the male than the female.

Dalton was a scientist who overcame social disadvantages to earn a reputation as an accomplished researcher, with valuable achievements.

Hooke came from modest circumstances, but obtained a university education, while Newcomen and Watt were self-taught, from my observations. Dalton is an extreme example, both poor and largely self-educated. He was elected to the Royal Society in 1822 CE. Recognised with a lunar crater of 60 km diameter. Later he taught James Joule, a scientist whom we shall soon meet.

Humphry Davy

Now, we can meet Davy, another scientist of modest origins, born in 1778 CE, in the south-west of England, in Cornwall. As a young man, his mentor was a Quaker, like Dalton. We can regard him as a chemist, but Davy's interests included physics and engineering.

Throughout his life, he wrote poetry.

Is this point relevant, 221? Like music, no other civilisation in the galaxy composes rhyming verses from their language.

I have observed these beings composing and performing music and poetry since they acquired languages. Some exhibit talent for constructing or enacting pieces, but most derive pleasure from listening. Analysis suggests mathematical correlations exist with music, but this is not how it is designed. Davy's poetic nature is probably indicative of high intelligence, but this is not invariably true.

Hard to comprehend an activity that absorbs time and resources but provides no tangible benefit. This species possesses peculiarities that remain perplexing, but the cumulative performance appears unique.

221 pondered his evolving opinion that the Homo sapiens brain might be the most complex machine in the galaxy. Now he understood Jimbo's distinction between complex and complicated. Harrison's intricate watches were complicated but could be rebuilt with care, but asteroids interacting with planets, where it is impossible to deduce the starting condition, exhibit complexity. We must return to Davy.

He received a school education and, aged about 0.017 kyE, entered an apprenticeship with a local surgeon, working in the pharmacy and studying chemistry. He immediately became an experimentalist. By 1797 CE, he had learned the French language and read Lavoisier's work. During this period, he received tuition in chemistry from the son of James Watt, named Gregory, introduced 9 seconds ago. Through him, he obtained employment as a laboratory supervisor in the city of Bristol, researching the medical applications of gases.

Until then Davy had aspired to a medical career, with study in Edinburgh planned, but became absorbed in his gaseous research. This included investigating the medicinal properties of 'laughing gas', as the client colloquially describes it.

Why this name, 221?

The substance is nitrous oxide, or N_2O in the local nomenclature. It has been used by therapists in medical or dental procedures because it reduces pain and anxiety. Feelings of euphoria, and therefore laughter, are also engendered in the species by the release of dopamine. James Watt became interested in Davy's N_2O research and was a frequent visitor.

Between his gas experiments, Davy also researched 'galvanism', a technical term that is rarely used in the present-day.

~ This is a new term to me, 221, but I have heard of galvanic protection.

=> *They both refer to the application of electric currents emanating from chemical reactions. Its relevance to Davy was the use of currents in medical therapy. Galvani was an Italian researcher who demonstrated that the leg of a deceased frog could be made to twitch by an electric current. Observers speculated that life might be created or re-commenced.*

~ Just like Frankenstein?

=> *221 felt the discussion was drifting.*

In 1801 CE Davy was interviewed at the Ri by a committee including Cavendish and appointed to a post encompassing chemistry lectures, laboratory supervision, and journal editing. I was present at Davy's first presentation on galvanism, which was well-received. Successive events attracted ever more interest. Davy was no mere lecturer, but more akin to a performer. Hundreds squeezed into the auditorium to witness the show.

~ Jimbo appreciated the front-row seat that 221 possessed in the hall and wondered how this was possible with such a large crowd, all demanding a better view. He soon realised that 221 was assisting with the equipment used in the lecture. Davy was a percussive presenter, inviting spectators to assist in noisy experiments. Some received a small electric shock, provoking laughter. At times, he spoke loudly, then quietly to gain attention, when making a scientific point.

He stressed that his research was uncovering his god's design, which appealed to the females, who nodded solemnly.

221 remembered attending the congested lectures given by Adam Smith and Joseph Black in Edinburgh, 0.05 kyE before. Davy's performances were similar, but bigger and noisier, with noticeably more females present.

A good story, 221, but after 0.9 seconds we have not learned of Davy's scientific revelations. What are you going to tell us?

In 1802 CE, Davy introduced the incandescent light, demonstrated with a primitive electric battery during a lecture at the Ri, using a platinum filament.

This invention, his high public profile, and widespread popularity enabled his election to the Royal Society in 1804 CE. 221 recalled that the botanist Joseph Banks had been President.

Will we meet Banks?

Unfortunately, not. He travelled, promoting international scientific cooperation, but our simulations do not indicate this was critical to Homo sapiens development.

In 1806 CE Davy presented a more powerful light to the Royal Society, using an electric arc between two electrodes.

Inventiveness is evident here, 221. Before this, the client used candles or oil lamps for illumination?

Generally, within buildings, but gas streetlights were being introduced.

Davy's contributions included the isolation of several elements, principally through electrolysis. The first was potassium in 1807 CE, and shortly afterwards, sodium. Note that these metals are designated K and Na in the local chemistry nomenclature. An exchange of data between 221 and the Intelligence ensued, confirming their identities. In 1808 CE Davy advised the Royal Society that he had isolated four more elements, barium, calcium, strontium and magnesium, designated Ba, Ca, Sr and Mg respectively.

Chlorine had been identified in 1774 CE by the Swedish chemist, Scheele, but not isolated as a discrete element. In 1809 CE, Gay-Lussac tried unsuccessfully to decompose compounds containing chlorine, but in 1810 CE, Davy confirmed that chlorine was an element, designated Cl.

~ You know that sodium chloride, or salt as we commonly call it, has been a valuable commodity here for a long time, used in food preparation and diluted in water at health resorts or spas? I recently learned about salt mining, while visiting Worcestershire with my parents.

=> 221 remembered Londinium, and the practice of the Roman soldiers, who received part of their payment in salt, to barter it at markets for beer and fresh food. The sweet smell of beer, the odour of caged animals, and smouldering remnants of grilled meat was unforgettable. While the Roman officials and traders preferred Mediterranean wine, the soldiers enjoyed the weaker native beer, which they drank copiously. He knew their source of the commoditised salt was a Roman settlement named Salinae, or Salt-Works, and recalled its location at present-day Droitwich.

In 1812 CE, Davy was injured while experimenting with nitrogen trichloride, or NCl_3, and consequently needed an assistant. He appointed Michael Faraday, who became a renowned scientist.

Can we assume that he is going to be introduced to us, 221?

Yes, he is on the agenda.

Despite his contributions to chemistry, he is remembered by the British for his invention in 1815 CE of the Davy lamp, which was a safety device for use in flammable atmospheres such as mines. The lamp had two functions, providing illumination in an environment where explosions or asphyxiation were possible, but also indicating the presence of methane.

By methane, we understand you are referring to CH_4? Your earlier reports indicate that it was identified in 1778 CE, by the scientist, Alessandro Volta.

Unfortunately, Volta is not included in our itinerary, but he also researched electrical phenomena.

We may need to consider Volta later, but please continue with the description of the Davy lamp.

The lamp consists of a wick, with the flame enclosed within a mesh screen.

What is a wick, 221? How does the flame burn?

A wick is simply a string of braided cloth or vegetable matter, consisting of fibres twisted into a single strand. The liquid fuel, in this case, vegetable oil, is conveyed by capillary action along the wick to supply the flame at the tip.

The wick and fuel are both vegetable matter, and the fuel delivery applies a physical principle. No need for pumps and power supplies. Elegant.

221 was surprised by the interest shown by the Energy Masters in what seemed a straightforward concept but reflected on the cleverness of Davy's design. A mesh screen acts as a flame-arrestor, enabling air to support continued combustion, but prevents the flame from reaching the external environment and igniting any explosive methane-air mixture or coal dust present.

What is the principle, 221?

The mesh absorbs heat from any flame travelling away from the source, in this case the burning wick, lowering the flammable mixture below its auto-ignition temperature, extinguishing the flame front. Aperture size varies with flammability. In this application, fine mesh is required. A critical aspect is maintenance since damage to the mesh compromises its functionality.

We still have difficulty with the concept, 221. Even if the risk of explosions can be removed, a methane-rich atmosphere is incompatible with *Homo sapiens* physiology. Subterranean cavities on Earth are susceptible to the accumulation of other gases such as CO_2, according to our analysis. How did Davy's lamp help in these circumstances?

The behaviour of the flame provided a warning to the miners. CO_2 is heavier than air, with a density, at normal temperature and pressure, of 1.8 kg/m³ compared to 1.2 kg/m³ for the combined gases that constitute air, so it accumulates at lower levels in a mine. If such a pocket exists, then the flame will be extinguished because of the low oxygen content. Those present can avoid these pockets. Other asphyxiant gases, such as carbon monoxide, with a density close to air, also extinguish the flame. Methane content generates a blue flame, warning the miners of a hazard nearby.

This therefore eliminated related fatalities from British mines?

Not completely, but it helped. The risk posed by damaged lamps was one issue. Another was the degraded performance of the flame-arrestor in rapid air flows. I believe the later introduction of improved ventilation had a greater effect, and subsequently the use of electric arc lighting. Davy was a leader in developing arc lighting, as I outlined 0.9 seconds ago.

Davy's career continued to attract public interest, even more so when he was elected to the post of President of the Royal Society in 1820 CE, a position he held for 0.006 kyE until declining health prevented his continuance.

We know this to be an accolade, 221. Your files record that his distinguished predecessors included Wren, 0.14 kyE, and Newton, 0.117 kyE earlier. If occupancy reflects professional accomplishments, then we conclude that Newton is ahead with 0.024 kyE as President.

Newton was the outstanding philosopher of his era, so his presidency was unchallenged. My impression from observing Homo sapiens interactions is that political dexterity is important, to reconcile competing interests and allocate recognition reasonably. I suspect that neither Wren nor Davy enjoyed their tenure. Banks held the presidency for 0.042 kyE, and while a capable scientist, I think his skill was in sustaining relationships between professional factions within the organisation.

During Davy's period as President, his former assistant, Faraday was elected as a member of the Royal Society. We will consider his contributions soon, but another visit to continental Europe is recommended first to consider parallel progress.

Σ77 seconds

Carl Friedrich Gauss

We can now return to Gauss, who shared Laplace's interest in the least-squares theorem. Born in 1777 CE in an area that became northern Germany, his contributions encompass mathematics, physics, and astronomy. Like Dalton, from a materially poor background, a prodigy who was recognised and given a formal education, attending the University of Göttingen until 1798 CE.

As a scholar, he was dissatisfied with details left unexplained but possessed less interest in teaching others. The methods he used to obtain answers were sometimes opaque, so his published work seems incomplete compared with his insights. In this sense, he shared the approach of Newton and perhaps Laplace, who innovated to address problems, and discounted the importance of their intuition and logic.

He was a religious man, with his own opinions, disinclined to accept dogmas.

Perhaps we can consider a few of his achievements?

His most notable astronomical contribution relates to the tracking of an asteroid known as Ceres. This is the largest such body in this system, with a diameter of 945 km, and sometimes described as a dwarf planet. A brief exchange between 221 and the Intelligence confirmed its identity.

We know it, 221. It is the 25th largest object within Neptune's orbit, and its mass is 1.2% of the Moon. First identified by Gauss?

Not exactly. We might say that he rediscovered it. The object was found by the Italian astronomer, Giuseppe Piazzi, in 1801 CE, but his observational opportunity was fleeting because it disappeared behind the Sun.

We did not meet Piazzi, 221. Was this an oversight?

No. Although Professor of Astronomy at Palermo University, our simulations have not indicated any critical content in his research. 221 recalled meeting Piazzi in London in 1779 CE, when he visited the instrument-maker, Ramsden. It was fortuitous that 221 had obtained employment with a prestigious manufacturer, because 0.002 kyE later Herschel discovered Uranus, and sought craftsmen for his telescope-building enterprise. 221 had strong credentials.

Can we return to Gauss and his rediscovery of Ceres?

The challenge was to find the object again, after its unobservable transit. Despite limited data, Gauss modelled its path, enabling astronomers to locate it. For this, he devised an intricate trigonometrical method.

A consequence of the achievement was his appointment as Professor of Astronomy at Göttingen in 1807 CE, a post he held for the remainder of his life, another 0.048 kyE. The workshops within the university were well-equipped, 221 remembered from his employment, engaged as an instrument-maker. His experience had spanned Galileo, Newton, and Herschel, and now he could include Gauss in his résumé.

By the time of his 1809 treatise, his preferred approach had evolved, now with more emphasis on the least-squares method in managing observations. I think that he developed this method independently of Legendre's work. Gauss's assumption that observational data is normally distributed was soon justified by Laplace's central limit theorem. His dissertation simplified the mathematical treatments applied to celestial mechanics, still relevant to the present-day.

Gauss also made some fundamental contributions to algebra and number theory, and provided proofs for conjectures of both Kepler and Descartes.

Can you briefly explain Kepler's conjecture, and Gauss's contribution, 221?

Kepler stated that no arrangement of equally sized spheres occupying space has a greater average density than the cubic and hexagonal close packing arrangements, of about 74%.

~ What does packing density mean, 221? I'm familiar with packing steel components in boxes to the maximum extent. Is it the same idea?

=> *Pretty much, Jimbo. The hard part is proving the conjecture though.*

~ I once wrote software to nest the most two-dimensional components within a steel sheet, but I had no way of proving it was the maximum possible.

=> *Like Kepler's conjecture but his was a three-dimensional puzzle.*

~ At least the spheres are all the same. I was dealing with different-shaped components cut from the same sheet. Then my father purchased a laser profiling machine, which had nesting software embedded, so my work was redundant.

=> *"The journey, Not the destination matters… Jimbo." The distinguished TS Eliot said this. What you acquired from your research is still with you, if not the end product.*

~ This describes Gauss. He learned but did not share all his insights.

We understand the sentiment, 221. Can we now return to the conjecture?

Gauss proved Kepler's conjecture for the restricted case of the spheres being arranged in a regular lattice. A proof that addresses all possible arrangements would have to wait, 221 knew.

Proving even the restricted conjecture is impressive, 221. As with our discussion of the Laplace transform, we would address this problem numerically.

The frozen microbes could solve this, 221 speculated.

We should also note Gauss's work on magnetism. In cooperation with the physicist, Wilhelm Weber, he defined a unit of magnetism in relation to charge, mass, and time. In 1833 CE, they invented the electromechanical telegraph, enabling information to be transmitted over distances, using dedicated wires to carry electrical pulses. He promoted the study of Earth's magnetic field and formulated related mathematical theory.

We have another polymath in Gauss, 221. His contributions have been exceptional and could have been greater, had he shared more with his students.

Was your time in the university workshop the only opportunity to meet him?

He took little interest in the equipment that was manufactured, except for the telegraph. When I heard him speak, his lectures were rather uninformative because he described his conclusions but spoke less about his methods.

In 1839 CE, I had another chance. Gauss decided to learn the Russian language, and essentially taught himself, but he required a conversational partner, so I was able to assist for a few hours each week. By then, his health was declining, and although his oral Russian was adequate for everyday life, it did not extend to his philosophical interests.

We will study Gauss through your reports which go beyond the scope of our review. His optical research interests us, so too his topological work.

It appears that the client's civilisation is evolving, 221. You have already introduced the *Industrial Revolution*, and we know that both population and wealth have been increasing. This means more scientists are affordable, and consequently that greater specialisation will arise. We also note the development of statistical methods, essential to analysing complex problems. What should we expect? More of the same, a change in direction, or something exotic?

Probably all three. Existing disciplines are advancing, improved methods are being applied, while new fields unfold. We are leaving the Enlightenment.

This seems a bad idea. Being enlightened is a good thing, especially for a species that believes in the supernatural and pursues military technology.

We have learned much about *Homo sapiens* philosophical progress over the *Enlightenment*, and identified scholars we could not examine, but what of the population as a whole. What has happened over the past 0.15 kyE?

We can discern that their numbers have grown. Our sensors indicate there were almost 10^9 of these beings by 1800 CE, an increase of about 43% during the Enlightenment era.

Is this global, or concentrated in certain regions?

Most of the growth occurred in Asia, which grew by 67%, to represent 65% of the total. By contrast, Europe has only grown by about 14%, to about 20% of the global aggregate.

Why should this be, 221? We understand that Europe has enjoyed scientific leadership over this period, and even before, so it was richer.

As a region becomes more prosperous, the fertility rate tends to drop, not directly because of per capita wealth, but related factors, notably education and medical science. A driver of their present-day population growth is longevity, which has risen dramatically, doubling in only ten generations.

We wonder whether an increasing lifespan is a consequence of the client's accelerating scientific capabilities or a driver of it. What is your opinion?

I think we can see a positive feed-back loop working here. Advancing medical science means average lifespans have increased. A major influence on this average has been reduced child mortality through science and education, but also because people live longer. Increased longevity means that individuals remain active and useful and can contribute more.

You mean there are more old scientists?

In part, but the effect extends beyond scientists. Other professions, such as teaching and healthcare, can invest in maintaining skills for longer.

For about the next 0.05 kyE we will experience what some describe as Romanticism, or the Age of Reflection, which we may consider as applying throughout 1800-1850 CE.

Can you explain how this period of *Reflection* differs from the *Enlightenment*. How do you characterise this, 221?

At least for the Intelligence, there is nothing too different. We will still find outstanding scientists, and more researchers, in widening fields. Romanticism had several dimensions, but for our purposes, an important aspect is that scientists emphasised respect for nature, and this informed their research. We can regard both John Herschel and Gauss as intellectuals with this outlook.

To us, there is little difference from earlier philosophers. All were dedicated, motivated by curiosity and sometimes commercial advantage, and intelligent.

221 began to regret introducing Romanticism as it did not explain the client's astonishing progress. We need not spend our time on this, particularly as it was a transitory phase, superseded by Positivism, which stressed observation, rational thought, and logic.

Then you know that we are *Positivists*, not *Romantics*, 221.

There were outputs from Romanticism that influenced research. We have seen the wider use of statistical analysis, with applications in astronomy. A second was an interest in the human's relationship with nature, and growth in biological science, which we will encounter shortly.

Before this, we will observe another step in the evolution of the Homo sapiens knowledge, in thermodynamics. The work of Watt and Black and the later ideas of Laplace and Lavoisier has already been noted.

Sadi Carnot

We should consider the contribution of Carnot, whose birthplace was Paris, in 1796 CE. The son of a mathematician. He trained to become a military engineer, but from 1819 CE he devoted himself to philosophical pursuits, though nominally remaining an army officer.

Watt's steam engines, and similar machines, had existed for 0.043 kyE when Carnot commenced his full-time scientific studies. By then, what the client terms internal combustion engines were being considered, including a hydrogen-

fuelled device to power a vehicle, designed by the Swiss engineer, Isaac de Rivaz in 1807 CE. We have previously noted that Huygens presented a conceptual design for such an engine in 1680 CE, although not utilising hydrogen.

Research with higher pressure steam systems had been pursued, but the efficiency, in the sense of mechanical work output compared to the energy input, remained below 5%. Watt opposed higher pressures, you will remember, on safety grounds.

More problematic was the absence of a theoretical basis from which efficiency improvements could be found, and limits understood.

Carnot abstracted the notion of an idealised heat engine from the intricacies of the steam engine, enabling a clearer understanding of the behaviour of this thermodynamic system, and objective calculations to be performed. He demonstrated that the efficiency of a heat engine is determined by the respective temperatures of the two heat stores between which the engine runs. He addressed this through a thought experiment that connected two imaginary engines of differing efficiencies and demonstrated that if achievable, it would be a perpetual motion system, therefore impossible.

The Carnot cycle, as it became known to the client, is the most efficient possible because it assumes no heat loss between engine components running at different temperatures. Other losses, primarily friction, are assumed not to exist.

In practice, heat is conducted, and friction exists: irreversible losses.

He also concluded that the working fluid, whether steam or an alternative, is irrelevant to the efficiency, so only a matter of convenience.

~ I have met these ideas in my studies, 221, including the Carnot cycle. The first constraint that he noted, which was perhaps already known, is that no more mechanical work, or kinetic energy, can be obtained from an engine than the input heat energy. This relates to the law of conservation of energy, equivalent to the first law of thermodynamics, and states that if heat is recognised as a form of energy, then the total energy of a system plus its surroundings is conserved. Assuming no matter transfer, the change in internal energy of a system can be stated as:

$$\Delta E = Q - W$$

with Q and W being the heat and work terms.

=> *Very impressive, Jimbo, your description is good, but you are ahead of the story. You don't realise that when he wrote his book, these laws had not yet been formulated, making his insights more impressive. In Carnot's era, heat was thought to be a mysterious substance named caloric.*

=> *Conservation of energy, as a physical law, was researched by his successors for another 0.025 kyE or more, before it was accepted.*

~ I hadn't got to my main point, which was the other constraint that Carnot identified. He postulated that leaving aside losses, there is also a theoretical maximum to the amount of heat energy available to provide useful work. This led to the second law of thermodynamics.

=> *The second law was also developed later, but Carnot was on the right track. Sadly, he did not live long enough to contribute further.*

His conclusions have merit, 221, but seem obvious to us. Given that we are Energy Masters, we possess a deep understanding of the nature of heat.

We know that at this time, the Homo sapiens theory of heat was inadequate.

From your reports, 221, we believe their theory was unambiguously wrong.

Perhaps so, but the contribution of the Carnot cycle is a notable achievement, built upon by later scientists.

How was his theory promulgated and received?

Carnot published one work, Reflections on the Motive Power of Fire, *in 1824 CE, which took the form a popular book aimed at a wide readership, rather than a scholarly treatise. The mathematical aspects were minimised; I believe he wanted to reach the populace, consistent with the social climate of the era.*

We assume the book title and your earlier introduction of the *Age of Reflection* is coincidental?

221 had missed this but believed the remark to be humorous.

Initially, his book made little impact, perhaps because the readership did not include many professional scientists, but it became more widely known. His conclusion that increasing the temperature differential, through a higher temperature at the heat source, became important because it rationalised the potential of superheated steam, and influenced engine design.

We understand from your reports that you never met Carnot, 221, but seem very familiar with his book.

Yes, because I helped to rewrite it shortly after Carnot's death in 1832 CE, making it more suitable for the scientific community.

We assume that you did not add to the philosophical content.

My contribution was to help another distinguished scholar, who added to the substance, furthering Carnot's ideas. His careful work was unappreciated; such is the existence of an Energy Operative, 221 knew.

Benoît Clapeyron

We will remain in the thermodynamics domain to consider the contributions of Clapeyron, born in Paris in 1799 CE, and a contemporary of Carnot. He was both a physicist and an engineer. Along with Carnot and others, he founded the Homo sapiens science of thermodynamics.

How is this field defined, 221?

Several definitions have arisen as knowledge accumulated, but the themes are heat and the transfer of energy.

~ I can offer a suggestion. Thermodynamics describes interactions between heat and other forms of energy, considering parameters including time, pressure, temperature, and volume.

=> *Is this a formal definition from your studies, Jimbo?*

~ No, but it's what I've learned.

While our structures that describe nature differ, the content mirrors Jimbo's description. Can we return to Clapeyron now?

He came to my attention in 1830 CE, when he was managing the construction of a railway in the western suburbs of Paris. The project involved infrastructure and the production of rail vehicles, including steam engines, manufactured to Clapeyron's design.

We have the impression that this was not a large rail network.

In modern terms, the client might regard it as a suburban line, but it was the first in the region. Present-day France has one of the most advanced railway systems on Earth.

My interest was in his theoretical work, from around 1834 CE. He published Memoir on the Motive Power of Heat, which was a revision to Carnot's work of 0.01 kyE earlier, written in a scientific format, and updated to reflect the terminology of the age. He included an indicator diagram, a chart originated by

Watt, which illustrated pressure and volume at successive stages of the Carnot cycle. The Memoir made Carnot's concept accessible to scientists and engineers.

You helped with this rewrite, 221. What did you contribute?

When I heard of Clapeyron's plans to revise Reflections, I obtained a contract with the publisher to check the work for accuracy. Publishers avoid being associated with badly prepared books, and the technical content of Memoir was beyond their expertise.

Giving you a chance to study Clapeyron's insights and methods, we believe.

He took a methodical approach to science, decomposing complicated questions into smaller ones where possible, and then reintegrating his solutions.

An example was his formulation of the ideal gas law, built upon the earlier theories of Boyle, Charles, and Gay-Lussac, that can be written as:

$$PV = nR$$

which relates pressure, volume, and temperature, with n defining the amount of gas present. R is the ideal gas constant.

This involved experimentation to recheck the individual laws and then synthesis of the combined law. He evaluated this model with various gases and obtained consistent results. The client uses the term 'ideal' because gases found in nature do not follow the paradigm precisely, but it is adequate for most terrestrial purposes, such as steam engines.

How did you follow his studies, 221?

Clapeyron was an energetic scholar so continued researching while Memoir was prepared for publication. I visited his laboratory frequently on behalf of the publisher and as a scientifically literate participant, discussed his work.

Regarding *Memoir*, how was it received?

It was more widely read, and scientists utilised the concepts. Later, the publisher identified a constraint, that it was available only in the French language. After about 0.009 kyE it was decided to create a German translation, so I was invited to cooperate with a publisher in Leipzig, under the supervision of Johann Poggendorff. I was the participant fluent in both languages.

Who was Poggendorff?

A respected scholar, originally from Hamburg in what is now Germany, who researched electricity and magnetism. He invented the mirror galvanometer in

1826 CE, used to detect electric currents. More advanced forms of the device, involving lasers, are still used. His involvement with the Memoir translation was through his association with the Leipzig publisher as editor of Annalen der Physik und Chemie from 1824 CE, a role he continued for 0.052 kyE. It became one of the foremost scientific journals and is still published, now in English.

221 recognised that they had wandered from thermodynamics.

Poggendorff seems to have been a serious contributor, 221. Journalism was important because he acted as a multiplier, transferring knowledge, probably adding impetus to the client's scientific acceleration.

He is not on our agenda, for reasons of time. We should note him as another scientist we may need to consider later.

You gave Memoir a second push, 221. First, you worked for the French publisher to revise Carnot's original work, then you produced a German-language version for the Leipzig publisher. Regrettably, we do not require journalistic skills within the Intelligence. Maybe we need a house magazine?

221 remained uncertain how to respond to these humorous asides, so was happy to hear from Jimbo.

~ I tried writing a journal for my father's business, but he didn't like it. When I wrote about customers, it was too sensitive. I penned an introduction to our suppliers, but he said it was commercially confidential. When I composed a piece on engineering and production, he said it was secret. Then I tried writing about the employees, but he said it was private. I think he was concerned about rivals making job offers to them.

=> What happened?

~ He asked me to write about the competition, then he told me it was not to be disclosed. Afterwards, he advised me to write software in future.

=> Valuable experience, Jimbo. Writing is an excellent way to organise your thoughts. 221 recalled his scribing at Lincoln Cathedral about 0.6 kyE ago, close to the beginning of his penmanship with the client.

Crucial points arise from Clapeyron's development of Carnot's earlier insights that we should not miss. Most significant was his elaboration of Carnot's Principle, showing that a limit exists to the efficiency of conversion of heat to work, leading to the second law of thermodynamics. The preparation of Memoir enabled Clapeyron to provide a precise statement of the Principle, which today would be expressed as: no heat engine operating between a defined heat source and sink can have an efficiency greater than a reversible engine working between the same source and sink. Jimbo introduced this earlier, but we should appreciate that the concept became essential to advances in diverse fields, from astrophysics to mechanical engineering.

~ I used to have the NASA statements of the three thermodynamic laws on my wall. For the second law: *the total entropy of a system plus its environment cannot decrease; it can remain constant for a reversible process but must always increase for an irreversible process.* A simple description of a complicated idea.

=> *You have also introduced entropy, a new idea. Can you explain?*

~ The concept and term were advanced by a physicist called Clausius.

Will we meet Clausius, 221? Entropy is a pivotal idea, whether the *Homo sapiens* derivation or in our more abstract sense.

We have insufficient time to fully explore his contributions now but should discuss this aspect of his work. His statement of the second law, translated into English is: a cyclic transformation whose only final result is to transfer heat from a body at a given temperature to a body at a higher temperature is impossible.

A similar statement was given by the Scottish physicist, William Thompson.

If we cannot meet Clausius or Thompson, then we are fortunate to have Jimbo available to explain entropy.

~ I referred to entropy increasing. In our terms, the change in entropy is a measure of the availability, or otherwise, of thermal energy to be converted into mechanical work. Like heat, we are concerned with the change rather than the absolute value. Analogous to potential energy, I like to think.

=> *An example is needed, Jimbo. We understand the notion of irreversibility in practical situations but want to know why entropy increases.*

~ If we have two separate jars containing gases, and therefore many gas molecules, when we mix them, the entropy of the combined gas exceeds that of the two gases we started with. Why is this? My father eats confectionary, although it's bad for him. In his office, he has a spiral-shaped jar of pineapple chunks, which are yellow, and another contains bullseyes, which are mainly black. The most that he ever has is thirty in each jar because that's how many are in a bag. We can say the possible positions of the items in each jar is 30 factorial. You are familiar with this term?

=> *Very familiar, Jimbo. 30! is 30x29x28x…1.*

~ Yes, but with two jars the value becomes $(30!)^2$, which is a large number.

=> *Approximately 7.02×10^{64}.*

~ If we then mix the contents, we have 60 units and therefore 60! possible positions, which is a substantially larger number.

=> *Roughly 8.32×10^{81}.*

~ The two jars represent what is termed the macrostate of the gases, and the positions of the items are the microstates of the individual molecules. Once the gases are mixed, or the confections are combined, then many more possible microstates exist.

=> *About 1.18×10^{17} more, Jimbo.*

~ For the molecules, the increase in microstates after mixing would be much larger. This growth is equivalent to entropy increasing. My lecturer used an analogy with coloured playing cards, of which we have 26 red and 26 black, in two piles, but I thought you might not be familiar with cards.

=> *True, Jimbo, but we don't eat pineapple chunks or bullseyes either.*

Jimbo has introduced us to the field of statistical mechanics, developed by the Austrian philosopher, Ludwig Boltzmann. We will not have an opportunity to review his contributions, but I did meet him. You have my reports. His ideas on entropy were initially unconvincing to many of his peers because they did not yet have proof that atoms existed. We will find that later scientists applied his ideas to great effect.

Is it not strange that many scientists did not accept the existence of atoms, given the work of Dalton and Davy that we have reviewed? Presumably, other researchers also provided evidence.

Some scholars saw atomic theory as a convenient means of understanding matter, without conceding the presence of such small particles, which they had never seen.

We enjoyed Jimbo's analogies with the confections and playing cards, although we have no experience of their use.

221 reflected that this was the only species that played games, whether with cards, balls, clubs, or rackets. As they had already pondered the client's unique interest in music and poetry, he did not want this question open to evaluation.

Perhaps Jimbo could explain a little more of his entropy knowledge, to extend our understanding of the *Homo sapien*s view of this phenomenon?

~ I imagine that most people have no opinion because they have never heard of the concept. Only scientists, and maybe not all comprehend it.

=> *Where do you see evidence of entropy at work in ordinary life?*

~ If I hit a golf ball with a club, it gains kinetic energy as it accelerates and potential energy as it rises into the air. This energy has been transferred from my body. It then loses potential energy as it returns to the surface and rolls along the grass. All this is in accordance with Newton's laws but does not describe the situation completely.

=> *Something is missing, Jimbo?*

~ Yes, the ball rolls for a while, then stops. We started with a positive value for kinetic energy after the ball was struck and, even assuming the conversion from kinetic to potential and back again is perfect, we have lost all the kinetic energy once the ball ceases to roll. Conservation of energy seems not to apply, but of course, it does.

=> *Where has the energy gone, Jimbo? The ball is at rest, so possesses no kinetic energy, and is back on the surface from which it started, so has no potential energy.*

~ The answer lies in the conversion of mechanical work, as represented by the ball in motion, into heat through air resistance, vibration as the ball bounces, and friction between the rolling ball and the grass, which eventually stops it.

=> *Therefore, the surroundings receive an energy input.*

~ Correct, but the process is irreversible. We cannot recover this heat, or convert it into mechanical work, without expending even more energy. Entropy has increased.

=> *We liked your example, Jimbo, even though our knowledge of golf is inadequate. I read the rules and learned the game began in Scotland.*

~ Maybe I can ask a question now? One supposed outcome of entropy is that the amount of disorder in the universe increases steadily and is irreversible. A friend studying astrophysics told me this. A consequence would be that eventually, the entire universe will be in thermodynamic equilibrium and experience so-called heat death, probably just a mass of gas at a common energy level. No further potential for useful work, such as the steam engine performs, would be possible.

=> *Yes, Jimbo, I am familiar with this notion, which has been postulated by several Homo sapiens philosophers. I first met this idea on Earth in 1777 CE, through the work of the French astronomer, Jean Bailly. Thompson considered this about 0.06 kyE later, arising from his development of the second law. It merits a longer discussion than we can accommodate, but you would have to be patient to observe it.*

~ How patient do you reckon, 221? How long have we got?

=> *If your friend's hypothesis were correct, she would have to wait for the last large black hole to decay, so roughly 10^{97} kyE. Maybe you can engineer a solution before then.*

~ Thanks, 221. I wondered how you knew my astrophysics friend is a she.

=> *You were referring to Stephanie, or to another female student?*

Time for us to move on, 221. We are coming towards the end of our budget. The contributions from Jimbo were stimulating, quite different from how we evolved our notions of entropy.

~ One aspect you have missed is that Thomson made many valuable contributions, both in theoretical science and engineering.

=> *Yes, Jimbo, we know this, but time is limited. The Energy Masters have my reports.*

~ Whether he can be regarded as Scottish, given his birthplace was Belfast in what is now Northern Ireland, I don't know, but you should note that he was honoured for his achievements, becoming Lord Kelvin. The recognition became global when it was decided that a temperature unit from absolute zero should be the kelvin, or K.

221 recalled the comments of Boyle in 1665 CE, his first evidence that Homo sapiens scholars had considered the notion of absolute zero when he wrote:

"There is some body or other that is of its own nature supremely cold and by participation of which all other bodies obtain that quality."

=> I know Thomson's career, Jimbo. He became Lord Kelvin 1892 CE, aged 0.066 kyE. During this period, he was President of the Royal Society, 0.063 kyE after Davy. 221 remembered that Kelvin had been buried close to Newton in Westminster Abbey. A measure of his stature.

Thermodynamics has provided a trio of philosophers of whom we should learn more, 221. Clausius, Boltzmann, and Thompson, or perhaps Kelvin, should be included in our list. Then you mentioned the thoughtful astronomer, Bailly.

For the remainder of our review, I will refer to Thomson as Kelvin.

Σ83 seconds

Michael Faraday

As Jimbo has returned us to the British Isles with his reminders of Kelvin, I propose that we consider the contributions of Faraday, whom I introduced as an assistant to Davy. We will learn that his work extended much further, initiating huge changes to the client's civilisation.

Faraday was born in 1791 CE, in an area that became part of London. His family was not wealthy, so he received only a basic education. He was largely self-taught, initially through reading. His opportunity came when aged only 0.014 kyE, he became an apprentice to a bookseller, giving him access to a wide range of books.

Although Faraday's background was modest, he had learned to read. An encouraging trend.

He had an interest in science and by this period, numerous books were available, making the sciences publicly accessible. Jane Marcet's Conversations on Chemistry, published in 1805 CE, was particularly inspirational. He regarded her as his first science tutor.

Is this writer of importance to us? We favour the wide dissemination of scientific ideas.

In the present-day, she would be described as an educationalist, but in her era, she was more. Her work addressed chemistry, natural philosophy, and economics, and was written in an informal style that made it easier for the uninformed reader.

An intelligent approach, 221, but apart from being a writer, was she a scientist? How did she obtain the knowledge to write these books?

My understanding is limited, but her husband, Alexander Marcet, engaged in scientific research after obtaining a medical degree in Edinburgh. He became a member of the Royal Society. She read drafts of his books and papers, giving her insights. She was an attendee of Davy's lectures. I am unsure how she obtained a grasp of economics, but she was able to explain the ideas of Smith, and those of other economists. There were similar writers. I believe that the Age of Reflection encouraged this trend. It also explains her support for females training as scientists.

Her daughter, Francois Marcet, was a physicist, working in her father's home country of Switzerland.

What was her field, 221? Should we review her contributions?

She built upon earlier work of Gay-Lussac and others, researching the superheating of water. Her experimental apparatus became well-known and enabled steam vapour pressure to be determined over a range of superheated temperatures. This was valuable in the design of high-pressure steam engines, far removed from Watt's earlier systems.

She was another thermodynamicist.

221 realised that they had travelled a long way from the life of Faraday and remembered that his reports detailed Jane Marcet's religious writing. Time to move on, before the Energy Masters asked why she wrote about the supernatural.

Around 1812 CE, aged 0.02 kyE, Faraday began attending Davy's lectures at the Ri, which had been running for about 0.011 kyE and become notable occasions, both scientifically and socially. He sent Davy his voluminous notes of the lectures, which were well-received. As we learned, after sustaining injuries while experimenting, Davy invited Faraday to become his assistant in 1813 CE.

Faraday's early research was conjoined with Davy's, primarily chemistry. He was associated with Davy's isolation of chlorine as an element and went on to detect new compounds, C_2Cl_6 and C_2Cl_4. In 1825 CE, he discovered C_6H_6, known to the client as benzene. A data exchange between 221 and the Energy Masters ensued. Faraday also furthered Dalton's study into the nature of gases, showing by liquefaction that gases are vapours emanating from liquids that possess low boiling points. His electrochemical work determined the principles of electrolysis, and a related law: the amount of material produced at an electrode during an electrochemical reaction is directly proportional to the total conducted charge.

~ It would be simpler to replace 'total conducted charge' with the 'product of average current and time'.

=> *This is an alternative formulation of the law, Jimbo, and can be represented by the equation:*

$$n = It/Fz$$

where It is the product of current and time, F is the Faraday constant which represents the magnitude of electric charge per mole and z is the number of electrons transferred per ion, or valence. n is the number of moles produced at the electrode. To obtain the mass of the substance, multiply by the molar mass.

Another elegant example of *Homo sapiens* science, 221. Faraday determined this by experimentation, according to your reports. Our approach reflects a theoretical analysis using statistical methods, but the result is identical.

We should appreciate that Faraday's education did not include advanced mathematics, so his research methods were practical.

You also found this constraint in William Herschel's career.

Mathematical limitations arise when the scientist has not received a university education. Is this an accurate observation, 221?

Partially, I think. These scholars were specialists, so a university education was desirable, but the field of study is relevant. Leibniz developed calculus, in parallel with Newton, but his education was in abstract philosophy and then law. His mathematical prowess grew through having Huygens as a mentor.

The *Homo sapiens* requirement is to have a good teacher, whether inside a university or not.

~ Teachers are essential to us. We cannot download information directly from a central source, we need to learn. Some educationalists believe that 'learning by doing' is best, rather than only reading or listening in a classroom. Young minds require stimulation. Much of my science education involved conducting experiments, even though the teacher knew the result.

There may be a learning point for us here, 221. If we compare Jimbo's education with proven galactic civilisations, it is singular. Some do download a package that gives them everything they need to know at the beginning of their existence, or even arrive in a conscious state with knowledge embedded. Others share a common mind. The Intelligence arguably has a single psyche, although our lengthy existence means convolutions exist. You are both part of us but capable of independent thought.

His nominally autonomous intellect told 221 that they were far from the achievements of Faraday, and time was passing.

Nevertheless, 221, we suspect that these random routes to knowledge over the client's history may help explain their acceleration, because fresh minds addressing a familiar problem with different neural connections may provide new insights. How else can we explain Newton's *Principia*?

Returning to Faraday, we have not yet reached his major contributions. He had been elected to the Royal Society in 1824 CE and appointed as Professor of Chemistry at the Ri in 1833 CE, not long after the end of Davy's life.

This recognition is encouraging, 221, but is it relevant to Faraday's career?

He was a religious man, given to modesty and simplicity, and averse to titles.

His beliefs seem like the Quakers you described.

Perhaps so, but my reason for raising this aspect was his dedication to research and persistence.

In 1819 CE, the revelations of the Danish physicist, Hans Christian Ørsted, who is credited by the client with discovering electromagnetism, became known. Ørsted's had linked electricity, a recently discovered phenomenon that was incompletely understood, with magnetism, which had been known for longer. 221 recalled Aristotle describing it, and he was not the first. Both Indian and Chinese philosophers knew of this property. The Islamic scholars had discussed magnets, and he recalled Halley demonstrating a magnetic compass in 1691 CE.

Responses to the relationship between electricity and magnetism were immediate, with insights provided by Gauss and Biot, and another distinguished French scientist, André-Marie Ampère.

We should include Ampère within our list of scientists we have yet to meet.

Faraday created the first electric drive in 1821 CE, by converting electrical energy into a rotating mechanical output, beginning the electromagnetic revolution. He adapted the ideas of Davy, and William Wollaston, another British scientist.

We have not been introduced to Wollaston, 221. Presumably his accomplishments were insufficient for him to figure in your itinerary.

No, like Ampère, a major contributor. He discovered two chemical elements, palladium, and rhodium: Pd and Rh. Both have present-day applications.

Then, include his name on our list, 221.

Faraday's greatest discovery was electromagnetic induction. If an electrically conductive material moves through a magnetic field, then an electric current will flow. Before this, only a battery could provide a current. This was the basis of the electric motor, which converts electricity into motion, and the electric generator, in which a mechanical input produces an electric current.

We see from your reports that Faraday made this discovery in 1831 CE, about 0.01 kyE after his first electrical breakthrough. This was a long period, given *Homo sapiens* impetuosity.

His work at the Ri was directed by Davy and encompassed other areas but included research into electromagnetism. There was also pressure to provide material for the public lectures.

It is surprising that other researchers failed to discover induction before Faraday. Surely, they were interested.

The Italian scientist, Francesco Zantedeschi, conducted related research around the same time, but Faraday developed the ideas more fully. Zantedeschi also detected a relationship between light and magnetism, probably 0.03 kyE before a theoretical basis was established.

The American scientist, Joseph Henry, made similar discoveries to Faraday independently, but did not publish his results until later. Henry was highly regarded and became the first secretary of the Smithsonian Institution.

~ His research was recognised in the unit of inductance, the henry or H.
=> *Quite correct, Jimbo. You and Henry share something. Please consider.*

William Sturgeon, a British scientist, researched electromagnets, and in 1832 CE, built the first electric motor incorporating a commutator.

What is a commutator, 221? A new term for us. An electrical component?

221 wondered how to explain the mechanical operation of an electrical device to the Energy Masters.

~ Perhaps I may offer a comment, 221? A commutator is a switch used in motors and generators to reverse the direction of current flow between the external circuitry and the rotor. Every half turn, the direction is reversed, providing a continuous torque. From my limited knowledge, I think this technology is obsolescent, because of solid-state electronic controls. These require less maintenance, therefore, more economical.

Here we find the commercial imperative driving technology, 221. The search for cost savings created a superior scientific solution. Uncommon in our galaxy.

I did examine Sturgeon's invention. While he developed an electric motor, in France a related concept proposed by Ampère resulted in an electrical generator, or dynamo.

With these ingenious devices and the *Industrial Revolution* continuing, we assume there was a rapid transformation, 221?

Compared with others in the galaxy, it was rapid, but constraints existed. With no electrical distribution yet available, expensive batteries were needed to power electric motors in factories, but the client soon overcame this limitation.

We are also pleased to meet an American philosopher, 221. He was not first, but perhaps was one of the few in this field.

The earlier efforts of the polymath, Benjamin Franklin, whose endeavours were multitudinous, included research into the nature of electricity from about 1746 CE. He was elected to the Royal Society in 1756 CE.

The competitive but collective efforts of the species continue to impress us, 221. We suppose that if time permitted, we could fully engage ourselves with American scientists.

This is another inventive, entrepreneurial society, like Europe, adding scale and critical mass to research. We have space for five more scholars but should complete our review of Faraday's accomplishments.

He continued to explore electrical phenomena, and contrary to prevailing scientific opinion concluded that there were not different kinds of electricity, and its nature depended on its intensity and quantity.

~ We can term intensity as potential difference, and quantity as current?
=> *Correct, Jimbo.*

He investigated static electricity and revealed that a charge exists on the exterior of a conductor but has less effect on the interior. This led to an electrical shield, or Faraday Cage, which bears his name to the present-day. Such shields are used to protect sensitive equipment.

Your reports of Faraday's research are of high quality, 221. Excellent descriptions of his experiments and lectures. We wonder how you obtained this detailed knowledge.

I obtained employment at the Ri once Davy became interesting and continued during the career of Faraday.

This was a busy time for you, 221. In addition to working at the *Ri* you were cooperating with Clapeyron in the preparation of Memoir, while assisting Gauss in telegraph development.

My role with Faraday would now be described as a technician, but I helped with the design of experiments and preparation of equipment. It was easy to appreciate their methods because Davy and Faraday were enthusiastic experimenters, making their research observable. It was harder to follow the ideas of theoreticians who provided solutions without explaining their reasoning. Newton possessed this trait, as did Gauss and some of the mathematicians we met.

Homo sapiens understanding of electricity at this stage was empirical.

This will be corrected shortly when we meet another outstanding philosopher, James Clerk Maxwell, in Edinburgh.

~ Faraday's work has been acknowledged in the unit of capacitance, the farad or F, the ability of a body to store electrical charge.

=> *In practice, you often work with µF or even pF. One farad is a lot of charge for your situation, but for the behaviour of the galaxy, quite modest.*

~ Similarly, Ampère is recognised in the unit of electrical current.

=> *Correct again, Jimbo. Since 1881 CE. I remember the related meeting in Paris.* 221 wondered whether to introduce the origins of volts, ohms, and coulombs, but decided to leave the Energy Masters to peruse his reports.

James Joule

I propose to remain in England to consider the work of Joule, who was born in the region of Lancashire, in 1818 CE. We can regard him as a physicist, although he was also a brewer, the only one I have introduced.

Joule was a producer of beer, we deduce, 221. A substance not found elsewhere in our galaxy.

221 reflected that beer had long been part of British culture, enjoyed by both the inhabitants and visitors alike. He remembered the Roman soldiers travelling through Londinium and those building Hadrian's Wall, consuming the local brew. At that time, about 1.9 kyE ago, the beer was made from honey, so a sweet scent emanated from their drinking vessels. Perhaps 0.07 kyE before Joule's existence, he had seen the attendees at Smith's lectures in Edinburgh seeking refreshment at nearby hostelries. Then he observed the crew of HMS Deptford enjoying beer in warmer climes.

Maybe your *Homo sapiens* associations mean that you too enjoy beer, 221, but not now. You will explain Joule's insights, we believe.

Joule was from a wealthy family and benefited from being tutored by distinguished scholars in his region. We noted that he received instruction from Dalton, but there were others. From a young age, he encountered contemporary scientific ideas. His early career was as a businessman and his interest in science might be described as a pastime, although there was an overlap. He understood the economics of his business and wondered whether it was financially attractive to replace the steam engines in his brewery with electric motors.

Can you explain what Joule might gain by replacing his steam engines, 221?

~ If the electric motors proved less expensive to operate, then Joule's overall cost of production would reduce by an amount. This saving, if significant, could enable him to lower his beer prices and perhaps sell more beer with unchanged profitability per unit.

=> *What does this mean, Jimbo?*

~ Every barrel of beer he sells has the same profit margin as before, say 10%, but now he might sell more barrels because the price is lower.

=> *If he sells more barrels does this mean people drink more beer?*

~ More likely is that he wins new customers who prefer his beer because it now costs less than rival products. Alternatively, he might maintain his existing prices and obtain an increased profit per barrel, say 11%. So, more income.

=> *This technical change affects his business, but his beer is the same?*

~ Yes, but another reason may have motivated Joule. His competitors, also seeking cost savings, perhaps with the same idea, placing him at a disadvantage.

=> *221 thought Jimbo's account clearer than Smith's Edinburgh lectures.*

A helpful explanation, 221, but we should return to Joule's research.

Joule concluded, through experimentation, that he should retain the steam engines. This is unimportant to the science, but his studies led to an electrical insight, known as a Joule's first law, in 1841 CE. It states that: the heat which is evolved by the proper action of any voltaic current is proportional to the square of the intensity of that current, multiplied by the resistance which it experiences.

~ I know this, but the form is different. In Joule's sense, we have $Q \propto I^2 Rt$ where Q is heat, I current, R is resistance and t is the time for which the electric current is applied. We often think in terms of power, meaning energy transferred per unit time, so we can develop an equation:

$$P = I^2 R$$

with the power term P, simply being Q/t.

~ This applies in a direct-current design. For alternating-current circuits common in the present-day, we need to consider mean values.

=> *Right again, Jimbo, but we don't have time for this now. In Joule's era, they were still trying to comprehend dc physics.*

How did he establish these relationships, 221?

Initially, he was investigating costs. He used the two alternative sources of motion to lift a mass through a defined distance and compared the cost of the fuels, coal for the steam boiler, and zinc for the battery supply. His experimentation advanced his understanding of energy further when he observed that a wire heated by an electric current raised the temperature of a known mass of water in which it was immersed by a measurable amount. Joule concluded that the chemical energy contained in the battery could be equated to heat, which was contrary to the prevailing scientific view that heat was a separate substance. His insight was that heat and mechanical work are equivalent.

When did these experiments take place, 221?

He published his results in 1843 CE.

Carnot's Reflections provided the basis for reaching Joule's conclusion in 1824 CE. Can we presume that Joule's thinking was readily accepted?

Not at first. He was isolated from the universities and professional institutions where these ideas were discussed, but Joule persevered, experimenting further to validate his theories.

By then I was taking a direct interest in Joule's efforts and heard criticism of his ideas. Some objections were theoretical, arising from the belief that the work of Carnot and Clapeyron had validated previous assumptions regarding heat. Kelvin demonstrated mathematically that the Carnot cycle was consistent with an equivalence of heat and work, but this happened later. Other concerns related to Joule's experiments, and the accuracy of his measurements, which was considered impractical, but my observations confirmed the validity of his results.

How did you achieve this, 221?

Joule employed an instrument-maker named Dancer, based in the nearby city of Liverpool. Dancer had research of his own, particularly into photographic methods. He produced bespoke devices for Joule, manufactured with precision for this era. I know this, because for a time Dancer employed me, so I worked with Joule while he experimented.

A fruitful route to these philosophers, 221. Galileo, Newton, Dalton, Gauss, Davy, and Faraday benefited from your skills, and Joule also.

His methods were easily grasped because he had a strong sense of measuring accuracy, and a related interest in his instrumentation. I believe this resulted from his brewing expertise.

Resistance to Joule's hypothesis, which became known as the kinetic theory of heat, also arose because it assumed molecular motion. As we have already noted, acceptance of atoms and molecules was not yet established. As a former student of Dalton, Joule was convinced of their existence and cited both Newton and Davy as scientists who shared his opinion. Other philosophers were becoming interested in his work by then. The German scientist, Hermann Helmholtz, wrote a treatise propounding the principle of conservation of energy in 1847 CE, which credited the research of Joule. Cooperation between Joule and Kelvin after 1852 CE, in which Joule conducted experiments and Kelvin analysed results, gradually convinced opinion of the validity of Joule's research.

A result of this work was what has become known as Joule's second law, which states: the internal energy of a defined mass of an ideal gas is independent of its volume and pressure, depending only on its temperature.

~ Remember that Kelvin was still called Thomson at this time.

=> *Yes, Jimbo, but I'm trying to avoid confusion. The British habit of awarding titles to people who then change their names is a complication.*

~ I know, but its relevance here is the Joule-Thomson effect, which was one of their experiments, important to developing Joule's second law.

Joule was instrumental in establishing conservation of energy as a physical law, which the client also interprets as their first law of thermodynamics.

This has been a complicated story, 221, throughout perhaps 0.1 kyE. Carnot presented a model of an ideal engine that is thermodynamically valid but built on a misconception of heat. Joule has demonstrated with his experiments that heat is one form of energy, which is conserved, and tried to explain it at the atomic level. We see from your reports that his postulations regarding molecular behaviour were incomplete, but this is understandable. Many other scientists have been involved. At the conclusion are *Homo sapiens* models of nature's processes that are rational, but the path from beginning to end is hard to discern. Quite unlike the other civilisations we have observed and sometimes assimilated.

The process is complicated, but the outcome has been reached perhaps $10^2 x$ more rapidly than the average of others I have observed.

From our experience of maturation lifecycles, we can say that your estimate of 10 kyE as the mean time to learn thermodynamics is optimistic. Assuming these lifecycles are normally distributed, we calculate the *Homo sapiens* achievement to be 4 standard deviations faster than the mean duration.

Within the best 0.003% mused 221. Maybe the fastest formulation of an energy conservation theory ever in this galaxy.

Even if we cannot fully follow their logic, the performance is admirable.

~ Joule is recognised by the international unit of energy, the joule, or J.

=> *You have multiple definitions of the joule. In mechanics, one joule is the energy transferred when a force of one newton acts on an object in the direction of its motion through a distance of one metre, so:* $1J = 1Nm$.

~ Joule's first law implies that one joule is the energy dissipated as heat when a current of one amp passes through a resistance of one ohm for one second.

=> *There is another, more fundamental definition relating to moving one unit of charge through a unit of electrical potential difference, so in your nomenclature a joule is one coulomb-volt, or:* $1J = 1C \cdot V$.

~ Remember Watt's recognition, in the unit of power, the watt or W.

=> *We didn't forget, Jimbo, it's just simpler after defining the joule. I think of it as the rate of energy transfer, or one joule per second, therefore we have:*

$1W = 1J/s = 1Nm/s$. *Related electromagnetic definitions also exist. I remember the joule and watt being adopted at an international congress in 1889 CE, which I attended in Paris.*

Σ86 seconds

James Clerk Maxwell

We will remain in Great Britain, returning to Edinburgh to meet Maxwell, born in 1831 CE. His family was prosperous and successful. From an early age, Maxwell showed curiosity about natural phenomena and mechanical devices. Although his parents lived in rural south-west Scotland, they decided that such precocity justified particular attention to his education, which he received initially at Edinburgh Academy.

We see from your reports that this school was another result of philanthropy, 221, opening in 1824 CE, so Maxwell was one of the earliest students. Their emphasis on classics, meaning Greek and Roman culture, did not deter Maxwell from acquiring scientific skills, fortunately for the client.

~ Jimbo remembered that Tony was a product of the Academy and wondered briefly whether he might be another Maxwell. Certainly, an excellent engineer.

Maxwell told me much later that an exhibition of electrical equipment he attended in Edinburgh with his father in 1841 CE inspired him. The sponsor of the event, Robert Davidson, was an engineer and entrepreneur from Aberdeen, who designed and built the first electric locomotive.

Steam locomotives existed, 221, but we are only 0.065 kyE after Watt's improved engine was launched, and already a new technology is available. Barely 0.01 kyE since Faraday's breakthrough. Presumably Davidson's design was well-received?

In terms of technology, perhaps, but commercially it was too expensive because it depended on batteries. His idea was ahead of electrical engineering science, so the client waited another 0.06 kyE for electrically propelled trains. If Davidson's achievement was to inspire Maxwell, this is sufficient.

Aged only 0.016 kyE, Maxwell attended Edinburgh University where he studied philosophy, logic, mathematics, and physics under luminaries of the era.

Are there philosophers who warrant our particular attention, 221?

Several if time permitted, which it does not. To mention one, James Forbes, who was appointed Professor of Natural Philosophy, aged 0.024 kyE. He researched heat and its relationship with Earth's atmosphere, the polarisation of infrared radiation, and earned respect as a glaciologist. Elected to the Royal Society in 1832 CE, he received awards for his scholarship.

Maxwell was fortunate to have such accomplished teachers. Presumably he found their insights demanding as a young man.

Apparently, he was untroubled by their content, which is evident from his contribution of papers to the RSE.

He subsequently attended Cambridge University, obtaining a degree in mathematics, and undertook research and teaching before his appointment as Professor of Natural Philosophy in Aberdeen, aged only 0.025 kyE.

This success would be even more impressive, 221, if you had not told us of Maclaurin's mathematics appointment in the same city at an even younger age.

That was about 0.14 kyE before Maxwell.

While in Aberdeen, he studied the composition of Saturn's rings, concluding that they consisted of small particles.

We doubt that he achieved this by observation, 221, because the client's technology was inadequate, so we infer he performed a mathematical analysis.

He examined the possibility of either solid or fluid rings and proved that neither would be stable, leaving the particulate option.

~ I remember the Voyager fly-bys of Saturn from 0.015 kyE ago. Perhaps this was my first year at school, but we received science lessons. The teacher projected images of the planet and its rings and asked us how long the information took to reach Earth.

=> *What did you think, Jimbo? Can you remember?*

~ My father had told me that light from the Sun takes about 8 minutes to arrive, and I knew Saturn is further away, so maybe I estimated 60 minutes.

=> *A reasonable guess. We assess an average of 82 minutes, although this fluctuates with variations in distance between the two planets. You were a young scientist.*

Maxwell's analysis is impressive, 221. He must have been familiar with Newton's work to reach this conclusion.

I believe so, but his most important work came later, after a move to King's College, a component of London University. During this time, he attended lectures at the Ri and met Faraday, who was 0.04 kyE senior to him in age.

Maxwell studied the relationship between electricity and magnetism after reading Faraday's 1839 CE treatise. In this, he had described electricity and magnetism geometrically. Other scientists looked for analogies with gravity. Maxwell's insight was to borrow from the mathematics of fluids and apply adjusted models to describe magnetic fields. He related this to electricity and the interaction between the phenomena. Where Faraday had perceived an electric field to consist of contours of force, Maxwell saw flow lines that possess speed and direction because of his fluid analogy.

In 1861 CE, he published On Physical Lines of Force, consolidating current knowledge into 20 differential equations. He was elected to the Royal Society.

Later, Maxwell deduced that the propagation speed of an electromagnetic field closely approximates to the speed of light, which he believed was not coincidental. He concluded that light is also an electromagnetic wave.

This is a critical point in Homo sapiens development, fundamental to our interest in the species. A temporal node of similar significance to Copernicus's treatise of 1543 CE that Earth is not the centre of the universe, and Newton's Principia in 1687 CE.

The client's perception of the universe had changed greatly in only 0.32 kyE, 221 considered.

I think Maxwell understood the significance of his discovery. Before his equations existed, scientists had not appreciated this link between electricity, magnetism, and light. His paper, A Dynamical Theory of the Electromagnetic Field, in 1864 CE stated: "that light is an electromagnetic disturbance propagated through the field according to electromagnetic laws." Given that light of different colours exists, and if it is understood that light is a wave phenomenon, it becomes possible to determine the respective wavelengths of these colours. Scientists already knew that energy existed just outside the visible spectrum in the infrared and ultraviolet wavelengths, but Maxwell's equations allowed for other wavelengths, above and below the visible spectrum.

We are only 0.06 kyE after Herschel discovered the infrared, and the client has a mathematical description of electromagnetic radiation.

As we shall observe shortly, Maxwell enabled the radio revolution and resulting present-day Homo sapiens technologies.

Maxwell's equations were refined into four partial differential equations that are still used today.

We think there is another fundamental aspect of Maxwell's research, 221. He has already provided a mathematical foundation for Faraday's discoveries, and revealed that light is an electromagnetic wave, but he has achieved something else. From our review, this is perhaps the only occasion, other than Newton, that a *Homo sapiens* philosopher has conjoined two physical phenomena within a single mathematical framework. Another temporal node.

221 observed that Maxwell's revelations had impressed the Energy Masters but knew the process of discovery still could not be discerned. Like their examination of thermodynamics, there was an opacity despite this being largely the work of one man.

You are correct, 221. We cannot now see inside Maxwell's brain, but his mind made connections and associations that others could not. It reminds us of Newton, who provided many insights, but we do not understand how.

We should note some of Maxwell's other achievements. He was another contributor to the client's thermodynamic knowledge through his research into gas kinetics. Unusually, in my experience of Maxwell, he conducted experiments before creating mathematical models. By 1866 CE, he had theory to describe the distribution of motion of gas particles. His work was later generalised by the scientist Boltzmann, whose ideas Jimbo has already introduced, providing theoretical explanations for the experiments of Joule and his collaborators.

Like earlier philosophers, Maxwell researched the nature of light, optical phenomena, and perception of colour. In 1861 CE, during his Ri lecture, he demonstrated colour photography for the first time.

In 1868 CE he submitted a paper regarding governors to the Royal Society.

Governors, 221?

A self-regulating control mechanism, first used to my knowledge to manage the speed of a windmill. The device I observed was called the Watt governor, which is an application of Newton's third law. When Watt's steam engines started being applied to rotating factory machinery, it became important to control their speed within tighter limits than in earlier reciprocating situations. The control system consists of two rotating balls attached to a vertical spindle, connected to the output shaft of the engine. A degree of automatic control is exerted by balancing the torque from the weight of the balls with the torque generated by their rotation.

The design is depicted in your report, 221. What was Maxwell's interest?

He provided the theoretical basis for the governor's operation, where previously empirical knowledge was the guiding principle. His paper exceeded the description of this mechanical configuration and provided concepts for a new discipline: control engineering. No doubt, Jimbo will study this.

~ The next academic year will be my introduction to the theory, although I have observed the operation of mechanical governors. Unusually for a mechanical device, I think they possess a certain beauty.

=> *Another new idea, 221 reflected, which they did not have time to explore.*

What can we learn about the species from Maxwell, 221? We can call him a polymath, even a giant, with ideas and skills comparable to Newton, but is there more? Many scientists exist, information is being shared faster, and technologies are advancing at a high velocity compared to evolution within the Intelligence. Are there dynamics we have missed?

~ An accurate description and if you look closely, you will find contributory factors that are accelerating progress, but there is no magic here. We have already discussed several reasons, including scale, education, literacy, female participation, and slightly more liberal attitudes. While religions still exist, they no longer dominate thought.

=> *Are there any new aspects, Jimbo?*

~ There is one influence, the American scientific and industrial presence, but this had little effect on Maxwell, I imagine.

=> *What about Maxwell, Jimbo? You are from the same city. Can you add to our understanding?*

~ Maybe two points, but I'm not sure if they help. He was a religious man, so, not fighting the church. When he explored nature, he probably saw it as the work of his god, like others we have considered.

=> *You are correct in this. He once said: "I have looked into most philosophical systems and I have seen none that will work without God." We have no sense of why Maxwell would say this but are unsurprised after meeting earlier scholars.*

~ The second point is more practical. Maxwell seemed to have been in a hurry, working on various projects in parallel, and moving between institutions quite rapidly. Perhaps he believed that his life would be relatively short. I think he died, still young.

=> *True, Jimbo. Like Pascal and Carnot. All are credited with lunar craters.*

This is valuable background knowledge, 221, but we think Jimbo's words were significant, when he stated, 'there is no magic'. We have been looking for an event, or person, or some chemistry, to explain the acceleration we have witnessed, but now we suspect there is no such factor. We must conclude that the startling *Homo sapiens* performance is their natural tempo. More evidence would help, but we are depleting our review time.

You have not explained your involvement with Maxwell, 221.

I became interested after he published his paper on Saturn in 1859 CE. The paper explained lucidly why his conclusion was the only viable one and showed him to be a gifted mathematical philosopher. In London, I encountered him at the Ri, but as a technician there was no chance to discuss his research.

I knew him later in his short life when he returned to Cambridge as Cavendish Professor of Physics.

Related to the philosopher Cavendish? We recall the family was wealthy.

His descendants founded the Cavendish laboratory and professorship in honour of the distinguished scientist. Another example of the client's philanthropy. Maxwell was the first professor. He installed much of the equipment, and personally took charge of the cataloguing of Cavendish's voluminous research notes. I became a librarian at the laboratory, assisting Maxwell with collating Cavendish's work. Unlike Maxwell, I had a thorough knowledge of his methods from modelling Earth's density, 0.075 kyE before.

How about Maxwell?

Fastidious, patient, courteous, and gentle. He would seem prosperous but unexceptional, except for his achievements.

No magic to be discerned.

We will remain in Edinburgh for a few milliseconds.

Charles Darwin

I propose to consider biology, to examine the research of Darwin, who was born in the English region of Shropshire, in 1809 CE. His father was a physician.

He attended Shrewsbury School before commencing a medical degree at Edinburgh University in 1825 CE. He was uninterested in much of the course and uncomfortable with surgical procedures. His studies did not go well. While in his second year, he was drawn to natural history, a childhood pursuit. He assisted the philosopher, Robert Grant, in observing invertebrate organisms living in the nearby River Forth.

Should we have allocated time to Grant, 221?

Unnecessary, I believe. He published some notable research regarding the lives of sea creatures, and later in London became a teacher of human anatomy, providing an accessible approach to the field. His greatest contribution was in nurturing Darwin's biological interests. Both Grant and Darwin's grandfather had expounded ideas about evolutionary processes.

Having witnessed Darwin's aversion to medicine, his father persevered with higher education, sending him to Cambridge in 1828 CE, to prepare for a future as a church official. He was not a zealous student but began collecting beetles, influenced by the botany professor, John Henslow, who became a mentor.

Can we confirm the nature of the beetle, 221? Our knowledge of Earth's natural history is incomplete.

Beetles are insects found throughout Earth's surface, except for the polar regions and oceans. Their order is the largest of any local lifeforms, with perhaps 400k species, representing nearly half of all known insects and perhaps a quarter of all creatures on the planet. More beetles remain to be discovered. They were important in the client's culture on occasions. Egyptian and Greek myths include beetles, recorded during my Insertions.

We have checked your files, 221, and now know sufficient of these creatures. Maybe we qualify as coleopterists?

His education at Cambridge was influenced by religious philosophy, but my understanding is that Darwin saw this as consistent with scientific research.

We expect that Darwin's later insights would diminish his faith in the supernatural, but our interest is primarily in his scientific achievements.

221 regretted introducing Homo sapiens beliefs into the dialogue.

Darwin graduated from Cambridge in 1831 CE, motivated to undertake scientific research, and particularly natural history. One source of this enthusiasm was John Herschel's recently published book, Preliminary Discourse. I learned this while talking with Darwin later in his career. He then spent a period in the region of Wales, undertaking a course in geology. Darwin had been introduced to geological theory during his studies in Edinburgh.

We thought he studied medicine.

In his second year, he enrolled in natural history, which included geology.

His short time in Wales was more practical, under the direction of the geologist, Adam Sedgewick, one of the founders of present-day geological science, at least on Earth.

We know these theories are universal, certainly within our galaxy, for those bodies composed of silicates. Known on Earth as silica or SiO_2, it represents almost 75% of the planet's crust and is found frequently on similar planets in other systems. The neighbouring planet, Mars, is rich in silica, although its surface is coated in the dust of iron oxides.

The composition of Mars was being revealed to his client, from probes already sent. Plans to deploy roving vehicles on the surface existed, but this was for the future. Meantime, they had drifted from Darwin's career.

Later in the year, after completing the survey work in Wales, an opportunity occurred for Darwin to join a Royal Navy survey expedition on HMS Beagle to chart the coastline of South America.

This would be a sailing ship at, we suppose, 221?

Yes, the Royal Navy and their American colleagues were experimenting with steam paddle frigates, but they were not in general use.

What size was Beagle?

27.5 metres in length and 7.5 metres wide, to accommodate a crew of 74. Darwin joined the ship as a civilian researcher. They departed at the end of 1831 CE on what was planned as a two-year expedition.

While the Navy surveyed the coast, Darwin explored the adjacent land, examining geological formations and collecting biological samples. He visited rainforests and searched for fossils. His observations of similarities and differences between living creatures on the Galápagos Islands, which were geologically new, encouraged him to theorise over the causes of this diversity. He met John Herschel in South Africa.

These would be two scholars with common perspectives perhaps?

I believe so. Herschel was 0.017 kyE older, but both were from prosperous English backgrounds, educated at Cambridge.

Herschel's father was originally German. Would that have made a difference? We like to understand these small points.

I don't think it is relevant. His father had succeeded in becoming respected in Great Britain, probably beyond all expectations. His family had assimilated. For us, the differences between the British and German societies are slight. More relevant is that both had successful fathers and received a high-quality education. They were living in the Age of Reflection, which fostered an interest in the natural world. Their meeting at the Cape was partly social, inevitable given the presence of garrulous naval officers, but they also discussed Herschel's botanical observations.

How do you know this, 221?

I received an assignment from a London publisher named Colburn, who was retained by the government to issue the account of the Beagle's voyage and research. My role was to review the scientific content.

Concurrent with your assistance to Clapeyron's publisher?

Slightly later, but close. The publisher was frustrated by the voyage's prolongation, which delayed publication. Significant sums had been spent in preparation, but without any immediate prospect of income. My visit to South Africa was to assess whether an interim report could be written before the ship's return. This was my suggestion. It proved impossible because Darwin's material was unprepared, but I interacted with the two philosophers.

Both instrument-making and publishing have been useful guises, 221.

During the voyage, Darwin had written regularly to his former tutor, John Henslow, describing his geological observations. Henslow compiled a paper drawn from Darwin's letters, which he circulated to prominent researchers. Darwin arrived in England in 1836 CE to find that he already possessed a high profile within the scientific community.

221, you previously told us this was a two-year excursion, commencing in 1831 CE. We appreciate the publisher's concern now.

Two years was the plan, but the extent of the work meant a prolonged trip.

On his return, a priority for Darwin was to seek expert help in cataloguing the animal and botanical collections accumulated during his travels. He was met on arrival by Charles Lyell, then President of the Geological Society, and through him, obtained assistance from the Royal College of Surgeons in London, for work on the fossil collection. He received help from Richard Owen, one of the foremost palaeontologists of the period.

We recall the last palaeontologist we met was Hooke, perhaps 0.19 kyE before, and wondered why they were unknown elsewhere in the galaxy. You provided persuasive answers, 221, but now we find these scientists are uncommon here, too.

There have been others since Hooke, but I had no reason to introduce them. Natural history on Earth has attracted many researchers who followed this science as a hobby, gathering samples without the scholarship of a professional scientist. Gradually, knowledge accumulated and a structured approach to research evolved. Both Darwin and Owen are examples of a specialist naturalist.

He presented a paper describing his circumnavigation to the Geological Society in London, addressing the South American landmass, in early 1837 CE. On the same day, he presented his bird and mammal specimens to the Zoological Society. In 1839 CE, he was elected to the Royal Society.

Apart from his engagements with the learned societies, participation in a social circle that included Lyell and Babbage, and marriage, Darwin divided his time between rewriting his journals for publication and pondering evolutionary processes. In 1839 CE, the Narrative of the Surveying Voyages was published. The first two volumes were written by the ship's officers, recounting the travels of HMS Beagle and a sister ship. The third volume consisted of Darwin's contribution, titled Journal and Remarks, containing his observations and comments on the geology, animals, and botany of the regions he visited. It was immediately popular and reissued by the publisher under a different title. A second edition was produced in 1845 CE, which included changes resulting from both the scientific interpretation of the samples and Darwin's developing reflections on evolution. Further editions followed, maintaining his reputation.

For 0.015 kyE after the publication of Narrative, Darwin provided new material, encompassing expert reports on the samples. In the background, he refined his ideas on evolution.

You were familiar with his thoughts during this time, 221?

Through my work with Colburn, I met Lyell, who was trying to encourage Darwin on his intellectual journey. While Lyell did not wholly agree, he knew his ideas were too important to be left unspoken. He sought a different publisher for Darwin's new work, so it would not be seen as an extension of the Beagle chronicles. I arranged for a publisher called Murray to become involved and again offered my services as a subject-matter specialist. Through this channel, assisted by Lyell, I facilitated Darwin's greatest work.

You helped to write his most notable book, 221?

Not really. I did some proofreading and made suggestions. Nothing more.

In 1859 CE, after sundry tribulations, his theories were published in On the Origin of the Species, attracting popular interest. The book was written to enable educated non-specialists to comprehend his thesis. It could not be dismissed as a work of fiction and was accessible with some study.

We appreciated your account of Darwin's work but should absorb his ideas.

The crux was that populations of living flora and fauna evolve over many generations through a process called natural selection. Earth's biota descended from common ancestors, and the branching of evolution led to distinct species. His principal points were that these did not evolve separately, and that the driver of change was natural selection.

This was not an entirely new idea, but the difference with Darwin's book was that he had amassed evidence during his travels, and from other researchers.

We have the impression that his book was controversial, 221. Why should this be? He was a respected scientific figure, providing a hypothesis supported by facts. Please explain.

The difficulty was that his model involved the Homo sapiens species as a product of evolutionary processes including natural selection. The prevailing view of many philosophers and the dominant local church was that the human was unique, separate, and distinct from other animals.

Once again, we observe the guardians of the supernatural obstructing progress, 221. We are no longer surprised, but remain puzzled by their influence, when their dogmas are progressively being supplanted by science. Can you explain Darwin's ideas? Natural selection is a new term for us, although we have probably encountered the process elsewhere.

I know Darwin's work, have heard him lecture, and listened to the opinions of scientists who utilised his theory, so understand the concept.

Evolution is the result of natural selection, which depends on variation. There is a random element to variation, in the sense that it is not driving in a single direction, such as improving the performance of a creature. The improvement trend arises from selection.

Where does this variation come from?

Genetic mutations that can take the species in various directions. A frequently cited example is the early hominids, ancestors of the Homo sapiens, in which mutation meant some possessed larger brains and others, smaller brains. If we accept brain size as synonymous with intelligence, selection favours the former, who become dominant.

We have seen this elsewhere in the galaxy, 221. Darwin was right. To have inferred this from observing animals and plants is an astonishing insight. We know of many civilisations who never deduced their origins, despite becoming technologically interesting to us. Some, less self-aware than this client, have not studied the question. Has Darwin's model been accepted in the present-day?

In the scientific community this is generally the case, but there are religious groups with powerful support that retain other beliefs.

~ Your account has fascinated me because I'm weak in the biological sciences. One unanswered question is how life began. So long as this remains unexplained, it leaves open the possibility that somebody started it. Maybe a god.

Jimbo raises an issue that deserves a response. Specifically for Earth, we cannot provide a definitive answer because we have not followed each event since the planet was formed. Nor elsewhere.

We know that there are several routes to life being initiated on a particular planet. One is through the carbon atom, which tends to form molecules at temperatures found on Earth-like planets. In the early phases, once they have cooled and solidified, we find CH_4, CO_2, H_2O, NH_3, perhaps some other organic gases, maybe some hydrogen but little oxygen.

We have observed three sources of these molecules. First is the capture of gases from the local nebula as a protoplanet forms. This is a gravitational effect. The lighter gases escape. Second is the product of volcanic activity. N_2 and S_2 become more prevalent during these eruptions. The third is large asteroids that bring CH_4 and H_2O. The second and third effects may be simultaneous. These are general comments, not specific to Earth.

The synthesis of more intricate organic molecules happens more readily in low-oxygen atmospheres. Over geologically significant periods, influenced by fluctuations in pressure, temperature, electrical discharges, and UV radiation, more complicated molecules are created, and occasionally these possess self-replicating properties, initiating the first stages of life.

I know that in the present-day, laboratories on Earth have simulated these early conditions but have not observed self-replication.

This process requires time, 221, as we know from our observations. It is useless to research within the scale of *Homo sapiens* lifespans.

Consider the statistics. We have roughly 10^{10} stars within our galaxy with planets that possess characteristics consistent with organic life. 10^{10} planets may seem a big number but consider the size of the opportunity. Assume that life must start within a window of 10^6 kyE on a planet, or not at all. We know this is pessimistic, but we can take a conservative approach here. On Earth it was later. With a time limit of 10^6 kyE available to each of 10^{10} planets, there are 10^{19} planet-years of opportunity for organic life to begin once within our galaxy. We have molecules synthesising larger molecules for 10 billion billion planet-years of opportunity, while we wait for a self-replicating molecule to evolve. Is this likely, or improbable? For the client, even as their scientific base expands, this is unknown. They only have one example of life starting, namely on Earth.

221 reflected that for the first time, he understood why some Homo sapiens religions preached that their species was unique, installed by a creator.

We see this too. Easy to be seduced into this belief. Harder for Copernicus, Galileo, and the other philosophers until Darwin to challenge.

The Intelligence has the advantages of time and a galactic perspective. We know the answer to the client's puzzle: life is pervasive in our galaxy. In other remote galaxies where the same physical laws prevail, life will also flourish.

221 noted that 0.5 seconds had so far been spent on something he understood but recognised the value of involving Jimbo in this aspect.

~ Jimbo also realised that the comments of the Energy Masters were for him. 221 knew all this because he was a part of the Intelligence. I have another question. Living cells can evolve in a suitable environment, apparently because the chance of self-replicating molecules developing from an organic cocktail is better than one in 10^{19}, maybe much better. It seems to me, though, that is only half of the picture. While self-replicating life is a necessary condition, to satisfy those who doubt that we could exist without a creator, the required condition is the evolution of intelligent life.

=> *A deep subject, Jimbo, because we need a common definition of intelligence. Taking you as the datum, then we could say that the majority of your species does not qualify, but if I took a sheepdog as the benchmark, then most could be deemed intelligent. Probably not all, though. For a millisecond, 221 worried that the Energy Masters might start a discussion about sheepdogs, but happily, this did not happen.*

Jimbo's observation is reasonable. If the galaxy had a cornucopia of single-celled life but *Homo sapiens* beings and the other complex creatures on Earth, all results of Darwin's natural selection, were unique, then the supernaturalists could claim that a god had guided their evolution.

Let's go back to the numbers and give Jimbo more of the picture. We identified a cautious budget of 10^{19} planet-years for life to start in our galaxy. Now we add the second condition of intelligent life. This must come from within the same budget because we have no more planets, and we have allocated only 10^6 kyE. We know that self-replicating life has occurred on about 10^8 occasions, which leaves a budget of 10^{11} for intelligence to develop. Using our definitions with no further canine analogies, we find that intelligent life has evolved roughly 10^7 times, but only half of these civilisations meet our interpretation of maturity, giving us about 5×10^6 occasions, as our organically derived clients.

Or in summary, once self-replication has been initiated, on about 10% of occasions, intelligence emerges, half of which matures.

~ You're saying that from your population of 10 billion suitable locations, about 1% produce self-replicating life, which means 100 million planets, and 10% of them evolve what you regard as intelligence, giving ten million, but only half achieve maturity. Therefore, five million intelligent civilisations have arisen within the galaxy, and probably more elsewhere.

=> *Yes, Jimbo, but there are some suppositions here. Note that we said there are 10^{10} stars with suitable planets. Some stars have several such planets, so the opportunity is greater.*

=> *We also have another route to organic life beginning. It is not necessary for self-replicating molecules to evolve independently. They can be delivered to the planet, ready for action.*

~ How? Are you saying they already existed elsewhere?

=> *Asteroids and comets, Jimbo. These bodies travel through space, carrying frozen water and hydrocarbons. Embedded within them can be self-replicating molecules.*

~ I have read these ideas, but they were science fiction.

=> *Truth is stranger than fiction, Jimbo. Your novelist, Mark Twain's opinion. He was correct.*

~ We could have existed elsewhere in the galaxy. Is that correct?

=> *In principle, yes, but you evolved here on Earth.*

~ How can you be sure?

=> *We know the lifeforms in the galaxy. Simplistic, but organic life has a signature, exclusive to the common ancestors that Darwin perceived, which the Intelligence recognises. Your mark only exists here. The Homo sapiens lifeform, the most intellectually advanced on Earth, certainly is unique, which is why your abnormal development intrigues us.*

221 realised that their absorbing discussion had consumed an unplanned 1.3 seconds of his budget.

We know this, but it has been useful. Not just for Jimbo, but for us to reflect on this client's unusual journey from hunter-gatherer to Darwin in $<10^2$ kyE. None of our 5×10^6 civilisations achieved this. Remember, 221, we are composed of many such earlier societies, so this species differs greatly from us.

There is more to learn before we conclude. One more trait to note, and then the inception of their electromagnetic exploits. Before that, we must finalise our understanding of Darwin.

Correct, but it is a pity we described only organic life to Jimbo. We should introduce him to inorganic life, so widespread and diverse.

What would Darwin have thought about inorganic evolution? No time for that now. For another 0.023 kyE, he continued his research, content to let others argue the merits of his theory while he gathered further evidence. We should meet another philosopher, Alfred Russel Wallace, a contemporary British scientist. While much of his research was distinct Darwin's, they shared similar views of evolution, construed independently.

Wallace studied the natural history of the Amazon rainforest in South America and the regions of Asia now known as Malaysia and Indonesia. While he and Darwin may be regarded as competitors, my impression was that they were collaborators. In 1858 CE, before Darwin published On the Origin of the Species, they jointly provided a related paper on evolution and natural selection. While Darwin received most of the credit for their theory, I believe that his career benefited from their cooperation. Although I did not meet Wallace, I learned from Darwin, who greatly respected him, that he was a philosopher attracted by unconventional ideas, of which natural selection was one.

He was also an environmentalist, concerned about the effects of industrial and agricultural expansion on the natural world. We will return to this theme, soon. It is apparent that he saw a relationship between vegetation and climate, and was concerned by deforestation.

Why was this happening, 221?

In his paper of 1878 CE, he addressed forest clearance for coffee cultivation, in the Indian subcontinent.

Prescient concerns, given the challenges the client now faces, and our simulations of the future for Earth's environment.

Wallace could claim to be the first Homo sapiens astrobiologist, who wrote seriously about the possibility of life on other planets.

What did he conclude, 221?

He confidently asserted that life in the local system must be confined to Earth because no liquid water could exist elsewhere.

We see weaknesses in the argument, but we have facts, whereas Wallace derived his conclusions from limited information.

He was doubtful about life adjacent to other stars, but this could only have been speculative, given that no adjoining planets were identified during his life.

We are impressed that scientists examined such celestial matters, with so few tools. The Herschel family had similar questions, we recall, and Huygens too.

How should we view Darwin?

His contribution to Homo sapiens science was huge. On the Origin of the Species has been described as one of the most influential books ever written. From within the limited scope of our review, I suggest that it stands with Newton's Principia and Smith's Wealth of Nations as transforming the client's understanding of nature and themselves.

Copernicus and Maxwell made contributions of equivalent magnitudes, it appears to us, as dispassionate observers. Galileo, too.

There were many, mused 221, but did not disagree with the Energy Masters.

At the end of his life, Darwin's remains were buried in Westminster Abbey alongside Newton and his old friend from South Africa, John Herschel. An Australian city, a regional capital, sustains his name. Many animal nomenclatures incorporate Darwin. Edinburgh University's biology school possesses a Darwin building, and Cambridge University, a Darwin college. A lunar crater bears his name; 122 km diameter. He will not be forgotten.

Σ93 seconds

John Muir

We will maintain the theme of natural history by meeting John Muir, born in the coastal town of Dunbar, to the east of Edinburgh, in 1838 CE. I regard him as a naturalist, botanist, geologist, and environmentalist. His early life consisted of a religious upbringing, but enjoyment of the local country and coastline. While still a child, his family emigrated to the newly established American state of Wisconsin, where they began farming. Later, he studied science at Wisconsin University. He learned sufficient geology and botany to inform his career.

Did Muir provide an invention or make a scientific discovery, 221? We cannot identify any specific achievement vital to *Homo sapiens* civilisation. Is there a philosophical aspect that we have missed?

Yes, there may be. 221 surprised himself with his assertion that the Energy Masters had neglected an essential facet of the client's disposition. We should appreciate the Homo sapiens relationship with Earth's natural environment, meaning the terrain and seas, and both plants and animals.

You have our attention, 221. This is not a dimension we have considered or encountered in other beings we regard as successful. You believe it is relevant to their remarkable advances, we assume.

Muir was not unique in encouraging respect for the natural world, but in his adopted home of North America, he was influential in maintaining what the client sometimes describes as wilderness. He published hundreds of articles and wrote twelve books. He encouraged the local political leadership to create national parks that would be protected from exploitation and founded an environmental organisation in 1892 CE. It has thrived ever since.

We have perused your reports, 221, and perceive that Muir was a motivated and energetic man, with a particular grasp of geology in his region. He sometimes convinced others to refrain from industrialisation to conserve nature, which seems inconsistent with recent *Homo sapiens* momentum. This intrigues us. Why sacrifice technological progress to protect unused resources? Why is this important, and how does it relate to their scientific acceleration?

221 wondered how to respond. He had read Muir's work and noted it was carefully prepared and possessed merit. Although he was not a great orator, he elaborated reasoned arguments modestly, and enthused his listeners. 221 could not express the importance of Muir's ideas, but felt they reflected a fundamental Homo sapiens characteristic. The Intelligence is a superb entity, he considered, enabling him to feel something is important without being able to articulate it.

We appreciate your difficulty, 221. Fortunately, Jimbo is present. He will explain what you sense. We are accustomed to his intuition and eloquence.

~ Jimbo recognised that the Intelligence, both the Energy Masters and 221, awaited his comments. I should remind you that we consist of a plethora of individuals, with independent and often conflicting opinions. It is not the case that we all appreciate the natural beauty of our planet and its inhabitants. Some prefer industrialisation, if profitable, irrespective of the environmental effects. Such people are perhaps a minority, but a powerful one in some regions. There are others living in poverty, who have no choice but to exploit their surroundings to survive. Their concern is to feed children, not long-term environmental damage. Finally, there is ignorance. We may not understand the impact of our actions if the consequences are not immediately obvious.

~ Despite these negatives, many of us, probably most, appreciate the natural splendour of our world and want it preserved. There are both emotional and rational reasons.

~ To consider the former, remember our roots. We were hunter-gatherers, living on the land and from its products. These small groups were in tune with nature, and the seasons. Perhaps we retain this affinity. If we accept Darwin's thesis, our heritage is even older, closer to nature.

=> *Are there examples? Is this just a feeling or is it reflected in behaviour?*

~ There are many. You can see countryside walks and trails, populated by city dwellers who enjoy nature at weekends. Volunteers act as guides, taking visitors into the woods or hills. We pick fruit, which is more time-consuming than buying it in the grocery store. Some watch birds or animals, not to catch them, but for their behaviour.

~ We have an agrarian past. Modern agriculture is productive, so a few farmers can feed a large population. In the future, these processes will become even more effective. Despite this, certainly among the British, most people like to own a garden and even grow vegetables This is not good economics, but people do it anyway.

=> *Why, Jimbo?*

~ Apart from our farming tradition, it's creative and brings them closer to nature. I have heard it said that gardening brings a sense of peace, so perhaps there are psychological benefits.

~ Then there is the sensory aspect. I explained that we appreciate beauty when we discussed art, but the Energy Masters seemed uninterested. We can admire spectacular terrain, or enjoy water shimmering in a river, or wind blowing through a forest, or a sunset. Or even a tree that stands for many of our lifespans.

=> *This is particularly hard for us, Jimbo. Darwin's natural selection should favour those who are productive, rather than dendrophiles.*

~ Maybe interacting with nature makes us productive.

~ Additionally, we feel a sense of responsibility, to maintain the planet for future generations, and for the other creatures that share it.

=> *We see the damage, Jimbo. The oceans are polluted with hydrocarbons and plastics. The ozone layer is depleted, and there is an existential problem with atmospheric warming, which will challenge your species.*

~ I didn't say we are perfect, or even successful, just that many of us feel responsible. We now have the Montreal Protocol, which addresses the ozone concern, both as an example of cooperation and effective science. Climate change has at least been acknowledged in the Kyoto Protocol, but many of us know this will be harder to solve.

=> *You will be driving an electric car soon, Jimbo.*

~ Which answers your question about an important forthcoming material. Lithium. You said it would be used for batteries. This technology will be essential for electrically powered vehicles. I understand that lithium is the preferred chemistry for these batteries.

=> *Correct, Jimbo. This element was detected by the Swedish chemist Johan Arfwedson in 1817 CE, but not isolated until the philosopher, William Brande, applied Davy's electrolysis method in 1821 CE.*

These are two additional scientists that we cannot meet now, 221. Nor are we able to address *Homo sapiens* uses for lithium, although we would like to. Perhaps Jimbo can continue explaining his relationship with the natural world?

221 noted the Energy Masters' patience and hoped Jimbo appreciated this.

~ These are emotional reasons for our attachment, but rational motives exist for respecting our planet, and not overusing resources. The most important is that this is our home. To be precise, our only home. We should take care of it, then it can look after us. We already know that some variables associated with climate change are non-linear, making the risks greater. My school reading list included *Only One Earth*, written 0.024 kyE ago, but the issues remain.

~ While our ultimate energy source is the Sun, we need biochemical processes to convert this into food, requiring care for our environment. Even more fundamental is access to unpolluted air and water.

~ Regarding the other creatures who share Earth with us, apart from being entitled to their existence, they may be useful. I am thinking mainly about their physiology, and what we can learn, but I'm ignorant of this field.

Jimbo has given us insights, 221. We note the rational arguments for taking care of the planet, but the emotional aspects are ones that may improve our understanding of *Homo sapiens* performance. You could not have explained this since you do not possess these feelings and neither do we. Perhaps the client's ancestry prolongs this behaviour, as Jimbo suggested, but not why their culture retains this vestige of their origins if it serves no purpose.

They listen to music and play games, too. These pursuits seem trivial but remain important. We know they have a complex brain and minds that make remarkable connections through opaque processes, so we assume seemingly irrational interests also emanate from the cerebrum.

We prefer to know, 221, rather than to assume, but within the confines of this review, we must accept these peculiarities are intrinsic to the species, together with their growing scientific capabilities.

Presumably, Muir would have agreed with Jimbo's comments?

I am sure, although he would not have been so succinct. He was a proponent of the natural world, with a mission to persuade others. He once wrote: "I care to live only to entice people to look at Nature's loveliness."

Examining Muir's contribution proved unexpected, 221. Through learning of his career, we have reassessed our knowledge of the *Homo sapiens* psyche and find deficiencies. Many contributors have been missed, but we already have a deeper appreciation of the client, if incomplete.

Guglielmo Marconi

Our final scientist reintroduces electromagnetism. We should travel to northern Italy to meet Marconi, who was born in 1874 CE into a wealthy family and lived near Bologna. For part of his childhood, he resided in England. An engineer, inventor, and entrepreneur.

He succeeded despite an unconventional education, which probably reflected the prosperity of his family. Several private tutors taught him, primarily mathematics and science. Marconi spoke fluent English and Italian. He did not pursue a formal university education, but through a friendship with the philosopher, Augusto Righi, gained access to resources at Bologna University.

What was Righi's specialism, 221?

He was Professor of Physics. Among his interests was electromagnetism, and one of the first to generate microwaves, widening the spectrum for exploitation. He was Marconi's mentor. Righi had pursued the research of the distinguished German scientist, Heinrich Hertz, who was the first to prove the existence of the electromagnetic waves predicted by Maxwell's equations, and to my knowledge, also the first to generate a radio signal.

It is unfortunate that we could not accommodate Hertz within our review, 221. We see vital contributions from your reports.

I followed his career closely, but his life ended at the age of 0.036 kyE. Otherwise, he would have achieved more.

~ You know that Hertz is recognised through the unit we use for frequency, the hertz, or Hz?

=> Yes, we do, Jimbo. One definition of the microwave spectrum investigated by Righi is 300 MHz - 300 GHz. You were probably going to remind us of the relationship between frequency and wavelength.

~ We can express it as: $\lambda = c/f$

where λ is the wavelength in metres, c is the speed of light, roughly 3×10^8 m/s and f is the frequency in hertz, formerly cycles per second. I assume this relationship remains valid throughout the galaxy.

=> Yes, and far beyond. Strange phenomena occur inside the black holes that interested Michell and Herschel, >0.2 kyE ago, though.

Righi wrote a valedictory article recording the work of Hertz in 1894 CE, referring to his electromagnetic achievements. This caught Marconi's attention. Righi may have encouraged him to investigate what was called wireless telegraphy. By this time, the scientific community was interested in radio waves, but viewed this as a natural phenomenon rather than an opportunity. The British physicist, Oliver Lodge, generated radio waves independently of Hertz and demonstrated the effect during his Ri lecture in the same year.

Marconi began conducting experiments at his home in Italy. This was before he came to my attention. He did not work within a formal setting, a scientific or engineering environment, so his activities were not apparent.

We understand, 221. Similar to Joule.

We note that Marconi was aged 0.020 kyE when he commenced his studies.

I think that he accessed concurrent scientific research though his university connections. Later, I inspected his experimental apparatus. The work of Hertz, Lodge, and the French physicist, Edouard Branly, seemed influential.

We see that Lodge and Branly were notable contributors, 221.

Marconi utilised their insights but furthered them through his research.

By the following year, his apparatus could send signals over several kilometres. Line-of-sight was not essential, which breached the understanding that radio waves were analogous to light, with a range limited to the horizon. Marconi knew he had a device with commercial and military applications.

This affliction is an inherent *Homo sapiens* trait, 221. It is pointless to criticise their fascination with warfare, as we cannot rationalise it.

221 had no wish to conclude on a negative note, which meant minimising the military content.

Marconi had two priorities. One was to acquire patents for his inventions. The other was to obtain funding that would enable his experiments to become working systems with practical uses. To achieve this, he came to England, where his discoveries attracted interest from both the British Post Office and the Admiralty, which controls the Royal Navy. In 1896 CE, he applied for a patent. He was supported by William Preece, then the Chief Electrical Engineer of the Post Office. The next year, Marconi's work became public knowledge through lectures given by Preece, including one at the Ri.

When did you become aware of Marconi's breakthrough, 221?

At the time of his patent application, and shortly afterwards when I observed a demonstration given to the government. This was not easy because no accredited position was immediately available, but I attended the event as a science correspondent for a newspaper. It was well-received, and the first of many evaluations, transmitting signals over progressively longer distances.

We are surprised the government allowed newspapers to report such an innovation, which had strategic importance.

The deal allowed reporters to attend but not share the news until authorised.

Once Marconi obtained funding, he assembled a small team to support his project. There were few candidates available with electrical knowledge, so I participated as a technician.

Demonstrations continued, including one for the Italian Government, while engineering proceeded at a high tempo. By 1898 CE, the system had sufficient power to be deployed, to connect a lighthouse with a lightship, about 19 km distant from the south-east coast of England. A few months later, it was instrumental in the first marine rescue.

During this period, Marconi was preoccupied with both technology and business. A transmitting station was built on England's south coast, on the Isle of Wight. 221 recalled the transmission mast being raised to a working height, >50 metres, which required help from the local inhabitants. The system could communicate with ships to a range of 64 km. 221 witnessed a visit by Lord Kelvin, who sent a message to Glasgow University via a receiving station in the town of Bournemouth, then through the post office telegraph network.

About 0.04 kyE before, 221 had observed Kelvin's role in laying undersea cables across the Atlantic Ocean.

You have reminded us of the scope of his contributions, 221. We think of him as a thermodynamicist because of his cooperation with Joule, and a mathematician, but he qualifies as an engineer too. You travelled on these voyages, 221; we hope your skills proved useful?

I worked as Kelvin's secretary, so was obliged to accompany him. He appreciated my language skills, when communicating with French and German philosophers, but was surprised that I followed his mathematical elaborations, as few others could.

Around this time, Faraday demonstrated that the data rate achievable along a cable depended on its design, which prompted Kelvin to consider the theoretical capacity. His concern was the impact of bandwidth on the financial viability of a transmission cable.

Again, we have *Homo sapiens* economic logic being applied, where other galactic civilisations would see a science project. It seems that Smith's *'invisible hand'* provided guidance.

221 noted that they had drifted from the agenda.

Marconi established a small factory, in the town of Chelmsford, 48 km north-east of London, and 35 km from Colchester. 221 had known the area long before the client discovered radio waves and remembered travelling via Caesaromagus as Chelmsford was then called, together with the Roman construction engineers on their journey to Camulodunum.

~ You know that *Caesaromagus* means Caesar's marketplace?

=> Yes, Jimbo, and that it was a small market, adjacent to a Roman fort. The soldiers could buy fruit there in summer, but beer all year long. Have you been to Chelmsford?

~ Only once when I visited a golf course. A small but important part of my father's business is supplying precision-machined components for radar applications. We don't talk about it. The customer is Marconi. He supplies a plant north of Edinburgh and another, larger one in Chelmsford. His relationship is long-established, so they invited him to a centenary event at the Chelmsford Golf Club, which was established in 1893 CE. I accompanied him. Good course and friendly people.

=> *221 reflected that golfers had played in Chelmsford before Marconi's arrival and wondered whether this was significant. Probably not.*

~ The inventor of radar was a Scot, descended from James Watt.

=> *I knew Robert Watson-Watt well, Jimbo. An outstanding scientist.*

Marconi then turned his attention to transatlantic wireless telegraphy.

Why was this of interest when cables already crossed the ocean floor, providing a telegraph connection?

It was the next technical challenge, but Marconi also saw a business opportunity in connecting shipping companies with vessels at sea. After various trials and frustrated efforts, a confirmed wireless signal was received from Nova Scotia, Canada in 1902 CE.

~ The signal was received on 17 December.

=> *Yes, Jimbo, is this of particular significance?*

~ I noticed a minor coincidence. Marconi became interested because of the work of Hertz, who researched the waves predicted by Maxwell's equations that established a theoretical basis for Faraday's discoveries, who was at one time assistant to Davy.

=> *Quite correct, but where is this leading?*

~ Davy's birthday was 17 December. He was born exactly 0.124 kyE before the signal crossed the ocean.

=> *What else, Jimbo?*

~ It's my birthday, too.

=> *Do you remember my question about Henry?*

~ You said we shared something. His birthday was also 17 December?

=> *Yes, it was. Three of you, from a group of seven scholars, share the same date. I estimate the probability of two or more having the same birthday is 1.6%.*

Can we learn something from this, 221 pondered, noting that Jimbo's birth was 0.075 kyE after the signal?

What we should learn is that time continues to pass. If we wanted to discuss the number 17 further, we see that Jimbo commenced university aged 0.017 kyE, slightly older than Maxwell. Can return to Marconi's exploits?

=> *221 noted that Davy was 0.199 kyE older than Jimbo.*

~ Jimbo thought about the Haddington golf course, 17th oldest in the world.

=> *Today is now the 17th day of the month.*

By 1900 CE, innovation meant that wireless telephony was feasible.

By this you mean the transmission of sound rather than discrete impulses provided by the telegraph.

Correct, although the sound is converted into impulses for transmission, then back again to audio by the receiver. This was first achieved in São Paulo, Brazil by the inventor Robert Landell, witnessed by journalists and the British Consul. His voice was transmitted for 8 km.

In 1912 CE, Marconi opened a factory in New Street, Chelmsford, which became Earth's first dedicated radio manufacturing facility, and in 1920 CE was the source of early British entertainment broadcasts. A research facility established by Marconi at the nearby village of Great Baddow was later used for regular broadcasts of news and entertainment. Parallel developments occurred in the United States. From these beginnings, the client's global broadcasting infrastructure evolved.

While Marconi enjoyed commercial success, he remained a dedicated researcher and inventor. In 1909 CE, he received the Nobel Prize for Physics, together with the German philosopher Karl Braun, for their contributions to wireless telegraphy.

This had become a top *Homo sapiens* award by this time?

The ninth year of awards; conferred most years since. Last time, two Americans were credited for particle physics research, 0.086 kyE after Marconi.

He was a leader, but from your reports we see that others participated.

I think Marconi was unusual in combining science with business, but many scientists worked in this field. I read their papers, but they were too numerous to meet individually. Apart from Europe, there were researchers in North America, Russia, and India with noteworthy contributions.

We appreciate these achievements, particularly those of Hertz and Marconi, exploiting the work of predecessors. As we learned, 221, '*on the shoulders of giants*'. We have stopped looking for magic. The client's intellectual progress over the review period is astounding by galactic standards.

Our requirement now is to reflect, to consider whether we have obtained an adequate sense of the client's situation. We know that time constraints mean that our picture is incomplete, with many scientists omitted.

~ I don't know what represents adequacy in understanding my species, because I don't fully comprehend the question you want to answer, but in my opinion, the gaps are large. Yes, you know that important figures are absent. Euler is an example, but there are other holes in your analysis.

=> *What would they be?*

~ You're interested in our progress, or acceleration as you call it. Much of the review has concentrated on astronomy, physics, chemistry, mathematics, and some engineering. It has enabled you to measure progress on these tracks, but there are trains running on other tracks.

=> *What does this mean, Jimbo?*

~ Simply that progress has been rapid in other areas. Medical science, a big subject in Edinburgh, has barely figured, but over this period we invented anaesthetics and antiseptics, and soon, x-rays and antibiotics. Not my field, so my comments represent a tiny part of what researchers have achieved.

=> *We know, Jimbo. Apart from time, my reason for avoiding medical developments is that they cannot be compared with other galactic inhabitants, who have differing physiologies, or none.*

Jimbo's point is valid, 221. You could not squeeze more into the review without affecting quality, but insights might be gleaned from other fields.

~ A second problem is that you stopped too soon. While much happened over 10^2 kyE, more has changed in the recent 0.1 kyE. Consider flight. We've progressed from early heavier-than-air machines to Moon landings in about 0.06 kyE. Or subjects that barely existed when your review stopped, such as relativity and quantum mechanics. Or digital computation, or seismology, or metallurgy, or nuclear fission, or nanotechnology.
=> *We appreciate your point, Jimbo. We have neglected important fields and missed the most interesting period.*
~ You also omitted the most interesting place, with its dynamism, the USA.

The message is clear. We will consider Jimbo's advice within our deliberations. We may have missed much but have learned immensely. Our next steps will be assessed, but meanwhile you must conclude the agreed client intervention, 221.

Σ97 seconds

37 seconds of interaction had elapsed since his call with Mr North. As the voices receded, Jimbo slipped into a deeper sleep for five more hours.

He had experienced 10^2 kyE of history in 97 seconds, all now embedded in his brain, which functioned optimally. The only peculiarity was the minute capacity now dedicated to communication with 221.

221 had consumed another 3 seconds in hyper-photonic exchanges with the Energy Masters during the review, providing sensor imagery with accompanying audio and olfactory inputs, facts, statistics, and projections in massive volumes, without troubling Jimbo, utilising his 100-second allocation. A paradigm from Earth was that Jimbo had seen 97 seconds of film promotions, while the Energy Masters absorbed the full-length movie in <3 seconds. Their understanding was deeper than Jimbo knew, but perhaps too narrow, as he suggested.

If he were a Homo sapiens, he might wonder whether his bosses appreciated the review, but as a component of the Intelligence, he believed they did not possess an inkling of satisfaction.

221 briefly interrogated the sensor outputs for Edinburgh and East Lothian, in preparation for Jimbo's morning.

Ten
1996 CE – About 05.45, 17 August, Edinburgh

Daybreak in Stirling Road. An afternoon in Haddington.
Jimbo had been awake for a while. The Sun would soon rise. Looking across the rooftops to the west, from his window, he watched the stars receding as the illumination strengthened. A cloudless start.

Normally an early riser, even at the weekend, he felt that today might be no ordinary Saturday. His parents would sleep until later. His father played golf at the weekend, but seemed bothered by yesterday's strange events, and might want another conversation. Better that he departed early.

Downstairs in the kitchen, Timothy stirred as Jimbo entered, but showed no interest in getting up. He heated two brown pita breads and opened the peanut butter jar. The ping of the microwave coincided with him returning the juice carton to the fridge. Before six, the nutrition had gone, including a second tumbler of orange. Crunchy peanut butter on warm pita was hard to beat. Flavour, protein, and brevity, combined.

He switched the radio on, thinking vaguely of Marconi, hoping to catch the news bulletin, but instead heard the beat of *Wannabe*. Timothy became attentive. A *Spice Girls* fan? Jimbo turned it off, as his phone started to vibrate. 06.01, which was after six.

"Hello, Jimbo. Are you ready for our excursion to East Lothian? I hope so. First, we need to make a call at the Institute. At 06.30, I will be outside in a green Range Rover." Then Mr North was gone.

Jimbo reflected that he hadn't uttered a word. Mr North didn't require a response. Was this arrogance or self-confidence? Or maybe he's busy.

"Gone to the Institute, back later" he wrote on the little whiteboard attached to the fridge. Susan would wonder why his car was still parked at the kerbside and worry. His father was more disturbed than he appeared.

He thought about 221, and immediately his voice was there, inside his head. While indistinguishable from conversation in the kitchen, Timothy appeared unaware of it, despite acute canine aural capabilities.

How are you, Jimbo? No ill effects from our little review last night, I hope. 221 already knew Jimbo's physiological state via his permanent presence in his head, but politeness costs nothing. One of Susan's expressions.

I'm fine, 221, but uncertain about how today will unfold. There are a few questions for you, though.

We have been entirely open, all along. What can you possibly need to know?

You've been open about the detail, I agree. The history lesson was fantastic. My unknowns are about the big picture. Lots of unknowns. What are you and the Energy Masters trying to achieve? If you have a galaxy to run, why are you preoccupied with chasing a few criminals around Edinburgh? If the Intelligence is $>10^7$ kyE old, why could it only afford 100 seconds for your review? Why do I seem so knowledgeable, like I've never forgotten anything? How do you know so much about me, even from childhood? How long will you be in my mind?

These are all simple points to answer, Jimbo, but not now. Mr North's vehicle is decelerating outside your home. Don't keep him waiting. Politeness costs nothing, you know.

Jimbo gasped audibly, attracting Timothy's momentary curiosity. The dog was dozing, Jimbo saw, realising that he didn't like peanut butter. Had it been his father's liver pâté on toast, then an alacritous Timothy would be evident.

There is a more urgent matter, Jimbo. Mr North does not want to detain Dr Gradac. He would prefer him to escape with the disks. This was discussed with Mr Fox last night. I think that he informed his leadership, then there was interaction with several people in London, and now silence. Prof. Raeburn was involved and had people working on the disks overnight.

Jimbo felt lost, involved in deep and dangerous intrigues, he believed.

Grabbing his outdoor jacket from one of the pegs in the porch and shoving his phone into the zippable inner pocket, Jimbo exited the house, quietly closing first the glass-panelled inner door and then the large pale-blue external door. Apart from an electric milk truck turning left into Zetland Place, the street remained in nocturnal stasis. A green Range Rover stood opposite the garden gate, partly obscured by Susan's large fuchsias, but with the diesel engine audible. The driver's window was open, framing the grinning face of a gentleman of indeterminate age, with little hair but aviator sunglasses, which seemed unnecessary, Jimbo considered.

"Back seat, mate," he advised, indicating with his thumb, superfluously.

Jimbo glanced at the tinted rear windows as he reached for the door, also noting the unusual non-reflective paint finish. The door swung open to reveal Mr North ensconced on the far side of the rear seat, phone in one hand and a coffee cup in the other. He was dressed for a day in the country, resplendent in a checked shirt, dark blue corduroy trousers, and a green, knee-length wax jacket. A regimental tie accompanied the shirt, with a steel-grey tie pin maintaining its position. On the seat lay a camouflage bush hat. The style was familiar to Jimbo, from the car parks on the premium side of Murrayfield Stadium, before an international rugby match, where such persons enjoyed expansive picnics before occupying expensive seats. Then he saw the distinctively shaped kukri, in a dull black scabbard, partly obscured by the hat. He hadn't seen them at Murrayfield.

"Back to the Institute, Gerry" ordered Mr North, disregarding Jimbo. "We can take the scenic route through the city centre. No great rush."

Gerry, performed a U-turn, heading south towards the centre. Jimbo noticed a similar green Range Rover still parked where he had seen it last night. His assumption that Mr North had flashed the lights was incorrect. Gerry waved to the occupants as his vehicle sped past.

"How are your parents, Jimbo?" enquired Mr North solicitously. "I imagine they were somewhat disconcerted by events. You allayed their fears?"

"I don't think they were entirely convinced by my story, to be frank. Getting out of bed in the middle of the night and driving to the Institute seemed odd to them." Then he remembered that Mr North also had doubts about his account.

"Inexplicable, Jimbo. My suspicion was that you were cooperating with Gradac, a participant in purloining the disks, willingly or under duress. Your arrival in the Grassmarket with the disks, pursued by armed thugs, could have been a pretence. Then your remarkable evaporation from the scene, and subsequent condensation at the Institute, still in possession of the disks, left us all uneasy. I suspected that the disks had been copied, but Prof. Raeburn assured me they are intact. Mr Fox's specialists examined them and concurred."

Jimbo would have preferred to discuss today, rather than re-examine the confusing events of yesterday. He saw that Gerry was following the conversation with apparent amusement, or maybe he always beamed.

"You live in a beautiful city, Jimbo" said Mr North unexpectedly. "It's a treat for us to spend time here. Better than some places we frequent," he added without elaboration.

Gerry introduced the Botanical Gardens on the right. "The fecundity of nature" he averred, apparently feeling further comment was unnecessary.

"He's just finished an English degree" interjected Mr North, with a slight twitch of the lips, as if to smile. "I encouraged him, and his employer paid."

"Education is the kindling of a flame, not the filling of a vessel" uttered Jimbo, vaguely aware this was translated from Greek.

Socrates, 221 advised.

"Before we leave the Institute for Haddington, I want you to make a placatory call to your parents. Tell them you had arranged to meet the police again, which is true, to provide any further information you have recalled. We surreptitiously involved you in our subterfuge, and by extension your parents, but the net effect of our efforts will be propitious. I have no desire to perturb them.

How did you become familiar with the writings of Socrates? The breadth of your scholarship surprises me. Wisdom from Ancient Greece, 24 centuries past, is hardly germane to an upcoming engineer. Perhaps Archimedes is relevant."

Jimbo felt perplexed. Evidently, his previous remark had not been ignored, wondered if Mr North had offered an apology, and why he employed unusual words. "Wisdom is always relevant" he heard himself say.

Mr North's lips twitched again. "Let us look forward, not back, Jimbo. I surmise that your account of yesterday remains extant. Further disputatious debate might impede today's proceedings. We have a plan of campaign. I assume you still possess Gradac's address in Haddington?"

"Hartington Well Steadings, on Hartington Lane. Maybe a farm."

Jimbo was surprised by the speed with which Mr North conveyed the information through his phone. The respondent seemed terse. The call ended after a few seconds.

"Mr Fox is checking, Jimbo. We trust that your memory is accurate."

Jimbo had not anticipated an immediate response, unlike Mr North, who received the call eagerly. This took longer. Jimbo looked up towards the castle as the big vehicle crossed Princes Street.

"The Empress of the North" proclaimed Gerry, eyeing Jimbo via his rear-view mirror. His advice was either disregarded or missed entirely by Mr North.

The words of Walter Scott, Jimbo. I knew him as president of the RSE.

Mr North remained engrossed, saying little, but listening intently. Then he ended the call and spoke immediately. "Farmhouse with outbuildings, sitting among trees, on the south-eastern edge of the town. Adjacent wooded area, leading nowhere. Surrounded by arable land. One road in, which goes no further. Complications caused by nearby new-build detached homes, perhaps 200 metres from the house, to the front aspect. When we reach the Institute, you can obtain a map from the police. Better brief the troops."

Jimbo realised that Mr North was addressing Gerry, who still smiled but appeared serious. He recalled 221 telling him that the military was arriving by helicopter. This seemed excessive to apprehend one man or let him escape.

Mr North seemed to read Jimbo's thoughts. "Obfuscation. Smoke and mirrors. Muddy the waters. Keep them guessing."

"How should we handle the residents, press, and police?" Gerry wondered.

Jimbo had by now recognised that Gerry was more than a driver.

"Mr Fox is already onto it. The residents will be advised of a small exercise in the area by weekend soldiers and asked to stay away. The press too, if they are interested. Handling the police should be a simple matter."

Jimbo had questions, but knew they were close to the Institute. Perhaps after their arrival. Mr North's tie was that of the Royal Air Force, not an army regiment, as he had assumed. "You were in the RAF, Mr North?"

"No, my father was, though. Flew Hurricanes."

"*Per ardua ad astra*" Gerry advised.

"Through adversity to the stars," Jimbo remarked, surprising both Gerry and Mr North. "The RAF's motto."

"Latin is an unusual skill for an engineering student in the UK, Jimbo. However, you're exceptional, I believe. *Per Mare, Per Terram.*" Mr North looked keenly.

"By sea, by land. The motto of the Royal Marines." The tie pin was in the shape of a commando knife, Jimbo saw. Gerry was watching him, serious but without hostility, Jimbo hoped, as the Range Rover reached the gates of the Institute. "So, you're Marines, members of the Royal Navy?"

Mr North gave another of his sombre chuckles. "Not now. Different tie but same boss, I suppose. Time brings all things to pass."

"Time and tide wait for no man" intoned Gerry.

"Chaucer" responded Jimbo, disconcerted by 221's intervention.

Mr North alighted from the left rear door of the vehicle, which Gerry's manoeuvring meant was close to the main entrance. He moved quickly, through the doors into the reception area, and left towards the Director's office.

Jimbo opened his door on the right, directly behind Gerry, who watched him leave without comment, smiling broadly in acknowledgement of Jimbo's thanks. As he closed the door, Jimbo saw that Mr North's hat and kukri had gone, which he supposed was reasonable since their owner had departed.

The car park was not as empty as might be expected early on a Saturday morning. He blinked in the bright sunlight, his eyes attuned to the tinted windows of the Range Rover. A blue sky, with high clouds gliding from west to east, but a persistent cool breeze. Gerry advanced his vehicle towards a parking bay, enabling Jimbo to walk straight into the building, several seconds after Mr North.

He didn't recognise Tessa immediately, her regular, formal two-piece office attire replaced by dark blue jeans, a denim blouse under a maroon woollen cardigan without buttons, a matching belt knotted at the front, and a blue headband. Tessa was a mathematician, with a doctorate in the statistics of software maintenance, he had read. In this building such credentials were unexceptional, but she brought practical organisational skills too, which were less prevalent. He had been interviewed by Tessa on his first visit to the Institute, before meeting Prof. Raeburn. She occupied an office next to the Director, a secretary positioned outside, who also acted as receptionist.

He sensed that her demeanour was warmer than yesterday. Perhaps his support for the Director, and cooperation with the Chief Inspector and Mr North, were reasons. Or simply because this time his clothes were not covered in mud. She proffered coffee, served in a porcelain cup and saucer. Although not a coffee aficionado, particularly here, the beverage commonly dispensed by a machine and evocative of plastic, he accepted, and trailed behind her into the Director's office. A wall clock advised an elapsed 45 minutes since departing Stirling Road.

The three older men were seated at the meeting table, engaged in a discussion that ceased as Jimbo arrived. He observed that all were in the same positions as yesterday, so he conformed, carefully positioning his coffee before sitting. Mr North's hat was on the table, his coat was neatly folded over an adjacent chair, but of his kukri, there was no sign.

"We have been defining the parameters of our conversation, and the day ahead, Jimbo" said the Director seriously. "As your employer at present, I have an obligation to ensure your welfare, so am naturally concerned at your involvement in the pursuit of criminals, which is conventionally the responsibility of these gentlemen and their colleagues." The Chief Inspector nodded. Mr North remained motionless. "I have their assurance that you will not be exposed to undue risk, and will return safely, later today.

Neither you nor I have a complete understanding of the picture that is unfurling. Mr North has agreed that as we are materially assisting their investigation, we should be adequately briefed." Mr Fox nodded again.

Jimbo noted that the Director no longer called him James. "I'm interested to learn more, and particularly how I can assist. Yesterday was a strange one, so I'd like to be better prepared today." Stranger than these three realise, he reflected.

It was Mr North who spoke. "Jimbo, you and Prof. Raeburn both know part of the story, but not all of it. My perception is that you are acquainted with slightly different parts, which overlap. I will endeavour to describe our current problem, or opportunity, as I see it.

At the behest of a state actor, that I know to be an Asian power, Gradac's mission is to acquire the cloning mathematics that Jimbo has been cataloguing. My description of Gradac as an entrepreneur, stealing and selling to order is accurate, but this state actor is his biggest customer by far. An alternative view might be that he is their employee. This might be a fine distinction, but to others, it is important. Gradac has enjoyed some successes, at the expense of our allies. His customer or employer has invested heavily, not just rewarding him generously, but with expensive infrastructure. My interest is not just to damage or destroy Gradac. A bigger opportunity is to discredit his sponsors within the state actor. This will embarrass them, reduce their current influence and future capabilities, and assuredly result in the permanent disappearance of Gradac. We can do this by allowing Gradac to escape the clutches of Chief Inspector Fox and his estimable associates and deliver the disks to his expectant customer."

Jimbo noted that Mr North paused, allowing the gravity of his plan to be absorbed. The effect was spoilt slightly by the chuckling of Prof. Raeburn. Mr Fox looked unhappy. Probably as a police officer, he wanted to apprehend the criminal, but had been overruled.

Jimbo, they have adjusted the contents of the disks. Our sensors have scanned them. The changes are inventive, although difficult to describe. The encryption has been enhanced slightly but could be tightened further.

"The disks don't matter, of course" said Jimbo briskly. "We could give Gradac any old disks, but he'll check. What matters is the information on the disks. I assume that what you are offering Gradac will be an adjusted version, enough to convince him, but useless to his client. Is this the plan?"

Mr North frowned slightly and continued. "Your perspicacity is unsurprising to me, Jimbo, but the ingenuity lies in the imaginative overnight work of Prof. Raeburn's mathematicians, working under pressure at short notice."

The Director looked ready to offer a lengthy explanation but apparently reconsidered, offering only a précis. "The information has been through a transformation, I'm advised. Superficially it is credible, but those trying to decompose the structure will find it impermeable without time and high-speed computing power. If penetrated, the biologists who examine the information will find it nonsensical. This will be a considerable time later."

His smile reminded Jimbo momentarily of Gerry's countenance. "Perhaps I may offer a suggestion? One of my concerns regarding the disks is the low level of security. I propose that we enhance the encryption level, both for credibility's sake, and to make them work for longer. What do you think?"

The Director and Mr North shared a glance. The former looked pleased while the latter appeared bemused. Before the Director could interject, Mr North responded. "This was the Institute's recommendation, which I opposed because it becomes difficult or impossible for Gradac to examine the contents. The Director persuaded me, suggesting this is a small problem that can be resolved this morning. Since it's also your idea, Jimbo, how would you satisfy Gradac?"

We can include your working disk, unencrypted, with the others, 221 suggested, unprompted but instantly.

"We could provide my working disk, with just basic security. He can access a small part of the model, but also find details of the file sizes and structure on the other disks, which he can check without breaking the encryption. We just need to ensure my working disk is adjusted to contain the same high-quality nonsense as the others."

The Director was on his feet, heading for the door and calling Tessa rather loudly, without feeling the need for further discussion.

"You are ahead of us, Jimbo" Mr North mused. "I'm relieved that my suspicion of you assisting Gradac was erroneous. I need you on our team.

Talking of teams, you should know that Prof. Raeburn and his colleagues stayed here overnight, working on the mathematical transformation that he mentioned.

It's a pity we didn't develop the notion of allowing our quarry to escape before yesterday. My fault, I'm afraid."

To Jimbo, this seemed an unusual display of humility from Mr North. Earlier, he had detected an apologetic tone when they discussed his parents, but this time it was unambiguous. He could see the Director through the open door, in a huddle with Tessa and a team leader named Samantha. Apart from being of Asian ethnicity and a prominent member of their badminton community, she was unknown to Jimbo. It occurred to him that Tessa and Samantha had worked during the night, while he received a history lesson from the Intelligence.

Mr Fox, who had barely spoken, had an idea that could not wait. "Jimbo, I know you're studying engineering, but have you considered a career with the police? We're always looking for talent."

"Funnily enough, somebody else suggested this to me recently. I should bear it in mind, but I don't graduate for a while, anyway."

Jimbo, my suggestion was not meant to be taken seriously. It was an attempt at irony, which is unknown elsewhere in our galaxy.

I understand, 221. You haven't answered my questions yet, though.

Mr North was restive, awaiting the return of the Director. The clock indicated 08.05. "Jimbo, has it occurred to you that Gradac might be trying to make contact? He cannot do so at present, because you're inside a screened building, but once we leave, I expect you will hear from him. For now, we can let his anxiety level increase. He will have deduced that his operatives were picked up in Edinburgh. There is nowhere for him to run without the disks because his client would not be sympathetic. He still assumes we wish to detain him. The fact that he is holding Dr Wagner is his leverage, as he sees it. He will want to trade his captive for the disks, plus an exit from the UK. Complicated to execute. My guess is that he hopes to hold you, as a second lever. This won't happen.

Jimbo realised that he was anxious about the prospect of confronting Gradac at his Haddington base.

I have been observing Dr Gradac's location in Haddington, Jimbo. So far as I can tell, there are only two persons inside the main building. There are four people in the nearby woods, though, and another four in the vegetation close to the access lane. This has happened in the past hour. They do not move but provide both thermal and electromagnetic signatures to our sensors. You should confirm that these are not part of his gang.

How to achieve this, Jimbo pondered for a second, or more? He couldn't say a galactic friend was looking down on Gradac's hideout.

"Gentlemen, would it be wise to ensure that Gradac cannot bring in help? You've arrested four, but Mr North told me he was unsure how much support he possesses. Should you put guards on the perimeter to stop anyone from entering or leaving?"

"If you don't want a police career, maybe you should consider becoming a military officer, Jimbo. You have a comprehensive grasp of the tactical situation. Since you gave me the address earlier, Gerry has deployed two picket teams at appropriate positions, close to our target. Reinforcements cannot enter."

Mr North seemed satisfied that this was an adequate explanation. Chief Inspector Fox thought otherwise.

"After receiving advice that Haddington was the location, we had officers performing roadside checks overnight on vehicles entering the town. As you might imagine, traffic is light over these hours, so we can guarantee that no villains gained access, at least by road. Our time was not wasted, though. We stopped two drivers who were in excess of the blood alcohol limit, one known housebreaker heading home with his evening's haul, and an escaped prisoner."

"Most gratifying" interjected the Director as he re-joined the meeting. "Jimbo's working disk will be adjusted and tested in less than an hour. The encryption on the others is being tweaked. After that, I will send my colleagues home. It's now 24 hours since they arrived."

"When all the disks are ready, I want to depart for Haddington. I'm mindful of the hostage's condition.

"Before then, perhaps you can clarify two uncertainties for me. One is the role of Dr Wagner. Why is he involved? Secondly, what is the plan for Haddington? How can you arrange a convincing exit for Gradac? This is not simple, I believe."

Mr North sipped his black coffee before responding. "I brought Ralph in for several reasons, Jimbo.

Previously, he worked for a friendly foreign intelligence service, but through his work became a drug addict, and was later dismissed. He was recruited into the service while working as an academic. His interests were in the mathematics of encryption, so you might imagine his relevance. We were at one time part of a joint project concerning the Middle East, so I got to know him well. My intention in bringing Ralph to the Institute was as a vulnerable target for Gradac after he became interested. Once he realised that his own nominal project limited his system access, he needed somebody else to circumvent this constraint. Ralph's weakness was obvious to Gradac, who used it to control him by interrupting the flow of medication I was supplying.

Gradac then found that Ralph's system authorisation was also limited, so couldn't access the cloning data. We expected Gradac would try harder to break the locks on Ralph's access. This would have been sufficient for us to entrap him, but he was wise to this. Gradac is nothing if not persistent, but so are we. This is where you come in, Jimbo. We established a stand-alone project within the Institute, which meant the information he required was physically here. From his perspective, this was almost too good to be true. Even more so when he learned from Ralph that Jimbo was his friend. This made Gradac see lots of possibilities, but it seems that his client was impatient, time was running out, and the disks in the desk were too tempting. He skilfully interrogated Jimbo while acting as a friendly neighbour driving him home, before deploying his break-in team. I have to admit, we had not anticipated this. We expected him to try using Ralph to copy the disks, but he took the direct route. Bold but unsuccessful, with thanks due to Jimbo's clairvoyance, though still not fully understood.

He interdicted Ralph and spirited him off to Haddington as a form of insurance. Although the break-in was unsuccessful, he felt unconnected but had leverage over Jimbo, because his friend Ralph was in trouble

In reality, Gradac has made mistakes.

We were monitoring his network access, and particularly his limited attempts to break out, both with his own user rights and those of Ralph. He also spent surprising time examining the details of your colleagues here. I recommend you discourage the staff from adding so much personal information onto your social forums, Director.

He was careless to leave mail lying in the car, indicating his East Lothian location. It occurred to me that this could be deliberate, but he gained nothing from this disclosure. If Gradac had appreciated Jimbo's eidetic capacity, he would have been more fastidious.

He was unwise to accompany his associates on their break-in. Despite regularly using an older Volvo for work, we were surprised to find that the BMW he drove is registered in his name. Very sloppy. The vehicle was caught on camera, of course.

Allowing or encouraging his associates to carry firearms was foolish. Who were they going to shoot? The whole point was to remain unseen. When one drew his weapon in the bar, it attracted immediate attention from the customers and, shortly thereafter, from Mr Fox's colleagues.

It was lazy of him not to check the relationship between Jimbo and Ralph. He'd never seen them together because there is no such friendship. His supposed leverage through detaining Ralph is less than he thought.

He was also too late in informing Jimbo that he was holding Ralph and should not involve the police. A whole day had passed.

Sending two more of his associates to Trinity was naïve, particularly as they barely speak English. We knew his address and made the connection with Jimbo's nearby home.

In summary, disappointing for a supposed international criminal maestro. You undoubtedly have more devious miscreants in Edinburgh, Chief Inspector.

My analysis is that he is under severe pressure to deliver. I will explain why this may be so."

Seven failure modes, Jimbo reflected. A relief to hear Mr North's comments because none of his evaluation was obvious.

"As to Jimbo's second question, allowing Gradac to escape with the disks but without making him suspicious is less certain, I agree, because we are not in complete control.

We do possess information that should steer our approach. Not so far away, off the Forth Estuary, is an oil supply vessel, that has been traversing the area for five days now. Except it's not supplying any oil rigs but does possess a hanger and helicopter. Additionally, it is not registered at any port remotely adjacent to the North Sea. It also has the habit of turning off its transponders at night, supposedly maintaining a cloak of anonymity.

This last action is pretty stupid. It is within the range of land-based radar, so its movements are tracked continuously. The transponder problem alone is a basis to intercept the vessel, even in international waters, but we prefer not to.

This is Gradac's way out.

The vessel is within easy helicopter range of the coast. It could make the round trip within one hour, picking their man up from a designated point and whisking him away, together with the disks. We have assets to prevent this, from land, sea, or air, but now our objective is to enable his departure.

Our problem is to let Gradac reach his prearranged pick-up location while securing the safe return of Ralph. This may require improvisation, but we have certain advantages. Most importantly, we know his collection point. For the last three nights, their helicopter has passed over a walled garden immediately to the north-east of Haddington, shortly after sunset, late enough to be inconspicuous but not so late as to attract undue local attention. About 21.25 is their schedule. Flying time from the adjacent coast to this point is less than one minute."

Mr Fox appeared anxious to contribute. "Acting on information received from Mr North, my officers visited the garden, which is disused and overgrown. They found a cache of marine flares secreted just inside one of the gates. The chain securing the gate, which was in poor condition, had recently been cut. I'm told the pyrotechnics are designed for local surface illumination. They would remain unseen by persons outside the garden walls, but visible from above."

After a nod of appreciation, Mr North resumed. "Amisfield Walled Garden was formerly part of an estate, belonging to a country home, long gone. Most of the land now forms Haddington Golf Club, a popular local course, I gather."

"I've played there" interrupted Jimbo. "It's to the east of the town. I didn't see a walled garden, though."

"Slightly further east, Jimbo" advised Mr North. "Estimated distance from Gradac's base is only four kilometres. The reason for the recent helicopter visits, we believe, is that Gradac has no direct contact with his shipborne accomplices. There is a date range when they fly over, hoping to see a flare, indicating his presence in the garden. This is the source of his time pressure. They can't keep the vessel off the coast indefinitely, without attracting attention, is their belief. Unfortunately for them, we were tracking the vessel long before it approached the Scottish shoreline."

Mr North had no opportunity to elaborate, due to the simultaneous arrival of Tessa and Gerry. Her reason was self-evident, the battered plastic box containing the disks, now including Jimbo's working disk, suitably doctored.

The Director rose from his chair, placed the disks on the table, and ambled away from the meeting, in quiet conversation with Tessa. "Back in a couple of minutes," he boomed, from the door.

Unusually large, observed Jimbo, as he examined Gerry. During their previous interaction, in the car, his dimensions were not apparent. He wasn't just tall or broad, but well-proportioned throughout. In all directions his size was far removed from the mean. Gerry didn't duck to enter the office, since the aperture was 2,040 mm in height. Working on an extension to his father's premises had introduced him to building standards. Doorways are typically 69 mm shorter in England. Gerry was better suited to Scotland, despite his London accent.

Goliath didn't wait to be invited. He slid onto a chair opposite Mr North. "We need to act soon, John. Our friend in Haddington is twitchy. He's walking around outside the house, with his mobile phone. Probably trying to call Jimbo."

Mr North nodded, attentive but relaxed.

"There's more. While he's got his phone in one hand, there's a weapon in the other. The boys tell me it's a Steyr TMP with the 30-round magazine. That's a machine pistol" he added with a grin, looking at Jimbo. "He's also got Dr Wagner outside, sitting on the grass. I think the message is clear. The boys are enjoying the fresh air, but they're hostage specialists, and they have a hostage in front of them. Without direction from us, they'll act. Wagner will be fine, and Gradac won't."

Jimbo noted that Gerry wasn't smiling now.

"These boys are your operatives, I assume, John?" Discussion of machine pistols in Haddington occasioned Mr Fox's complete attention.

"Yes, the ones I brought up from Poole overnight. Usually, they remove uninvited gunmen from parked aircraft, so a farmhouse is an easy problem.

Gerry is right, though. I believe our target is planning to leave tonight, but he hasn't obtained the disks and cannot communicate with Jimbo. It's time to make contact. Meantime, Gerry, tell your boys to stay put unless the position becomes critical. They don't need instructions from me."

"I need to put some officers in place now, I'm afraid. It's not acceptable to have a thug waving a machine gun around next to residences. In fact, it's not acceptable anywhere in my area."

The Chief Inspector was primed for action, Jimbo perceived.

"Andrew, it's an automatic pistol, not a machine gun. Very short effective range" said Mr North in a placatory tone. "However, I see the problem. Apart from anything else, it doesn't look good. If I'd recently invested in an expensive new home, I wouldn't want a gunman in the vicinity. Can I recommend that you ask some of your officers to go door to door, in plain clothes, advising that there might be some bangs and flashes, so please keep away from the frontage? You could also control the access to the neighbourhood, but further back, out of view of the farmhouse.

Come on, Jimbo. Let's go out and see if Gradac gives you a call. It's 09.15, so he expects you're awake. Even students get out of bed if they're hungry."

Gerry had already gone. Quickly and quietly.

As Jimbo reached the reception desk, he was startled to encounter a small crowd, perhaps a dozen in all, obstructing his route to the main door. It pleased him that Mr North was similarly surprised. He recognised most as work colleagues but knew few by name. Tessa and Samantha were at the front. The Director was making a speech of appreciation to his team, thanking them for committing to an unscheduled nightshift.

With their arrival from his office door, Prof. Raeburn turned sideways, extending a welcoming arm in their direction. "May I introduce your customer, the reason for your overnight efforts, Mr North. You'll be happy to learn that he wishes to buy you dinner, together with your partners, of course." A ripple of applause broke out, as the tired faces beamed at him.

Mr North responded evenly. "I owe you all more than dinner, but gratitude for your response and skills. If I were cleverer, then perhaps my understanding of your efforts would be greater, but please accept my thanks. Regarding the dinner, I have only a couple of comments. Hopefully, I can rely on Tessa for the arrangements. Two other attendees you could consider are my close friend, Jimbo Morrison, and my absent friend, Ralph Wagner. You should also show your appreciation to the Director because he plans to arrange taxis for everybody, so you arrive home safely, if not soberly. I wish you all a good morning, pleasant sleep, and a nice weekend." After a small bow and a nod to Prof. Raeburn, he strode out into the bright morning to louder applause.

Jimbo followed, phone in hand, puzzled by the scene just witnessed. "I didn't realise you were planning to buy them all dinner, Mr North. With so much else to consider, this is a thoughtful gesture. You don't know, I'm sure, that their work last night was effectively unpaid. These researchers are generously salaried but do not receive any overtime pay or shift allowances, so your dinner invitation is welcome. Particularly as they gave up time with their families."

Mr North lips twitched, as if to smile. "Have you considered, Jimbo, why Gradac's customer is trying to steal the information on the disks? Why is this intellectual property important to them? It has certain strategic value, but as with earlier breakthroughs, only a limited life. The information will be published and surely superseded by the next generation of research. It is valuable because of the innovators who developed it, people like your colleagues at the Institute, and the environment they work within. Our opponents cannot do this, so they resort to stealing brilliant ideas using opportunists such as Gradac. In the future, global networks may make this easier and require a different kind of criminal. My job is to protect their science from theft but more importantly, the culture that enables it. I know a bright spark like you understands this."

The Chief Inspector had joined them unbidden and heard Mr North's discourse. "Well said, John. Puts my efforts to lock up burglars into perspective."

The phone vibrated for perhaps a second before it rang, Jimbo noted. He glanced at Mr North, then pressed the loudspeaker function.

"Mr Morrison, this is Gradac. You are not easy to contact. As your phone was unavailable, I assume you have visited the Institute.

Ralph was unable to provide your home landline number, otherwise your family would have heard from me. I'm afraid Ralph is quite unwell, probably because I mislaid his medication, but his attitude is disappointing. Quite uncooperative. You should find some nicer friends.

Where are the disks? I want them this morning, remember? It's now 09.40. Make sure you're here by noon and come alone. Don't let Ralph down."

The phone connection was cut.

"He certainly prefers to do the talking, doesn't he? Jimbo didn't say a word." The voice was Gerry's, who had joined the group unnoticed by Jimbo. "He sounds stressed, which is bad for the hostage."

Mr North paused before he spoke. "He knows his associates were apprehended last night in Trinity. Therefore, he will also assume that Jimbo is not isolated, but has police help. While Ralph is a bargaining chip, he is also a constraint. Today may be his last chance to catch the helicopter. His phone calls and emails are being monitored, he expects, which also inhibits him. He believes we're unaware of the walled garden and the helicopter visits, so will not communicate anything relevant to his extraction.

He expects Jimbo to arrive with support, we can be open about this, but keep the picket close and concealed." Gerry nodded, his shovel-like hands on his hips.

"Gradac thinks he can trade Ralph's release for an uninhibited departure. In this he is correct but plans to deceive us with a surprise airborne withdrawal.

I didn't like his negative remarks about Ralph, almost as if he is justifying some drastic action to himself.

One point, Andrew, before we surrender the disks, I want Gradac's landline connection cut. While we think the files are too big to email in their entirety, I don't want him sending a sample off to his customer. We believe they will encounter severe difficulties with encryption and mathematics, but there's no need to take any risks."

The Chief Inspector nodded and headed back into the Institute.

"Suppose he points his gun at Ralph and demands his email connection back?" Jimbo wondered aloud.

"Then it's Goodnight Vienna for Gradac" pronounced Gerry, "or Goodnight Haddington. You'd be surprised by their speed, Jimbo. No worries."

Mr North turned to Jimbo, making an unexpected change of topic. "Please give your parents a call. I'm sure they're worrying. If necessary, I can speak to them. You're only a spectator. No reasons for concern. You'll be back home late evening, assuming you stay for the helicopter escape. We meet at the car in ten minutes. I need to confirm details with the Chief Inspector and thank the Director more formally."

The farmhouse telecommunications have been disconnected, Jimbo. I observe Dr Gradac running around outside the building. He seems to be checking the cable.

You've been very quiet, 221. They can easily cut the connection remotely. He knows this. He's eliminated the possibility of an accidental event, so now knows it's a deliberate act.

The people in the woods are soldiers, I learned from your discussion. Four are very close to him, but he does not see them. I listened to your conversations but did not understand it all. Why is Mr North buying dinners for the philosophers at the Institute? They seem neither poor nor hungry. This can only be a celebration, but what is the occasion? What has Vienna got to do with this morning? Dr Gradac is not an Austrian.

It seems we both have questions to answer, 221.

Jimbo's phone vibrated, then rang. Gradac again. He ignored it in Mr North's absence. Calling his parents would be time better spent, he knew.

Then he ambled across the car park towards the Range Rover and Gerry. The remnants of the unscheduled night shift dribbled from the main door, talking in small groups. They eyed him with curiosity but did not stop. He was a newcomer, still an outsider, younger by a few years, and unknown to the majority until this morning, but now connected with law enforcement agencies. A mystery man, Jimbo imagined, would be the shared opinion.

Gerry grinned, but Jimbo noticed that while his mouth smiled, his eyes did not. They were blue, restless, and like the rest of him, rather large. An earpiece was inserted on the left side of his head, and a cable ran under his blue sweater. "Soon you'll have a wireless version, no cable necessary," Jimbo advised, pointing at Gerry's ear. Then he realised that Gerry was listening, concentrating on the information being received.

Mr North strode to the vehicle, opened the rear door, and jumped inside. Gerry responded by inserting his frame into the driver's position.

Jimbo swiftly opened the other rear door and hopped in, behind Gerry once again. The hat and kukri had reappeared.

The drive to Haddington was uneventful. Weekend traffic on the bypass was light, with a short queue at the junction leading onto the A1, a major route that leads to London if you have the patience for a 400-mile drive.

645 km to be precise, Jimbo, and 461 minutes, assuming average conditions.

He knew this area well, within two minutes of the JHM facility, where the equipment maintenance plan was proceeding, he supposed. Mr North said nothing, and Gerry concentrated on the road ahead. It was only at the turn-off, Jimbo saw they were leading a small convoy, with Chief Inspector Fox in the car behind, then a marked police car. His phone rang. Gradac's number appeared in the green display. Jimbo looked at Mr North.

"Leave it. We'll arrive soon."

Gerry had studied the route to Hartington Lane, Jimbo concluded, wondering for a moment when the GPS navigation systems recently introduced on some premium Japanese models would be widely available. If everybody was like Gerry, then a small market, he mused. The signpost before the Haddington exit also indicated directions to Gladsmuir and Dunbar. Birthplaces of George Heriot and John Muir, he recalled. They turned off the main road, still designated A1, and down into the town. Its central area had probably been a market in the old days, Jimbo considered vaguely, while Gerry headed away from the centre, turning left at the traffic lights into Knox Place.

Within a minute, he turned left again, into a housing development, with the builder's name visible on flags fluttering outside a marketing office that defined the entrance to the estate. He stopped the Range Rover. A police car was parked nearby, with two officers who watched their arrival. Four more stood close to vehicles that occupied the builder's car park One of these officers was accompanied by a powerfully built dog.

You are close to the farm building, Jimbo. 400 metres from your position. Two people are inside again, and two groups of four soldiers close to the buildings. These soldiers seem very patient. They hardly move.

Yes, 221. Well-trained specialists. Do you know if Gradac has been using his mobile phone?

He has been silent since his two unanswered calls to you.

Mr North opened his door. "On foot from here, Jimbo. I don't particularly want Gradac to see our car. It may not matter, but let's be cautious."

The Chief Inspector joined them, while Gerry remained in the vehicle, accompanied by his earpiece. Mr Fox opened his mouth, as if to speak, but it was Mr North who took the lead. "My understanding is that the route between these new homes is U-shaped, and the bottom of the U is the frontage, facing roughly south across a field to the farm building. There are only homes on the north side of the frontage, so an unimpeded view of the farmhouse pertains, and vice versa. I'm happy for Gradac to see us.

The access lane is from the left, running diagonally south-west from Knox Place. I assume the lane pre-dates this new road. The woods are at the far end of the lane, adjoining the left side of the farm building from the perspective of the frontage, and extending behind. Gerry's colleagues are positioned alongside the lane, and somewhere in the woods, closer to the house. The local river, the Tyne, is further south, behind the farm, flowing west to east. Is my description correct?"

"It sounds right. I looked at the layout from a local map, on the way here, but it didn't include these new houses and roads. Your grasp of the layout is better than mine. You must have local knowledge."

"We both have our sources. You can check with the neighbourhood officers, perhaps? My appreciation of the terrain comes from the gentlemen secreted near the house." Mr North waved his left arm in a vaguely southern direction, although all that was visible were new houses.

Jimbo saw the kukri, and its scabbard, nestling inside his coat.

"Andrew, it would be good for Gradac to see a police presence. He will be pleased to identify a response from us. He wouldn't like to be ignored, I'm sure. Could you park a marked police car on the frontage road, just on the first bend, visible from the farm, but not too overt?"

The Chief Inspector spoke to a couple of uniformed police officers, who immediately headed for their vehicle.

Gerry had changed his footwear, Jimbo saw. Gone were the shiny brown brogues, replaced by laced, black boots that extended up to his calves, protecting the lower reaches of his olive dockers. A green windcheater covered his sweater now, more than vaguely military, but probably not standard issue. He was holding the box containing the disks.

"John, I'm off to see the boys now. Maybe they'll offer me a brew. Call when ready." Gerry jogged back into Knox Road, turned right, towards the town centre, then entered Hartington Lane on his right after about 100 metres.

Mr North watched him for a few seconds, before turning to Jimbo. "*Mens sana in corpore sano.*"

"A healthy mind in a healthy body," Jimbo's voice advised.

Written by Juvenalis, about 1.9 kyE ago. A poet I encountered.

Mr Fox re-joined Mr North and Jimbo. "The local officers confirmed the layout, John. I took the liberty of removing the keys from your Range Rover. This is a friendly town, but we can't be too careful" he smirked.

"Let's check the frontage. We can inspect these pristine homes on the way." Mr North stepped smartly out along the freshly laid pavement, passed the recently positioned street sign. Sandy Place.

Jimbo considered that they made an eclectic trio as they traipsed along the newly created road, passed neat brickwork, shining cars, and families enjoying the weekend. Mr North, slim, wiry, and leading the way, dressed for a day in the country, but too immaculate to be a rambler. Few wear smart, neatly pressed corduroys, and black shoes with shiny toecaps. Were cords meant to be pressed? The Chief Inspector, larger than his officers, in a rumpled blue-grey suit, blue tie slightly askew, and scuffed, comfortable-looking shoes. Then himself, student-style jeans with worn knees and a mustard-yellow denim shirt under a blue duffel jacket. The residents seemed aware of events across the field but unconcerned. A few smiled or exchanged a greeting. More than once, their path was blocked by a discarded child's bicycle. Mr North appeared to enjoy the tranquillity.

They proceeded about 150 metres south along Sandy Place, to the corner and the recently parked police car, where the right turn led them along the frontage. Houses to their right on the north side faced directly towards the field and farmhouse, perhaps 200 metres away, on their left. Beyond, to the hazy south, were the rolling green hills of the Scottish Borders. A black BMW was parked to the left of the stone farmhouse, at the end of a lane and adjacent to the woods. Now almost midday, the Sun was at its zenith, roughly above the farmhouse. Mr North contemplated the houses and families glimpsed during their perambulation. "*Esto perpetua*, Jimbo."

"May it be perpetual," Jimbo recalled from his unloved Latin lessons. It was as if he could remember anything ever experienced. Mr Fox looked perplexed, perhaps less by the Latin than the intent of the remark. Despite Mr North remaining an enigma, Jimbo presumed he was referring to the lives enjoyed by the proud owners of the splendid, lately completed homes.

Said by Paulo Sarpi, a Venetian scholar, ~0.4 kyE ago. A friend of Galileo.

The trio proceeded along the frontage, extending for 200 metres before bending again to the right and north, back to a second entrance from Knox Place.

You are being studied, Jimbo. The soldiers can see you, and so can Dr Gradac. He is watching from the shadow, inside the front door.

What about Dr Wagner, 221? Can you see him?

Our sensors indicate he is in a room at the back of the house. One more thing. Earlier, when Dr Gradac was outside, the soldiers from the wood attached devices to the house. It meant nothing to me, but now I perceive transducers were installed, because they are receiving signals from inside the house. Very smart.

Mr North continued along the frontage, Jimbo by his side, with Mr Fox to the rear. His phone was to his ear. "Gerry tells me we're being observed. Gradac has large and powerful binoculars. He knows you, Jimbo, so he is trying to deduce who we are. He may recognise Mr Fox, a senior police officer in Edinburgh, but I should be a mystery. Let's stroll to the next corner, then retrace our steps." He pulled his bush hat down a little further.

Jimbo felt tense. Something should happen. At the corner, his attention was distracted by a Jaguar sports car's presence on the drive of the first house on the west side, just after the turn. It was the new XK8 coupé, a red one. He was intrigued because the inaugural date was October, so this must be a pre-launch model. He ambled towards it, momentarily relieved of his anxiety. The promotional material had been headed '*The Cat is Back*'. A supercharged model, 0-60 mph in 5.2 seconds he recalled, with a 5-speed automatic gearbox.

That's 26.67 m/s, Jimbo. With a mass of 1644 kg, you could apply Newton's second law.

Thanks, 221, but not now. He looked through the side window, then saw that somebody was moving inside. A child's safety seat was being fitted onto the back seat by its owner, whose head and broad shoulders emerged from the other side, looking directly at him with a grin. "Beautiful car" Jimbo uttered, surprised. Just then a young woman, fair with blue eyes, appeared at the open door of the house, clutching a tiny infant. She also smiled. "Beautiful baby" he offered, stepping back into the Chief Inspector.

"If you want one of them, forget about a police career," Mr Fox advised. "Not even our reprobates can afford a new Jag."

Mr North beckoned them back to the corner, his hatted form silhouetted against the bright light behind him. He held his phone in one hand and a small telescopic spyglass in the other.

As he reached the corner, Jimbo felt his phone vibrate. Gradac. He looked at Mr North who took the device, exchanging it for the spyglass, and calmly opened the line, saying nothing.

"Who are you?" said the voice, confirming he was still watching the group.

"My name is North. Where is Dr Wagner? I'm here to take him home."

"Wagner isn't going anywhere until I receive the disks. Mr Morrison and I have an understanding. He's already late."

Mr North remained silent, which annoyed Gradac. "Did you not hear me? I want the disks now."

"If there's one thing I dislike more than rudeness, it's arrogance. You're exhibiting both. Would you like to start again?"

Gradac appeared at the door, holding his gun. "You see this?" The machine pistol was waved above his head. "This says I can ignore your stupid British conventions. It's either the disks or Wagner's day will get even worse."

"Then what? Dr Wagner may be damaged by you, but I still possess the disks. What next? Your situation is not good. It's not even logical. What happens if I give you the disks? Do you think I will let you go without returning Dr Wagner?"

"Give me the disks to examine. If the contents are what I expect, I'll leave Wagner for you after I depart. Send Mr Morrison over with the disks now."

"He's staying with me, but you can have a look at the disks. You'll find the box on the roof of your car."

Jimbo looked at the BMW with the spyglass, the box neatly positioned.

One of the soldiers put it there, Jimbo. Fast and silent.

Gradac ran to the side of the house, pointing his weapon and then edging warily towards the car. The adjacent bushes waved gently in the breeze, causing him to jump backwards, then approach the car for a second time. He grabbed the box and returned cautiously to the front door.

Mr North pushed the mute button on Jimbo's phone. "Now he knows we have assets close to him, which will concern him. Hopefully, this will distract him from examining the disks too thoroughly. He has about seven hours before heading for the walled garden." He disconnected the call and returned the phone. "Time for a little sustenance, I think. Gradac will be busy with the disks for a while, then call to express his unhappiness. Meantime, Gerry and his friends will be paying close attention."

His plans to appraise a local restaurant were ended by Mr Fox's invitation to visit the police station. The Chief Inspector called ahead to make arrangements. The trio strode beyond the parked Range Rover, turned right into Knox Place, then walked for ten minutes towards the town centre. The headquarters of the emergency services were on the right after the traffic lights. A fire engine sat in the forecourt, being hosed and cleaned. Behind the vehicle lay the entrance to the small but apparently busy police facility.

"I think this is abnormal for Haddington," Mr Fox explained apologetically. "Our presence has caused turmoil. The officers and staff are aware of the situation along the road. It's uncommon for military personnel to be deployed here, and rarer still for a hostage to be held by an armed man. Not so much rare, as unknown, I imagine. It's also pretty peculiar to have a Detective Chief

Inspector holding weekend tea parties." They sat together in a glazed office, looking out on a reception desk and the main entrance.

Jimbo saw uniformed and plain-clothes officers moving purposively in either direction along the thoroughfare. A police dog and handler trailed in. Hard to tell whether it was the creature present earlier, but dogs enjoy their food, he knew.

"Shift change" explained their host. Tea, coffee, biscuits, and packs of sandwiches from the local grocery arrived.

Hunger seemed to have crept up on him, Jimbo reflected. More than eight hours since breakfast, so no wonder. Two sandwiches and most of the biscuits later, he felt more awake. He saw that Mr North had only consumed half a cup of black coffee and a single digestive biscuit.

While Mr Fox shared his motoring opinions with Jimbo, Mr North's phone was held to his ear; listening but speaking little. "Gradac is working on a computer, according to Gerry's observations," he advised. "He's quickly been through all the disks, and now seems to be reviewing them more slowly. He'll be upset when he encounters the encryption." Anticipating a question, he added the soldiers had installed both microphones and cameras, providing video feed, watched from the adjacent woods. The trio sat together for another half hour, with Mr Fox occasionally leaving to receive news from his officers.

"Officers have visited the nearest properties, facing the farm. We've asked the occupants to stay away from the frontage. No reasons were given. Obviously, we're concerned to have an armed man directly across the field from them. I now have uniformed officers stationed at both ends of the frontage. We've refrained from introducing firearms specialists because of the soldiers nearby."

Mr North nodded, appearing sympathetic. "A policeman's lot is not a happy one, in the words of the song. You have more variables to balance than me, Andrew. I never would have succeeded in the police."

Jimbo's phone vibrated. Gradac again. He handed it swiftly to Mr North.

"Mr North, the disks you gave me are no good. The information has been encrypted, you knew this. Wagner is supposed to be an expert but is useless. I require unencrypted information immediately."

Mr North looked briefly at the clock on the wall before responding. Two hours had passed since their arrival at the police station. "Sorry, can't help you with that. The disks contain the information that your friends tried to steal from the Institute. You've received the same thing, just one day later."

"This is untrue. Mr Morrison has been working on the material. I have his working disk, which includes a record of his interactions with the data files. They were unencrypted then. I require the same information now. Please remember that Wagner is still my guest."

Jimbo observed that Mr North hesitated for a few seconds before responding, muting and then unmuting the phone. Was this uncertainty? Apparently not.

"I'm no expert in these matters, of course, but Mr Morrison advises that at the Institute, he accesses the disks via de-encryption software resident on the local network. This cannot be copied or otherwise downloaded onto a disk. Perhaps you would like to revisit the Institute?"

Gradac spoke harshly and loudly in a language unknown to Mr North, who moved the phone from his ear. The line was disconnected. "Now he'll threaten Ralph Wagner again, but it won't help. I've seen how Ralph reacts to being deprived of his medication. Quite useless to Gradac, except for leverage. I don't think he'll harm Ralph, so long as he's needed to facilitate a departure. This aspect is still unclear, which is worrisome." Mr North's phone buzzed in its usual subdued manner, requiring his attention.

"Gerry" he confirmed after some seconds. "Gradac is giving Ralph a rough time. No violence, but shouting and screaming, threats, and so forth. Apparently in the German language, Ralph's native tongue. A talented man, Dr Gradac. What we call a philomath. A new word for you, Jimbo?"

Mr Fox didn't know it and was sure nobody in the police station would either.

"Someone who possesses a love of learning" Jimbo responded promptly, recalling 221 describing James Watt and William Herschel as such.

Mr North looked quizzically at Jimbo. "*Graecum est; non legitur.*"

"It is Greek, it cannot be read." Jimbo was pretty sure his long-forgotten Latin tuition had not extended this far.

I thought you might appreciate a little help, Jimbo. You already know that I became familiar with Roman culture, including their language. William Shakespeare is credited with this expression, used in Julius Caeser. In 1599 CE, I read his final proof, finding few errors. 221 recalled Grosseteste's scribes uttering similar expressions, ~0.4 kyE before.

Philomath is from the Greek, so Mr North's remark is humour. Correct?

Probably, but with Mr North it's hard to tell.

"You're another philomath, Jimbo. Perhaps the only trait you share with Gradac. Have you studied other languages?"

"German, but it wasn't one of my strengths. I preferred the sciences."
"Maybe so, but it might be useful later, judging by Gerry's report."

Mr Fox, who had briefly left the room, returned accompanied by a gentleman in a white coat, proffering three helpings of fried fish and chips. "In Edinburgh, nowadays, they talk about French fries, but Paulo still calls them chips. This station is his best customer, so he delivers personally."

Despite their sedentary hours in the police station, Jimbo again felt hungry. Stress, he supposed. Mr North appeared more interested in this culinary arrival than the earlier sandwiches. His nose twitched in response to the pleasing aroma. He had almost finished his portion before the Chief Inspector was seated.

"Another helping, John? Paulo is just outside."

A polite refusal was accompanied by a request for coffee. "Delicious. Another reason for spending time in Scotland. Superior fish and local potatoes, I suspect. When you are finished, we should return to the frontage. Gerry is silent, meaning peace has descended on the farmhouse. I wonder if Gradac has made any phone calls. Can you check, Andrew?"

While the Chief Inspector was out, Mr North contacted Gerry. "Gradac is busy on the computer again, perhaps trying to crack the encryption. From what the Director told me, manual efforts might take millions of years and still not yield results. A combinatorial problem, he said."

"No phone calls, not even for fish and chips" Mr Fox quipped on his return.

The trio tramped back to Sandy Place. Now early evening, the Sun was in the west, and the inhabitants were on the move, in the opposite direction, for a Saturday evening in the bars and restaurants around the town. As they approached the residences, the throaty roar of the Jaguar was audible, seconds before the vehicle turned the corner, heading home via the frontage, its occupants unaware of the scene across the field. '*The Cat is Back*', Jimbo remembered.

Mr North was listening to Gerry. They walked slowly along the frontage, accompanied by two uniformed officers and the dog handler, with the Sun discernibly lower in the sky. Now 19.35. "Gradac is packing up. Still not clear what his intentions are, regarding us. Does he expect that we let him drive off into the sunset? Gerry is going to move the team from the lane down to the walled garden, just in case." A nondescript military jeep could be seen slowly reversing down the track, partially obscured by the vegetation. Within seconds, it was heading back to Knox Place, its human cargo hidden by a tarpaulin covering the rear of the vehicle. Shortly thereafter, Gerry appeared.

"Team 2 en route to the garden, John," he reported, with exaggerated formality. "You lot have been eating fish and chips," he added, sniffing the air. "Their instructions are to watch, take some video of the helicopter, but do nothing else unless told."

It occurred to Jimbo that he had not seen any of the soldiers, not a single glimpse, except the outsized Gerry, and it remained unclear whether he was a soldier, an intelligence officer like Mr North, or something in between.

"Andrew, you are positioning officers in cars on the roads leading out of Haddington? If Gradac changes his travel plans, we need to know."

"Correct. There are also two pursuit cars on the A1. I'll wait here with my officers until he departs and secure the farmhouse for evidence purposes. There is a specialist firearms unit in Haddington, now. I cannot have an armed man roaming the area without responding. They will remain unobtrusive unless circumstances change."

"Team 1 will stay close to the farmhouse until later, just in case of surprises. It might be as well if the police officers keep out of the woods, Mr Fox. We don't want any mishaps in the dark," Gerry advised.

Mr North's phone drew his attention with its customary murmur. He listened intently, seeking clarification several times, and checked his watch. 20.05.

Jimbo noted that Mr North wore his timepiece with the face on the inside of his wrist, another idiosyncrasy. His concealed kukri and the understated aggression of his dagger-shaped tie pin were others. The cufflinks had been the first, apart from his distinctive vocabulary. Jimbo looked at the upturned wrist, the cufflink visible in the fading light. A similar dagger, but inverted and smaller, with the words, *By Strength and Guile*. He had seen this before, so his impeccable memory provided three letters: SBS.

"Gradac's associates have launched their helicopter from the ship. On previous excursions it has followed a circuitous route, eventually arriving over Haddington, then apparently straight back to the ship. Tonight, should be no different. They will take about 60 minutes over a journey of less than 30. Presumably, they think we find this confusing," Mr North added with a slight shake of the head.

"You're watching this with ground-based radar?" Jimbo enquired, with technical interest, he realised.

"Yes, but we have other support, although restrained. There is a naval helicopter above the Forth estuary, which is quite common, so unlikely to alarm Gradac's rescuers. They don't know it is armed with Sea Skua, of course, but we aren't going to need these, I hope. There are also a couple of Tornado ADVs up there, too, providing top cover. I doubt the ship's radar can even detect them.

I think that ADV means Air Defence Variant, Jimbo.

Thanks, 221. I know the acronym, but it's good that you are listening.

Dr Gradac will depart soon. I am concerned he will harm Ralph, who is unable to help him.

Jimbo's phone rang. Mr North took it immediately.

"This is Gradac. I will leave you now, together with the disks. Don't try to stop me, you know I'm armed. Wagner will accompany me on the first stage of my journey. You will find him in the car. Assuming you don't obstruct me, I will not shoot him, despite being hopeless."

"My objective is the return of Dr Wagner. The disks are of secondary importance. You are personally responsible."

"Mr North, stay out of my way, your friends too. Regards to Mr Morrison. I'm sorry to have missed meeting his family." The line was disconnected.

"He sends his regards, Jimbo. Good that you didn't become chums. Andrew, our target is leaving. Tell the officers to stay at a discreet distance, visible to Gradac, but don't approach him. We must return to the vehicle."

Mr North set off a brisk pace along the frontage, Jimbo almost jogging to keep up. At the corner they stopped, watching the farmhouse.

As Jimbo peered into the gathering gloom, his night vision activated, providing a view of the farmhouse and terrain.

The spyglass came out, apparently effective in the twilight. Both saw Gradac, dressed in dark clothes, wearing a backpack, pushing a dishevelled, white-topped figure along the side of the farmhouse towards the black car. The rear boot lid opened and closed. The white figure had gone, and Gradac ran to the driver's door. A second later, they heard the engine start. "Ralph's in a bad way," muttered Mr North.

Jimbo turned to find himself alone. His night vision switched off as his eyes sensed the illuminated street, informing his brain accordingly. The receding figure of Mr North was sprinting north along Sandy Place, towards the flags and his green vehicle. Despite competitive running experience, Jimbo was surprised to find he could not gain on the older man, who was probably 30 metres ahead when he reached the car. Another surprise, that Gerry was already in the driver's seat, engine running. Barely inside when the Range Rover accelerated, Jimbo reached an upright position just as it turned rapidly, hard right onto Knox Place, sending him sliding across the seat, only to meet the firm resistance represented by Mr North.

"Try to keep up with the program," advised the driver.

The black limousine had already entered Knox Place, proceeding rapidly towards the traffic lights, passing a parked police car. It accelerated, the distance widening between it and the Range Rover, turning right into the town centre despite the red light. When Gerry reached the junction, the light was green. A right turn onto Court Street, passed the police station, and into the one-way system. Their quarry was visible but receding as it sped through another red light, over the river bridge, onto Whittingham Drive.

"This leads to the golf club. The road bends right, then the entrance is on the left" announced Gerry. Mr North was leaning forward, peering between the two front seats.

The black car disappeared from view as it traversed the bend. The Range Rover followed, with a police vehicle's flickering blue lights visible in the gathering darkness, perhaps 400 metres ahead on a slight incline. Gradac's vehicle had vanished.

"Hold tight" commanded Gerry as the vehicle swerved left through an archway into the golf club. "Hopefully, Mr Fox remembered to clear the course."

The route ahead was a single-track metalled lane with passing places and neatly maintained fairways extending on either side, rising gently for 400 metres north to the clubhouse and car park. A further 200 metres north-east, not discernible from the entrance, across the course and some rough ground lay the perimeter of the walled garden. No taillights were visible on the track ahead.

Jimbo, Dr Gradac's car turned immediately left, roughly west, after the entrance. He is not heading up the lane.

A turn of the head to obtain a rear window view enabled Jimbo to catch sight of the red taillights, as the vehicle bounced across the course, slightly behind them, 150 metres to their left. His night vision activated, providing a clear image.

"Over there," Jimbo found himself yelling, almost punching Mr North's head, as he pointed. He wondered momentarily how the greenkeeper would react to the tyre tracks tomorrow.

Gerry spun the wheel, accelerating the powerful 4-wheel drive vehicle across the course. "We need to be a bit careful here, the river is the boundary of the golf course on this side."

The terrain fell away suddenly, causing Gerry to brake hard, as they reached the riverbank, sloping down to the fast-flowing Tyne. There was no sign of Gradac or his car. Now almost dark, the surging river water reflected the light cast by Gerry's headlights.

Mr North was first out, and down a grassy bank to the water's edge. From somewhere he produced a torch. It was Gerry who spotted the red lights, bobbing along the river as the partially immersed limousine progressed to their right, dragged by the current, at least 100 metres distant and receding.

"Ralph Wagner's in there" growled Mr North, seemingly talking to himself. Then he stopped and considered.

It was Gerry who spoke. "Beyond the golf course, under a bridge, the river widens, becoming shallower. The car will not get beyond that point. Gradac has used this as a feint, to distract us from his escape. For sure, he's not in the car. The boys in the garden can stop him in a moment, though. They have the tools to bring down the helicopter, too. Just say the word."

Jimbo later recalled the cold, angry, but deliberate tone of Mr North.

"Think, Gerry. After all this, the best we can do is let Gradac go, carrying his dud disks. His employers will apply their own retribution, while being exposed and humiliated within their reprehensible hierarchy. Don't touch him or the helicopter."

As if on cue, the beating of the helicopter rotors resounded with increasing strength from the north, the machine circling on the far side of the clubhouse, proximate to the walled garden. "The boys advise that a flare has been ignited in the garden, so Gradac made it. No watery end for him."

The helicopter lights sunk from view, the noise attenuated. Seconds later the aircraft rose vertically, engine roaring, before banking left and heading north towards the nearby coast. Soon it was gone.

Jimbo had been aware of Mr North calling the Chief Inspector while the extraction of Gradac was proceeding. He vaguely heard him asking for a search team to attend the car in the river, then he noticed his tone change, from unhappiness to relief, combined with another emotion.

Mr North looked from Gerry to Jimbo, then back again. "That was Andrew Fox. He's been in the farmhouse. Gerry's boys found Ralph locked in a bedroom cupboard, seemingly asleep, but now shouting in what is probably German. None of the police officers can understand him, anyway.

I saw Ralph pushed into the rear luggage compartment of the car with my own eyes, through the telescope. Your team also reported this." Gerry nodded, puzzled. "Jimbo, I believe you observed this? So did the Chief Inspector. How did he leave the car, unseen by us, re-enter the farmhouse despite the presence of Gerry's team, then lock himself inside a cupboard, before falling asleep?

Jimbo, yesterday I suggested that perhaps you were assisted by a conjuror. Has he been involved again? I'm also wondering who is locked in the back of that car, if not Ralph Wagner. We should get back to the farmhouse."

Minutes later, they arrived, this time driving up the potholed lane directly to the farmhouse and an array of flashing blue lights, including those of an ambulance. Dr Wagner was calmer, sitting in a wheelchair, wrapped in a blanket, mumbling to himself.

Mr North spoke with him in fluent German, then turned to the assembled group, Jimbo, Gerry, and Mr Fox. "He saw his double, somebody who looked identical and dressed in the same clothes. This person touched him gently, and he remembers nothing more until a soldier unlocked the door. Inexplicable. Miraculous, in fact."

"I have another puzzle, I'm afraid," interjected the Chief Inspector. "The boot of the car, now stuck in the river, was locked, but empty. My officers attempted to rescue the occupant but found nobody."

He was going to kill Dr Wagner, Jimbo. This was part of his escape plan, maybe from the beginning. My ability to act is limited, but I made a rapid high-energy Insertion.

You replaced Dr Wagner, got pushed into the back of the car by Gradac, then evaporated, is that right, 221?

Precisely, Jimbo. I contravened our rules, too.

Jimbo faded into the background, so far as possible, leaving the professionals to investigate. Perhaps he could go home soon?

"The boys are leaving now. No need to say goodbye. They also have helicopters to catch, back home to Poole," Gerry advised.

Later, in the Range Rover, Jimbo and Mr North sat in reflective silence as Gerry drove west towards Edinburgh. The sky was clear, stars visible in the darkness before they reached the streetlamps of the conurbation. "I've loved the stars too fondly to be fearful of the night," announced Gerry, disconcerting Mr North, who remained in deep thought over the evening's events.

"Assuming you're not speaking personally, you are quoting something from your English course that I cannot identify for now," he admitted.

Gerry chuckled, seemingly less troubled by the mystery of Dr Wagner's resurrection. "It was said to me as a youngster, learning navigation, I remember. Certainly, our teacher didn't come up with it. Good with numbers, but hopeless with words. I've no idea, either. It just seemed right for our dark journey on a starry night."

"It was said by Galileo" Jimbo advised, without really needing to think. He recalled watching the old scientist at work, 0.4 kyE before. Meticulous in his methods, gently spoken, and obstinate in his beliefs.

"I'm beginning to think you're a time traveller, visiting us from the past, with your knowledge of the Ancient Greeks, Roman language, and now an Italian scientist from the Middle Ages. Could that be possible, Jimbo?"

"Galileo represented the essence of the Scientific Revolution, I like to think" asserted Jimbo with authority. They were travelling through the suburbs in the light traffic that pertained at 23.10. No chance to see the stars now.

Mr North turned in the seat to face Jimbo. "We will drop you off outside your home in some minutes. I think that we owe you thanks for rescuing the disks from the intruders at the Institute. If they'd succeeded, Gradac would have left earlier, with a lightly encrypted version of the genuine biological structures. So, thanks for that.

My inner voice is telling me that you helped spring Ralph from the back of the car, but logic tells me you could not, without an ethereal accomplice."

Jimbo, Mr North is a very clever man. He has detected my presence.

No 221, he has not, but logic has brought him to a reasonable conclusion.

"When you have eliminated the impossible, whatever remains, however improbable, must be the truth. Who said that, do you know?" asked Mr North, after a few contemplative minutes.

Gerry, with his remarkable directional sense, had decided that a late evening drive along Princes Street to the West End was needed, enabling a view of the floodlit castle to their left. At the Haymarket, he turned right, heading north towards Trinity.

"Sherlock Holmes, of course. Or more correctly, his creator, Sir Arthur Conan-Doyle, who lived here in Palmerston Place," Jimbo advised, as Gerry cruised between the distinctive and beautiful buildings.

Mr North shook his head and resumed his gaze out of the window.

"I do hope that we meet again, Mr North. This has been an unusual experience for me, quite different from summers helping my father in his business, always useful, but humdrum, I would say."

"Don't disregard humdrum so easily, young man. Gerry and I have more excitement than we need. A peaceful existence, remote from gangsters and criminal states, has a lot to recommend it. You can call me John, you know.

"We'll reconvene sooner than you think. On Monday, I will confer with the Director and his supervisory board at the Institute, to conclude this affair, and make a few suggestions. You may be invited. Perhaps a jacket and tie would be appropriate. Clothes make a man, you know. At least, Mark Twain thought so."

"*Vestis virum facit,*" Jimbo found himself saying.

Written by Erasmus, a Dutch scholar, almost 0.4 kyE ago, reflecting earlier ideas. I met him at Cambridge University.

"The apparel oft proclaims the man," opined Gerry, exhibiting his recently acquired Shakespearean erudition, now in Stirling Road.

At 23.40, Jimbo was back in the family home, a little more than 17 hours since his departure. He was pleased to see his parents waiting for him but dismayed that there might be questions. It appeared, though, that they were just relieved he was back. His father proffered a glass of red wine from the bottle he and Susan had started. A soft but substantial Italian beverage, reminding Jimbo of his introduction to Roman culture.

As they were finishing, his father introduced one snippet of news. "I had a call from Bill MacDonald, cancelling our Sunday morning golf. He must investigate the reasons for a car driving into the river at Haddington, coincidentally from the golf course. The strange part is that nobody was found in the car, nor was anybody rescued, and the car has not been reported missing. Funny things happen these days."

Jimbo wearily reached his room, to recharge his brain and mobile phone.

We can have a brief discussion later, Jimbo. You had a few minor questions, which I will answer. Soon, I have an interaction with the Energy Masters, who have comments after our review. I will be able to tell you more.

Thanks, 221. I appreciated your help, particularly in rescuing Dr Wagner. Alert me when the time is right. He lay down, his somnolence leading him immediately to slumber.

Eleven

1996 CE – The Milky Way – Galactic Review: Interim Exchange

Puzzlement begets indecision. Probably.
We are pleased to note the success of your intervention, 221. We surmise that your efforts to protect the mammal data from unethical applications proceeded to plan.
A positive conclusion, but the method adopted by the client was unique in my experience. We should not be surprised by innovation in their endeavours.
This is not apparent to us. Perhaps you can explain, but briefly. Our primary objective is to discuss the review.

221 believed the Intelligence was intrigued, but wary of losing focus. Simply that in any other civilisation I have encountered, those charged with protecting an asset would have extinguished the intruder directly, possibly by violent methods in which Homo sapiens societies are well-versed. However, what I observed was subtlety, an ability to devise a scheme through which the interloper will be destroyed by his sponsors, who would themselves be discredited.

This is not beyond our capabilities, 221.

No, it was relatively simple in concept but implemented with great skill. Notable is that their strategy was not the work of a single outstanding mind, but a collective social effort to secure the asset while aiming for long-term damage to their adversaries. I doubt this would have occurred to us, or to others we have assimilated. Or at least the ones I know.

Now, we should consider the singular nature of this species, our enhanced appreciation of it, and further action. Our methods are well known to you, 221. We are cautious and painstaking in understanding phenomena adequately, then decisive once the conclusion is clear and agreed.

We have synthesised the excellent material you presented and incorporated Jimbo's novel inputs. We will address several themes as a basis for comprehending the *Homo sapiens* species.

Our intention is to keep this exchange brief. We will present our observations and invite you, 221, to comment. We are mindful of your deeper knowledge.

The interest we have in assimilating any civilisation, or subset, relates to their potential contribution to the scientific work of the Intelligence. In the case of *Homo sapiens* scholars, it is apparent that their approach is rigorous and dynamic, and that progress is accelerating. Our concern is that we cannot dissect the process. What is driving the acceleration? Why do some individuals have inexplicable insights? How do they both compete and cooperate?

We conclude that examining further luminaries will enhance our perception. What is your opinion, 221?

I can introduce other philosophers, some whom we deliberately omitted but also contributors from recent times, from diverse fields, and North America. You may recall the recommendation of Jimbo.

This is essential.

The principal driver of scientific endeavour on Earth is commerce. Individuals and organisations dedicate time to science and technology, to provide a new or better product that can be traded profitably. This is rare in the galaxy. Most civilisations reach a point when exploring nature becomes their primary goal. This is not the case with *Homo sapiens* research.

Our conclusion is one of uncertainty. We wonder whether their development trajectory will ultimately become incompatible with our ethos.

221 recognised a threat to his client. If the rapid Homo sapiens advances continued, but in a manner incompatible with the Intelligence, they might ultimately become a danger. Meet some scientists from commercial environments. You will find their curiosity regarding nature little different from Gauss or Maxwell.

Encountering further scientists is an attractive conclusion.

I also recommend entrepreneurs and economists. You met Smith, but there are other valuable insights available.

We observed economics being applied to allocate resources. This enables rational *Homo sapiens* decision-making on the basis of incomplete information;

a new concept for us. We believe it contributes to their rapid progress. We must explore this further.

I recommend the entrepreneurs, and perhaps mathematicians too, as scholars to meet.

Military preparations are a source of concern. Extensive scientific research is driven by the need for weaponry and related equipment. We acknowledge that many advances in materials, ballistics, and electromagnetics are attributable to these efforts, but remain uncomfortable with beings that devote their wealth to destructive ends. The motives of the researchers in this domain are unclear to us.

We cannot assimilate a species whose priority is warfare. This is contrary to our goals. We require a persuasive argument.

I should have explained that a relatively small proportion of Homo sapiens wealth is spent today on military activity. If we consider the British, whose reputation as warriors is disproportionate to their modest population, we find they spend more on education or healthcare than on their military. My advice is to meet scientists engaged in research with military applications. You will find that they too are driven by an interest in natural phenomena.

The continued credence given to supernatural beings is a puzzle. In other civilisations, scientific progress gradually demolishes such notions, but *Homo sapiens* beliefs persist. We acknowledge Jimbo's assertion that religious thought is not a bad thing if it inspires individuals to behave ethically. Our observation is that as science has advanced, the proponents of the supernatural have lost influence, so are not a constraint. These tendencies are irrelevant to our interests and can be disregarded.

221 was relieved to end discussion of an aspect he did not understand either.

Environmental degradation is troubling to us. The *Homo sapiens* species does not yet possess interplanetary capabilities, meaning they only have one home. This small rock in a hostile universe is their spaceship. Despite scientific achievements and knowledge of the natural processes that govern their living conditions, a durable environment seems of limited interest. We know this is unsustainable and suspect that they do, too. Both illogical and incompatible with becoming an advanced civilisation. Our projections indicate crises, unfolding within 0.1 kyE, if they do not respond.

This is now accepted, particularly by the young and better educated. The Montreal Protocol provides evidence that they can act rationally. My observation is that the issue is not scientific, but sociological. In some of their societies, governance is weak, or corrupt, or unaccountable, so the unscrupulous inflict damage for short-term gain, irrespective of fellow citizens.

We cannot assimilate a species that destroys its own home. Such disrespect for nature is irreconcilable with our interests.

My recommendation is that we examine their recent efforts.

This would be encouraging. We recognised Jimbo's familiarity and concern while examining Muir's career, but the sensors indicate continuing degradation.

This is an Interim Exchange. Now is not the time for a decision. You know our options are wide. Previously, we have occasionally assimilated only individuals with useful attributes into our consciousness. If an opportunity is particularly attractive, we have assimilated an entire population; relevant if they possess a common psyche, but not the situation on Earth. We even assimilate societies into a simulated world, meaning they are not aware of their changed circumstances, but their evolution is more closely discernible. We can leave a species entirely alone if we regard them as irrelevant to our needs. They will eventually fade away. Or finally, we can destroy a civilisation if we see a threat to us, or to other promising galactic inhabitants. As yet we are undecided.

We are appreciative of your efforts with this complex but stimulating species and expect to learn more.

221 was surprised to receive the Energy Masters' approbation and knew they had noted his earlier frustration regarding the rewrite of Carnot's Reflections.

Your remaining task is to apprise Jimbo of his new circumstances. His response will be interesting. We hope he reacts with unequivocal enthusiasm. Only one other *Homo sapiens* has enjoyed such a privilege.

Twelve
1996 CE – 01.30, 18 August, Edinburgh

Explanations from 221. Revelations, too.
Hello Jimbo, you are resting after an interesting day.
An unusual Saturday, seeing a new Jaguar, eating in the police station, the unpleasantness of Gradac, and your ingenuity in rescuing Ralph Wagner.

Since we last spoke, I have been describing events to the Energy Masters. They were impressed by my account.
More importantly, you wanted help with several questions. It is my practice to avoid losing information, so I noted the points to assist our discussion. I also have further news that will interest you.

You asked what we are trying to achieve, referring specifically to me but also the Energy Masters. Our roles are different, so I will start at the top and work downwards. The Intelligence has existed for nearly our galaxy's duration, assembled from the combined consciousnesses of civilisations present then, cultivated by the originators and successional societies ever since. For $>10^7$ kyE in your terms, the Intelligence has researched our galaxy, acquiring a deep understanding of its scale, physical processes, contents, and inhabitants. The Energy Masters were leading scholars from among the originators. As further civilisations were assimilated, talent was subsumed to become Energy Masters.
There must be a lot of them by now, I imagine.
Yes and no. Certainly, there have been many new entrants, but do not view the Energy Masters as individuals. While they have access to their experiences and knowledge, they possess a single mind, with collective wisdom synthesised into a shared sagacity.
So, this is a very old, erudite, and powerful intellect, which knows everything important about our galaxy and probably far beyond. Perhaps like a god?

I wouldn't recommend saying that, Jimbo. At present, the Energy Masters have a high opinion of you. Don't spoil it.

What do they do?

221 recognised that limits existed to his knowledge of the Energy Masters and their work, constraining his explanation.

This is best viewed as several distinct areas. One is simply maintaining the Intelligence. Like any complicated machine, it needs care and upgrades. This is a big task. Most of my aggregated career had been spent on this. A significant upgrade, perhaps after an assimilation, can take 10^2 kyE.

Second is the management of our energy sources and consumption. We have multiple options, of course, such as stars and black holes, but there is a lot of unused energy lying around. Much of the control process has been automated, but it still requires supervision and development, every 10^3 kyE or so. The Second Law of Thermodynamics applies, though. There is no free lunch, even for the Intelligence, Jimbo.

The third is what you might call talent-spotting. Monitoring intelligent life as it evolves, identifying candidates to be assimilated into the Intelligence when they are ready. My job on Earth has been to evaluate the suitability of your species to join us. Of course, this is not my decision, I'm just the guy on the ground providing data.

What do they think, 221? Are we suitable?

The Energy Masters are impressed by the recent speed and quality of scientific advancement but are unsure about the process. The objective is to find new ideas and methods that add capability, which they suspect Homo sapiens science offers. Unfortunately, they are a bit nervous about your continued fascination with weapons. For now, they remain undecided. I will be asked to provide further information.

How does assimilation happen, 221? Does it hurt?

There are many variations, Jimbo, depending on the situation. None of them hurt. Either individuals or whole societies can be assimilated. This needs a longer discussion.

Fourth, and most fundamental, is research. This might be what you call our raison d'être. The previous three areas are inputs, enabling our investigations concerning nature. 221 realised he knew little, never having been a researcher.

At our inception, the originating civilisations had more advanced technology than Homo sapiens today, although at one time their philosophical knowledge was at your present-day level, long before the Intelligence existed. Since then, our understanding has grown immensely, but there is still more to learn.

You mentioned one research theme earlier, when you introduced what your astrophysics friend described as the heat death of the universe. This is an area of current activity, but I'm not involved. I sometimes read the reports. Unlike your theoreticians, our interest is in engineering countermeasures, which is a big challenge. We are optimistic.

Heading downwards to me, I'm an Energy Operative, a discrete entity, like a project manager, within a shared community. I'm looking after the Homo sapiens project, watching your progress, and filing reports. Most of my existence has been spent on internal maintenance roles. You could consider me as a technician. Recently, the Energy Masters gave me a few external projects, but monitoring your species is now a full-time task. A lot is happening on Earth, certainly compared with 10^2 kyE ago. If I do well here, then maybe I will be given something bigger.

How old are you, 221?

An odd question, Jimbo. In one sense, I have no age because I'm not a physical being. In another, I have access to ideas and memories that extend towards the age of the galaxy. If you consider me as a partly independent entity within the Intelligence, then perhaps 7×10^4 kyE is my age, much younger than Earth but far older than Homo sapiens. I have observed some of your evolution and all the recent history. It's a mixed story, some good but other parts horrible.

Over the past 2 kyE, I have come to admire the tempo and imagination of your scientists, whose achievements are rare in our galaxy.

Hopefully, you realise the Intelligence is large in operational scale, but takes an interest in detail. This brings us to your perceptive question regarding the incompatibility of managing a galactic operation and crime prevention in Edinburgh. More precisely, why is the Intelligence concerned to prevent a gangster stealing some mammal cloning data? Is that right?

Yes, precisely. It seems incongruous that an entity so old, with a vast territory, is concerned by these trivial local activities. It cannot be that our science interests you if the Intelligence is so advanced.

Correct, Jimbo, but allow me to explain. My project management job is not confined to reporting notable events, but also uses simulation tools to predict where trends are leading. Occasionally a significant juncture arises, called a temporal node. These are singular events, with decisive outcomes, leading the civilisation in one direction or another. Mammal cloning technology is important to Homo sapiens development, but the critical question is its application. Our projections indicated that in the possession of an ambitious and unaccountable power, it would be misused, leading to a catastrophic conflict. We were concerned to prevent this because you possess attributes that might be useful to the Intelligence. So, we became involved, a rare occurrence. Our intervention was pursued through you.

Your interest was therefore not altruistic, but to secure a promising asset, a bit like a farmer protecting chickens from the fox?

Exactly so, Jimbo. It is inaccurate to view the Intelligence as a charitable organisation, doing good in the galaxy. Its sole interest is in uncovering scientific truths, which requires it to survive, build, and maintain suitable infrastructure. Sometimes there are nice outcomes, but these are collateral effects. The reality is that our scale makes it essential to maintain focus, not becoming distracted. Time and energy are vital dimensions because, although large, both may be limited, which is why the Energy Masters set a budget of 100 seconds for their review.

Your assertion that this is a small share of $>10^7$ kyE is mathematically correct but erroneous. We have been actively observing Earth for about 10^2 kyE, and only the accelerating occurrences of the past 0.5 kyE have stimulated close attention. Finally, Jimbo, understand that we did not really require 100 seconds to conduct our review. Most of this, about 97 seconds, was to allow your participation. We conducted the review in English, slower than our normal processes. The Intelligence could examine my files and ask further questions in ~3 seconds. You did not notice, but the 100 seconds was discontinuous interaction, interspersed with interruptions, caused by the multitasking necessities of the Energy Masters. Contributing 97 seconds is an expression of thanks. From our perspective, this is a big thank-you.

I see; Jimbo's response, but he was unsure whether he did.

We know your species possesses an impressive brain, more capable than you realise, able to store significant amounts of information, although the recall capability could be improved, and communicate faster than you appreciate. We manipulate information quickly, but when it comes to conclusions or decisions, we are relatively slow. You seem able to make good decisions without having acquired or remembered all the facts.

My memory recall seems much improved, 221. Why is this?

I made a few small adjustments that make a huge difference. Effectively, you can now recall every experience in your life without difficulty. This explains your knowledge of Latin from >0.01 kyE ago, a subject you did not enjoy and believed you had forgotten entirely. I admit to helping with vocabulary you never learned, but the rest was already stored in your brain.

221 knew they were approaching a sensitive part of the conversation. There are older memories that you have. Do you remember your mother, Jimbo?

Susan, of course. I was drinking wine with her and my father earlier.

No, Jimbo, I mean your biological mother. You and she shared the same location in space and time for only a few months after your birth.

Jimbo had seen photographs of Margaret, but never remembered her in life, smiling and talking to him. Until now, he realised. The lady with the baby in Haddington came to a mind for a moment. Then the voice, similar to Susan's, but slightly softer. Margaret was talking to him, while an infant, he knew. This had been in his head all along, but now he could recall his mother. His hands were flexing, tightening into balls then relaxing, like a baby, he imagined.

These are special memories for you, Jimbo. I know this despite not experiencing Homo sapiens sentiments. They have been unlocked.

It will take me time to become used to this, 221. Not just the memory recall, but access to my mother. I am lucky to have my father, and Susan, who are very caring, but remembering Margaret is special.

I'm glad you're pleased, Jimbo, but there is more to explain about Margaret, if you're ready for a short story.

I'm anxious to learn anything you know.

A few months after your birth, Margaret went back to work as a researcher at the university. You know she was a physicist, I am sure. Quite outstanding, contributing within a team on quantum mechanical questions, cooperating with other scientists around the world. She worked in the building you refer to as JCMB, the James Clerk Maxwell Building, close to your engineering facilities.

We use the computing resources there, and the common room.

Margaret had her own studies, too, in the curious area of matter teleportation. Even now, 0.02 kyE later, little Homo sapiens research is active in the field. Margaret was ahead of her time, Jimbo, and built a device that she believed could transfer matter, small amounts over short distances. Unfortunately, she was too successful. One evening, as she tested it, there was an explosion. In your terms, she had created a tiny fusion reaction, but even such a small effect was enough to destroy the laboratory and the corner of the building and ignite the adjacent gas main.

She was vaporised by the explosion.

There is more. The process initiated by her experiment ended with an explosion, but she had already gone.

Gone?

Matter teleportation, Jimbo. She accidentally sent herself to somewhere else.

Where? This is important to me, 221.

Margaret travelled rapidly to a destination that your theoreticians ponder. She entered another dimension. In life, you experience four dimensions, described using Cartesian coordinates for three, and time, as a fourth. Mathematicians define relationships in more dimensions, but for you, these have no physical meaning.

Fortunately, our understanding is deeper, although not exhaustive. There are other dimensions, we don't know how many, but certainly a few. We can regard them as wrinkles in space-time, residues from what you call the Big Bang. We have found little practical use for them, but we know where some are located. Most are small, nanoscale in your terms, while the biggest we studied would comfortably fit inside a one-kilometre diameter sphere. Margaret materialised in one large enough to accommodate her body, which was fortunate. Less lucky is that these exist as vacuums and at a temperature close to zero kelvin.

Can there be anything left to tell?

Allow me to continue, Jimbo. I had followed Margaret's work closely, both the quantum mechanics and the matter teleportation. When the explosion occurred, we knew the cause and found her within milliseconds, but could not rescue her. The energy required made this impossible, even for the modest mass of her body. What we could do was extract information, which has either no mass or very little, depending on the format. We extracted her mind and excellent reasoning capabilities. Her consciousness is now within the Intelligence.

You're telling me that my mother, Margaret, is frozen somewhere in another dimension, but that her mind is now with you. Is this correct?

Yes, Jimbo, but there was another development.

221's disclosures were hard to accept. For his entire life until now, he had believed his mother was gone. Wrong, it seemed. Now there was still more.

Once Margaret's mind was suitably installed within our structure, we invited her to continue working as a researcher, pursuing our quests. Her speed of reasoning and formulation of theories was astonishing by our lugubrious standards, but with hindsight this should have been no surprise, given our knowledge of your species. Consequently, she almost immediately became an Energy Master, the fastest induction in our history.

She entered this group of the wisest, doing the things you described earlier?

Yes, so she joined our 100-second dialogue. You talked with your mother.

I need time to get accustomed to all this, 221. If everything you have told me about Margaret is accurate, then my problem is that I cannot share it with anyone. If I did, they wouldn't believe me for an instant.

Mr North might, but I don't advise you inform him.

You now have the answer to another of your questions, Jimbo. How did we know so much about your childhood? My interest has been to examine scientific advances, assessing how your leading philosophers work, not necessarily monitoring a schoolboy. The Energy Masters, because of Margaret, were concerned to follow your progress. I know that Margaret and Susan were good friends from their school days, and although one studied languages and the other physics at university, they remained close. Margaret was relieved to have Susan help your father after her departure, and for you too. Complicated for Susan to replace her friend, and difficult for Margaret to observe but remain uninvolved.

I suppose this relationship explains my employment at the Institute. Your knowledge of me would be greater than any other option.

True, Jimbo, but you also met our selection criteria. We discussed this during the review. It was very important to make the right choice, not just to protect the data but because of the nature of our cooperation.

In what way?

Your final question addresses this aspect when you enquired about the longevity of our relationship. Within our review, I described many occasions when Insertions let me scrutinise something or someone of interest. This is our usual method, energy-efficient, flexible, and temporary.

There is an alternative, though. What we call an Assumption, which we use when the situation is complicated or uncertain, and perhaps lengthy. It is rare, being more energy-intensive to initiate and irreversible. The brain of the target becomes a small extension of the Intelligence. While living, assuming a limited duration, the target will forever possess an inner voice, often helpful, but maybe sometimes a distraction. If the target's life ends, meaning its physical manifestation ceases operation, then the consciousness continues within the Intelligence, forever.

I think the difference between Insertions and Assumptions is clear, 221, even if I don't have a clue how you achieve these things. Why are you telling me this?

Don't you know, Jimbo? You were our target. You have been Assumed. I expect you will have a successful career, helped by a great memory and a friendly ethereal companion, and a long life.

So began Jimbo's Assumption.

Brief Thoughts

This has been a story, one which includes a rapid journey through some of our *Homo sapiens* scientific evolution. Edinburgh was the setting because of its association with mammal-cloning, history of scholarship, and exceptional beauty. Jimbo seems appreciative of his surroundings.

Probably, 221 has not been among us, looking over our shoulder, scribing here and instrument-making over there. Probing, patient, puzzled, and tireless. Only probably, though. How would we know?

To us, the galaxy is large and ancient; about 10^5 light-years in diameter and ~13 billion Earth-years old. Could an ethereal entity have evolved over this unimaginable period, extending its reach to our tiny home? Possessing an understanding of nature beyond our capabilities and utilising it. We cannot exclude the possibility. Truth, we learned, is stranger than fiction.

The galactic model that explains the existence, across history, of 5×10^6 intelligent civilisations is consonant with the story. Some variables were elaborated, making it easy for the reader to adjust the model and examine what this means for our species. Are we alone, or is life abundant? Or somewhere in between? One day we will know.

For the meantime, a structured approach is provided by the *Drake equation*, >60 years after Frank Drake first tabled the model:

$$N = R_* \cdot f_p \cdot n_e \cdot f_l \cdot f_i \cdot f_c \cdot L$$

Alternative methods can be explored.

Look out for the career of Jimbo Morrison, helped by his nebulous associate. His long life has just begun.